John Vanbrugh, William C. Ward

Sir John Vanbrugh

Vol. 1

John Vanbrugh, William C. Ward

Sir John Vanbrugh
Vol. 1

ISBN/EAN: 9783337398699

Printed in Europe, USA, Canada, Australia, Japan

Cover: Foto ©Raphael Reischuk / pixelio.de

More available books at **www.hansebooks.com**

EDITED BY

W. C. WARD

IN TWO VOLUMES

VOLUME II.

LONDON

LAWRENCE & BULLEN

16 HENRIETTA STREET, COVENT GARDEN, W.C.

1893

CONTENTS OF VOL. II.

THE FALSE FRIEND.

VOL. II.

INTRODUCTION TO "THE FALSE FRIEND."

The False Friend was produced, about the end of January,
or beginning of February, 1702, at the Theatre Royal in
Drury Lane. It was published, in 4to, and without the
author's name, on the 10th of February of the same year.
The title page of the original edition reads as follows :—
"*The False Friend, a Comedy. As it is Acted at the
Theatre-Royal in Drury-lane, By his Majesty's Servants.
London: Printed for Jacob Tonson, within Gray's Inn Gate,
next Gray's Inn Lane,* 1702."
Genest was mistaken in supposing *The False Friend* to
have been taken from Dancourt's comedy of *La Trahison
Punie,* which was first produced on the 28th of November,
1707,* nearly six years later than Vanbrugh's play. Both
plays were, in fact, borrowed from the same source—a
Spanish comedy, entitled *La Traicion busca el Castigo,*
published at Madrid in 1640, and written by Don Francisco
de Rojas y Zorrilla, one of the great dramatists of Spain.
But *The False Friend,* it is certain, was not taken directly
from the Spanish. In the year 1700, Le Sage translated
La Traicion busca el Castigo, and published his translation

---

* Frères Parfaict : *Histoire du Théâtre François,* vol. xiv., p. 454.

under the title of *Le Traître Puni.** Le Sage has taken some liberties with his text, occasionally altering or abbreviating the dialogue, and introducing one entirely new character—that of Galindo, Don Garcie's servant. He has, moreover, reduced the verse of the Spanish author to prose, and divided the three "jornadas" into five acts; but he has followed faithfully the general plan of his original. A collation of the plays puts it beyond doubt that Vanbrugh's comedy was translated from the French of Le Sage : *The False Friend* is, in general, closely imitated from *Le Traître Puni*, and in many places the translation is absolutely literal.

There are, however, two or three passages in *The False Friend* which prove that Vanbrugh was not unacquainted with the Spanish comedy; for in these he has introduced matter which is to be found in *La Traicion busca el Castigo*, but not in Le Sage's translation. A single example may be given.

In the first act of *The False Friend*, Guzman addresses Don John in the following words :

"You are the Argus of our street, and the spy of Leonora ; whether Diana, by her borrowed light, supplies the absence of the *astre* of day, or that the shades of night cover the earth with impenetrable darkness; you still attend

---

* The following note by Le Sage is prefixed to *Le Traître Puni* in his *Recueil de Pièces mises au Théâtre François*, Paris, 1739. "Cette pièce qui a pour titre en Espagnol : *La Traicion busca el Castigo* (La trahison cherche le châtiment), est de Don Francisco de Rojas. Je la traduisis en 1700, et la fis imprimer telle qu'elle est ici. M. Dancourt dans la suite la mit en vers, et la donna au Théâtre François sous le titre de *La Trahison Punie.*"

till Aurora's return, under the balcony of that adorable beauty."

The passage in Le Sage is very brief:

"Vous êtes l'argus de notre rue. Dans quelque lieu que Léonor porte ses pas, vous la suivez comme son ombre."

But in the Spanish play we find :

> "Vos solo desentendido,
> O mal advertido jóven,
> Argos hecho de su calle,
> Sois lince de sus balcones,
> Desde que luciente el alba
> En nuestro oscuro horizonte
> Sumiller de plata al sol
> La rubia cortina corre,
> Hasta que para enmendar
> Lo que ha borrado la noche,
> De luces prestadas borda
> Montes la diosa triforme.
> De su balcon y su puerta
> Sois estátua tan inmóvil
> Que ni la luz os extraña
> Ni la sombra os desconoce."

Vanbrugh has changed the names of several of the characters. Don Andrés de Alvarado corresponds in the Spanish play to Vanbrugh's Don John ; Don Juan Osorio is called in *The False Friend* Don Pedro ; Don García de Torrellas is Vanbrugh's Don Guzman ; Mogicon becomes Lopez ; and Doña Juana and Inés are re-named, respectively, Isabella and Jacinta. Don Felix and Leonor retain their original names. In Le Sage's version the characters are

named as in the Spanish play, with the exception of Doña
Juana, who is called Isabelle.

One scene alone in *The False Friend*—the first of the
fourth act, between Guzman and Jacinta—is originally
Vanbrugh's : I am afraid it cannot be reckoned a brilliant
effort of his genius. He has made some consequent
alterations in the subsequent scene, in which Guzman con-
verses with Jacinta, and afterwards with Leonora, through
the hole in the wall. With Le Sage, Don Garcie (Guzman)
frankly avows that he sought Leonora's chamber at night
" pour satisfaire son amour." He makes no attempt, as
with Vanbrugh, to convince her of his innocence ; sullenly
accepts his dismissal ; and ends by promising that she
shall never see him more. In the Spanish piece he speaks
to much the same purpose as with Le Sage.

It will not, perhaps, be impertinent to add a few words
respecting Dancourt and *La Trahison Punie.* Florent
Carton Dancourt (or d'Ancourt) was born at Fontainebleau
in 1661, and died in 1725. He possessed considerable
talent as a dramatist, especially as a writer of comedy, and
two of his plays—*La Maison de Campagne* and *Les
Bourgeoises à la Mode*—were translated by Vanbrugh. His
translation of *La Traicion busca el Castigo*, published under
the title of *La Trahison Punie*, has, at least, more intrinsic
merit than the English translation of Vanbrugh, or the
French of Le Sage ; although it differs from the original
more considerably than either. It is a comedy in five acts,
and in verse. However incapable Dancourt may have been
of doing justice to the poetic character of the Spanish play,
it can hardly be denied that he has made one or two happy
alterations in the plot. The unpleasant business of the

assassination is certainly better managed by Dancourt, whose villain meets his death by misadventure at the hands of the bravos whom he has himself engaged to murder his rivals. With Dancourt, finally, the lovers, Léonor and Don Garcie, are happily united at the conclusion of the piece ; whereas his predecessors, by bestowing the hand of the heroine upon a man for whom she has no sort of affection, leave the lovers miserable, and the audience dissatisfied.

A tragedy entitled *The False Friend*, by Mary Pix, was produced at Lincoln's Inn Fields in 1699, and published the same year. Except in the title, it bears no resemblance whatever to Vanbrugh's play.

DRAMATIS PERSONÆ.

MEN.

Don Felix, a Gentleman of *Valencia* ...	Capt. *Griffin.*
Don Pedro,	Mr. *Wilks.**
Don Guzman, } Lovers of *Leonora* ...	{ Mr. *Mills.*
Don John,	Mr. *Cibber.*
Lopez, Servant to *Don John*	... Mr. *Pinkethman.*
Galindo, Servant to *Don Guzman* ...	... Mr. *Bullock.*

WOMEN.

Leonora, Daughter to *Don Felix*	... Mrs. *Rogers.*
Isabella, her Friend, and Sister to *Guzman*	Mrs. *Kent.*
Jacinta, Woman to *Leonora*	... Mrs. *Oldfield.*

SCENE.—*At* VALENCIA.

* Robert Wilks, one of the most distinguished actors of his day, came of a good family in Ireland, and was born at Rathfarnham, near Dublin, in 1670. His strong inclination to the stage induced him, after the battle of the Boyne, to throw up a profitable post in the Secretary's office, in order to become an actor ; and he made his first public appearance in Dublin, in the character of Othello. About 1691 he came to London, and performed at the Theatre Royal, but soon returned to Dublin, where he was greatly admired. In 1698 he was again at the Theatre Royal in London, where he continued to act during the remainder of his stage-career. He played the part of Pedro, in Vanbrugh's alteration of *The Pilgrim*, in 1700. At a subsequent period, Wilks was associated with Cibber and Dogget, and later, with Cibber and Booth, in the management of the Theatre Royal. He died at his house in Bow Street, Covent Garden, Sept. 27, 1732.

PROLOGUE.

SPOKEN BY CAPT. GRIFFIN.

You dread reformers of an impious age,
You awful cat-a-nine-tails to the stage,
This once be just, and in our cause engage.
To gain your favour, we your rules obey,
And treat you with a moral piece to-day;
So moral, we're afraid 'twill damn the play.
　For though y'have long been leagued (as people tell)
T'reduce the power exorbitant of hell;
No troops you send, t'abate it in this field,
But leave us still expos'd, to starve or yield.　　　　10
Your scouts indeed sometimes come stealing in,
T'observe this formidable camp of sin,
And whisper, if we'll piously declare,
What aids you then will send to help us through the war.
　To this we answer, We're a feeble state,
And cannot well afford to love or hate,
So should not meddle much in your debate.
But since your cause is good, thus far we'll go,
When Portugal declares, we'll do so too.*

---

* This was written in 1702. The Peace of Ryswick was of short duration. Louis XIV. placed his grandson on the throne of Spain, and, on the death of the exiled James II., openly recognized James's son as King of England, in defiance of the treaty. A new alliance was concluded between England, Holland, and the Emperor, although war was not actually declared by England until May, 1702; some two months after the accession of Queen Anne. In 1703, after long hesitation, Portugal joined the confederacy against France and Spain.

Our cases, as we think, are much alike,   20
And on the same conditions we should strike ;
Send to their aid a hundred men-of-war,
To ours a hundred squadrons of the fair ;
Rig out your wives and daughters all around,
(I mean wh' are fit for service, tight and sound)
And for a proof our meaning is sincere,
See but the ships are good, and if you fear
A want of equipage, we'll man 'em here.
    These are the terms, on which you may engage
The poet's fire, to batter from the stage.   30
Useful ally ! whose friendship lets you in
Upon the weak and naked side of sin ;
Against your old attack, the foe's prepar'd,
Well fortified, and always on his guard ;
The sacred shot you send are flung in vain ;
By impious hands, with insolent disdain,
They're gather'd up, and fir'd at you again.
Through baffled toils, and unsuccessful cares,
In slaughter, blood, and wounds, and pious snares,
Y'have made a Flanders war these fifteen hundred years.   40
Change then your scheme, if you'll your foe annoy,
And the infernal Bajazet destroy :
Our aid accept,
We've gentler stratagems which may succeed ;
We'll tickle 'em, where you would make 'em bleed :
In sounds less harsh we'll teach 'em to obey ;
In softer strains the evil spirit lay,
And steal their immorality away.

THE FALSE FRIEND.

A COMEDY.

ACT I.

SCENE I.—Don John's *Lodgings.*

Enter Don John *beating* Lopez.

Lop. Hold, sir, hold; there's enough in all conscience; I'm reasonable, I ask no more; I'm content.

Don John. Then there's double content, you dog, and a brace of contents more into the bargain. Now is't well?

[*Striking again and again.*

Lop. O mighty well, sir, you'll never mend it; pray leave it as 'tis.

Don John. Look you, you jackanapes, if ever I hear an offer at your impertinent advice again—

Lop. And why, sir, will you stifle the most useful of my qualifications? 10

Don John. Either, sirrah, I pass for a very great blockhead with you, or you are pleased to reckon much upon my patience.

Lop. Your patience, sir, indeed is great; I feel at this time forty proofs on't upon my shoulders. But really, sir I would advise you to—

Don John. Again ! I can bear thee no longer. Here, pen and ink, I'll give thee thy discharge. Did I take you for a valet, or a privy-counsellor, sir?   19

Lop. 'Tis confessed, sir, you took me but for humble employment ; but my intention was agreeably to surprise you with some superior gifts of nature to your faithful slave. I profess, my noble master, a most perfect knowledge of men and manners. Yours, gracious sir, (with all respect I speak it) are not irreprehensible. And I'm afraid, in time, sir, I am indeed, they'll wriggle you into some ill-favoured affair, whence with all my understanding I shall be puzzled to bring you off.

Don John. Very well, sir.

Lop. And therefore, sir, it is, that I (poor Lopez as I am) sometimes take leave to moralize.   31

Don John. Go, go, moralize in the market-place; I'm quite worn out. Once more, march.

Lop. Is the sentence definitive ?

Don John. Positive.

Lop. Then pray let us come to account, and see what wages are due.

Don John. Wages ! Refund what you have had, you rascal you, for the plague you have given me.

Lop. Nay, if I must lose my money, then let me claim another right ; losers have leave to speak. Therefore advance, my tongue, and say thy pleasure ; tell this master of mine, he should die with shame at the life he leads : so much unworthy of a man of honour. Tell him—   44

Don John. I'll hear no more.

Lop. You shall indeed, sir.

Don John. Here, take thy money and begone.

Lop. Counters all ; adieu, you glistening spangles of the
world ! farewell, ye tempters of the great ; not me ! Tell
him—

Don John. Stay.

Lop. Go on.—Tell him he's worse among the women,
than a ferret among the rabbits ; at one and all, from the
princess to the tripe-woman ; handsome, ugly, old women
and children, all go down.   55

Don John. Very well.

Lop. It is indeed, sir, and so are the stories you tell 'em
to bring 'em to your matters. The handsome, she's all
divinity to be sure ; the ugly, she's so agreeable, were it not
for her virtue, she'd be overrun with lovers ; the light airy
flipflap, she kills him with her motions ; the dull, heavy-
tailed maukin, melts him down with her modesty ; the
scragged lean pale face, has a shape for destruction ; the fat
overgrown sow, has an air of importance ; the tall awkward
trapes, with her majesty wounds ; the little short trundle-
tail, shoots a *je-ne-sais-quoi :* in a word, they have all something for him—and he has something for 'em all.

Don John. And thus, you fool, by a general attack, I
keep my heart my own ; lie with them that like me, and
care not sixpence for them that don't.   70

Lop. Well said, well said, a very pretty amusement
truly ! But pray, sir, by your leave, (ceremony aside) since
you are pleased to clear up into conversation, what mighty
matters do you expect, from boarding a woman you know
is already heart and soul engaged to another ?

Don John. Why, I expect her heart and soul should
disengage in a week. If you live a little longer with me,
sirrah, you'll know how to instruct your next master to the

purpose : and therefore that I may charitably equip you for
a new service, now I'm turning you out of my own, I'll let
you know, that when a woman loves a man best, she's in the
most hopeful way of betraying him ; for love, like fortune,
turns upon a wheel, and is very much given to rising and
falling.   84

Lop.   Like enough.   But as much upon the weathercock
as the ladies are, there are some the wind must blow hard
to fetch 'em about.   When such a sturdy hussy falls in your
honour's way, what account may things turn to then, an't
please ye ?

Don John.   They turn to a bottle, you puppy.

Lop.   I find they'll always turn to something ; but when
you pursue a poor woman only to make her lover jealous,
what pleasure can you take in that ?

Don John.   That pleasure.

Lop.   Look you there again !   95

Don John.   Why, sirrah, d'you think there's no pleasure
in spoiling their sport, when I can't make my own ?

Lop.   Oh ! to a good-natured man, be sure there must ;
but suppose, instead of fending and proving with his mistress,
he should come to—a—parrying and thrusting with you ;
what becomes of your joy then, my noble master ?

Don John.   Why, do you think I'm afraid to fight, you
rascal ?

Lop.   I thought we were talking of what we loved, not
what we feared, sir.   105

Don John.   Sir, I love everything that leads to what I
love most.

Lop.   I know, sir, you have often fought upon these
occasions.

Don John. Therefore that has been no stop to my pleasures.

Lop. But you have never been killed once, sir ; and when that happens, you will for ever lose the pleasure of—

Don John. [*Striking him.*] Breaking your head, you rascal, which will afflict me heartily.—[*Knocking at the door.*] See who knocks so hard. 116

Lop. Somebody that thinks I can hear no better than you think I can feel.

Enter DON GUZMAN.

Don Guz. Don John de Alvarada, is he here ?

Lop. There's the man.—[*Aside.*] Show me such another, if you can find him.

Don Guz. Don John, I desire to speak with you alone.

Don John. You may speak before this fellow, sir ; he's trusty.

Don Guz. 'Tis an affair of honour, sir.

Don John. Withdraw, Lopez. 126

Lop. [*Aside.*] Behind the door I will, and no farther. This fellow looks as if he came to save me a broken head.
[*Retires.*

Don Guz. I call myself Don Guzman de Torrellas, you know what blood I spring from ; I am a cadet, and by consequence not rich ; but I am esteemed by men of honour : I have been forward to expose myself in battles abroad, and I have met with applause in our feasts at home.

Lop. So much by way of introduction. [*Aside.*

Don John. I understand your merit, sir, and should be glad to do as much by your business. 136

Don Guz.   Give attention, and you'll be instructed.   I love Leonora, and from my youth have done so.   Long she rejected my sighs, and despised my tears, but my constancy at last has vanquished.   I have found the way to her heart, and nothing is wanting to complete my joy, but the consent of her father, whom I cannot yet convince that the wants in my fortune are recompensed by the merits of my person.

Lop.   He's a very dull fellow indeed.   [*Aside.*

Don Guz.   In the meanwhile, the object of my vows is a sharer in my grief, and the only cordial we have is the pleasure of a secret conversation, through a small breach I have made in a thin partition that divides our lodgings.   I trust you, Don John, with this important secret ; friend or enemy, you are noble, therefore keep it, I charge your honour with it.   151

Lop.   You could not put it in better hands.   [*Aside.*

Don Guz.   But more ; my passion for this lady is not hid ; all Valencia is acquainted with my wishes, and approves my choice.   You alone, Don John de Alvarada, seeming ignorant of my vows, dare traverse my amour.

Don John.   Go on.

Lop.   These words import war ; lie close, Lopez.

                                                            [*Aside.*

Don Guz.   You are the Argus of our street, and the spy of Leonora ; whether Diana, by her borrowed light, supplies the absence of the *astre* of day,* or that the shades of night

---

* *I.e.*, the sun.   I have adhered to the reading of the first edition : in later editions, the French word *astre*, which Vanbrugh rather affectedly employs instead of the English "star," is converted into "Astrea," and the passage becomes absolute nonsense.

cover the earth with impenetrable darkness; you still attend till Aurora's return, under the balcony of that adorable beauty.   164

Don John.   So.

Don Guz.   Wherever she moves, you still follow as her shadow, at church, at plays; be her business with heaven or earth, your importunity is such, you'll share it.

Lop.   He is a forward fellow, that's the truth on't.
                                                              [*Aside.*

Don Guz.   But what's still farther, you take the liberty to copy me; my words, my actions, every motion is no sooner mine, but yours. In short, you ape me, Don; and to that point, I once designed to stab myself, and try if you would follow me in that too.   174

Lop.   No, there the monkey would have left you. [*Aside.*

Don Guz.   But to conclude.

Don John.   'Tis time.

Don Guz.   My patience, Don, is now no more; and I pronounce, that if henceforth I find you under Leonora's window, who never wished, fond man, to see you there, I, by the ways of honour, shall fix you in another station. I leave you to consider on't.   Farewell.   [*Exit.*

Don John.   Hold, sir, we had e'en as good do this honourable deed now.   184

Re-enter LOPEZ.

Lop.   No, pray, sir, let him go, and maybe you mayn' have occasion to do it at all.

Don John.   I thought at first the coxcomb came upon another subject, which would have embarrassed me much more.

Lop. Now this was a subject would have embarrassed me enough in all conscience.

Don John. I was afraid he came to forbid me seeing his sister Isabella, with whom I'm upon very good terms.   194

Lop. Why, now, that's a hard case, when you have got a man's sister, you can't leave him his mistress.

Don John. No, changeling, I hate him enough, to love every woman that belongs to him : and the fool has so provoked me by his threatening, that I believe I shall have a stroke at his mother before I think myself even with him.

Lop. A most admirable way to make up accounts, truly !

Don John. A son of a whore ! 'sdeath, I did not care sixpence for the slut before, but now I'll have her maidenhead in a week, for fear the rogue should marry her in ten days.   207

Lop. Mum; here's her father : I'll warrant this old spark comes to correct our way of living too.

Enter DON FELIX.

Don Fel. Don John—

Don John. Don Felix, do I see you in my poor dwelling ? Pray, to what lucky accident do I owe this honour ?

Don Fel. That I may speak to you without constraint, pray send away your servant.

Lop. [*Aside.*] What the pox have I done to 'em, they are all so uneasy at my company ?   217

Don John. Give us chairs, and leave the room.

Lop. [*Aside.*] If this old fellow comes to quarrel with us too, he'll at least do us less harm.

Don Fel. Won't you retire, friend?   [*Looking behind.*

Don John. Begone, sirrah !

Lop. [*Aside.*] Pox take ye, you old prig you! But I shall be even with you !   [*Hides himself.*

Don Fel. You know me, sir ?

Don John. I do, sir.   226

Don Fel. That I call myself—

Don John. Don Felix.

Don Fel. That I am of the house of—

Don John. Cabrera, one of the first of Valencia.

Don Fel. That my estate is—

Don John. Great.

Don Fel. You know that I have some reputation in the world.   234

Don John. I know your reputation equals your birth.

Don Fel. And you are not ignorant, that heaven for the consolation of my grey hairs has given me an only daughter, who is not deformed.

Don John. Beauteous as light.

Don Fel. Well shaped, witty, and endowed with—

Don John. All the good qualities of mind and body.

Don Fel. Since you are satisfied with all this, hearken, I pray, with attention, to the business that brings me hither.

Don John. I shall.   245

Don Fel. We all know, Don John, some by their own experience, some by that of others, how nice a gentleman's honour is, and how easily tarnished ; an *éclaircissement* managed with prudence, often prevents misfortunes that

C 2

perhaps might be upon the point of attending us. I have thought it my duty to acquaint you, that I have seen your designs upon my daughter. You pass nights entire under her window, as if you were searching an opportunity to get into my house ; there is nobody in the town but has taken notice of your proceedings ; you give the public a subject for disadvantageous discourse ; and though in reality Leonora's virtue receives no prejudice by it, her reputation daily runs some risk. My years have taught me to judge right of things : and yet I have not been able to decide what your end can be ; you can't regard my daughter on a foot of gallantry, you know her virtue and my birth too well ; and for a wife you seem to have no thought, since you have yet made no demand to me : what then is your intention? You have heard, perhaps, I have hearkened to a gentleman of Toledo, a man of merit. I own I have, and I expect him daily here ; but, Don John, if 'tis that which hinders you from declaring in form, I'll ease you of a great deal of trouble, which the customs of the world impose upon these occasions, and, in a word, I'll break with him, and give you Leonora.   270

Lop. [*Aside.*] Good.

Don Fel. You don't answer me! what is't that troubles you ?

Don John. That I have been such a sot, old gentleman, to hear you with so much patience.   [*Rising.*

Don Fel. How, Don! I'm more astonished at your answer than I was with your silence.

Don John. Astonished! why, han't you talked to me of marriage? He asks me to marry, and wonders what I complain of!   280

Don Fel. 'Tis well—'tis well, Don John, the outrage is violent! You insult me in your own house. But know, sir—   [*Rising.*

Don John. But know, sir, there needs no quarrel, if you please, sir; I like your daughter very well; but for marrying her—serviteur.

Don Fel. Don Guzman de Torrellas has not less merit than you, Don.

Don John. Agreed; what then?

Don Fel. And yet I have refused him my daughter.

Don John. Why, then you have used him better than you have done me, which I take very unkindly.   292

Don Fel. I have used you, sir—

Don John. Used me, sir! you have used me very ill, to come into my own house to seduce me.

Don Fel. What extravagance!

Don John. What persecution!

Don Fel. Am I then to have no other answer?

Don John. Methinks you have enough in all conscience.

Don Fel. Promise me at least, you'll cease to love my daughter.   301

Don John. I won't affront your family so far neither.

Lop. Egad, my master shines to-day.   [*Aside.*

Don Fel. Know, Don, that I can bear no more.

Lop. If he could, I think there's no more to lay upon him.

Don Fel. If I find you continue to importune Leonora, I shall find a way to satisfy my offended honour, and punish your presumption.

Don John. You shall do what you please to me, provided you don't marry me.   311

Don Fel. Know, Alvarada, there are ways to revenge such outrageous affronts as these.

Don John. I won't marry.

Don Fel. 'Tis enough.   [*Exit.*

Re-enter LOPEZ.

Lop. [*Aside.*] So, the old fellow's gone at last, and has carried great content along with him.

Don John. Lopez!

Lop. Sir—

Don John. What dost think? he would have married me!   321

Lop. Yes, he had found his man.   But you have been even with him.

Don John. What, thou hast heard us then?

Lop. Or I were no valet.   But pray what does your honour intend to do now?   Will you continue the siege of a place, where 'tis probable they will daily augment the fortifications, when there are so many open towns you may march into without the trouble of opening the trenches?

Don John. I am going, Lopez, to double my attacks : I'll beat up her quarters six times a-night, I am now down-right in love ; the difficulties pique me to the attempt, and I'll conquer or I'll die.   334

Lop. Why, to confess the truth, sir, I find you much upon my taste in this matter ; difficulties are the rocambole* of love, I never valued an easy conquest in my life.   To

---

* *i.e.*, seasoning.

rouse my fire, the lady must cry out (as softly as ever she can), Have a care, my dear, my mother has seen us; my brothers suspect me; my husband may surprise us: O, dear heart, have a care, I pray! Then I play the devil: but when I come to a fair one, where I may hang up my coat upon a peg, get into my gown and slippers—

Don John. Impudent rogue! [*Aside.*

Lop. See her stretched upon the couch in great security, with—My dear, come kiss me, we have nothing to fear; I droop, I yawn, I sleep. 347

Don John. Well, sir, whatever you do with your fair one, I am going to be very busy with mine; I was e'en almost weary of her, but Guzman and this old fellow have revived my dying fire; and so, have at her.

Lop. 'Tis all mighty well, sir, mighty well, sir, as can be in the world. But if you would have the goodness to consider *en passant*, or so, a little now and then, about swords and daggers, and rivals, and old fellows, and pistols and great guns, and such-like baubles, only now and then at leisure, sir, not to interrupt things of more consequence.

Don John. Thou art a cowardly rascal, I have often considered that. 359

Lop. Ay, that's true, sir, and yet a blunderbuss is presently discharged out of a garret window.

Don John. Come, no more words; but follow me.— How now! what impertinence have we here now to stop me?

Enter Don Pedro.

Lop. 'Tis Don Pedro, or I'm a dog.

Don John. Impossible! Don Pedro returned!

Don Ped. 'Tis I, my dearest friend; I'm come to forget all the miseries of a long absence, in one happy embrace.

[*They embrace.*

Don John. I'm overjoyed to see you.   369

Don Ped. Mine's not to be expressed.—What, friend Lopez here still! how dost do, Lopez? What, dost not know me?

Lop. As well as my father's seal, sir, when he sends me a bill of exchange.

Don Ped. Just as he was, I find, galliard still.

Lop. I find it very unwholesome to be otherwise, sir.

Don John. You have then quitted the service in Flanders, I suppose?

Don Ped. I have so, friend; I have left the ensigns of Mars, and am listing myself in a softer militia.

Don John. Explain, pray.   381

Don Ped. Why, when your father's death obliged you to leave Brussels, and return hither to the plentiful fortune he left you, I stayed in Flanders, very triste for your loss, and passed three years in the trade of war. About two months since, my father writ to me from Toledo, that he was going to marry me very advantageously at Valencia. He sent me the picture of the lady, and I was so well pleased with it, that I immediately got my *congé*, and embarked at Dunkirk; I had a quick passage to the Groyne, from whence, by the way of Madrid, I am come hither with all the speed I could. I have, you must know, been two days in town, but I have lain *incognito*, that I might inform myself of the lady's conduct I'm to marry; and I have discovered that she's served by two cavaliers of birth and merit. But though they have both given many proofs of a most violent passion, I have found for the quiet of my honour, that this virtuous lady, out of modesty or prudence, has shown a perfect indifference to them and their gallantries ; her fortune is considerable, her birth is high, her manners irreproachable, and her beauty so great, that nothing but my love can equal it. 401

Don John. I have hearkened to you, Don Pedro, with a great deal of attention, and Heaven's my witness, I have a mighty joy in seeing you ; but the devil fetch me, it makes my heart bleed to hear you are going to be married.

Don Ped. Say no more of that, I desire you ; we have always been friends, and I earnestly beg we ever may be so ; but I am not come to ask counsel about my marriage ; my party is taken, and my inquiries⸝have so much heightened my desire, that nothing can henceforth abate it. I must therefore expect from you, dear friend, that you won't oppose it, but that you'll aid me in hastening the moment of my happiness. 414

Don John. Since 'tis so impossible for you to resolve for your own good, I must submit to what you'll have me. But are not we to know the name of this piece of rarity, that is to do you this good turn?

Don Ped. You'll know it presently ; for I'm going to carry you to her house.

Don John. You shall tell me at least who are her two gallants.

Don Ped. One, they could not tell me his name ; t'other is—But before we talk any more of these affairs, can you let me dispose of Lopez, till the return of a servant I sent three days ago to— 426

Don John. Carry news of you to papa, I suppose?

Don Ped. You are right; the good man is thirty leagues off, and I have not seen him this six years.

Don John. Lopez, do you wait upon Don Pedro.

Lop. With all my heart.—[*Aside.*] It's at least a suspension of boxes o' th' ear, and kicks o' th' backside.

Don Ped. Then, honest Lopez, with your master's leave, go to the new inn, the King of France on horseback, and see if my servant's returned; I'll be there immediately, to charge thee with a commission of more importance.   436

Lop. I shall perform your orders, sir, both to your satisfaction and my own reputation.   [*Exit.*

Don John. Very quaint.—Well, old acquaintance, we are going to be married then? 'Tis resolved: ha?

Don Ped. So says my star.

Don John. The foolishest star that has said anything a great while.

Don Ped. Still the same, I see! or, more than ever, resolved to love nothing.

Don John. Love nothing! why, I'm in love at this very time.   447

Don Ped. With what?

Don John. A woman.

Don Ped. Impossible!

Don John. True.

Don Ped. And how came you in love with her?

Don John. Why, I was ordered not to be in love with her.

Don Ped. Then there's more humour than love in't.

Don John. There shall be what you please in't: but I shan't quit the gentlewoman till I have convinced her there's something in't.   458

Don Ped. Mayn't I know her name?

Don John. When you have let me into your conjugal affection.

Don Ped. Pray stay here but till I have sent Lopez to my father-in-law : I'll come back and carry you with me in a moment.

Don John. I'll expect you.

Don Ped. Adieu, dear friend ; may I in earnest see you quickly in love.   467

Don John. May I, without a jest, see you quickly a widower.—[*Exit* DON PEDRO.] He comes, he says, to marry a woman of quality that has two lovers.—If it should be Leonora?—But why she? There are many, I hope, in that condition in Valencia.—I'm a little embarrassed about it, however.—

> Friendship, take heed ; if woman interfere,
> Be sure the hour of thy destruction's near.

[*Exit.*

ACT II.

SCENE I.—LEONORA'S *Apartment.*

Enter LEONORA, ISABELLA, *and* JACINTA.

Leo. Dear Isabella, come in. How I am plagued with this troublesome wretch !—Jacinta, have you shut the outward gates ?

Jac. I have, madam.

Leo. Shut the window too ; we shall have him get in there by and by.

Isab. What's this you are in such apprehensions of, pray ?

Leo. Nothing worth naming.

Isab. You dissemble : something of love in the case, I'll warrant you.   11

Leo. The reverse on't; 'tis aversion. My impertinent star has furnished me with a lover for my guard, who is never from my window ; he persecutes me to distraction ; I affront him fifty times a day, which he receives with a bow down to the ground : in short, all I can do is doing nothing at all : he still persists in loving me, as much as I hate him.

Isab. Have a care he don't get the better on't, for all that; for when a man loves a woman well enough to persevere, 'tis odds but she at last loves him well enough to make him give it over. But I think I had as good take off my scarf ; for since my brother Don Guzman knows I'm with you, he won't quarrel at my return for the length of my visit. 24

Leo. If he should, I should quarrel with him, which few things else would make me do. But methinks, Isabella, you are a little melancholy.

Isab. And you a little thoughtful.

Leo. Pray tell me your affliction.

Isab. Pray don't conceal yours.

Leo. Why truly, my heart is not at ease.

Isab. Mine, I fear, never will.

Leo. My father's marrying me against my inclination.

Isab. My brother is hindering me from marrying with mine. 35

Leo. You know I love your brother, Don Guzman.

Isab. And you shall know, I'm uneasy for Don John de Alvarada.

Leo. Don John !

Isab. The same.

Leo. Have you any reason to hope for a return ?

Isab. I think so.

Leo. I'm afraid, my dear, you abuse yourself.

Isab. Why ?

Leo. Because he is already in love with— 45

Isab. Who ?

Leo. Me.

Isab. I would not have you too positive in that, madam, for I am very sure that—

Leo. Madam, I am very sure that he's the troublesome guest I just now complained of : and you may believe—

Isab. Madam, I can never believe he's troublesome to anybody.

Leo. O dear madam ! But I'm sure I'm forced to keep
my windows shut, till I'm almost dead with heat, and that I
think is troublesome.   56

Isab. This mistake is easily set right, Leonora. Our
houses join, and when he looks at my window, you fancy
'tis at yours.

Leo. But when he attacks my door, madam, and almost
breaks it down, I don't know how in the world to fancy 'tis
yours.

Isab. A man may do that to disguise his real inclination.

Leo. Nay, if you please, believe he's dying for you. I
wish he were; then I should be troubled no more with him.
—Be sure, Jacinta, you don't open a window to-night.

Isab. Not while I'm here at least ; for if he knows that,
he may chance to press in.   68

Leo. Look you, Isabella, 'tis entirely alike to me, who
he's fond of; but I'm so much your friend, I can't endure
to see you deceived.

Isab. And since I have the same kindness for you,
Leonora, know in short, that my brother is so alarmed at
his passion for me, that he has forbid him the street.

Leo. Bless my soul! and don't you plainly see by that
he's jealous of him upon my account?

Isab. [*Smiling.*] He's jealous of his honour, madam,
lest he should debauch his sister.

Leo. I say, he's jealous of his love, lest he should
corrupt his mistress.   80

Isab. But why all this heat? If you love my brother,
why are you concerned Don John should love me ?

Leo. I'm not concerned ; I have no designs upon him, I
care not who he loves.

Isab. Why then are you angry ?

Leo. Why do you say he does not care for me ?

Isab. Well, to content you then, I know nothing certain but that I love him.

Leo. And to content you, I know nothing so certain, as that I neither love him, nor never can love him. And so I hope we are friends again. 91

Isab. Kiss me, then, and let us never be otherwise.

Leo. Agreed.—[*They kiss.*] And now, my dear, as my misfortune's nearest, I am first to be pitied. I am the most wretched woman living. My father every moment expects a gentleman from Flanders, to whom he has resolved to marry me. But neither duty, nor prudence, nor danger, nor resolution, nor all I can summon to my aid, can drive your brother from my heart; but there he's fixed to ruin me. 100

Jac. Madam, here's Don Guzman at the chamber-door; he begs so passionately to come in, sure you can't refuse him.

Leo. Heavens ! but does he consider to what he exposes me ?

Jac. Madam, he considers nothing; if he did, I'd say he were an impudent fellow to pretend to be in love with you.

Leo. Shall I venture, Isabella ?

Isab. You know best.

Enter DON GUZMAN.

Jac. Marry, methinks he knows best of us all, for here he comes. 111

Don Guz. Forgive me, lovely Leonora; 'tis the last time perhaps that I may beg your pity. My rival is not

far ; excess of modesty is now our ruin. Break through it,
for this moment you have left, and own to your old father
how you love. He once did so himself; our scene of
sorrow may perhaps recall some small remembrance of his
tender years, and melt him into mercy.

Leo.   Alas ! Don Guzman !

Jac.   O Heavens ! madam—   120

Leo.   What's the matter ?

Jac.   Y'are undone, here's your father.

Isab.   What an unlucky accident !

Leo.   Has he seen Don Guzman ?

Jac.   Nay, the deuce knows.

Isab.   Where shall he hide himself ?

Jac.   In the moon, if he can get thither.

Enter DON FELIX.

Don Guz.   I must e'en stand it now.

Don Fel.   Good news, my daughter, good news;   I
come to acquaint you, that—How now ? what's the meaning
of this ?   Don Guzman in my daughter's chamber !

Don Guz.   I see your surprise, sir, but you need not
be disturbed ; 'twas some sudden business with my sister
brought me here.   134

Don Fel.   'Tis enough, sir.   I'm glad to find you here ;
you shall be a witness that I know how to preserve the
honour of my family.

Don Guz.   What mean you, sir ?

Don Fel.   To marry Leonora this moment.

Don Guz.   How say you ?

Don Fel.   I say you shall have nothing left to ask of me.

Don Guz.   Is't possible ?   O Heavens ! what joy I feel !

Don Fel. Leonora, prepare your hand and heart.

Leo. They both are ready, sir; and in giving me the man I love, you charge me with a debt of gratitude can never be repaid.   146

Don Guz. [*Kneeling.*] Upon my knees I thank the best of men, for blessing me with all that's blest in woman.

Isab. How well that kind, that gentle look becomes him.

Jac. Now methinks he looks like an old rogue. I don't like his looks.   [*Aside.*

Enter LOPEZ.

Lop. To all whom it may concern, greeting. Don Pedro Osorio, acknowledging himself most unworthy of the honour intended him, in the person of the fair Leonora, addresses himself (by me his small ambassador) to the generosity of Don Felix, for leave to walk in and take possession.   157

Don Fel. I had already given order for his entrance.

Don Guz. What is't I hear?

Leo. Support me!

Isab. She faints.

Don Guz. Look, tyrant, here, and if thou canst, be cruel!   [*Holding her.*

Don Fel. Bring in Don Pedro.   [*Exit* LOPEZ.

Don Guz. Barbarian!

Jac. Look up, madam, for Heaven's sake! since you must marry the fellow, e'en make the most on't.

Leo. Oh!   168

Enter DON PEDRO *and* DON JOHN.

Jac. So—how d'ye do now? Come, cheer up. See, here he comes.—By my troth, and a pretty turned fellow.—

[*Aside.*]   He'll set all to rights by to-morrow morning, I'll answer for him.

Don Fel.   Don Pedro, you are welcome ; let me embrace you.

Don Ped.   In what terms, sir, shall I express what I owe you for the honour you do me ? and with what prospect of return can I receive this inestimable present ?—Your picture, madam, made what impression art could stamp, but nature has done more.   What wounds your sex can give, or ours receive, I feel.   180

Don Fel.   Come, son (for I'm in haste to call you so)— but what's this I see ?   Alvarada here !   Whence, sir, this insolence ; to come within my doors after you know what has passed ?   Who brought you here?

Don Ped.   'Twas I, sir.

Don Fel.   But do you know that he—

Don Ped.   Sir, he's the best of my friends.

Don Fel.   But do you know, I say, that he would—

Don Ped.   Hinder this marriage, 'tis true.

Don Fel.   Yes, because he designed—   190

Don Ped.   I know his design, sir ; 'tis to hinder all his friends from marrying.   Pray forgive him.

Don Fel.   Then to prevent for ever his designs here, come hither, Leonora, and give Don Pedro your hand.

Don John.   Keep down, my kindling jealousy : I've something tortures me I never felt till now.   [*Aside.*

Don Ped. [*To* LEONORA.]   Why this backwardness, madam ?   Where a father chooses, a daughter may with modesty approve.   Pray give me your hand.

Don Guz.   I cannot see it.   [*Turning from 'em.*

Don Fel. [*Aside to* LEONORA.]   Are you distracted ?

Will you let him know your folly? Give him your hand,
for shame!   203

Leo.   Oh! Don Guzman, I am yours.

        [Sighing, and giving carelessly her hand.

Don Guz.   Madam!   *[Turning.*

Don Fel.   What a fatal slip!   *[Aside.*

Leo.   'Twas not to you I spoke, sir.

Don Ped.   But him it was she named, and thought on
too, I fear.   I'm much alarmed.   *[Aside.*

Don Fel. [*To* LEONORA.]   Repair what you have done,
and look more cheerful on him.

Leo.   Repair what you have done, and kill me.   212

Don Fel.   Fool!

Leo.   Tyrant!

Jac.   A very humdrum marriage this.   *[Aside.*

Don Guz.   Pray, sister, let's retire; for I can bear the
sight no longer.

Isab.   My dear, farewell! I pity you indeed.

Leo.   I am indeed an object of your pity.

        [Exeunt DON GUZMAN *and* ISABELLA.

Don Fel.   Come daughter, come my son, let's to the
church and tie this happy knot.

Don Ped.   I'll wait upon you, sir.   222

  [Exit DON FELIX, *leading* LEONORA, JACINTA *following.*

Don John.   I love her, and I'll love her still. Fate, do
thy worst, I'll on.   *[Aside.*

Don Ped.   To name another man, in giving me her
hand!   *[Aside.*

Don John.   How am I racked and torn with jealousy!

                      [Aside.

                  D 2

Don Ped. 'Tis doubtless so, Don Guzman has her heart.   [*Aside.*

Don John. [*Aside.*] The bridegroom's thoughtful. The lady's trip has furnished him with some matrimonial reflections. They'll agree with him at this time, perhaps, better than my company. I'll leave him.—[*Aloud.*] Don Pedro, adieu ! we shall meet again at night.   234

Don Ped. Pray stay ; I have need of a friend's counsel.

Don John. What, already ?

Don Ped. Already.

Don John. That's to say, you have already enough of matrimony.

Don Ped. I scarce know what I have, nor am I sure of what I am.

Re-enter LOPEZ.

Lop. [*To* Don PEDRO.] An't please your honour, yonder's your man Bertrand just arrived ; his horse and he so tired of one another, that they both came down upon the pavement at the stable-door.   245

Don Ped. [*To* DON JOHN.] He brings news from my father.

Lop. I believe he does, and hasty news too ; but if you stay till he brings it hither, I believe it will come but slowly. But here's his packet ; I suppose that will do as well as his company. [*Gives a letter.*]

Don Ped. [*Reads to himself.*] My dear friend, here's ill news.

Don John. What's the matter ?

Don Ped. My poor old father's dying.   255

Don John. I'm mighty sorry for't ; 'tis a weighty stroke

I must confess ; the burden of his estate will almost bear you down. But we must submit to Heaven's good will.

Don Ped. You talk, Alvarada, like a perfect stranger to that tenderness methinks every son should feel for a good father. For my part, I've received such repeated proofs of an uncommon affection from mine, that the loss of a mistress could scarce touch me nearer. You'll believe me, when you see me leave Leonora a virgin, till I have seen the good old man.   265

Don John. That will be a proof indeed; Heaven's blessing must needs fall upon so dutiful a son ; but I don't know how its judgments may deal with so indifferent a lover.

Don Ped. Oh, I shall have time enough to repair this seeming small neglect. But before I go, pray a word or two with you alone.—Lopez, wait without.—[*Exit* LOPEZ.] You see, my dearest friend, I am engaged with Leonora ; perhaps I have done wrong ; but 'tis gone too far to talk or think of a retreat ; I shall go directly from this place to the altar, and there seal the eternal contract. That done, I'll take post to see my father, if I can, before he dies. I leave then here a young and beauteous bride ; but that which touches every string of thought, I fear I leave her wishing I were Guzman. If it be so, no doubt he knows it well ; and he that knows he's loved by Leonora, can let no fair occasion pass to gain her : my absence is his friend, but you are mine, and so the danger's balanced. Into your hands, my dear, my faithful Alvarada—[*Embracing him*] I put my honour, and I put my life ; for both depend on Leonora's truth. Observe her lover, and—neglect not her. You are wise, you are active, you are brave and true. You have all the qualities that man should have for such a trust ;

and I by consequence have all the assurance man can have, you'll, as you ought, discharge it.   289

Don John.   A very hopeful business you would have me undertake—keep a woman honest !—Udsdeath ! I'd as soon undertake to keep Portocarrero honest.*   Look you, we are friends, intimate friends ;—you must not be angry if I talk freely.   Women are naturally bent to mischief, and their actions run in one continued torrent till they die.   But the less a torrent's checked, the less mischief it does ; let it alone, perhaps 'twill only kiss the banks and pass ; but stop it, 'tis insatiable.

Don Ped.   I would not stop it; but could I gently turn its course where it might run, and vent itself with innocence, I would.   Leonora of herself is virtuous ; her birth, religion, modesty, and sense, will guide her wishes where they ought to point.—But yet, let guards be what they will, that place is safest that is ne'er attacked.   304

Don John.   As far as I can serve you, in hindering Guzman's approaches, you may command me.

Don Ped.   That's all I ask.

Don John.   Then all you ask is granted.

Don Ped.   I am at ease ; farewell !

Don John.   Heaven bring you safe to us again !—[*Exit* DON PEDRO.]   Yes, I shall observe her, doubt it not.   I

---

* Cardinal Louis Portocarrero was particularly odious to the people of England as the head of the French interest in Spain, and a principal in the intrigues which resulted in the accession of Philip, Duke of Anjou, second son of the Dauphin, to the throne of that country, at the end of the year 1700.   In 1704 a scandalous History (so-called) of the Cardinal was published in London, under the title of *The History Political and Gallant of the famous Card. Portocarrero, Archbishop of Toledo.   Done out of French.*

wish nobody may observe me; for I find I'm no more master of myself. Don Guzman's passion for her adds to mine; but when I think on what Don Pedro'll reap, I'm fire and flame! Something must be done; what, let love direct, for I have nothing else to guide me.   316

Re-enter LOPEZ.

Lop. [*Aside.*] Don Pedro is mounting for his journey, and leaves a young, warm, liquorish hussy, with a watery mouth, behind him.—Hum—if she falls handsomely in my master's way, let her look to her——'st—there he is. Doing what?—thinking? That's new; and if any good comes on't, that will be newer still.

Don John. [*Aside.*] How! abuse the trust a friend reposes in me? and while he thinks me waking for his peace, employ the stretch of thought to make him wretched?   326

Lop. Not to interrupt your pious meditations, sir, pray have you seen——Seen what, fool? Why, he can't see thee. Egad, I believe the little blind bastard has whipped him through the heart in earnest.

Don John. [*Aside.*] Pedro would never have done this by me.—How do I know that? Why,—he swore he was my friend.—Well, and I swore I was his.—Why then, if I find I can break my oath, why should not I conclude he would do as much by his?   335

Lop. [*Aside.*] His countenance begins to clear up: I suppose things may be drawing to a conclusion.

Don John. [*Aside.*] Ay, 'tis just so; and I don't believe he would have debated the matter half so long as I have done: egad, I think I have put myself to a great expense of morality about it.   I'm sure, at least, my stock's out.   But I have a fund of love, I hope may last a little longer.—[*Seeing* LOPEZ.]   Oh, are you there, sir?   343

Lop.   I think so, sir.   I won't be positive in anything.

Don John.   Follow me ; I have some business to employ you in, you'll like.   [*Exit.*

Lop.   I won't be positive in that neither.   I guess what you are going about ;—there's roguery a-foot !   This is at Leonora, who I know hates him : nothing under a rape will do't.—He'll be hanged ; and then what becomes of thee, my little Lopez ?   Why, the honour to a—dingle dangle by him ; which he'll have the good-nature to be mighty sorry for.   But I may chance to be beforehand with him : if we are not taken in the fact, they'll perhaps do him the honour to set a reward upon his head.   Which if they do, Don, I shall go near to follow your moral example, secure my pardon, make my fortune, and hang you up for the good of your country.

[*Exit.*

ACT III.

SCENE I.—*A Room in* DON FELIX'S *House.*

Enter DON FELIX, DON PEDRO, LEONORA, *and* JACINTA.

Don Fel. How, son! obliged to leave us immediately, say you?

Don Ped. My ill fortune, sir, will have it so.

Leo. [*Aside.*] What can this be?

Don Fel. Pray what's the matter? You surprise me.

Don Ped. This letter, sir, will inform you.

Don Fel. [*Reads.*] *My dear son, Bertrand has brought me the welcome news of your return, and has given me your letter; which has in some sort revived my spirits in the extremity I am in. I daily expect my exit from this world. 'Tis now six years since I have seen you; I should be glad to do it once again before I die. If you will give me that satisfaction, you must be speedy. Heaven preserve you!*—'Tis enough. The occasion I'm sorry for, but since the ties of blood and gratitude oblige you, far be it from me to hinder you. Farewell, my son! may you have a happy journey, and if it be Heaven's will, may the sight of so good a son revive so kind a father! I leave you to bid your wife adieu. [*Exit.*

Don Ped. I must leave you, my lovely bride; but 'tis with bitter pangs of separation. Had I your heart to cheer me on my way, I might, with such a cordial, run my course; but that support you want the power to give me. 22

Leo. Who tells you so?

Don Ped. My eyes and ears, and all the pains I bear.

Leo. When eyes and ears are much indulged, like favourite servants, they are apt to abuse the too much trust their master places in 'em.

Don Ped. If I am abused, assist me with some fair interpretation of all that present trouble and disquiet, which is not in my power to overlook, nor yours to hide.

Leo. You might, methinks, have spared my modesty; and, without forcing me to name your absence, have laid my trouble there.   33

Don Ped. No, no, my fair deluder, that's a veil too thin to cover what's so hard to hide; my presence, not my absence, is the cause. Your cold reception at my first approach prepared me for the stroke; and 'twas not long before your mouth confirmed my doom: *Don Guzman, I am yours!*

Leo. Is't then impossible the mouth should utter one name for another?

Don Ped. Not at all, when it follows the dictates of the heart.   42

Leo. Were it even so, what wrong is from that heart received, where duty and where virtue are its rulers?

Don Ped. Where they preside, our honour may be safe, yet our minds be on the rack.

Leo. This discourse will scarce produce a remedy; we'll end it therefore if you please, and leave the rest to time. Besides, the occasion of your journey presses you.

Don Ped. The occasion of my delay presses you, I fear, much more; you count the tedious minutes I am with you, and are reduced to mind me of my duty to free yourself from my sight.   53

Leo. You urge this thing too far, and do me wrong. The sentiments I have for you áre much more favourable than your jealousy suffers 'em to appear. But if my heart has seemed to lean another way, before you had a title to it, you ought not to conclude I shall suffer it to do so long.

Don Ped. I know you have virtue, gratitude, and truth; and therefore 'tis I love you to my ruin. Could I believe you false, contempt would soon release me from my chains, which yet I can't but wish to wear for ever: therefore, indulge at least your pity to your slave; 'tis the soft path in which we tread to love. I leave behind a tortured heart to move you :—   65

> Weigh well its pains, think on its passion too,
> Remember all its torments spring from you;
> And if you cannot love, at least be true.   [*Exit.*

Jac. Now, by my troth, madam, I'm ready to cry. He's a pretty fellow, and deserves better luck.

Leo. I own he does: and his behaviour would engage anything that were unengaged. But, alas! I want his pity more than he does mine.   73

Jac. You do? Now, I'm of another mind. The moment he sees your picture, he's in love with you; the moment he's in love with you, he embarks; and, like lightning, in a moment more he's here: where you are pleased to receive him with a *Don Guzman, I am yours!* Ah—poor man!

Leo. I own, Jacinta, he's unfortunate, but still I say my fate is harder yet. The irresistible passion I have for Guzman renders Don Pedro, with all his merit, odious to me. Yet I must in his favour make eternal war against the strength of inclination and the man I love.   83

Jac. [*Aside.*] Um—If I were in her case, I could find

an expedient for all this matter. But she makes such a bustle with her virtue, I dare not propose it to her.

Leo. Besides, Don Pedro possesses what he loves, but I must never think on poor Don Guzman more.   [*Weeping.*

Jac. Poor Don Guzman, indeed ! We han't said a word of the pickle he's in yet. Hark ! somebody knocks—at the old rendezvous. It's he, on my conscience.

Leo. Let's be gone ; I must think of him no more.

Jac. Yes, let's be gone ; but let's know whether 'tis he or not first.   94

Leo. No, Jacinta ; I must not speak with him any more. —[*Sighing.*] I'm married to another.

Jac. Married to another ? well, married to another ; why, if one were married to twenty others, one may give a civil gentleman an answer.

Leo. Alas ! what wouldst thou have me say to him ?

Jac. Say to him ? why, one may find twenty things to say to a man. Say, that 'tis true you are married to another, and that a—'twould be a sin to think of anybody but your husband, and that—you are of a timorous nature, and afraid of being damned ; and that a—you would not have him die neither ; that a—folks are mortal, and things sometimes come strangely about, and a widow's a widow, and—   108

Leo. Peace, Levity !—[*Sighing.*] But see who 'tis knocks.

Jac. Who's there ?

Isab. [*Behind the scenes.*] 'Tis I, Isabella.

Leo. Isabella ! What do you want, my dear ?

Isab. Your succour, for Heaven's sake, Leonora. My brother will destroy himself.

Leo. Alas! it is not in my power to save him.

Isab. Permit him but to speak to you, that possibly may do.   118

Leo. Why have not I the force to refuse him?

Don Guz. [*Behind the scenes.*] Is it you I hear, my poor lost mistress? Am I so happy once more to meet you, where I so often have been blest?

Jac. Courage, madam, say a little something to him.

Don Guz. Not one kind word to a distracted lover? No pity for a wretch you have made so miserable?

Leo. The only way to end that misery, is to forget we ever thought of happiness.

Don Guz. And is that in your power? Ah, Leonora, you never loved like me!   129

Leo. How I have loved, to Heaven I appeal! But Heaven does now permit that love no more.

Don Guz. Why does it then permit us life and thought? Are we deceived in its omnipotence? Is it reduced to find its pleasures in its creatures' pain?

Leo. In what, or where, the joys of Heaven consist, lies deeper than a woman's line can fathom; but this we know, a wife must in her husband seek for hers, and therefore I must think of you no more. Farewell.   [*Exit.*

Don Guz. Yet hear me, cruel Leonora.   139

Jac. It must be another time then, for she's whipped off now. All the comfort I can give you is, that I see she durst not trust herself any longer in your company. But hush, I hear a noise, get you gone, we shall be catched.

Leo. [*Within.*] Jacinta!

Jac. I come, I come, madam.   [*Exit.*

SCENE II.—*A Room in the same.*

Enter LOPEZ.

Lop. If I mistake not, there are a brace of lovers intend to take some pains about madam, in her husband's absence. Poor Don Pedro! Well, methinks a man's in a very merry mood that marries a handsome wife. When I dispose of my person, it shall be to an ugly one: they take it so kindly, and are so full of acknowledgment; watch you, wait upon you, nurse you, humour you, are so fond, and so chaste. Or if the hussy has presumption enough to think of being otherwise, away with her into the mountains fifty leagues off; nobody opposes. If she's mutinous, give her discipline; everybody approves on't. Hang her! says one, he's kinder than she deserves; Damn her! says another, why does not he starve her? But if she's handsome, Ah the brute! cries one; Ah the Turk! cries t'other: Why don't she cuckold him? says this fellow; Why does not she poison him? says that; and away comes a packet of epistles to advise her to't. Ah, poor Don Pedro! But enough. 'Tis now night, all's hush and still: everybody's a-bed, and what am I to do? Why, as other trusty domestics, sit up to let the thief in. But I suppose he won't be here yet; with the help of a small nap beforehand, I shall be in a better condition to perform the duty of a sentinel when I go to my post. This corner will just fit me. Come, Lopez, lie thee down, short prayers, and to sleep. 24

[*He lies down.*

Enter JACINTA, *with a candle in her hand.*

Jac. So, I have put my poor lady to bed with nothing but sobs, tears, sighs, wishes, and a poor pillow to mumble, instead of a bridegroom, poor heart! I pity her; but everybody has their afflictions, and by the beads of my grandmother, I have mine. Tell me, kind gentlemen, if I have not something to excite you? Methinks I have a roguish eye, I'm sure I have a mettled heart. I'm soft, and warm, and sound, may it please ye. Whence comes it then, this rascal Lopez, who now has been two hours in the family, has not yet thought it worth his while to make one motion towards me? Not that the blockhead's charms have moved me, but I'm angry mine han't been able to move him. I doubt I must begin with the lubber; my reputation's at stake upon't, and I must rouse the drone somehow.   38

Lop. [*Rubbing his eyes and coming on.*] What a damned condition is that of a valet! No sooner do I, in comfortable slumber, close my eyes, but methinks my master's upon me with fifty slaps o' th' back, for making him wait in the street. I have his orders to let him in here to-night, and so I had 'e'en—who's that?—Jacinta?—Yes. A caterwauling?—like enough.

Jac. The fellow's there; I had best not lose the occasion.   [*Aside.*

. *Lop.* The slut's handsome; I begin to kindle. But if my master should be at the door—why, there let him be till the matter's over.   [*Aside.*   50

    Jac. Shall I advance?   [*Aside.*

    Lop. Shall I venture?   [*Aside.*

    Jac. How severe a look he has!   [*Aside.*

Lop.   She seems very reserved.   [*Aside.*

Jac.   If he should put the negative upon me.   [*Aside.*

Lop.   She seems a woman of great discretion ; I tremble.

[*Aside.*

Jac.   Hang it, I must venture.   [*Aside.*

Lop.   Faint heart never won fair lady.   [*Aside.*

Jac.   Lopez !

Lop.   Jacinta !

Jac.   O dear heart ! is't you ?

Lop.   Charming Jacinta ! fear me not.

Jac.   [*Aside.*]   O ho ! he begins to talk soft,—then let us take upon us again.   64

Lop.   Cruel Jacinta, whose mouth (small as it is) has made but one morsel of my heart.

Jac.   [*Aside.*]   It's well he prevents me.   I was going to leap about the rascal's neck.

Lop.   Barbare Jacinta, cast your eyes
       On your poor Lopez, ere he dies.

Jac.   [*Aside.*]   Poetry too !   Nay, then I have done his business.

Lop.   Feel how I burn with hot desire,
       Ah ! pity me, and quench my fire.
       Deaf, my fair tyrant, deaf to my woes ?
       Nay then, barbarian, in it goes.   76

[*Drawing a knife.*

Jac.   Why, how now, Jack-sauce ? why, how now, Presumption ?   What encouragement have I given you, Jack-a-lent, to attack me with your tenders ?   I could tear your eyes out, sirrah, for thinking I am such a one.   What indecency have you seen in my behaviour, Impudence, that you should think me for your beastly turn, you goat you ?

Lop. Patience, my much offended goddess, 'tis honourably I would share your bed.   84

Jac. Peace, I say—Mr. Liquorish. I, for whom the
most successful cavaliers employ their sighs in vain, shall I
look down upon a crawling worm ?   Pha !—see that crop-
ear there, that vermin, that wants to eat at a table would set
his master's mouth a-watering !

Lop. May I presume to make an humble meal upon
what savoury remnants he may leave ?

Jac. No.

Lop. 'Tis hard ! 'tis wondrous hard !

Jac. Leave me.

Lop. 'Tis pitiful, 'tis wondrous pitiful !

Jac. Begone ! I say.—   96
        Thus ladies 'tis, perhaps, sometimes with you ;
        With scorn you fly the thing which you pursue.
                                            [*Aside.—Exit.*

Lop. 'Tis very well, Mrs. Flipflap, 'tis very well ; but do
you hear—Tawdry, you are not so alluring as you think you
are—Comb-brush, nor I so much in love !—your maidenhead may chance to grow mouldy with your airs ;—the pox
be your bedfellow ! there's that for you.—Come, let's think
no more on't, sailors must meet with storms ; my master's
going to sea too. He may chance to fare no better with the
lady than I have done with her Abigail : there may be foul
weather there too.   I reckon at present he may be lying by
under a mizen at the street door, I think it rains too for his
comfort. What if I should leave him there an hour or two
in fresco, and try to work off the amour that way ? No ;
people will be physicked their own way. But perhaps I
might save his life by't—yes, and have my bones broke for

being so officious; therefore, if you are at the door, Don
John, walk in and take your fortune.   [*Opens the door.*

Enter DON JOHN.

Don John.   Hist! hist!   115

Lop.   Hist! hist!

Don John.   Lopez!

Lop.   [*Aside.*]   The devil!—[*Aloud.*]   Tread softly.

Don John.   Are they all asleep?

Lop.   Dead.

Don John.   Enough; shut the door.

Lop.   'Tis done.

Don John.   Now begone.

Lop.   What! shut the door first, and then begone?
Now methinks I might as well have gone first, and then
shut the door.   126

Don John.   I bid you begone, you dog! do you find the
way.

Lop.   [*Aside.*]   Stark mad, and always so when a
woman's in chase.—[*Aloud.*]   But, sir, will you keep your
chief minister out of the secrets of your state?   Pray let me
know what this night's work is to be.

Don John.   No questions, but march.

Lop.   Very well.—[*Goes to the door, and returns.*]   But,
sir, shall I stay for you in the street?

Don John.   No, nor stir out of the house.

Lop.   So.   Well, sir, I'll do just as you have ordered
me; I'll be gone, and I'll stay; and I'll march, and I won't
stir, and—just as you say, sir.   139

Don John.   I see you are afraid, you rascal you.

Lop.   Passably.

Don John. Well, be it so; but you shan't leave the house, sir; therefore begone to your hogsty, and wait farther orders.

Lop. [*Aside.*] But first I'll know how you intend to dispose of yourself.   [*Hides behind the door.*

Don John. All's hush and still; and I am at the point of being a happy—villain. That thought comes uninvited: —then like an uninvited guest let it be treated: begone, intruder! Leonora's charms turn vice to virtue, treason into truth; nature, who has made her the supreme object of our desires, must needs have designed her the regulator of our morals. Whatever points at her, is pointed right. We are all her due, mankind's the dower which Heaven has settled on her; and he's the villain that would rob her of her tribute. I therefore, as in duty bound, will in, and pay her mine.   157

Lop. [*Aside.*] There he goes, i'faith; he seemed as if he had a qualm just now; but he never goes without a dram of conscience-water about him, to set matters right again.

Don John. This is her door. 'Tis locked; but I have a smith about me will make her staple fly.

[*Pulls out some irons, and forces the lock.*

Lop. [*Aside.*] Hark! hark! if he is not equipped for a housebreaker too. Very well, he has provided two strings to his bow; if he 'scapes the rape, he may be hanged upon the burglary.   166

Don John. There, 'tis done. So: no watchlight burning?—[*Peeping into her chamber.*] All in darkness? So much the better; 'twill save a great deal of blushing on both sides. Methinks I feel myself mighty modest, I tremble too; that's not proper at this time. Be firm, my courage, I have business for thee.—So—how am I now?—pretty well. Then by your leave, Don Pedro, I must supply your neglect. You should not have married till you were ready for consummation; a maidenhead ought no more to lie upon a handsome bride, than an impeachment upon an innocent minister.   [*Exit into the chamber.* 177

 Lop. [*Coming forwards.*] Well done, well done; Gad a-marcy, my little Judas! Unfortunate Don Pedro! thou hast left thy purse in the hands of a robber; and while thou art galloping to pay the last duty to thy father, he's at least upon the trot to pay the first to thy wife. Ah, the traitor! What a capilotade* of damnation will there be cooked up for him! But softly: let's lay our ear to the door, and pick up some curiosities.—I hear no noise.—There's no light; we shall have him blunder where he should not do, by and by.—Commit a rape upon her tea-table perhaps, break all her china, and then she'll be sure to hang him. But hark! —now I hear—nothing; she does not say a word; she sleeps curiously. How if she should take it all for a dream now? or her virtue should be fallen into an apoplex?— Where the pox will all this end?   192

 Leo. [*Within.*] Jacinta! Beatrix! Fernandes! Murder! murder! help! help! help!

 Lop. Now the play begins; it opens finely.

 Leo. [*Within.*] Father! Alphonso! Save me! O save me!

 Lop. Comedy or tragedy for a ducat! for fear of the latter, decamp Lopez.   [*Exit.*

---

* A "capilotade" is a hotchpotch: "sorte de ragoût fait de morceaux de viandes déjà cuites."—*Littré.*

SCENE III.—LEONORA's *Bedchamber.*

LEONORA *discovered in a gown,* holding DON JOHN *by the sleeve.*

Leo.   Whoever you are, villain, you shan't escape me ; and though your efforts have been in vain, you shan't fail to receive the recompense of your attempt.— Help, ho, help there ! help !

[DON JOHN *breaks from her, but can't find the door.*

Don John. [*Aside.*]   'Sdeath, I shall be undone ! where is this damned door ?

Leo.   He'll get away : a light there, quickly !

Enter DON GUZMAN, *with his sword drawn.*

Don Guz.   Where are you, fair angel ? I come to lose my life in your defence.   9

Don John. [*Aside.*]   That's Guzman's voice ; the devil has sent him.   But we are still in the dark ; I have one tour yet, impudence be my aid.—[*Aloud.*]   Lights there, ho ! Where is the villain that durst attempt the virtuous Leonora?

Don Guz.   His life shall make her satisfaction.

Don John.   Or mine shall fall in his pursuit.

Don Guz.   'Tis by my hands that she shall see him die.

Don John.   My sword shall lay him bleeding at her feet.

Leo. [*Aside.*]   What can this mean? But here's lights at last, thank the just bounteous Heaven.

Don John.   Enter with the light there ; but secure the door, lest the traitor 'scape my vengeance.   21

Enter DON PEDRO *with a light, he finds* LEONORA *between 'em ; both their swords drawn.*

Leo. O Heavens ! what is't I see?

Don John. Don Pedro here !

Don Ped. [*Aside.*] What monstrous scene is this !

Don Guz. [*Aside.*] What accident has brought him here ?

Don John. [*Aside.*] Now I'm intrigued indeed.

[DON PEDRO *steps back, and shuts the door.*

Don Ped. [*Aside.*] This mystery must unfold before we part. What torments has my fate provided me ? Is this the comfort I'm to reap, to dry my tears for my poor father's death ?—[*Aloud.*] Ah, Leonora !   31

Leo. [*Aside.*] Alas ! where will this end ?

[*Falling into a chair.*

Don Ped. [*Aside.*] Naked ! and thus attended at the dead of night !—my soul is froze at what I see. Confusion sits in all their faces, and in large characters I read the ruin of my honour and my love.—[*Aloud.*] Speak, statues, if you yet have power to speak, why at this time of night you are found with Leonora ?—None speak ?—Don John, it is from you I ought to know.

Don John. My silence may inform you.

Don Ped. Your silence does inform me of my shame, but I must have some information more ; explain the whole.   43

Don John. I shall. You remember, Don Pedro—

Don Ped. Be quick.

Don John. You remember you charged me before you went—

Don Ped. I remember well, go on.

Don John. With the care of your honour.

Don Ped. I did : dispatch.

Don John. Very well ; you see Don Guzman in this apartment, you see your wife naked, and you see me, my sword in my hand ; that's all.

Don Ped. [*Drawing upon* DON GUZMAN.] 'Tis here then I am to revenge my wrongs.   55

Don Guz. Hold !

Don Ped. Villain, defend thyself !

Leo. O Heaven !

Don Guz. Yet hear me.

Don Ped. What canst thou say ?

Don Guz. The truth, as holy Heaven itself is truth. I heard the shrieks and cries of Leonora ; what the occasion was I knew not, but she repeated 'em with so much vehemence, I found, whatever her distress might be, her succour must be sudden ; so leaped the wall that parts our houses, and flew to her assistance. Don John can, if he please, inform you more.   67

Don Ped. [*Aside.*] Mankind's a villain, and this may be true. Yet 'tis too monstrous for a quick conception. I should be cautious how I wrong Don John. Sure 'tis not right to balance. I yet have but their words against their words : I know Don John for my friend, and Guzman for my rival. What can be clearer ? Yet hold : if Leonora's innocent, she may untangle all.—[*Aloud.*] Madam, I should be glad to know (if I have so much interest left) which way your evidence will point my sword ?

Leo. My lord, I'm in the same perplexity with you. All I can say is this, one of 'em came to force me, t'other to save me: but the night confounding the villainy of the guilty with the generosity of the innocent, I still am ignorant to which I owe my gratitude or my resentment.   82

Don Guz. But, madam, did you not hear me cry I came to help you?

Leo. I own it.

Don John. And did you not hear me threaten to destroy the author of your fears?

Leo. I can't deny it.

Don Guz. What can there be more to clear me?

Don John. Or me?

Don Ped. Yet one's a villain still.—[*Aside.*] My confusion but increases: yet why confused? It is, it must be Guzman. But how came Don John here? Right. Guzman has said how he came to her aid, but Alvarada could not enter but by treason.—[*Aloud.*] Then perish—

Don Guz. Who?   96

Don John. Who?

Don Ped. Just gods! instruct me who.

[*Knocking at the door.*

Don Fel. [*Within.*] Let me in, open the door!

Leo. 'Tis my father.

Don Ped. No matter, keep the door fast.—[*Aside.*] I'll have this matter go no farther, till I can reach the depth on't.—[*Aloud.*] Don Guzman, leave the house; I must suspend my vengeance for a time.

Don Guz. I obey you; but I'll lose my life, or show my innocence.   [*Exit.*

Don Fel. [*Within.*] Open the door; why am I kept out?   108

Don Ped. Don John, follow me by this back way.—
And you, Leonora, retire. [*Exit* Leonora.

Don John. [*Aside.*] If Don Guzman's throat were cut,
would not this bustle end ?—Yes.—Why, then, if his throat
be not cut, may this bustle end me. [*Exeunt.*

ACT IV.

SCENE I.—*A Room in* DON GUZMAN'S *House.*

Enter DON GUZMAN *and* GALINDO.

Don Guz. [*Musing.*] Galindo !

Gal. Sir !

Don Guz. Try if you can see Jacinta ; let her privately know I would fain speak with her.

Gal. It shall be done, sir. [*Exit.*

Don Guz. Sure villainy and impudence were never on the stretch before ! This traitor has racked 'em till they crack. To what a plunge the villain's tour has brought me! Pedro's resentment must at last be pointed here. But that's a trifle ; had he not ruined me with Leonora, I easily had passed him by the rest.—What's to be done ? Which way shall I convince her of my innocence ? The blood of him who has dared declare me guilty, may satisfy my vengeance, but not aid my love. No, I am lost with her for ever—

Enter JACINTA.

Speak, is't not so, Jacinta ? Am I not ruined with the virtuous Leonora ?　　　　　　　　　　　　　　　　16

Jac. One of you, I suppose, is.

Don Guz. Which dost thou think ?

Jac. Why, he that came to spoil all ; who should it be ?

Don Guz. Prithee be serious with me if thou canst for one small moment, and advise me which way I shall take to convince her of my innocence, that it was I that came to do her service?

Jac. Why, you both came to do her service, did not you? 26

Don Guz. Still trifling?

Jac. No, by my troth, not I.

Don Guz. Then turn thy thoughts to ease me in my torment, and be my faithful witness to her, that Heaven and Hell and all their wrath I imprecate, if ever once I knew one fleeting thought, that durst propose to me so impious an attempt. No, Jacinta, I love her well; but love with that humility, whatever misery I feel, my torture ne'er shall urge me on to seize more than her bounty gives me leave to take.

Jac. And the murrain take such a lover and his humility both, say I. Why sure, sir, you are not in earnest in this story, are you? 39

Don Guz. Why dost thou question it?

Jac. Because I really and seriously thought you innocent.

Don Guz. Innocent! what dost thou mean?

Jac. Mean! why, what should I mean? I mean that I concluded you loved my lady to that degree, you could not live without her: and that the thought of her being given up to another made your passion flame out like mount Etna. That upon this, your love got the bridle in his teeth, and ran away with you into her chamber, where that impertinent spy upon her and you, Don John, followed, and prevented farther proofs of your affection. 51

Don Guz. Why sure—

Jac. Why sure, thus I thought it was, and thus she thinks it is. If you have a mind in the depth of your discretion to convince her of your innocence—may your innocence be your reward. I'm sure, were I in her place, you should never have any other from me.

Don Guz. Was there then no merit in flying to her assistance when I heard her cries?

Jac. As much as the constable and the watch might have pretended to—something to drink.

Don Guz. This is all raillery; 'tis impossible she can be pleased with such an attempt.   63

Jac. 'Tis impossible she can be pleased with being reduced to make the attempt upon you.

Don Guz. But was this a proper way to save her blushes?

Jac. 'Twas in the dark, that's one way.

Don Guz. But it must look like downright violation.

Jac. If it did not feel like it, what did that signify? Come, sir, waggery apart, you know I'm your servant, I have given you proofs on't. Therefore don't distrust me now if I tell you, this quarrel may be made up with the wife, though perhaps not with the husband. In short, she thinks you were first in her chamber, and has not the worse opinion of you for it; she makes allowance for your sufferings, and has still love enough for you, not to be displeased with the utmost proofs you can give, that you have still a warm remain for her.   79

Don Guz. If this be true, and that she thought 'twas me, why did she cry out to expose me?

Jac. Because at that time she did not think 'twas you.

Will that content you ? And now she does think 'twas you,
your business is to let her think so on ; for, in a word, I can
see she's concerned at the danger she has brought you into,
and I believe would be heartily glad to see you well out
on't.

Don Guz. 'Tis impossible she can forgive me. 88

Jac. Oons !—Now Heaven forgive me, for I had a great
oath upon the very tip of my tongue ; you'd make one mad
with your impossibles, and your innocence, and your
humilities. 'Sdeath, sir, d'you think a woman makes no
distinction between the assaults of a man she likes and one
she don't ? My lady hates Don John, and if she thought
'twas he had done this job, she'd hang him for't in her own
garters ; she likes you, and if you should do such another,
you might still die in your bed like a bishop, for her.

Don Guz. Well, I'll dispute no farther. I put myself
into thy hands. What am I to do next ? 99

Jac. Why, do as she bids you ; be in the way at the old
rendezvous, she'll take the first occasion she can to speak to
you ; and when you meet, do as I bid you, and instead of
your innocent and humble, be guilty and resolute. Your
mistress is now married, sir, consider that. She has changed
her situation, and so must you your battery. Attack a maid
gently, a wife warmly, and be as rugged with a widow as you
can. Good bye t'ye, sir. [*Exeunt several ways.*

SCENE II.—LEONORA'S *Apartment.*

Enter DON PEDRO.

Don Ped. In what distraction have I passed this night ! Sure I shall never close my eyes again. No rack can equal what I feel. Wounded in both my honour and my love ; they have pierced me in two tender parts. Yet, could I take my just revenge, it would in some degree assuage my smart. Oh, guide me, Heaven, to that cordial drop !— Hold ! a glance of light, I think, begins to—yes—right. When yesterday I brought Don John hither, was not Don Felix much disturbed ?—He was. And why ?—That may be worth inquiring. But something more occurs. At my arrival in this city, was I not told two cavaliers were warm in the pursuit of Leonora ? One I remember well they named ; 'twas Guzman : the other I am yet a stranger to. I fear I shall not be so long—'tis Alvarada ; O the traitor ! —yet I may wrong him much. I have Guzman's own confession that he passed the wall to come to Leonora.— Oh, but 'twas to her assistance.—And so it might, and he a villain still. There are assistances of various sorts.—What were her wants ? That's dark. But, whatsoe'er they were, he came to her assistance. Death be his portion for his ready service ! 21

Enter DON FELIX.

Don Fel. You avoid me, Don Pedro ; 'tis not well. Am I not your father, have you not reason to believe I am your friend?

Don Ped. I have.

Don Fel. Why do you not then treat me like a father

and a friend ? The mystery you make to me of last night's disturbance, I take unkindly from you.   Come, tell me your grief, that, if I can, I may assuage it.

Don Ped. Nothing but vengeance can give me ease.

Don Fel. If I desire to know your wrongs, 'tis to assist you in revenging 'em.   32

Don Ped. Know then, that last night in this apartment I found Don Guzman and Don John.

Don Fel. Guzman and Alvarada !

Don Ped. Yes ; and Leonora almost naked between them, crying out for aid.

Don Fel. Were they both guilty ?

Don Ped. One was come to force her, t'other to rescue her.

Don Fel. Which was the criminal ?

Don Ped. Of that I yet am ignorant.   They accuse each other.

Don Fel. Can't your wife determine it ?   44

Don Ped. The darkness of the night put it out of her power.

Don Fel. But I perhaps may bring some light to aid you.   I have part in the affront : and though my arm's too old and weak to serve you, my counsel may be useful to your vengeance.   Know then, that Don Guzman has a long time pursued my daughter ; and I as resolutely refused his suit : which however has not hindered him from searching all occasions to see and speak to her.   Don John, on his side—

Don Ped. Don John's my friend, and I am confident—

Don Fel. That confidence destroys you. Hear my charge, and be yourself his judge. He too has been a pressing suitor to my daughter.   57

Don Ped. Impossible !

Don Fel. To me myself he has owned his love to her.

Don Ped. Good gods ! Yet still this leaves the mystery where it was ; this charge is equal.

Don Fel. 'Tis true ; but yonder's one (if you can make her speak) I have reason to believe can tell us more.—Ho, Jacinta !

Enter JACINTA.

Jac. Do you call me, sir ? 65

Don Fel. Yes ; Don Pedro would speak with you.— [*Aside to* DON PEDRO.] I'll leave you with her ; press her both by threats and promises, and if you find your wife in fault, old as I am, her father too, I'll raise my arm to plunge this dagger in her breast; and by that *fermeté* convince the world my honour's dearer to me than my child. [*Exit.*

Don Ped. [*Aside.*] Heaven grant me power to stifle my rage, till 'tis time to let my vengeance fly !—Jacinta, come near : I have some business with you. 75

Jac. [*Aside.*] His business with me at this time can be good for nothing, I doubt.—[*Aloud.*] What commands have you, sir, for me ? for I'm not very well.

Don Ped. What's your disorder ?

Jac. A little sort of a something towards an ague, I think.

Don Ped. You don't seem so ill but you may tell me—

Jac. Oh, I can tell you nothing, sir, I assure you.

Don Ped. You answer me before you hear my question. That looks as if you knew—

Jac. I know that what you are going to ask me is a secret I'm out at. 86

Don Ped. [*Offering her a purse.*] Then this shall let thee into it.

Jac. · I know nothing of the matter.

Don Ped. Come, tell me all, and take thy reward.

Jac. I know nothing of the matter, I say.

Don Ped. [*Drawing his sword.*] Speak ! or by all the flame and fire of hell eternal—

Jac. O Lard ! O Lard ! O Lard !

Don Ped. Speak, or th'art dead.

Jac. But if I do speak, shan't I be dead for all that ?

Don Ped. Speak, and thou art safe.   97

Jac. Well—O .Lard !—I'm so frighted !—But if I must speak then—O dear heart !—give me the purse.

Don Ped. There.

Jac. Why truly, between a purse in one's hand—and—a sword in one's guts, I think there's little room left for debate.

Don Ped. Come, begin, I'm impatient.

Jac. Begin ? let me see ; where shall I begin ? at Don Guzman, I think.

Don Ped. What of him ?

Jac. Why, he has been in love with my lady these six years.   109

Don Ped. I know it, but how has she received him ?

Jac. Received him ? Why—as young maids use to receive handsome fellows ; at first ill, afterwards better.

Don Ped. [*Aside.*] Furies !—[*Aloud.*] Did they ever meet ?

Jac. A little.

Don Ped. By day or night ?

Jac. Both.

Don Ped. Distraction !   Where was their rendezvous ?

Jac. Where they could not do one another much good.

Don Ped. As how ?   120

Jac. As through a hole in a wall.

Don   Ped.   The strumpet banters me.—Be serious,
insolence, or I shall spoil your gaiety ; I'm not disposed to
mirth.

Jac. Why, I am serious, if you like my story the better
for't.

Don Ped. [*Aside.*] How miserable a wretch am I !

Jac. I tell you there's a wall parts their two houses, and
in that wall there's a hole.   How the wall came by the hole,
I can't tell ; mayhap by chance, mayhap by no chance ;
but there 'tis, and there they use to prattle.   131

Don Ped. And this is truth ?

Jac. I can't bate you a word on't, sir.

Don Ped. When did they meet there last ?

Jac. Yesterday ; I suppose 'twas only to bid one another
adieu.

Don Ped. Ah, Jacinta, thou hast pierced my soul !

Jac. [*Aside.*]   And yet I han't told you half I could tell
you, my don.

Don Ped. Where is this place you speak of?

Jac. There 'tis, if you are curious.   141

Don Ped. When they would speak with one another,
what's the call ?

Jac. Tinkle, tinkle.

Don Ped. A bell ?

Jac. It is.

Don Ped. Ring !

Jac. What do you mean, sir ?

Don Ped. [*Hastily.*] Ring!

Jac. 'Tis done.   [*She makes the signal.*

Don Ped. [*Aside*]. I'll make use of her to examine him.
—[*Aloud.*] Does he come?   152

Jac. Not yet.

Don Ped. Pull again.

Jac. You must give him time, sir; my lady always does
so.

Don Ped. I hear something.

Jac. 'Tis he.

Don Guz. [*Within.*] Who's there?

Don Ped. [*Softly.*] Say you are Leonora.

   [*Dumb show of her unwillingness, and his threatening.*

Jac. [*Softly.*] 'Tis Leonora.

Don Guz. What are your commands, madam? Is it
possible so unfortunate a wretch as I can be capable of
serving you?   164

   [Don Pedro *whispers* Jacinta, *who seems backward to
      speak.*

Jac. I come to ask you, how you could so far forget that
infinite regard you have professed, to make an attempt so
dangerous both to yourself and me; and which, with all
the esteem and love I have ever borne you, you scarce
could hope I ever should forgive you?

Don Guz. Alas, my hopes and fears were vanished too.
My counsel was my love and my despair. If they advised
me wrong, of them complain, for it was you who made 'em
my directors.

Don Ped. [*Aside.*] The villain owns the fact. It seems
he thinks he has not much to fear from her resentment.
Oh, torture!   176

F 2

Enter LEONORA.

Jac. [*Aside.*] So, she's here; that's as I expected : now we are blown up.

Leo. [*Aside, not seeing them.*] If I don't mistake, I heard Don Guzman's call. I can't refuse to answer it; forgive me, gods, and let my woman's weakness plead my cause.— How ! my husband here ! Nay, then—

Don Ped. You seem disordered, madam ; pray what may be the cause ?

Leo. [*Confused.*] I don't know really ; I'm not—I don't know that—   186

Don Ped. You did not know that I was here, I guess.

Leo. Yes, I did, and—came to speak with you.

Don Ped. I'm not at present in a talking humour, but if your tongue is set to conversation, there's one behind the wall will entertain you.

Don Guz. But is it possible, fair Leonora, that you can pardon my attempt ?

Don Ped. [*To* LEONORA.] You hear him, madam ; he dares own it to you.   196

Leo. [*Aside.*] Jacinta winks ; I guess what scene they have been acting here. My part is now to play. —[*To* DON PEDRO.] I see, sir, he dares own it : nor is he the first lover has presumed beyond the counte- nance he ever has received. Pray, draw near, and hear what he has more to say : it is my interest you should know the depth of all has ever passed between us.—[*To* DON GUZMAN.] I fain would know, Don Guzman, whether in the whole conduct of my life, you

have known one step that could encourage you to hope
I ever could be yours, but on the terms of honour which
you sought me ?   208

Don Guz. Not one.

Leo. Why then should you believe I could forgive the
taking that by force, which you already were convinced I
valued more the keeping than my life ?

Don Guz. Had my love been as temperate as yours,
I with your reason had perhaps debated. But not in
reason, but in flames, I flew to Leonora.   215

Leo. If strong temptation be allowed a plea, vice, in
the worst of shapes, has much to urge. No, could
anything have shaken me in virtue, it must have been
the strength of it in you. Had you shone bright enough
to dazzle me, I blindly might have missed the path I
meant to tread : but now you have cleared my sight for
ever. If therefore from this moment more you dare to
let me know one thought of love, though in the humblest
style, expect to be a sacrifice to him you attempt to wrong.
Farewell !   [*She retires from him.*

Don Guz. Oh, stay and hear me ! I have wronged myself, I'm innocent ; by all that's sacred, just, and good, I'm
innocent !   228

Don Ped. [*Aside.*] What does he mean ?

Don Guz. I have owned a fact I am not guilty of ;
Jacinta can inform you ; she knows I never—

Jac. I know ! the man's mad. Pray be gone, sir, my
lady will hear no more.—I'll shut him out, madam, shan't
I ?

Leo. I have no farther business with him.

[JACINTA *shuts up the hole.*

Enter ISABELLA *hastily.*

Isab.   O Heavens, Leonora, where are you?—Don Pedro, you can assist me better.

Leo.   What's the matter?   238

Don Ped.   What is it, madam, I can serve you in?

Isab.   In what the peace of my whole life consists, the safety of my brother.   Don John's servant has this moment left me a letter for him, which I have opened, knowing there is an animosity of some time between 'em.

Don Ped.   Well, madam?

Isab.   O dear, it is a challenge, and what to do I know not!   If I show it my brother, he'll immediately fly to the place appointed: and if I don't, he'll be accused of cowardice.   One way I risk his life, t'other I ruin his honour.   249

Don Ped.   What would you have me do, madam?

Isab.   I'll tell you, sir: I only beg you'll go to the place where Don John expects him; tell him I have intercepted his letter, and make him promise you he'll send no more. By this generous charity you may hinder two men (whose piques are on a frivolous occasion) from murdering one another; and by this good office you'll repay the small debt you owe my brother for flying last night to Leonora's succour; and doubly pay the obligation you have to me upon the same occasion.   259

Don Ped.   What obligation, madam?   I am ignorant; pray inform me.

Isab.   'Twas I, sir, that first heard Leonora's cries, and raised my brother to her aid.   Pray let me receive the same assistance from your prudence, which you have had from

my care and my brother's generosity. But pray lose no
time. Don John is perhaps already on the spot, and not
meeting my brother, may send a second message, which may
be fatal.

Don Ped. Madam, be at rest; you shall be satisfied,
I'll go this moment. I'll only ask you first whether you are
sure you heard my wife call out for succour, before your
brother passed the wall?   272

Isab. I did; why do you ask that question?

Don Ped. I have a reason, you may be sure.—[*Aside.*]
Just Heaven, I adore thee! the truth at last shines clear,
and by that villain Alvarada I'm betrayed. But enough,
I'll make use of this occasion for my vengeance.—[*To*
ISABELLA.] Where, madam, is it Don John is waiting?

Isab. But here, in a small field behind the garden.

Don Ped. [*Aside.*] His blood shall do me reason for
his treachery.

Isab. Will you go there directly?

Don Ped. I will. Be satisfied.   [*Exit.*

Leo. You weep, Isabella.

Isab. You see my trouble for a brother, for whom I
would die, and a lover for whom I would live. They both
are authors of my grief.

Leo. They both are instruments of my misfortune.

[*Exeunt.*

ACT V.

SCENE I.—*A Field adjoining* DON FELIX'S *Garden.*

Enter LOPEZ.

Lop. O ho, my good signor Don John, you are mistaken
in your man !   I am your humble valet, 'tis true, and I am
to obey you : but when you have got the devil in your body,
and are upon your rantipole adventures, you shall Quixote
it by yourself for Lopez. Yonder he is, waiting for poor
Guzman, with a sword of a fathom and a half, a dagger for
close engagement; and (if I don't mistake) a pocket pistol
for extraordinary occasions.   I think I am not in the wrong
to keep a little out of the way.   These matters will end in a
court of justice, or I'm wrong in my foresight.   Now that
being a place where I am pretty well known, and not over-
much reputed, I believe 'tis best, neither to come in for
prisoner nor evidence.   But hold ; yonder comes another
Toledo.   Don Guzman, I presume ; but I presume wrong ;
'tis—who is't ? Don Pedro, by all the powers! What the pox
does he here, or what the pox do I here?   I'm sure as matters
stand, I ought to fly him like a creditor ; but he sees me,
'tis too late to slip him.   18

Enter DON PEDRO.

Don Ped. How now, Lopez, where are you going?

Lop. I'm going, sir, I—I'm going—if you please I'm going about my business.

Don Ped. From whence do you come?

Lop. Only—only, sir, from—taking the air a little; I'm mightily muddled with a whur—round about in my head for this day or two; I'm going home to be let blood, as fast as I can, sir.

Don Ped. Hold, sir, I'll let you blood here.—[*Aside.*] This rascal may have borne some part in this late adventure. He's a coward, I'll try to frighten it out of him.—[*Aloud.*] You traitor you, y'are dead!   30

    [*Seizing him by the collar, and drawing his poniard.*

Lop. Mercy, Don Pedro!   [*Kneeling.*

Don Ped. Are you not a villain?

Lop. Yes, if you please.

Don Ped. Is there so great a one upon earth?

Lop. With respect to my master; no.

Don Ped. Prepare then to die.

Lop. Give me but time, and I will. But noble Don Pedro, just Don Pedro, generous Don Pedro, what is it I have done?   39

Don Ped. What if thou darest deny, I'll plunge this dagger deep into thy throat, and drive the falsehood to thy heart again. Therefore take heed, and on thy life declare; didst thou not this last night open my doors to let Don Guzman in?

Lop. Don Guzman!

Don Ped. Don Guzman? Yes, Don Guzman, traitor, him!

Lop. Now may the sky crush me, if I let in Don Guzman.   49

Don Ped. Who did you let in then? It wan't your master sure! if it was him, you did your duty, I have no more to say.

Lop. Why then, if I let in anybody else, I'm a son of a whore. [*Rising.*

Don Ped. Did he order you beforehand, or did you do't upon his knocking?

Lop. Why, he—I'll tell you, sir, he—pray put up that brilliant; it sparkles so in my eyes, it almost blinds me.— [DON PEDRO *puts up his poniard.*] Thank you, sir.—Why, sir, I'll tell you just how the matter was, but I hope you won't consider me as a party? 61

Don Ped. Go on, thou art safe.

Lop. Why then, sir, when (for our sins) you had left us, says my master to me, Lopez, says he, go and stay at old Don Felix's house, till Don Pedro returns, they'll pass thee for his servant, and think he has ordered thee to stay there. And then says he, dost hear, open me the door by Leonora's apartment to-night, for I have a little business, says he, to do there.

Don Ped. [*Aside.*] Perfidious wretch! 70

Lop. Indeed, I was at first a little wresty, and stood off; being suspicious (for I knew the man) that there might be some ill intentions. But he knew me too, takes me upon the weak side; whips out a long sword; and by the same means makes me do the thing as you have made me dis- cover it.—[*Aside.*] There's neither liberty nor property in this land, since the blood of the Bourbons came amongst us.

Don Ped. Then you let him in, as he bid you?

Lop. I did: if I had not, I had never lived to tell you the story. Yes, I let him in. 80

Don Ped. And what followed ?

Lop. Why, he followed.

Don Ped. What ?

Lop. His inclinations.

Don Ped. Which way ?

Lop. The old way ; to a woman.

Don Ped. Confound him !

Lop. In short, he got to madam's chamber, and before he had been there long (though you know, sir, a little time goes a great way in some matters), I heard such a clutter of small shot, murder ! murder ! murder ! rape ! fire ! help ! and so forth—But hold, here he comes himself, and can give you a more circumstantial account of the skirmish.

[*Exit.*

Don Ped. I thank thee, Heaven, at last, for having pointed me to the victim I am to sacrifice.   95

Enter DON JOHN.

Villain, defend thyself !   [*Drawing.*

Don John. What do you mean ?

Don Ped. To punish a traitor.

Don John. Where is he ?

Don Ped. In the heart of a sworn friend.

Don John. [*Aside.*] I saw Lopez go from him ; without doubt he has told him all.—[*Aloud.*] Of what am I suspected ?

Don Ped. Of betraying the greatest trust that man could place in man.   105

Don John. And by whom am I accused ?

Don Ped. By me. Have at thy traitor's heart.

Don John. Hold ! and be not quite a madman ! Pedro,

you know me well. You know I am not backward upon these occasions, nor shall I refuse you any satisfaction you'll demand; but first, I will be heard, and tell you, that for a man of sense, you are pleased to make very odd conclusions.

Don Ped. Why, what is't possible thou canst invent to clear thyself?   115

Don John. To clear myself! Of what? I'm to be thanked for what I have done, and not reproached. I find I have been an ass, and pushed my friendship to that point, you find not virtue in yourself enough to conceive it in another. But henceforward I shall be a better husband on't.

Don Ped. I should be loath to find ingratitude could e'er be justly charged upon me : but after what your servant has confessed—   124

Don John. My servant! right, my servant! the very thing I guessed. Fie, fie, Don Pedro! is't from a servant's mouth a friend condemns a friend? or can servants always judge at what their masters' outward actions point? But some allowances I should make for the wild agitations you must needs be in. I'm therefore calm, and thus far pass all by.

Don Ped. If you are innocent, Heaven be my aid, that I may find you so. But still—   133

Don John. But still you wrong me, if you still suspect. Hear then, in short, my part of this adventure. In order to acquit myself of the charge you laid upon me in your absence, I went last night, just as 'twas dark, to view the several approaches to the house where you had left your wife; and I observed not far from one of the back doors

two persons in close eager conference. I was disguised, so
ventured to pass near 'em, and by a word or two I heard, I
found 'twas Guzman talking to Jacinta. My concern for
your honour made me at first resolve to call him to an
immediate account. But then reflecting that I might possibly o'erhear some part of their discourse, and by that judge
of Leonora's thoughts, I reined my passion in; and by the
help of an advancing buttress, which kept me from their
sight, I learned the black conspiracy. Don Guzman said,
he had great complaint to make ; and since his honourable
love had been so ill returned, he could with ease forgive
himself, if by some rougher means he should procure what
prayers, and tears, and sighs had urged in vain.   152

Don Ped. Go on.

Don John. His kind assistant closed smoothly with him,
and informed him with what ease that very night she'd
introduce him to her chamber. At last they parted with
this agreement, that at some overture * in a wall, he should
expect her to inform him when Leonora was in bed, and all
the coast was clear.

Don Ped. Dispatch the rest.—[*Aside.*]   Is't possible
after all he should be innocent !   161

Don John. I must confess the resolution taken made me
tremble for you. How to prevent it now and for ever was
my next care. I immediately ordered Lopez to go lie at
Don Felix's and to open me the door when all the family
were in bed. He did as I directed him. I entered, and
in the dark found my way to Leonora's apartment ; I found

---

* *i.e.*, opening.

the door open, at which I was surprised. I thought I heard some stirring in her chamber, and in an instant heard her cry to aid. At this I drew, and rushed into the room; which Guzman alarmed at, cried out to her assistance. His ready impudence, I must confess, at first quite struck me speechless; but in a moment I regained my tongue, and loud proclaimed the traitor.   174

Don Ped. Is't possible!

Don John. Yet more: your arrival hindering me at that time from taking vengeance for your wrong, I at this instant expect him here, to punish him (with Heaven's righteous aid) for daring to attempt my ruin with the man, whose friendship I prefer to all the blessings Heaven and earth dispense. And now, Don Pedro, I have told you this, if still you have a mind to take my life, I shall defend it with the self-same warmth I intended to expose it in your service.   [*Draws.*

Don Ped. [*Aside.*] If I did not know he was in love with Leonora, I could be easily surprised with what he has told me. But—but yet 'tis certain he has destroyed the proofs against him; and if I only hold him guilty as a lover, why must Don Guzman pass for innocent? Good Gods, I am again returning to my doubts!   190

Don John. [*Aside.*] I have at last reduced him to a balance, but one lie more tossed in will turn the scale.— [*Aloud.*] One obligation more, my friend, you owe me; I thought to have let it pass, but it shall out. Know then, I loved, like you, the beauteous Leonora; but from the moment I observed how deep her dart had pierced you, I tore my passion from my bleeding heart, and sacrificed my happiness to yours. Now I've no more to plead; if

still you think your vengeance is my due, come pay it
me.   200

Don Ped. Rather ten thousand poniards strike me dead.
O Alvarada! Can you forgive a wild distracted friend?
Gods! whither was my jealous frenzy leading me? Can
you forget this barbarous injury?

Don John. I can: no more. But for the future, think
me what I am, a faithful and a zealous friend. Retire, and
leave me here. In a few moments I hope to bring you
farther proofs on't. Guzman I instantly expect; leave me
to do you justice on him.

Don Ped. That must not be. My revenge can ne'er be
satisfied by any other hand but this.   211

Don John. Then let that do't. You'll in a moment
have an opportunity.

Don Ped. You mistake, he won't be here.

Don John. How so?

Don Ped. He has not had your challenge. His sister
intercepted it, and desired I'd come to prevent the quarrel.

Don John. What then is to be done?

Don Ped. I'll go and find him out immediately.

Don John. Very well: or hold—[*Aside.*] I must hinder
'em from talking, gossiping may discover me.—[*Aloud.*] Yes:
let's go and find him: or, let me see—ay—'twill do better.

Don Ped. What?   223

Don John. Why, that the punishment should suit the
crime.

Don Ped. Explain.

Don John. Attack him by his own laws of war.—'Twas
in the night he would have had your honour, and in the
night you ought to have his life.

Don Ped.   His treason cannot take the guilt from mine.

Don John.   There is no guilt in fair retaliation.   When
'tis a point of honour founds the quarrel, the laws of sword-
men must be kept, 'tis true : but if a thief glides in to seize
my treasure, methinks I may return the favour on my dagger's
point, as well as with my sword of ceremony six times as
long.   236

Don Ped.   Yet still the nobler method I would choose ;
it better satisfies the vengeance of a man of honour.

Don John.   I own it, were you sure you should succeed :
but the events of combats are uncertain.   Your enemy may
'scape you : you perhaps may only wound him ; you may
be parted.   Believe me, Pedro, the injury's too great for a
punctilio satisfaction.

Don Ped.   Well, guide me as you please, so you direct
me quickly to my vengeance.   What do you propose ? 245

Don John.   That which is easy, as 'tis just to execute.
The wall he passed, to attempt your wife, let us get over to
prevent his doing so any more.   'Twill let us into a private
apartment by his garden, where every evening in his
amorous solitudes he spends some time alone, and where I
guess his late fair scheme was drawn.   The deed done, we
can retreat the way we entered ; let me be your pilot, 'tis
now e'en dark, and the most proper time.

Don Ped.   Lead on ; I'll follow you.

Don John. [*Aside.*]   How many villainies I'm forced to
act, to keep one secret !   [*Exeunt.*

SCENE II.—Don Guzman's *Apartment.*

Don Guzman *discovered sitting.*

Don Guz. With what rigour does this unfaithful woman treat me! Is't possible it can be she, who appeared to love me with so much tenderness? How little stress is to be laid upon a woman's heart! Sure they're not worth those anxious cares they give.—[*Rising.*] Then burst my chains, and give me room to search for nobler pleasures. I feel my heart begin to mutiny for liberty; there is a spirit in it yet, will struggle hard for freedom: but solitude's the worst of seconds.—Ho, Sancho! Galindo! who waits there? Bring some lights. Where are you?   10

Enter Galindo, *rubbing his eyes, and drunk.*

Gal. I can't well tell. Do you want me, sir?

Don Guz. Yes, sir, I want you. Why am I left in the dark? what were you doing?

Gal. Doing, sir? I was doing—what one does when one sleeps, sir.

Don Guz. Have you no light without?

Gal. [*Yawning.*] Light!—No, sir,—I have no light. I'm used to hardship. I can sleep in the dark.

Don Guz. You have been drinking, you rascal, you are drunk!   20

Gal. I have been drinking, sir, 'tis true, but I am not drunk. Every man that is drunk, has been drinking; confessed. But every man that has been drinking, is not drunk. Confess that too.

Don Guz. Who is't has put you in this condition, you sot?

Gal. A very honest fellow : Madam Leonora's coach-man, nobody else. I have been making a little debauch with Madam Leonora's coachman ; yes.

Don Guz. How came you to drink with him, beast ?

Gal. Only *par complaisance*, sir. The coachman was to be drunk upon madam's wedding ; and I, being a friend, was desired to take part.   32

Don Guz. And so, you villain, you can make yourself merry with what renders me miserable !

Gal. No, sir, no ; 'twas the coachman was merry : I drank with tears in my eyes. The remembrance of your misfortunes made me so sad, so sad, that every cup I swallowed, was like a cup of poison to me.

Don Guz. Without doubt.

Gal. Yes ; and to mortify myself upon melancholy matters, I believe I took down fifty. Yes.   41

Don Guz. Go fetch some lights, you drunken sot you !

Gal. I will if I can find the door, that is to say.—The devil's in the door ! I think 'tis grown too little for me.— [*Feeling for the door, and running against it.*] Shrunk this wet weather, I presume.   [*Exit.*

Don Guz. Absence, the old remedy for love, must e'en be mine ; to stay and brave the danger were presumption. Farewell, Valencia, then ! and farewell, Leonora ! And if thou canst, my heart, redeem thy liberty ; secure it by a farewell eternal to her sex.   51

Re-enter GALINDO, *with a candle.*

Gal. Here's light, sir.—[*He falls and puts it out.*] So !

Don Guz. Well done ! You sottish rascal, come no more in my sight.   [*Passing angrily into another chamber.*

Gal. These boards are so uneven!—You shall see now I shall neither find the candle—nor the candlestick; it shan't be for want of searching however.—[*Rising and feeling about for the candle.*] O ho, have I got you? Enough, I'll look for your companion to-morrow.

Enter DON PEDRO *and* DON JOHN.

Don Ped. Where are we now? 60

Don John. We are in the apartment I told you of—softly—I hear something stir.—Ten to one but 'tis he.

Gal. Don't I hear somewhat?—No.—When one has wine in one's head, one has such a bustle in one's ears.

Don Ped. [*To* DON JOHN.] Who is that talking to himself?

Don John. 'Tis his servant, I know his voice, keep still.

Gal. Well; since my master has banished me his sight, I'll redeem by my obedience what I have lost by my debauch. I'll go sleep twelve hours in some melancholy hole where the devil shan't find me. Yes. [*Exit.*

Don John. He's gone; but hush, I hear somebody coming. 74

Don Guz. Ho, there! will nobody bring light?

[*Behind the scene.*

Don Ped. 'Tis Guzman.

Don John. 'Tis so, prepare.

Don Ped. Shall I own my weakness? I feel an inward check; I wish this could be done some other way.

Don John. Distraction all! is this a time to balance? Think on the injury he would have done you, 'twill fortify your arm, and guide your dagger to his heart.

G 2

Don Ped. Enough, I'll hesitate no more; be satisfied, hark ! he's coming. 84

DON GUZMAN *passes the stage.*

Don Guz. I think these rogues are resolved to leave me in the dark all night. [*Exit.*

Don John. Now's your time; follow him, and strike home.

Don Ped. To his heart, if my dagger will reach it.

[*Exit.*

Don John. [*Aside.*] If one be killed, I'm satisfied ; 'tis no great matter which.

Re-enter DON GUZMAN, DON PEDRO *following him with his dagger ready to strike.*

Don Guz. My chamber-door's locked, and I think I hear somebody tread.—Who's there?—Nobody answers. But still I hear something stir. Hollo there ! Sancho, are you all drunk ? Some lights here quickly. 95

[*Passes by the corner where* DON JOHN *stands, and goes off the stage ;* DON PEDRO *following him.*

Don Ped. [*Aside.*] I think I'm near him now.—Traitor, take that ! my wife has sent it thee. [*Stabs* DON JOHN.

Don John. Ah, I'm dead !

Don Ped. Then thou hast thy due.

Don John. I have indeed, 'tis I that have betrayed thee.

Don Ped. And 'tis I that am revenged on thee for doing it.

Don John. I would have forced thy wife.

Don Ped. Die then with the regret to have failed in thy attempt. 106

Don John. Farewell, if thou canst forgive me— [*Dies.*

Don Ped. I have done the deed: there's nothing left but to make our escape. Don John, where are you? let's be gone, I hear the servants coming.

[*Knocking at the door.*

Lop. [*Without.*] Open there quickly, open the door!

Don Ped. That's Lopez, we shall be discovered. But 'tis no great matter, the crime will justify the execution. But where's Don John?—Don John, where are you?

[*Knocking at the door.*

Lop. [*Without.*] Open the door there, quickly!— Madam, I saw 'em both pass the wall, the devil's in't if any good comes on't.   117

Leo. [*Without.*] I am frightened out of my senses!— Ho, Isabella!

Don Ped. 'Tis Leonora.—She's welcome.—With her own eyes let her see her Guzman dead.

Enter DON GUZMAN, LEONORA, ISABELLA, JACINTA, *and* LOPEZ, *with lights.*

Don Ped. Ha! what is't I see? Guzman alive? Then who art thou?   [*Looking on* DON JOHN.

Don Guz. Guzman alive! Yes, Pedro, Guzman is alive.

Don Ped. Then Heaven is just, and there's a traitor dead.

Isab. [*Weeping.*] Alas, Don John!   126

Lop. [*Looking upon* DON JOHN.] Buenas noches!

Don Guz. What has produced this bloody scene?

Don Ped. 'Tis I have been the actor in't; my poniard, Guzman, I intended in your heart. I thought your crime deserved it: but I did you wrong, and my hand, in searching the innocent, has by Heaven's justice been directed to the guilty.   Don John, with his last breath, confessed himself the offender.   Thus my revenge is satisfied, and you are cleared.

Don Guz. Good Heaven, how equitable are thy judgments!

Don Ped. [*To* LEONORA.] Come, madam, my honour now is satisfied, and if you please my love may be so too.

Leo. If it is not,

You to yourself alone shall owe your smart,

For where I've given my hand, I'll give my heart.

[*Exeunt omnes.*

EPILOGUE.

WHAT say you, sirs, d'ye think my lady'll 'scape?
'Tis devilish hard to stand a favourite's rape.
Should Guzman, like Don John, break in upon her,
For all her virtue, Heaven have mercy on her!
Her strength, I doubt,'s in his irresolution,
There's wondrous charms in vigorous execution.
Indeed you men are fools, you won't believe
What dreadful things we women can forgive:
I know but one we never do pass by,
And that you plague us with eternally;   10
When in your courtly fears to disoblige,
You won't attack the town which you besiege.
Your guns are light, and planted out of reach:
D'ye think with billets-doux to make a breach?
'Tis small-shot all, and not a stone will fly;
Walls fall by cannon, and by firing nigh:
In sluggish dull blockades you keep the field,
And starve us ere we can with honour yield.
In short——
We can't receive those terms you gently tender,   20
But storm, and we can answer our surrender.

THE COUNTRY HOUSE.

INTRODUCTION TO THE "THE COUNTRY HOUSE."

Genest supposes *The Country House* to have been first produced at some time between 1697 and 1703 : the earliest performance, however, recorded by him, took place at the Theatre Royal, Drury Lane, on the 16th of June, 1705. It was first published, in 12mo, and without the author's name, on the 17th of March, 1715. * The names of the actors are not given. The title-page of the original edition reads as follows : "*The Country House. A Farce. As Acted at both Theatres with great Applause. London : Printed for W. Meares at the Lamb, and Jonas Browne at the Black Swan, without Temple-Bar. MDCCXV.*"

This slight, but rather amusing, farce is a translation of *La Maison de Campagne*, a comedy by Dancourt, first represented on the 27th of August, 1688. † Vanbrugh has divided the single act of the French play into two acts. His translation is pretty close throughout ; not slavishly exact, but never straying far from the sense of the original.

---

* The *Post Boy* of March 15-17, 1715, contains the following announcement : "This Day is publish'd, The Country-House, a Farce, as acted at Both Theatres, with applause. Printed for W. Mears and J. Brown without Temple Bar."

† Frères Parfaict : *Hist. du Théâtre François*, vol. xiii., p. 87.

DRAMATIS PERSONÆ.

MEN.

Monsieur *Barnard*.
Monsieur *Griffard*, Brother to M. *Barnard*.
Erast, in Love with *Mariane*.
Dorant, Son to M. *Barnard*.
The Marquis.
The Baron *de Messy*.
Janno, Cousin to M. *Barnard*.
Colin, Servant to M. *Barnard*.
Charly, a Boy.
A Soldier.
Servant to *Erast*.
A Cook.
Three Gentlemen, friends to *Dorant*.

WOMEN.

Madame *Barnard*.
Mariane, her Daughter.
Mawkin, Sister to *Janno*.
Lisett, Servant to *Mariane*.

[SCENE.—A Country House in FRANCE.]

THE COUNTRY HOUSE.

A FARCE.

ACT I.

SCENE.—*A Room in* Monsieur BARNARD'S *Country-House.*

Enter ERAST *and his* Servant, LISETT *following.*

Lis. Once more I'll tell ye, sir, if you've any consideration in the world for her, you must begone this minute.

Erast. My dear Lisett, let me but see her, let me but
speak to her only.

Lis. You may do what you will; here you are in our
house, and I do believe she's as impatient to see you as you
can be to see her; but—

Erast. But why won't you give us that satisfaction
then?

Lis. Because I know the consequence; for when you
once get together, the devil himself is not able to part ye;
you'll stay so long till you're surprised, and what shall
become of us then?   13

Serv. Why, then we shall be thrown out at the window,
I suppose.

Lis. No, but I shall be turned out of doors.

Erast. How unfortunate am I! these doors are open to all the world, and only shut to me.

Lis. Because you come for a wife, and at our house we don't care for people that come for wives—

Serv. What would you have us come for then?

Lis. Because such people generally want portions.

Serv. Portions! No, no, never talk of portions! my master nor I neither don't want portions; and if you'd follow my advice, a regiment of fathers should not guard her. 25

Lis. What's that?

Serv. Why, if you'll contrive that my master may run away with your mistress, I don't much care, faith, if I run away with you.

Lis. Don't you so, rogue's face! But I hope to be better provided for.

Erast. Hold your tongue.—But where is her brother? He is my bosom friend, and would be willing to serve me.

Lis. I told you before that he has been abroad a-hunting, and we han't seen him these three days; he seldom lies at home, to avoid his father's ill humour; so that it is not your mistress only that our old covetous cuff teases:—there's nobody in the family but feels the effects of his ill humour: —by his good will he would not suffer a creature to come within his doors, or eat at his table;—and then if there be but a rabbit extraordinary for dinner, he thinks himself ruined for ever. 42

Erast. Then I find you pass your time comfortably in this family.

Lis. Not so bad as you imagine neither, perhaps; for, thank Heaven, we have a mistress that's as bountiful as he's stingy, one that will let him say what he will, and yet does what she will.   But hark, here's somebody coming; it is certainly he.

Erast.   Can't you hide us somewhere?

Lis.   Here, here, get you in here as fast as you can.

Serv.   Thrust me in too.   [*She puts 'em into the closet.*

Enter MARIANE.

Lis.   Oh, is it you?   53

Mar.   So, Lisett, where have you been?   I've been looking for ye all over the house.   Who are those people in the garden with my mother-in-law?   I believe my father won't be very well pleased to see 'em there.

Lis.   And here's somebody else not far off, that I believe your father won't be very well pleased with neither.—Come, sir, sir!   [*Calls.*

Re-enter ERAST and Servant.

Mar.   O Heavens!

Lis.   Come, lovers, I can allow you but a short bout on't this time; you must do your work with a jerk—one whisper, two sighs, and a kiss; make haste, I say, and I'll stand sentry for ye in the meantime.   [*Exit.*

Mar.   Do you know what you expose me to, Erast? What do you mean?   67

Erast.   To die, madam, since you receive me with so little pleasure.

Mar.   Consider what would become of me, if my father should see you here.

Erast.   What would you have me do?

Mar.   Expect with patience some happy turn of affairs. My mother-in-law is kind and indulgent to a miracle; and her favour, if well managed, may turn to our advantage;

and could I prevail upon myself to declare my passion to her, I don't doubt but she'd join in our interest.   77

Erast.   Well, since we've nothing to fear from her, and your brother, you know, is my intimate friend, therefore you may conceal me somewhere about the house for a few days. I'll hide anywhere.

Serv.   Ay, but who must have the care of bringing us victuals?   [*Aside.*

Erast.   Thrust us into the cellar, up into the garret: I don't care where it is, so that it be but under the same roof with you.   86

Serv.   But I don't say so, for that jade Lisett will have the feeding of us, and I know what kind of diet she keeps.— I believe we shan't be like the fox in the fable, our bellies won't be so full but we shall be able to creep out at the same hole we got in at.   [*Aside.*

Erast.   Must I then begone? must I return to Paris?

Re-enter LISETT.

Lis.   Yes, that you must, and immediately too, for here's my master coming in upon ye.

Erast.   What shall I do?

Lis.   Begone this minute.   96

Mar.   Stay in the village till you hear from me, none of our family know that you are here.

Erast.   Shall I see you sometimes?

Mar.   I han't time to answer you now.

Lis.   Make haste, I say; are you bewitched?

Erast.   Will you write to me?

Mar.   I will if I can.

Lis.   Begone, I say; is the devil in you?—[*Thrusting*

ERAST *and* Servant *out.*]   Come this way, your father's just stepping in upon us.   [*Exeunt.*

Enter Monsieur BARNARD *beating* COLIN.

Mon. Barn. . Rogue ! rascal ! did not I command you ? Did not I give you my orders, sirrah ?   108

Col.   Why, you give me orders to let nobody in ; and madam, her gives me orders to let everybody in—why, the devil himself can't please you both, I think.

Mon. Barn.   But, sirrah, you must obey my orders, not hers.

Col.   Why, the gentlefolks asked for her, they did not ask for you—what do ye make such a noise about ?

Mon. Barn.   For that reason, sirrah, you should not let 'em in.

Col.   Hold, sir, I'd rather see you angry than her, too ; for when you're angry you have the de'il in ye, that's true enough ; but when madam's in a passion she has the de'il and his dam both in her belly.   121

Mon. Barn.   You must mind what I say to you, sirrah, and obey my orders.

Col.   Ay, ay, measter—but let's not quarrel with one another—you're always in such a plaguy humour.

Mon. Barn.   What are these people that are just come ?

Col.   Nay, that know not I—but as fine folk they are as ever eye beheld, Heaven bless 'em !

Mon. Barn.   Did you hear their names ?

Col.   Noa, noa, but in a coach they keam all besmeared with gould, with six breave horses, the like on 'em ne'er did I set eyes on.—'Twould do a man's heart good to look on those fine beast, measter.   133

Mon. Barn.   How many persons are there?

Col.   Four—two as fine men as ever woman bore, and two as dainty deames as a man would desire to lay his lips to.

Mon. Barn.   And all this crew sets up at my house?

Col.   Noa, noa, measter, the coachman is gone into the village to set up his coach at some inn, for I told him our coach-house was full of faggots, but he'll bring back the six horses, for I told him we had a rare good steable.

Mon. Barn.   Did you so, rascal? did you so?   143

[Beating him.

Col.   Doant, doant, sir, it would do you good to see those cattle, in faith they look as if they had ne'er kept Lent.

Mon. Barn.   Then they shall learn religion at my house. —Sirrah, do you take care they sup without oats to-night.— What will become of me! Since I bought this damned country-house, I spend more in a summer than would maintain me seven year.

Col.   Why, if you spend money, han't you good things for it all the whole country raund?—Come they not all to see you? Mind how you're beloved, measter.   153

Mon. Barn.   Pox take such love!—

Re-enter LISETT.

How now, what do you want?

Lis.   Sir, there's some company in the garden with my mistress, who desire to see you.

Mon. Barn.   Devil take 'em, what business have they here? But who are they?

Lis.   Why, sir, there's the fat abbot that always sits so long at dinner, and drinks his two bottles by way of whet.

Mon. Barn. I wish his church was in his belly, that his guts might be half full before he came.—And who else?

Lis. Then there's the young marquis that won all my lady's money at cards.   165

Mon. Barn. Pox take him too!   .

Lis. Then there's the merry lady that's always in good humour.

Mon. Barn. Very well.

Lis. Then there's she that threw down all my lady's china t'other day, and then laughed at it for a jest.

Mon. Barn. Which I paid above fifty pounds for in earnest.—Very well, and pray how did madam receive all this fine company?—With a hearty welcome, and a curtsey with her bum down to the ground, ha?   175

Lis. No, indeed, sir, she was very angry with 'em.

Mon. Barn. How! angry with 'em, say you?

Lis. Yes, indeed, sir, for she expected they would have stayed here a fortnight, but it seems things happen so unluckily that they can't stay here above ten days.

Mon. Barn. Ten days! how! what! four persons with a coach and six, and a kennel of hungry hounds in liveries, to live upon me ten days!   [*Exit* Lisett.

Enter Soldier.

So, what do you want?

Sol. Sir, I come from your nephew, captain Hungry.

Mon. Barn. Well, what does he want?   186

Sol. He gives his service to you, sir, and sends you word that he'll come and dine with you to-morrow.

Mon. Barn. Dine with me! no, no, friend, tell him I don't dine at all to-morrow, it is my fast-day, my wife died on't.

Sol.   And he has sent you here a pheasant and a couple of partridges.

Mon. Barn.   How's that, a pheasant and partridges, say you?—Let's see—very fine birds, truly.—Let me consider—to-morrow is not my fast-day, I mistook ; tell my nephew he shall be welcome.—[*To* COLIN.]   And d'ye hear? do you take these fowl and hang them up in a cool place—and take this soldier in, and make him drink—make him drink, do ye see—a cup,—ay, a cup of small beer—do ye hear?

Col.   Yes, sir.—Come along ; our small beer is rare good.

[*Exit.*

Sol.   But, sir, he bade me tell ye that he'll bring two or three of his brother officers along with him.   202

Mon. Barn.   How's that! officers with him—here, come back—take the fowls again ; I don't dine to-morrow, and so tell him.—[*Gives him the basket.*]   Go, go!

[*Thrusting him out.*

Sol.   Sir, sir, that won't hinder them from coming, for they retired off the camp, and because your house is near 'em, sir, they resolve to come.

Mon. Barn.   Go, begone, rogue !—[*Thrusts him out.*] There's a rogue now, that sends me three lean carrion birds, and brings half-a-dozen rogues to eat them !   211

Enter Monsieur GRIFFARD.

Mon. Griff.   Brother, what is the meaning of these doings?   If you don't order your affairs better, you'll have your fowl taken out of your very yard, and carried away before your face.

Mon. Barn.   Can I help it, brother?   But what's the matter now?

Mon. Griff. There's a parcel of fellows have been hunting about your grounds all this morning, broke down your
hedges, and are now coming into your house.—Don't you
hear them ?   221

Mon. Barn. No, I did not hear them : but who are
they ?

Mon. Griff. Three or four rake-helly officers, with your
nephew at the head of 'em.

Mon. Barn. Oh, the rogue ! he might well send me
fowl.—But is it not a vexatious thing, that I must stand
still and see myself plundered at this rate, and have a
carrion of a wife that thinks I ought to thank all these rogues
that come to devour me ?   But can't you advise me what's
to be done in this case ?   231

Mon. Griff. I wish I could, for it goes to my heart to see
you thus treated by a crew of vermin, who think they do you
a great deal of honour in ruining of you.

Mon. Barn. Can there be no way found to redress
this ?

Mon. Griff. If I were you, I'd leave this house quite,
and go to town.

Mon. Barn. What, leave my wife behind me ? ay, that
would be mending the matter indeed !

Mon. Griff. Why don't you sell it, then ?   241

Mon. Barn. Because nobody will buy it ; it has got as
ill a name as if it had the plague ; it has been sold over and
over, and every family that has lived in it has been ruined.

Mon. Griff. Then send away all your beds and furniture,
except what is absolutely necessary for your family ; you'll
save something by that, for then your guests can't stay with
you all night, however.

Mon. Barn. I've tried that already, and it signified nothing :—for they all got drunk and lay in the barn, and next morning laughed it off for a frolic.   251

Mon. Griff. Then there is but one remedy left that I can think of.

Mon. Barn. What's that ?

Mon. Griff. You must e'en do what's done when a town's afire, blow up your house that the mischief may run no farther.—But who is this gentleman ?

Mon. Barn. I never saw him in my life before, but for all that, I hold fifty pound he comes to dine with me.

Enter the Marquis.

Marq. My dear M. Barnard, I'm your most humble servant.   262

Mon. Barn. I don't doubt it, sir.

Marq. What is the meaning of this, M. Barnard? You look as coldly upon me as if I were a stranger.

Mon. Barn. Why truly, sir, I'm very apt to do so by persons I never saw in my life before.

Marq. You must know, M. Barnard, I'm come on purpose to drink a bottle of wine with you.

Mon. Barn. That may be, sir ; but it happens that at this time I am not at all dry.

Marq. I left the ladies at cards, waiting for supper ; for my part, I never play ; so I come to see my dear M. Barnard ; and I'll assure you, I undertook this journey only to have the honour of your acquaintance.   275

Mon. Barn. You might have spared yourself that trouble, sir.

Marq. Don't you know, M. Barnard, that this house of yours is a little paradise ?

Mon. Barn. Then rot me if it be, sir !

Marq. For my part, I think a pretty retreat in the country is one of the greatest comforts in life ; I suppose you never want good company, M. Barnard ?

Mon. Barn. No, sir, I never want company ; for you must know I love very much to be alone. 285

Marq. Good wine you must keep above all things ; without good wine and good cheer I would not give a fig for the country.

Mon. Barn. Really, sir, my wine is the worst you ever drank in your life, and you'll find my cheer but very indifferent.

Marq. No matter, no matter, M. Barnard ; I've heard much of your hospitality, there's a plentiful table in your looks—and your wife is certainly the best woman in the world. 295

Mon. Barn. Rot me if she be, sir !

Re-enter Colin.

Col. Sir, sir, yonder's the baron de Messy has lost his hawk in our garden ; he says it is perched upon one of the trees ; may we let him have'n again, sir ?

Mon. Barn. Go tell him, that—

Col. Nay, you may tell him yourself, for here he comes.

Enter the Baron De Messy.

Baron. Sir, I'm your most humble servant, and ask you a thousand pardons that I should live so long in your neighbourhood, and come upon such an occasion as this to pay you my first respects. 305

Mon. Barn. It is very well, sir ; but I think people may be very good neighbours without visiting one another.

Baron. Pray, how do you like our country?

Mon. Barn. Not at all, I am quite tired on't.

Marq. Is it not the baron ? it is certainly he.

Baron. How ; my dear marquis ! let me embrace you.

Marq. My dear baron, let me kiss you.

[*They run and embrace.*

Baron. We have not seen one another since we were schoolfellows before.

Marq. The happiest rencounter ! 315

Mon. Griff. These gentlemen seem to be very well acquainted.

Mon. Barn. Yes, but I know neither one nor t'other of them.

Marq. Baron, let me present to you one of the best-natured men in the world—M. Barnard here, the flower of hospitality !—I congratulate you upon having so good a neighbour.

Mon. Barn. Sir !

Baron. It is an advantage I am proud of. 325

Mon. Barn. Sir !

Marq. Come, gentlemen, you must be very intimate ; let me have the honour of bringing you better acquainted.

Mon. Barn. Sir !

Baron. Dear Marquis, I shall take it as a favour if you'll do me that honour.

Mon. Barn. Sir !

Marq. With all my heart.—Come, baron, now you are here, we can make up the most agreeable company in the world.—Faith, you shall stay and pass a few days with us.

Mon. Barn. Now methinks this son of a whore does the honours of my house to a miracle.   [*Aside.*

Baron. I don't know what to say, but I should be very glad you'd excuse me.   339

Marq. Faith, I can't.

Baron. Dear marquis!

Marq. Egad, I won't.

Baron. Well, since it must be so—but here comes the lady of the family.

Enter Madame BARNARD.

Marq. Madam, let me present to you the flower of France.

Baron. Madam, I shall think myself the happiest person in the world in your ladyship's acquaintance; and the little estate I have in this country I esteem more than all the rest, because it lies so near your ladyship.   350

Mad. Barn. Sir, your most humble servant.

Marq. Madam, the baron de Messy is the best-humoured man in the world. I've prevailed with him to give us his company a few days.

Mad. Barn. I'm sure you could not oblige M. Barnard or me more.

Mon. Barn. That's a damned lie, I'm sure.   [*Aside.*

Baron. I'm sorry, madam, I can't accept of the honour —but it falls out so unlucky,—for I've some ladies at my house that I can't possibly leave.   360

Marq. No matter, no matter, baron; you have ladies at your house, we have ladies at our house—let's join companies. —Come, let's send for them immediately; the more the merrier.

Mon. Barn.   An admirable expedient, truly !

Baron.   Well, since it must be so, I'll go for them myself.

Marq.   Make haste, dear baron, for we shall be impatient for your return.   369

Baron.   Madam, your most humble servant.—But I won't take my leave of you—I shall be back again immediately.—Monsieur Barnard, I'm your most humble servant ; since you will have it so, I'll return as soon as possible.   [*Exeunt* Baron *and* Marquis.

Mon. Barn.   I have it so ! 'sbud, sir, you may stay as long as you please; I'm in no haste for ye.   Madam, you are the cause that I am not master of my own house.

Mad. Barn.   Will you never learn to be reasonable, husband ?   379

Re-enter the Marquis.

Marq.   The baron is the best-humoured man in the world, only a little too ceremonious, that's all.—I love to be free and generous : since I came to Paris I've reformed half the court.

Mad. Barn.   You are of the most agreeable humour in the world.

Marq.   Always merry.—But what have you done with the ladies ?

Mad. Barn.   I left them at cards.

Marq.   Well, I'll wait upon 'em.   But, madam, let me desire you not to put yourself to any extraordinary expense upon our accounts.—You must consider we have more than one day to live together.   392

Mad. Barn.   You are pleased to be merry, marquis.

Marq. Treat us without ceremony. Good wine and poultry you have of your own ; wild-fowl and fish are brought to your door :—you need not send abroad for anything but a piece of butcher's meat, or so.—Let us have no extra-ordinaries. [*Exit.*

Mon. Barn. If I had the feeding of you, a thunderbolt should be your supper. 400

Mad. Barn. Husband, will you never change your humour? If you go on at this rate, it will be impossible to live with ye.

Mon. Barn. Very true ; for in a little time I shall have nothing to live upon.

Mad. Barn. Do you know what a ridiculous figure you make?

Mon. Barn. You'll make a great deal worse, when you han't money enough to pay for the washing of your smocks.

Mad. Barn. It seems you married me only to dishonour me ; how horrible this is ! 411

Mon. Barn. I tell ye, you'll ruin me. Do you know how much money you spend in a year?

Mad. Barn. Not I truly, I don't understand arithmetic.

Mon. Barn. Arithmetic, O Lud ! O Lud ! Is it so hard to comprehend, that he who spends a shilling and receives but sixpence, must be ruined in the end?

Mad. Barn. I never troubled my head with accounts, nor never will; but if you did but know what ridiculous things the world says of ye— 420

Mon. Barn. Rot the world !—'Twill say worse of me when I'm in a jail.

Mad. Barn. A very Christian-like saying, truly.

Mon. Barn. Don't tell me of Christian !—Adsbud, I'll

turn Jew, and nobody shall eat at my table that is not cir-
cumcised.

Re-enter LISETT.

Lis.   Madam, there's the duchess of Twangdillo just set
down near our door, her coach was overturned.

Mad. Barn.   I hope her grace has received no hurt?

Lis.   No, madam, but her coach is broke.   430

Mon. Barn.   Then there's a smith in town may mend it.

Lis.   They say 'twill require two or three days to fit it
up.

Mad. Barn.   I'm glad on't with all my heart, for then I
shall enjoy the pleasure of her grace's good company.—I
wait upon her.

Mon. Barn.   Very fine doings !   [*Exeunt severally.*

ACT II.

SCENE.—*The same.*

Enter Monsieur BARNARD.

Mon. Barn. Now Heaven be my comfort, for my house
is hell :—How now, what do you want? who are you?

Enter a Servant *with a portmanteau.*

Serv. Sir, here's your cousin Janno and cousin Mawkin
come from Paris.

Mon. Barn. What a plague do they want?

Enter JANNO, *leading in* MAWKIN.

Jan. Come, sister, come along.—Oh, here's cousin Barnard.—Cousin Barnard, your servant.—Here's my sister
Mawkin and I are come to see you.

Mawk. Ay, cousin, here's brother Janno and I are come
from Paris to see you. Pray how does cousin Mariane do?

Jan. My sister and I waunt well at Paris; so my father
sent us here for two or three weeks to take a little country
air.   13

Mon. Barn. You could not come to a worse place; for
this is the worst air in the whole country.

Mawk. Nay, I'm sure, my father says it is the best.

Mon. Barn. Your father's a fool; I tell ye, 'tis the worst.

Jan. Nay, cousin, I fancy you're mistaken now; for I

begin to find my stomach come to me already; in a fortnight's time you'll see how I'll lay about me.

Mon. Barn. I don't at all doubt it.   21

Mawk. Father would have sent sister Flip and little
brother Humphrey, but the calash would not hold us all,
and so they don't come till to-morrow with mother.

Jan. Come, sister, let's put up our things in our chamber; and after you have washed my face, and put me on a
clean neckcloth, we'll go and see how our cousins do.

Mawk. Ay, come along, we'll go and see cousin
Mariane.

Jan. Cousin, we shan't give you much trouble, one bed
will serve us; for sister Mawkin and I always lie together.

Mawk. But, cousin; mother prays you that you'd order
a little cock-broth for brother Janno and I, to be got ready
as soon as may be.   34

Jan. Ay, *à propos*, cousin Barnard, that's true; my
mother desires that we may have some cock-broth to drink
two or three times a-day between meals, for my sister and I
are sick folks.

Mawk. And some young chickens too, the doctor said,
would bring us to our stomachs very soon.

Jan. You fib now, sister, it waunt young chickens, so it
waunt, it was plump partridges, sure the doctor said so.

Mawk. Ay, so it was, brother.—Come, let's go see our
cousins.   44

Jan. Ay, come along, sister.—Cousin Barnard, don't
forget the cock-broth.

      [*Exeunt* JANNO *and* MAWKIN, Servant *following*.

Mon. Barn. What the devil does all this mean! Mother,
and sister Flip and little brother Humphrey, and chickens,

and partridges, and cock-broth, and fire from hell to dress
'em all.

Enter COLIN.

Col. O measter ! O measter !—you'll not chide to-day,
as you are usen to do ; no, marry will you not ; see now
what it is to be wiser than one's measter !

Mon. Barn. What would this fool have ?   54

Col. Why, thanks, and money to boot, an folk were
greateful.

Mon. Barn. What's the matter ?

Col. Why, the matter is, if you have store of company in
your house, why, you have store of meat to put in their bellies.

Mon. Barn. How so ? how so ?

Col. A large and steately stag, with a pair of horns of
his head, Heaven bless you, your worship might be seen to
wear 'em, comes towards our geate a puffing and blowing
like a cow in hard labour.—Now, says I to myself, says I,
if my measter refuse to let this fine youth come in, why,
then, he's a fool d'ye see.—So I opens him the geate, pulls
off my hat with both my hands, and said, You're welcome,
kind sir, to our house.   68

Mon. Barn. Well, well !

Col. Well, well, ay, and so it is well, as you shall straight-
way find.—So in a trots, and makes directly towards our
barn, and goes bounce, bounce, against the door, as boldly
as if he had been measter on't :—he turns'n about and
thawcks'n down in the stra, as who would say, Here will I
lay me till to-morrow morning.—But he had no fool to deal
with : for to the kitchen goes I, and takes me down a
musket, and, with a brace of balls, I hits'n such a slap in

the face, that he ne'er spoke a word more to me.—Have I
done well or no, measter?   79

Mon. Barn.   Yes, you have done very well for once.

Col.   But this was not all, for a parcel of dogs came
yelping after their companion, as I suppose; so I goes to
our back-yard door, and, as many as came by, shu! says I,
and drive 'em into the garden; so there they are as safe as
in a pownd—ha! ha!—But I can but think what a power
of pasties we shall have at our house, ha! ha!   [*Exit.*

Mon. Barn.   I see Providence takes some care of me:
this could never have happened in a better time.

Enter Cook.

Cook.   Sir, sir, in the name of wonder, what do you
mean? is it by your orders that all those dogs were let into
the garden?   91

Mon. Barn.   How!

Cook.   I believe there's forty or fifty dogs tearing up the
lettuce and cabbage by the root; I believe before they've
done, they'll root up the whole garden.

Mon. Barn.   This is that rogue's doings.

Cook.   This was not all, sir, for three or four of 'em came
into the kitchen, and tore half the meat off the spit that was
for your worship's supper.

Mon. Barn.   The very dogs plague me!   100

Cook.   And then there's a crew of hungry footmen
devoured what the dogs left, so that there's not a bit left for
your worship's supper; not a scrap, not one morsel, sir.

[*Exit.*

Mon. Barn.   Sure I shall hit of some way to get rid of
this crew.

Re-enter COLIN.

Col. Sir, sir, here's the devil to do without; yonder a parcel of fellows swear they'll have our venison, and 'sblead, I swear they shall have none on't; so stand to your arms, measter.   109

Mon. Barn. Ay, you've done finely, rogue, rascal, have you not?   [*Beating him.*

Col. 'Sblead, I say they shan't have our venison! I'll die before I'll part with it.   [*Exit.*

Enter Monsieur GRIFFARD.

Mon. Griff. Brother, there's some gentlemen within ask for you.

Mon. Barn. What gentlemen? who are they?

Mon. Griff. The gentlemen that have been hunting all this morning, they're now gone up to your wife's chamber.

Mon. Barn. The devil go with 'em!   119

Mon. Griff. There's but one way to get rid of this plague, and that is, as I told you before, to set your house on fire.

Mon. Barn. That's doing myself an injury, not them.

Mon. Griff. There's dogs, horses, masters, and servants, all intend to stay here till to-morrow morning, that they may be near the woods to hunt the earlier:—besides, I overheard 'em, they're in a kind of a plot against you.

Mon. Barn. What did they say?

Mon. Griff. You'll be angry if I should tell ye.

Mon. Barn. Can I be more angry than I am?   129

Mon. Griff. Then they said, it was the greatest pleasure in the world to ruin an old lawyer in the country, who had got an estate by ruining honest people in town.

Mon. Barn. There's rogues for ye!

Mon. Griff. I'm mistaken if they don't play you some trick or other.

Mon. Barn. Hold, let me consider.

Mon. Griff. What are you doing?

Mon. Barn. I'm conceiving, I shall bring forth presently.— Oh, I have it! it comes from hence, wit was its father, and invention its mother; if I had thought on't sooner, I should have been happy.   141

Mon. Griff. What is it?

Mon. Barn. Come, come along, I say; you must help me to put it in execution.

Enter LISETT.

Lis. Sir, my mistress desires you to walk up; she is not able, all alone, to pay the civilities due to so much good company.

Mon. Barn. O the carrion! What, does she play her jests upon me too?—but, mum, he laughs best that laughs last.   150

Lis. What shall I tell her, sir, will you come?

Mon. Barn. Yes, yes, tell her I'll come, with a pox to her!   [*Exit with* Monsieur GRIFFARD.

Lis. Nay, I don't wonder he should be angry;—they do try his patience, that's the truth on't.

Enter MARIANE.

What, madam, have you left your mother and the company?

Mar. So much tittle-tattle makes my head ache; I don't wonder my father should not love the country, for besides the expense he's at, he never enjoys a minute's quiet.

Lis. But let's talk of your own affairs:—have you writ to your lover?   161

Mar.   No, for I have not had time since I saw him.

Lis.   Now you have time then, about it immediately, for he's a sort of a desperate spark, and a body does not know what he may do if he should not hear from you.   Besides you promised him, and you must behave yourself like a woman of honour, and keep your word.

Mar.   I'll about it this minute.

Enter Charly.*

Char.   Cousin, cousin, cousin, where are you going? Come back, I have something to say to you.   170

Lis.   What does this troublesome boy want?

Char.   What's that to you what I want?   Perhaps I have something to say to her that will make her laugh.—Why sure !   What need you care?

Mar.   Don't snub my cousin Charly.—Well, what is't?

Char.   Who do you think I met as I was coming here, but that handsome gentleman I've seen at church ogle you like any devil?

Mar.   Hush, softly, cousin.

Lis.   Not a word of that for your life.   180

Char.   Oh, I know, I should not speak on't before folks ; you know I made signs to you above, that I wanted to speak to you in private, did not I, cousin?

Mar.   Yes, yes, I saw you.

Char.   You see I can keep a secret.—I am no girl, mun.—I believe I could tell ye fifty, and fifty to that, of my sister Sis.—Oh, she's the devil of a girl !—but she gives me

---

*Vanbrugh has divided the single part of Cousin Chonchon between the two characters of Janno and Charly.

money and sugar-plums—and those that are kind to me fare the better for it, you see, cousin.

Mar. I always said my cousin Charly was a good-natured boy.   191

Lis. Well, and did he know you?

Char. Yes, I think he did know me—for he took me in his arms, and did so hug me and kiss me!—Between you and I, cousin, I believe he's one of the best friends I have in the world.

Mar. Well, but what did he say to you?

Char. Why, he asked me where I was going; I told him I was coming to see you; You're a lying young rogue, says he, I'm sure you dare not go see your cousin:—for you must know my sister was with me, and it seems he took her for a crack, and I being a forward boy, he fancied I was going to make love to her under a hedge, ha! ha!   203

Mar. So!

Char. So he offered to lay me a louis-d'or that I was not coming to you; so, Done! says I—Done! says he,—and so 'twas a bet, you know.

Mar. Certainly.

Char. So my sister's honour being concerned, and having a mind to win his louis-d'or, d'ye see—I bade him follow me, that he might see whether I came in or no.—But he said he'd wait for me at the little garden door that opens into the fields, and if I would come through the house and meet him there, he'd know by that whether I had been in or no.   215

Mar. Very well.

Char. So I went there, opened the door, and let him in—

Mar. What then?

Char. Why, then he paid me the louis-d'or, that's all.

Mar. Why, that was honestly done.

Char. And then he talked to me of you, and said you had the charmingest bubbies, and every time he named 'em, Ha! says he, as if he had been supping hot milk-tea.

Mar. But was this all?   225

Char. No, for he had a mind, you must know, to win his louis-d'or back again; so he laid me another that I dare not come back and tell you that he was there; so, cousin, I hope you won't let me lose, for if you don't go there and tell him that I've won, he won't pay me.

Mar. What, would you have me go and speak to a man?

Char. Not for any harm, but to win your poor cousin a louis-d'or. I'm sure you will—for you're a modest young woman, and may go without danger.—Well, cousin, I'll swear you look very handsome to-day, and have the prettiest bubbies there; do let me touch 'em, I'll swear I must.   238

Mar. What does the young rogue mean? I swear I'll have you whipped.   [*Exeunt* CHARLY *and* MARIANE.

Re-enter COLIN.

Col. Ha! ha! odd, the old gentleman's a wag, i'faith, he'll be even with 'em for all this, ha!——

Lis. What's the matter? what does the fool laugh at?

Col. We an't in our house now, Lisett, we're in an inn: ha! ha!

Lis. How in an inn?

Col. Yes, in an inn; my measter has gotten an old

rusty sword and hung it up at our geate, and writ under-
neath with a piece of charcoal with his own fair hand, *At
the Sword Royal ; Entertainment for Man and Horse ;* ha !
ha !—   251

Lis.   What whim is this ?

Col.   Thou and I live at the Sword Royal, ha ! ha !

Lis.   I'll go tell my mistress of her father's extravagance.

[*Exit.*

Re-enter Monsieur BARNARD *and* Monsieur GRIFFARD.

Mon. Barn.   Ha ! ha ! yes, I think this will do.—Sirrah,
now you may let in all the world ; the more the better.

Col.   Yes, sir.—Odsflesh ! we shall break all the inns in
the country :—for we have a breave handsome landlady, and
a curious young lass to her daughter.—Oh, here comes my
young measter.—We'll make him chamberlain—ha ! ha !

Enter DORANT.

Mon. Barn.   What's the matter, son ?   How comes it
that you are all alone ?   You used to do me the favour to
bring some of your friends along with ye.   263

Dor.   Sir, there are some of 'em coming ; I only rid
before to beg you to give 'em a favourable reception.

Mon. Barn.   Ay, why not ?   It is both for your honour
and mine ; you shall be master.

Dor.   Now, sir, we have an opportunity of making all the
gentlemen in the country our friends.

Mon. Barn.   I'm glad on't with all my heart ; pray how
so ?

Dor.   There's an old quarrel to be made up between
two families, and all the company is to meet at our
house.   274

Mon. Barn. Ay, with all my heart ; but pray what is the quarrel ?

Dor. O, sir, a very ancient quarrel ; it happened between their great-grandfathers about a duck.

Mon. Barn. A quarrel of consequence truly !

Dor. And 'twill be a great honour to us if this should be accommodated at our house.

Mon. Barn. Without doubt.

Dor. Dear sir, you astonish me with this goodness ; how shall I express this obligation ? I was afraid, sir, you would not like it.   285

Mon. Barn. Why so ?

Dor. I thought, sir, you did not care for the expense.

Mon. Barn. O Lord, I am the most altered man in the world from what I was, I'm quite another thing, mun ! But how many are there of 'em ?

Dor. Not above nine or ten of a side, sir.

Mon. Barn. Oh, we shall dispose of them easily enough.

Dor. Some of 'em will be here presently ; the rest I don't expect till to-morrow morning.   295

Mon. Barn. I hope they're good companions, jolly fellows, that love to eat and drink well ?

Dor. The merriest, best-natured creatures in the world, sir.

Mon. Barn. I'm very glad on't, for 'tis such men I want. —But come, brother, you and I will go and prepare for their reception.   [*Exit with* Monsieur GRIFFARD.

Dor. Bless me, what an alteration is here ! How my father's temper is altered within these two or three days ! Do you know the meaning of this ?   `   305

Col.   Why, the meaning on't is, ha ! ha !—

Dor.   Can you tell me the cause of this sudden change, I say ?

Col.   Why, the cause on't is, ha ! ha !—

Dor.   What do you laugh at, sirrah ? do you know?

Col.   Ha !—Because the old gentleman's a droll, that's all.

Dor.   Sirrah, if I take the cudgel—

Col.   Nay, sir, don't be angry for a little harmless mirth. —But here are your friends.   314

Enter three Gentlemen.

Dor.   Gentlemen, you are welcome to Pasty Hall.—See that these gentlemen's horses are taken care of.

                                          [*Exit* COLIN.

1st Gent.   A very fine dwelling this.

Dor.   Yes, the house is tolerable.

2nd Gent.   And a very fine lordship belongs to it.

Dor.   The land is good.

3rd Gent.   This house ought to have been mine ; for my grandfather sold it to his father, from whom your father purchased it.

Dor.   Yes, the house has gone through a great many hands.   325

1st Gent.   A sign there has been always good house-keeping in it.

Dor.   And I hope there ever will.

Re-enter Monsieur BARNARD *and* Monsieur GRIFFARD,
                dressed like Drawers.

Mon. Barn.   Gentlemen, do you call ? will you please to see a room, gentlemen ?—Here, somebody take off the gentlemen's boots there.

Dor. Father! uncle! what is the meaning of this?

Mon. Barn. Here, show a room.—Or will you please walk into the kitchen first, and see what you like for dinner.

1st Gent. Make no preparations, sir; your own dinner will suffice. 336

Mon. Barn. Very well, I understand ye. Let's see, how many are there of ye?—[*Counting them.*] One, two, three, four: well, gentlemen, it is but half-a-crown a-piece for yourselves, and sixpence a-piece for your servants; your dinner shall be ready in half an hour. Here, show the gentlemen into the Apollo.

2nd Gent. What, sir, does your father keep an inn?

Mon. Barn. The Sword Royal, at your service, sir.

Dor. But, father, let me speak to ye; will you shame me? 346

Mon. Barn. My wine is very good, gentlemen, but, to be plain with ye, it is dear.

Dor. Oh, I shall run distracted!

Mon. Barn. You seem not to like my house, gentlemen; you may try all the inns in the country, and not be better entertained; but I own my bills run high.

Dor. Gentlemen, let me beg the favour of ye——

1st Gent. Ay, my young squire of the Sword Royal, you shall receive some favours from us!

Dor. Dear Monsieur La Garantière! 356

1st Gent. Here, my horse there!

Dor. Monsieur La Rose!

2nd Gent. Damn ye, you prig!

Dor. Monsieur Trofignac!

3rd Gent. Go to the devil!

[*Exeunt the three* Gentlemen.

Dor.   Oh, I'm disgraced for ever !

Mon. Barn.   Now, son, this will teach you how to live.

Dor.   Your son ! I deny the kindred ; I'm the son of a whore, and I'll burn your house about your ears, you old rogue you !   [*Exit.*

Mon. Barn.   Ha ! ha !—   367

Mon. Griff.   The young gentleman's in a passion.

Mon. Barn.   They're all gone for all that, and the Sword Royal's the best general in Christendom.

Enter ERAST'S Servant *talking with* LISETT.

Lis.   What, that tall gentleman I saw in the garden with ye ?

Serv.   The same, he's my master's uncle, and ranger of all the king's forests.   He intends to leave my master all he has.   375

Mon. Barn.   Don't I know this scoundrel ? What, is his master here ?—What do you do here, rascal ?

Serv.   I was asking which must be my master's chamber.

Mon. Barn.   Where is your master ?

Serv.   Above stairs with your wife and daughter ; and I want to know where he's to lie, that I may put up his things.

Mon. Barn.   Do you so, rascal?

Serv.   A very handsome inn this.—Here, drawer, fetch me a pint of wine.   385

Mon. Barn.   Take that, rascal ; do you banter us ?

          [*Kicks him out.*

Enter Madame BARNARD.

Mad. Barn.   What is the meaning of this, husband ? Are not you ashamed to turn your house into an inn ?—

and is this a dress for my husband, and a man of your character?

Mon. Barn.   I'd rather wear this dress than be ruined.

Mad. Barn.   You're nearer being so than you imagine; for there are some persons within that have it in their power to punish you for your ridiculous folly.   394

Enter ERAST *leading in* MARIANE.

Mon. Barn.   How, sir, what means this? who sent you here?

Erast.   It was the luckiest star in your firmament that sent me here.

Mon. Barn.   Then I doubt, that at my birth, the planets were but in a scurvy disposition.

Erast.   The killing one of the king's stags, that run hither for refuge, is enough to overturn a fortune much better established than yours.   However, sir, if you consent to give me your daughter, for her sake I will secure you harmless.   405

Mon. Barn.   No, sir; no man shall have my daughter, that won't take my house too.

Erast.   Sir, I will take your house; pay you the full value on't, and you shall remain as much its master as ever.

Mon. Barn.   No, sir, that won't do neither; you must be master on't yourself, and from this minute begin to do the honours on't in your own person.

Erast.   Sir, I do consent.

Mon. Barn.   Upon that condition, and in order to get rid of my house, here, take my daughter.—And now, sir, if you think you've a hard bargain, I don't care if I toss you in my wife, to make you amends.   417

————Since all things now are sped,
My son in anger, and my daughter wed,
My house dispos'd of, which was the cause of strife,
I now may hope to lead a happy life,
If I can part with my engaging wife.

                                    [*Exeunt omnes.*

THE CONFEDERACY.

INTRODUCTION TO "THE CONFEDERACY."

The Confederacy was first produced on the 30th of October, 1705, at the theatre built by Vanbrugh in the Haymarket. Genest states that it was acted ten times, but I find, from announcements in the *Daily Courant*, that the last performance took place on T,uesday, the 6th of November: on the following day Dryden's *Indian Emperor* was given. *The Confederacy* was published, in 4to, and without the author's name, on the 15th of November, 1705.* The title-page of the original edition reads as follows: " *The Confederacy. A Comedy. As it is Acted at the Queen's Theatre in the Hay-Market. By Her Majesty's Sworn Servants. By the Author of The Relapse, Provok'd Wife, and Æsop. London, Printed for Jacob Tonson, within Gray's-Inn Gate next Gray's-Inn Lane. 1705.*"

This admirable comedy is a translation of *Les Bourgeoises à la Mode*, a comedy by Dancourt, acted for the first time on the 15th of November, 1692. The French play, like

---

* The following announcement appeared in the *London Gazette* of November 12-15, 1705. "This day is published, The Confederacy: A Comedy. As it is Acted at the Queen's Theatre in the Hay-Market, by Her Majesty's Sworn Servants. Written by the Author of the Relapse, Provok'd Wife, and Æsop. Printed for Jacob Tonson within Gray's-Inn Gate next Gray's-Inn Lane."

the English, is in five acts and in prose. It is a witty and well-constructed piece, and Vanbrugh has followed it, upon the whole, very closely throughout. He has changed the scene from Paris to London, and altered, accordingly, the names of the characters; but he has rendered not only the particulars of the plot, but, for the most part, even the detail of the dialogue with considerable fidelity. At the same time, it must be allowed that Vanbrugh has everywhere improved upon his original. Rarely as he has departed from the track of his predecessor, he has yet interpreted the text with such singular felicity, and added so many little touches of wit or humour, that the French play, with all its merit, will appear to the reader chiefly valuable in having given rise to the English translation. Three scenes in *The Confederacy* belong to Vanbrugh alone :—the opening scene of the play, between Mrs. Amlet and Mrs. Cloggit; the first scene of the third act, between Dick Amlet and his mother; and the second scene of the fifth act, as far as the entrance of the goldsmith.

Vanbrugh was not the first English dramatist who borrowed from *Les Bourgeoises à la Mode.* In April, 1703, a comedy entitled *The Fair Example; or the Modish Citizens*, by Richard Estcourt, the actor, was produced at Drury Lane. This piece, which was not published till 1706, contains certain characters and incidents imitated from Dancourt's comedy. In the ironical dedication to Manager Rich, which precedes *The Fair Example*, Estcourt alludes to Vanbrugh's translation, and to the priority of his own play. But the resemblance between the two plays is very distant, and confined to a few scenes: there is nothing in *The Confederacy* to show that its author was even acquainted with *The Fair Example ;* nor, indeed, does Estcourt hint at any indebtedness to himself on the part of Vanbrugh. Estcourt has taken from Dancourt the notion of his two citizens, Whimsey and Symons, each of whom makes love to the other's wife. From the same source he has derived the character of a gentleman adventurer, who is discovered, in the last scene, to be the son of Mrs. Furnish, the milliner. But the details of his piece frequently differ from those of Dancourt's, and in the more serious portion of its fable, *The Fair Example* presents no resemblance whatever to *Les Bourgeoises à la Mode.*

DRAMATIS PERSONÆ.

MEN.

Gripe, ⎱
Moneytrap, ⎰ Two rich Money Scriveners ⎰ Mr. *Leigh.*
Mr. *Dogget.*

Dick, a Gamester, Son to Mrs. *Amlet* ... ... Mr. *Booth.* *

Brass, his Companion, passes for his *Valet de* ⎱
Chambre ... ...⎰ Mr. *Pack.*

Clip, a Goldsmith ... ... Mr. *Mimes.*

Jessamin, Foot-boy to *Clarissa.*

WOMEN.

Clarissa, Wife to *Gripe,* an expensive luxurious ⎱
Woman, a great Admirer of Quality ... ...⎰ Mrs. *Barry.*

Araminta, Wife to *Moneytrap,* very intimate with ⎱
Clarissa, of the same Humour ... ...⎰ Mrs. *Porter.*

Corinna, Daughter to *Gripe* by a former Wife, a ⎱
good Fortune, young, and kept very close by ⎰ Mrs. *Bradshaw.*
her Father ... ...⎰

Flippanta, Clarissa's Maid ... ... Mrs. *Bracegirdle.*

Mrs. *Amlet,* a Seller of all Sorts of private Affairs ⎱
to the Ladies ... ...⎰ Mrs. *Willis.*

Mrs. *Cloggit,* her Neighbour... ... ... Mrs. *Baker.*

[SCENE.—In LONDON.]

---

* Barton Booth was born in 1681, and educated at Westminster. Like Wilks, he made his first appearance in Dublin, where he played Oroonoko in 1698. He was engaged at Lincoln's Inn Fields in 1700, and his reputation increased, until it was raised to the highest pitch by his performance of Cato, in Addison's tragedy, in the year 1713. According to Cibber, Othello was Booth's masterpiece. He died May 8, 1733.

PROLOGUE.

YE gods! what crime had my poor father done,
That you should make a poet of his son?
Or is't for some great services of his,
Y'are pleased to compliment his boy—with this?

> [*Showing his crown of laurel.*

The honour, I must needs confess, is great,
If, with his crown, you'd tell him where to eat.
'Tis well.—But I have more complaints—look here!

> [*Showing his ragged coat.*

Hark ye :—D'ye think this suit good winter wear?
In a cold morning, whu—at a lord's gate,
How you have let the porter let me wait!   10
You'll say, perhaps, you knew I'd get no harm,
You'd given me fire enough to keep me warm.
Ah !—
A world of blessings to that fire we owe ;
Without it I'd ne'er made this princely show.
I have a brother too, now in my sight,

> [*Looking behind the scenes.*

A busy man amongst us here to-night :
Your fire has made him play a thousand pranks,
For which, no doubt, you've had his daily thanks ;
He 'as thank'd you, first, for all his decent plays,   20
Where he so nick'd it, when he writ for praise.

Next, for his meddling with some folks in black,
And bringing—souse !—a priest upon his back ;
For building houses here t'oblige the peers,
And fetching all their house about his ears ;
For a new play, he 'as now thought fit to write,
To soothe the town —which they—will damn to-night.
   These benefits are such, no man can doubt
But he'll go on, and set your fancy out,
Till, for reward of all his noble deeds,   30
At last like other sprightly folks he speeds :
Has this great recompense fix'd on his brow
At fam'd Parnassus ; has your leave to bow,
And walk about the streets—equipp'd—as I am now.

THE CONFEDERACY.

A COMEDY.

ACT I.

SCENE I.—*Covent Garden.*

Enter Mrs. AMLET *and* Mrs. CLOGGIT, *meeting.*

Mrs. Aml. Good-morrow, neighbour; good-morrow, neighbour Cloggit! How does all at your house this morning?

Mrs. Clog. Thank you kindly, Mrs. Amlet, thank you kindly; how do you do, I pray?

Mrs. Aml. At the old rate, neighbour, poor and honest; these are hard times, good lack!

Mrs. Clog. If they are hard with you, what are they with us? You have a good trade going, all the great folks in town help you off with your merchandise.   10

Mrs. Aml. Yes, they do help us off with 'em indeed; they buy all.

Mrs. Clog. And pay?

Mrs. Aml. For some.

Mrs. Clog. Well, 'tis a thousand pities, Mrs. Amlet, they are not as ready at one as they are at t'other: for, not to wrong 'em, they give very good rates.

Mrs. Aml. Oh, for that, let us do 'em justice, neighbour; they never make two words upon the price, all they haggle about is the day of payment.   20

Mrs. Clog. There's all the dispute, as you say.

Mrs. Aml. But that's a wicked one. For my part, neighbour, I'm just tired off my legs with trotting after 'em; besides, it eats out all our profit. Would you believe it, Mrs. Cloggit, I have worn out four pair of pattens with following my old lady Youthful, for one set of false teeth, and but three pots of paint.

Mrs. Clog. Look you there now!

Mrs. Aml. If they would but once let me get enough by 'em, to keep a coach to carry me a-dunning after 'em, there would be some conscience in it.   31

Mrs. Clog. Ay, that were something. But now you talk of conscience, Mrs. Amlet, how do you speed amongst your city customers?

Mrs. Aml. My city customers! now by my truth, neighbour, between the city and the court (with reverence be it spoken) there's not a—to choose. My ladies in the city, in times past, were as full of gold as they were of religion, and as punctual in their payments as they were in their prayers; but since they have set their minds upon quality, adieu one, adieu t'other, their money and their consciences are gone, Heavens knows where. There is not a goldsmith's wife to be found in town, but's as hard-hearted as an ancient judge, and as poor as a towering duchess.   44

Mrs. Clog. But what the murrain have they to do with quality? why don't their husbands make 'em mind their shops?

Mrs. Aml. Their husbands! their husbands, sayest

thou, woman? Alack! alack! they mind their husbands, neighbour, no more than they do a sermon.

Mrs. Clog. Good lack a-day, that women born of sober parents should be prone to follow ill examples! But now we talk of quality, when did you hear of your son Richard, Mrs. Amlet? My daughter Flipp says she met him t'other day in a laced coat, with three fine ladies, his footman at his heels, and as gay as a bridegroom.   56

Mrs. Aml. Is it possible? Ah the rogue! Well, neighbour, all's well that ends well; but Dick will be hanged.

Mrs. Clog. That were pity.

Mrs. Aml. Pity indeed; for he's a hopeful young man to look on; but he leads a life—Well—where he has it, Heaven knows; but they say, he pays his club with the best of 'em. I have seen him but once these three months, neighbour, and then the varlet wanted money; but I bid him march, and march he did to some purpose; for in less than an hour back comes my gentleman into the house, walks to and fro in the room, with his wig over his shoulder, his hat on one side, whistling a minuet, and tossing a purse of gold from one hand to t'other, with no more respect (Heaven bless us!) than if it had been an orange. Sirrah, says I, where have you got that? He answers me never a word, but sets his arms akimbo, cocks his saucy hat in my face, turns about upon his ungracious heel, as much as to say kiss —and I've never set eye on him since.   75

Mrs. Clog. Look you there now; to see what the youth of this age are come to!

Mrs. Aml. See what they will come to, neighbour. Heaven shield, I say; but Dick's upon the gallop. Well,

I must bid you good-morrow! I'm going where I doubt I shall meet but a sorry welcome.

Mrs. Clog.   To get in some old debt, I'll warrant you?

Mrs. Aml.   Neither better nor worse.

Mrs. Clog.   From a lady of quality?

Mrs. Aml.   No, she's but a scrivener's wife; but she lives as well and pays as ill as the stateliest countess of 'em all.

[*Exeunt several ways.*

———

SCENE II.—*The Street before* GRIPE'S *House.*

Enter BRASS.

Brass.   Well, surely through the world's wide extent, there never appeared so impudent a fellow as my school-fellow Dick.   Pass himself upon the town for a gentleman, drop into all the best company with an easy air, as if his natural element were in the sphere of quality; when the rogue had a kettle-drum to his father, who was hanged for robbing a church, and has a pedlar to his mother, who carries her shop under her arm!—But here he comes.

Enter DICK AMLET.

Dick.   Well, Brass, what news?   Hast thou given my letter to Flippanta?   10

Brass.   I'm but just come; I han't knocked at the door yet.   But I have a damned piece of news for you.

Dick.   As how?

Brass.   We must quit this country.

Dick.   We'll be hanged first.

Brass. So you will if you stay.

Dick. Why, what's the matter?

Brass. There's a storm a-coming.

Dick. From whence?

Brass. From the worst point in the compass; the law.   21

Dick. The law! why, what have I to do with the law?

Brass. Nothing; and therefore it has something to do with you.

Dick. Explain.

Brass. You know you cheated a young fellow at picquet t'other day, of the money he had to raise his company.

Dick. Well, what then?

Brass. Why, he's sorry he lost it.

Dick. Who doubts that?   30

Brass. Ay, but that is not all, he's such a fool to think of complaining on't.

Dick. Then I must be so wise to stop his mouth.

Brass. How?

Dick. Give him a little back; if that won't do, strangle him.

Brass. You are very quick in your methods.

Dick. Men must be so that will dispatch business.

Brass. Hark you, colonel, your father died in's bed?

Dick. He might have done, if he had not been a fool.

Brass. Why, he robbed a church.   41

Dick. Ay, but he forgot to make sure of the sexton.

Brass. Are not you a great rogue?

Dick. Or I should wear worse clothes.

Brass. Hark you, I would advise you to change your life.

Dick. And turn ballad-singer ?

Brass. Not so neither.

Dick. What then ?

Brass. Why, if you can get this young wench, reform, and live honest.   51

Dick. That's the way to be starved.

Brass. No, she has money enough to buy you a good place, and pay me into the bargain for helping her to so good a match.   You have but this throw left to save you, for you are not ignorant, youngster, that your morals begin to be pretty well known about town ; have a care your noble birth and your honourable relations are not discovered too ; there needs but that to have you tossed in a blanket, for the entertainment of the first company of ladies you intrude into ; and then, like a dutiful son, you may daggle about with your mother, and sell paint : she's old and weak, and wants somebody to carry her goods after her.   How like a dog will you look, with a pair of plod shoes, your hair cropped up to your ears, and a bandbox under your arm !   66

Dick. Why, faith, Brass, I think thou art in the right on't ; I must fix my affairs quickly, or madam Fortune will be playing some of her bitch-tricks with me.   Therefore I'll tell thee what we'll do ; we'll pursue this old rogue's daughter heartily ; we'll cheat his family to purpose, and they shall atone for the rest of mankind.

Brass. Have at her then !   I'll about your business presently.   74

Dick. One kiss—and success attend thee.   [*Exit.*

Brass. A great rogue !—Well, I say nothing : but when I have got the thing into a good posture, he shall sign and seal, or I'll have him tumbled out of the house like a cheese.—Now for Flippanta. [*Knocks at* GRIPE's *door.*

Enter FLIPPANTA.

Flip. Who's that? Brass!

Brass. Flippanta!

Flip. What want you, rogue's face?

Brass. Is your mistress dressed?

Flip. What, already! Is the fellow drunk? 84

Brass. Why, with respect to her looking-glass, it's almost two.

Flip. What then, fool?

Brass. Why then it's time for the mistress of the house to come down, and look after her family.

Flip. Prithee don't be an owl. Those that go to bed at night may rise in the morning; we that go to bed in the morning rise in the afternoon.

Brass. When does she make her visits then?

Flip. By candle-light; it helps off a muddy complexion; we women hate inquisitive sunshine. But do you know that my lady is going to turn good housewife? 96

Brass. What, is she going to die?

Flip. Die?

Brass. Why, that's the only way to save money for her family.

Flip. No; but she has thought of a project to save chair-hire.

Brass. As how?

Flip. Why, all the company she used to keep abroad, she now intends shall meet at her own house. Your master has advised her to set up a basset-table. 106

Brass. Nay, if he advised her to't, it's right; but has she acquainted her husband with it yet?

Flip. What to do? when the company meet, he'll see 'em.

Brass. Nay, that's true, as you say; he'll know it soon enough.

Flip. Well, I must be gone; have you any business with my lady?

Brass. Yes; as ambassador from Araminta, I have a letter for her.   116

Flip. Give it me.

Brass. Hold!—and as first minister of state to the colonel, I have an affair to communicate to thee.

Flip. What is't?—quick !

Brass. Why—he's in love.

Flip. With what?

Brass. A woman—and her money together.

Flip. Who is she?

Brass. Corinna.

Flip. What would he be at ?   126

Brass. At her—if she's at leisure.

Flip. Which way ?

Brass. Honourably. He has ordered me to demand her of thee in marriage.

Flip. Of me !

Brass. Why, when a man of quality has a mind to a city fortune, wouldst have him apply to her father and mother ?

Flip. No.

Brass. No; so I think. Men of our end of the town are better bred than to use ceremony. With a long periwig we strike the lady ; with a you-know-what we soften the maid; and when the parson has done his job, we open the affair to the family. Will you slip this letter into her prayer-book, my little queen? It's a very passionate one—it's sealed with a heart and a dagger ; you may see by that what he intends to do with himself.   142

Flip. Are there any verses in it? If not, I won't touch it.

Brass. Not one word in prose ; it's dated in rhyme.

[*She takes it.*

Flip. Well, but—have you brought nothing else?

Brass. Gad forgive me, I'm the forgetfullest dog !—I have a letter for you too ;—here, 'tis in a purse, but it's in prose ; you won't touch it.

Flip. Yes, hang it, it is not good to be too dainty.

Brass. How useful a virtue is humility !—Well, child, we shall have an answer to-morrow, shan't we?   151

Flip. I can't promise you that ; for our young gentle-woman is not so often in my way as she would be. Her father (who is a citizen from the foot to the forehead of him) lets her seldom converse with her mother-in-law and me, for fear she should learn the airs of a woman of quality. But I'll take the first occasion.—See, there's my lady ; go in and deliver your letter to her.   [*Exeunt.*

SCENE III.—*A Parlour.*

Enter CLARISSA, *followed by* FLIPPANTA *and* BRASS.

Clar. No messages this morning from anybody, Flip-panta? Lard, how dull that is ! Oh, there's Brass !—I did not see thee, Brass. What news dost thou bring?

Brass. Only a letter from Araminta, madam.

Clar. Give it me.—Open it for me, Flippanta, I am so lazy to-day. [*Sitting down.*

Brass. [*Aside to* FLIPPANTA.] Be sure now you deliver my master's as carefully as I do this.

Flip. Don't trouble thyself, I'm no novice.

Clar. [*To* BRASS.] 'Tis well; there needs no answer, since she'll be here so soon. 11

Brass. Your ladyship has no farther commands, then?

Clar. Not at this time, honest Brass.—[*Exit* BRASS.] Flippanta!

Flip. Madam.

Clar. My husband's in love.

Flip. In love!

Clar. With Araminta.

Flip. Impossible!

Clar. This letter from her is to give me an account of it. 21

Flip. Methinks you are not very much alarmed.

Clar. No; thou knowest I'm not much tortured with jealousy.

Flip. Nay, you are much in the right on't, madam, for jealousy's a city passion; 'tis a thing unknown amongst people of quality.

Clar. Fie! a woman must indeed be of a mechanic mould, who is either troubled or pleased with anything her husband can do to her. Prithee mention him no more; 'tis the dullest theme. 31

Flip. 'Tis splenetic indeed. But when once you open your basset-table, I hope that will put him out of your head.

Clar. Alas, Flippanta! I begin to grow weary even of the thoughts of that too.

Flip. How so?

Clar. Why, I have thought on't a day and a night already; and four-and-twenty hours, thou knowest, is enough to make one weary of anything.

Flip. Now, by my conscience, you have more woman in you than all your sex together: you never know what you would have.   43

Clar. Thou mistakest the thing quite. I always know what I lack, but I am never pleased with what I have. The want of a thing is perplexing enough, but the possession of it is intolerable.

Flip. Well, I don't know what you are made of, but other women would think themselves blest in your case; handsome, witty, loved by everybody, and of so happy a composure to care a fig for nobody. You have no one passion but that of your pleasures; and you have in me a servant devoted to all your desires, let 'em be as extravagant as they will. Yet all this is nothing; you can still be out of humour.   55

Clar. Alas! I have but too much cause.

Flip. Why, what have you to complain of?

Clar. Alas! I have more subjects for spleen than one. Is it not a most horrible thing that I should be but a scrivener's wife? Come, don't flatter me; don't you think nature designed me for something *plus élevée?*

Flip. Nay, that's certain; but on t'other side, methinks you ought to be in some measure content, since you live like a woman of quality, though you are none.   64

Clar. O fie! the very quintessence of it is wanting.

Flip. What's that?

Clar. Why, I dare abuse nobody: I'm afraid to affront people, though I don't like their faces; or to ruin their reputations, though they pique me to it by taking ever so much pains to preserve 'em : I dare not raise a lie of a man, though he neglects to love me ; nor report a woman to be a fool, though she's handsomer than I am. In short, I dare not so much as bid my footman kick the people out of doors, though they come to ask me for what I owe 'em.   74

Flip. All this is very hard indeed.

Clar. Ah, Flippanta, the perquisites of quality are of an unspeakable value!

Flip. They are of some use, I must confess ; but we must not expect to have everything. You have wit and beauty, and a fool to your husband ; come, come, madam, that's a good portion for one.

Clar. Alas ! what signifies beauty and wit, when one dares neither jilt the men nor abuse the women ? 'Tis a sad thing, Flippanta, when wit's confined ; 'tis worse than the rising of the lights. I have been sometimes almost choked with scandal, and durst not cough it up, for want of being a countess.   87

Flip. Poor lady !

Clar. Oh ! liberty is a fine thing, Flippanta; it's a great help in conversation to have leave to say what one will. I have seen a woman of quality, who has not had one grain of wit, entertain a whole company the most agreeably in the world, only with her malice. But 'tis in vain to repine; I can't mend my condition till my husband dies; so I'll say no more on't, but think of making the most of the state I am in.

Flip. That's your best way, madam ; and in order to it,

pray consider how you'll get some ready money to set your basset-table a-going; for that's necessary. 98

Clar. Thou sayest true; but what trick I shall play my husband to get some, I don't know: for my pretence of losing my diamond necklace has put the man into such a passion, I'm afraid he won't hear reason.

Flip. No matter; he begins to think 'tis lost in earnest: so I fancy you may venture to sell it, and raise money that way.

Clar. That can't be, for he has left odious notes with all the goldsmiths in town.

Flip. Well, we must pawn it, then.

Clar. I'm quite tired with dealing with those pawn-brokers.

Flip. [*Aside.*] I'm afraid you'll continue the trade a great while, for all that. 111

Enter Jessamin.

Jes. Madam, there's the woman below that sells paint and patches, iron-bodice, false teeth, and all sorts of things to the ladies; I can't think of her name. [*Exit.*

Flip. 'Tis Mrs. Amlet; she wants money.

Clar. Well, I han't enough for myself, it's an unreasonable thing she should think I have any for her.

Flip. She's a troublesome jade.

Clar. So are all people that come a-dunning.

Flip. What will you do with her? 120

Clar. I have just now thought on't. She's very rich, that woman is, Flippanta; I'll borrow some money of her.

Flip. Borrow! sure, you jest, madam.

Clar. No, I'm in earnest; I give thee commission to do it for me.

Flip. Me !

Clar. Why dost thou stare, and look so ungainly ? don't I speak to be understood?

Flip. Yes, I understand you well enough ; but Mrs. Amlet— 130

Clar. But Mrs. Amlet must lend me some money; where shall I have any to pay her else ?

Flip. That's true ; I never thought of that truly. But here she is.

Enter Mrs. AMLET.

Clar. How d'you do? how d'you do, Mrs. Amlet? I han't seen you these thousand years, and yet I believe I'm down in your books.

Mrs. Aml. Oh, madam, I don't come for that, alack !

Flip. Good-morrow, Mrs. Amlet.

Mrs. Aml. Good-morrow, Mrs. Flippanta. 140

Clar. How much am I indebted to you, Mrs. Amlet ?

Mrs. Aml. Nay, if your ladyship desires to see your bill, I believe I may have it about me.—There, madam, if it ben't too much fatigue to you to look it over.

Clar. Let me see it, for I hate to be in debt—[*Aside.*] where I am obliged to pay.—[*Reads.*] Imprimis, *For bolstering out the Countess of Crump's left hip*—Oh, fie ! this does not belong to me.

Mrs. Aml. I beg your ladyship's pardon, I mistook, indeed ; 'tis a countess's bill I have writ out to little pur-pose. I furnished her two years ago with three pair of hips, and am not paid for 'em yet. But some are better customers than some.—There's your ladyship's bill, madam. 153

Clar. [*Reads.*] *For the idea of a new-invented commode.**

---

* Head-dress.

—Ay, this may be mine, but 'tis of a preposterous length. Do you think I can waste time to read every article, Mrs. Amlet? I'd as lief read a sermon.

Mrs. Aml. Alack-a-day, there's no need of fatiguing yourself at that rate; cast an eye only, if your honour pleases, upon the sum total.

Clar. Total; fifty-six pound—and odd things.

Flip. But six-and-fifty pound!

Mrs. Aml. Nay, another body would have made it twice as much; but there's a blessing goes along with a moderate profit.   165

Clar. Flippanta, go to my cashier, let him give you six-and-fifty pound. Make haste: don't you hear me? six-and-fifty pound. Is it so difficult to be comprehended?

Flip. No, madam, I—I comprehend six-and-fifty pound, but—

Clar. But go and fetch it, then.

Flip. [*Aside.*] What she means I don't know; but I shall, I suppose, before I bring her the money.   [*Exit.*

Clar. [*Setting her hair in a pocket-glass.*] The trade you follow gives you a great deal of trouble, Mrs. Amlet?   175

Mrs. Aml. Alack-a-day, a world of pain, madam, and yet there's small profit, as your honour sees by your bill.

Clar. Poor woman! Sometimes you make great losses, Mrs. Amlet?

Mrs. Aml. I have two thousand pounds owing me, of which I shall never get ten shillings.

Clar. Poor woman! You have a great charge of children, Mrs. Amlet?

Mrs. Aml. Only one wicked rogue, madam, who, I think, will break my heart.   185

Clar. Poor woman !

Mrs. Aml. He'll be hanged, madam—that will be the end of him. Where he gets it, Heaven knows ; but he's always shaking his heels with the ladies, and his elbows with the lords. He's as fine as a prince, and as gim* as the best of 'em ; but the ungracious rogue tells all he comes near that his mother is dead, and I am but his nurse.

Clar. Poor woman !

Mrs. Aml. Alas, madam, he's like the rest of the world ; everybody's for appearing to be more than they are, and that ruins all.   196

Clar. Well, Mrs. Amlet, you'll excuse me, I have a little business ; Flippanta will bring you your money presently. Adieu, Mrs. Amlet !

Mrs. Aml. I return your honour many thanks.—[*Exit* CLARISSA.] Ah, there's my good lady, not so much as read her bill. If the rest were like her, I should soon have money enough to go as fine as Dick himself.

Enter DICK AMLET.

Dick. Sure Flippanta must have given my letter by this time ; I long to know how it has been received.   205

Mrs. Aml. Misericorde ! what do I see !

Dick. [*Aside.*] Fiends and hags—the witch my mother !

Mrs. Aml. Nay, 'tis he ; ah, my poor Dick, what art thou doing here ?

Dick. [*Aside.*] What a misfortune !

Mrs. Aml. Good Lard ! how thou art bravely decked. But it's all one, I am thy mother still ; and though thou art

---

* Neat, spruce, well-dressed.—*Johnson.*

a wicked child, nature will speak. I love thee still; ah,
Dick! my poor Dick!   [*Embracing him.*

Dick.   Blood and thunder! will you ruin me?   215
                                          [*Breaking from her.*

Mrs. Aml.   Ah, the blasphemous rogue, how he swears!

Dick.   You destroy all my hopes.

Mrs. Aml.   Will your mother's kiss destroy you, varlet?
Thou art an ungracious bird; kneel down and ask me
blessing, sirrah.

Dick.   Death and furies!

Mrs. Aml.   Ah, he's a proper young man; see what a
shape he has! ah, poor child!

           [*Running to embrace him, he still avoiding her.*

Dick.   Oons, keep off! the woman's mad. If anybody
comes, my fortune's lost.   225

Mrs. Aml.   What fortune? ha! speak, graceless! Ah,
Dick, thou'lt be hanged, Dick!

Dick.   Good dear mother now, don't call me Dick
here.

Mrs. Aml.   Not call thee Dick? is it not thy name?
What shall I call thee? Mr. Amlet? ha? Art not thou a
presumptuous rascal? Hark you, sirrah, I hear of your
tricks; you disown me for your mother, and say I am but
your nurse. Is not this true?   234

Dick.   No, I love you; I respect you;—[*Taking her
hand.*] I am all duty. But if you discover me here, you
ruin the fairest prospect that man ever had.

Mrs. Aml.   What prospect? ha? Come, this is a lie
now.

Dick.   No, my honoured parent; what I say is true, I'm
about a great fortune. I'll bring you home a daughter-in-

law, in a coach and six horses, if you'll but be quiet: I
can't tell you more now.

Mrs. Aml.   Is it possible?

Dick.   'Tis true, by Jupiter!   245

Mrs. Aml.   My dear lad!—

Dick.   For Heaven's sake!—

Mrs. Aml.   But tell me, Dick—

Dick.   I'll follow you home in a moment, and tell you all.

Mrs. Aml.   What a shape is there!—

Dick.   Pray mother, go.

Mrs. Aml.   I must receive some money here first, which
shall go for thy wedding-dinner.

Dick.   Here's somebody coming.—[*Aside.*]   'Sdeath,
she'll betray me!   [*He makes signs to his mother.*

Re-enter FLIPPANTA.

Dick.   Good-morrow, dear Flippanta: how do all the
ladies within?   257

Flip.   At your service, colonel; as far at least as my
interest goes.

Mrs. Aml.   Colonel!—Law you now, how Dick's
respected!   [*Aside.*

Dick.   Waiting for thee, Flippanta, I was making
acquaintance with this old gentlewoman here.

Mrs. Aml.   The pretty lad! he's as impudent as a page.
                                                             [*Aside.*

Dick.   Who is this good woman, Flippanta?

Flip.   A gin of all trades; an old daggling cheat, that
hobbles about from house to house to bubble the ladies of
their money.   I have a small business of yours in my pocket,
colonel.   269

Dick. An answer to my letter?

Flip. So quick indeed! No, it's your letter itself.

Dick. Hast thou not given it then yet?

Flip. I han't had an opportunity; but 'twon't be long first. Won't you go in and see my lady?

Dick. Yes, I'll go make her a short visit. But, dear Flippanta, don't forget: my life and fortune are in your hands.

Flip. Ne'er fear, I'll take care of 'em.

Mrs. Aml. How he traps 'em! let Dick alone. [*Aside.*

Dick. [*To* Mrs. AMLET.] Your servant, good madam.

Mrs. Aml. Your honour's most devoted.—[*Exit* DICK AMLET.] A pretty, civil, well-bred gentleman this, Mrs. Flippanta. Pray who may he be? 282

Flip. A man of great note; Colonel Shapely.

Mrs. Aml. Is it possible! I have heard much of him indeed, but never saw him before. One may see quality in every limb of him: he's a fine man truly.

Flip. I think you are in love with him, Mrs. Amlet.

Mrs. Aml. Alas, those days are done with me; but if I were as fair as I was once, and had as much money as some folks, Colonel Shapely should not catch cold for want of a bedfellow. I love your men of rank, they have something in their air does so distinguish 'em from the rascality. 292

Flip. People of quality are fine things indeed, Mrs. Amlet, if they had but a little more money; but for want of that, they are forced to do things their great souls are ashamed of. For example—here's my lady—she owes you but six-and-fifty pounds—

Mrs. Aml. Well?

Flip. Well, and she has it not by her to pay you.

Mrs. Aml. How can that be?

Flip. I don't know; her cash-keeper's out of humour, he says he has no money. 302

Mrs. Aml. What a presumptuous piece of vermin is a cash-keeper! Tell his lady he has no money!—Now, Mrs. Flippanta, you may see his bags are full, by his being so saucy.

Flip. If they are, there's no help for't; he'll do what he pleases, till he comes to make up his yearly accounts.

Mrs. Aml. But madam plays sometimes, so when she has good fortune, she may pay me out of her winnings.

Flip. Oh, ne'er think of that, Mrs. Amlet; if she had won a thousand pounds, she'd rather die in a jail than pay off a farthing with it. Play-money, Mrs. Amlet, amongst people of quality, is a sacred thing, and not to be profaned. The deuce!—'tis consecrated to their pleasures, 'twould be sacrilege to pay their debts with it. 316

Mrs. Aml. Why, what shall we do then? for I han't one penny to buy bread.

Flip. I'll tell you—it just now comes in my head: I know my lady has a little occasion for money at this time; so—if you'll lend her—a hundred pound—do you see, then she may pay you your six-and-fifty out of it.

Mrs. Aml. Sure, Mrs. Flippanta, you think to make a fool of me!

Flip. No, the devil fetch me if I do.—You shall have a diamond necklace in pawn. 326

Mrs. Aml. O ho, a pawn! That's another case. And when must she have this money?

Flip. In a quarter of an hour.

Mrs. Aml. Say no more. Bring the necklace to my house, it shall be ready for you

Flip. I'll be with you in a moment.

Mrs. Aml. Adieu, Mrs. Flippanta.

Flip. Adieu, Mrs. Amlet.— [*Exit* Mrs. AMLET.] So— this ready money will make us all happy. This spring will set our basset going, and that's a wheel will turn twenty others. My lady's young and handsome; she'll have a dozen intrigues upon her hands before she has been twice at her prayers. So much the better; the more the grist, the richer the miller. Sure never wench got into so hopeful a place! Here's a fortune to be sold, a mistress to be debauched, and a master to be ruined. If I don't feather my nest, and get a good husband, I deserve to die both a maid and a beggar. [*Exit.*

ACT II.

SCENE I.—*A Room in* GRIPE'S *House.*

Enter CLARISSA *and* DICK AMLET.

Clar. What in the name of dulness is the matter with you, colonel? You are as studious as a cracked chemist.

Dick. My head, madam, is full of your husband.

Clar. The worst furniture for a head in the universe.

Dick. I am thinking of his passion for your friend Araminta.

Clar. Passion!—dear colonel, give it a less violent name.

Enter BRASS.

Dick. Well, sir, what want you?

Brass. [*Aside to* DICK AMLET.] The affair I told you of goes ill. There's an action out.   11

Dick. The devil there is!

Clar. What news brings Brass?

Dick. Before Gad I can't tell, madam; the dog will never speak out.—[*To* BRASS.] My lord what d'ye call him waits for me at my lodging: is not that it?

Brass. Yes, sir.

Dick. Madam, I ask your pardon.

Clar. Your servant, sir.—[*Exeunt* DICK AMLET *and* BRASS.] Jessamin!   [*She sits down.*

Enter Jessamin.

Jes.   Madam !   21

Clar.   Where's Corinna ?   Call her to me, if her father han't locked her up ; I want her company.

Jes.   Madam, her guitar-master is with her.   [*Exit.*

Clar.   Psha ! she's taken up with her impertinent guitar man.   Flippanta stays an age with that old fool, Mrs. Amlet. And Araminta, before she can come abroad, is so long a-placing her coquette-patch, that I must be a year without company.   How insupportable is a moment's uneasiness to a woman of spirit and pleasure !   30

Enter Flippanta.

Oh, art thou come at last ? Prithee, Flippanta, learn to move a little quicker, thou knowest how impatient I am.

Flip.   Yes, when you expect money.   If you had sent me to buy a prayer-book, you'd have thought I had flown.

Clar.   Well, hast thou brought me any after all ?

Flip.   Yes, I have brought some.   There— [*Giving her a purse.*] the old hag has struck off her bill, the rest is in that purse.

Clar.   'Tis well ; but take care, Flippanta, my husband don't suspect anything of this ; 'twould vex him, and I don't love to make him uneasy : so I would spare him these little sort of troubles, by keeping 'em from his knowledge.   43

Flip.   See the tenderness she has for him ! and yet he's always complaining of you.

Clar.   'Tis the nature of 'em, Flippanta ; a husband is a growling animal.

Flip.   How exactly you define 'em !

Clar. Oh ! I know 'em, Flippanta ; though I confess my poor wretch diverts me sometimes with his ill humours. I wish he would quarrel with me to-day a little, to pass away the time, for I find myself in a violent spleen.

Flip. Why, if you please to drop yourself in his way, six to four but he scolds one rubbers with you.   54

Clar. Ay, but thou knowest he's as uncertain as the wind, and if instead of quarrelling with me, he should chance to be fond, he'd make me as sick as a dog.

Flip. If he's kind, you must provoke him ; if he kisses you, spit in's face.

Clar. Alas ! when men are in the kissing fit, (like lap-dogs) they take that for a favour.

Flip. Nay, then I don't know what you'll do with him.

Clar. I'll e'en do nothing at all with him.—Flippanta !

[*Yawning.*

Flip. Madam !   65

Clar. My hoods and scarf, and a coach to the door.

Flip. Why, whither are you going ?

Clar. I can't tell yet, but I would go spend some money since I have it.

Flip. Why, you want nothing that I know of.

Clar. How awkward an objection now is that ! as if a woman of education bought things because she wanted 'em. Quality always distinguishes itself ; and therefore, as the mechanic people buy things, because they have occasion for 'em, you see women of rank always buy things, because they have not occasion for 'em. Now there, Flippanta, you see the difference between a woman that has breeding, and one that has none. O ho, here's Araminta come at last.   78

Enter Araminta.

Lard, what a tedious while you have let me expect you! I was afraid you were not well ; how d'ye do to-day ?

Aram.   As well as a woman can do, that has not slept all night.

Flip.   Methinks, madam, you are pretty well awake, however.

Aram.   Oh, 'tis not a little thing will make a woman of my vigour look drowsy.

Clar.   But prithee what was't disturbed you ?

Aram.   Not your husband, don't trouble yourself; at least, I am not in love with him yet.

Clar.   Well remembered, I had quite forgot that matter. I wish you much joy, you have made a noble conquest indeed.   92

Aram.   But now I have subdued the country, pray is it worth my keeping ?   You know the ground, you have tried it.

Clar.   A barren soil, Heaven can tell.

Aram.   Yet if it were well cultivated, it would produce something, to my knowledge.   Do you know 'tis in my power to ruin this poor thing of yours ?   His whole estate is at my service.

Flip.   Cods-fish ! strike him, madam, and let my lady go your halves.   There's no sin in plundering a husband, so his wife has share of the booty.   102

Aram.   Whenever she gives me her orders, I shall be very ready to obey 'em.

Clar.   Why, as odd a thing as such a project may seem, Araminta, I believe I shall have a little serious discourse with you about it.   But, prithee, tell me how you have passed the night? for I am sure your mind has been roving upon some pretty thing or other.

Aram. Why, I have been studying all the ways my brain could produce, to plague my husband.   111

Clar. No wonder indeed you look so fresh this morning, after the satisfaction of such pleasing ideas all night.

Aram. Why, can a woman do less than study mischief, when she has tumbled and tossed herself into a burning fever for want of sleep, and sees a fellow lie snoring by her, stock-still, in a fine breathing sweat?

Clar. Now see the difference of women's tempers! If my dear would make but one nap of his whole life, and only waken to make his will, I should be the happiest wife in the universe. But we'll discourse more of these matters as we go, for I must make a tour among the shops.

Aram. I have a coach waits at the door, we'll talk of 'em as we rattle along.   124

Clar. The best place in nature; for you know a hackney-coach is a natural enemy to a husband.

[*Exeunt* CLARISSA *and* ARAMINTA.

Flip. What a pretty little pair of amiable persons are there gone to hold a council of war together! Poor birds! What would they do with their time if the plaguing their husbands did not help 'em to employment! Well, if idleness be the root of all evil, then matrimony's good for something, for it sets many a poor woman to work. But here comes Miss. I hope I shall help her into the holy state too ere long. And when she's once there, if she don't play her part as well as the best of 'em, I'm mistaken. Han't I lost the letter I'm to give her?—No, here 'tis; so, now we shall see how pure nature will work with her, for art she knows none yet.

Enter CORINNA.

Cor. What does my mother-in-law want with me, Flippanta? They tell me she was asking for me.   139

Flip. She's just gone out, so I suppose 'twas no great business.

Cor. Then I'll go into my chamber again.

Flip. Nay, hold a little, if you please. I have some business with you myself, of more concern than what she had to say to you.

Cor. Make haste then, for you know my father won't let me keep you company ; he says you'll spoil me.

Flip. I spoil you ! He's an unworthy man to give you such ill impressions of a woman of my honour.   149

Cor. Nay, never take it to heart, Flippanta, for I don't believe a word he says. But he does so plague me with his continual scolding, I'm almost weary of my life.

Flip. Why, what is't he finds fault with?

Cor. Nay, I don't know, for I never mind him ; when he has babbled for two hours together, methinks I have heard a mill going, that's all. It does not at all change my opinion, Flippanta, it only makes my head ache.

Flip. Nay, if you can bear it so, you are not to be pitied so much as I thought.   159

Cor. Not pitied ! Why, is it not a miserable thing, such a young creature as I am should be kept in perpetual solitude, with no other company but a parcel of old fumbling masters, to teach me geography, arithmetic, philosophy, and a thousand useless things? Fine entertainment, indeed, for a young maid at sixteen ! Methinks one's time might be better employed.

Flip. Those things will improve your wit.

Cor. Fiddle, faddle! han't I wit enough already? My mother-in-law has learned none of this trumpery, and is not she as happy as the day's long? 170

Flip. Then you envy her, I find?

Cor. And well I may. Does she not do what she has a mind to, in spite of her husband's teeth?

Flip. [*Aside.*] Look you there now, if she has not already conceived that as the supreme blessing of life!

Cor. I'll tell you what, Flippanta; if my mother-in-law would but stand by me a little, and encourage me, and let me keep her company, I'd rebel against my father to-morrow, and throw all my books in the fire. Why, he can't touch a groat of my portion; do you know that, Flippanta? 180

Flip. [*Aside.*] So—I shall spoil her! Pray Heaven the girl don't debauch me!

Cor. Look you: in short, he may think what he pleases, he may think himself wise; but thoughts are free, and I may think in my turn. I'm but a girl, 'tis true, and a fool too, if you'll believe him; but let him know, a foolish girl may make a wise man's heart ache; so he had as good be quiet. —Now it's out.

Flip. Very well, I love to see a young woman have spirit, it's a sign she'll come to something. 190

Cor. Ah, Flippanta! if you would but encourage me, you'd find me quite another thing. I'm a devilish girl in the bottom; I wish you'd but let me make one amongst you.

Flip. That never can be till you are married. Come, examine your strength a little. Do you think you durst venture upon a husband?

Cor. A husband! Why, a—if you would but encourage

me. Come, Flippanta, be a true friend now. I'll give you
advice when I have got a little more experience. Do you
in your very conscience and soul think I am old enough to
be married? 201

Flip. Old enough! why, you are sixteen, are you not?

Cor. Sixteen! I am sixteen, two months, and odd days,
woman. I keep an exact account.

Flip. The deuce you are!

Cor. Why, do you then truly and sincerely think I am
old enough?

Flip. I do upon my faith, child.

Cor. Why, then, to deal as fairly with you, Flippanta, as
you do with me, I have thought so any time these three
years. 211

Flip. Now I find you have more wit than ever I thought
you had; and to show you what an opinion I have of your
discretion, I'll show you a thing I thought to have thrown in
the fire.

Cor. What is it, for Jupiter's sake?

Flip. Something will make your heart chuck within you.

Cor. My dear Flippanta!

Flip. What do you think it is?

Cor. I don't know, nor I don't care, but I'm mad to
have it. 221

Flip. It's a four-cornered thing.

Cor. What, like a cardinal's cap?

Flip. No, 'tis worth a whole conclave of 'em. How do
you like it? [*Showing the letter.*

Cor. O Lard, a letter!—Is there ever a token in it?

Flip. Yes, and a precious one too. There's a handsome
young gentleman's heart.

Cor. A handsome young gentleman's heart!—[*Aside.*]
Nay, then, it's time to look grave.   230

Flip. There.

Cor. I shan't touch it.

Flip. What's the matter now?

Cor. I shan't receive it.

Flip. Sure you jest.

Cor. You'll find I don't. I understand myself better
than to take letters when I don't know who they are from.

Flip. I'm afraid I commended your wit too soon.

Cor. 'Tis all one, I shan't touch it, unless I know who
it comes from.   240

Flip. Heyday! open it and you'll see.

Cor. Indeed I shall not.

Flip. Well—then I must return it where I had it.

Cor. That won't serve your turn, madam. My father
must have an account of this.

Flip. Sure you are not in earnest?

Cor. You'll find I am.

Flip. So, here's fine work! This 'tis to deal with girls
before they come to know the distinction of sexes!

Cor. Confess who you had it from, and perhaps, for this
once, I mayn't tell my father.   251

Flip. Why then, since it must out, 'twas the colonel. But
why are you so scrupulous, madam?

Cor. Because if it had come from anybody else, I would
not have given a farthing for it.

                    [*Twitching it eagerly out of her hand.*

Flip. Ah, my dear little rogue!—[*Kissing her.*] You
frightened me out of my wits.

Cor. Let me read it, let me read it, let me read it, let

me read it, I say.—Um, um, um,—*Cupid's*,—um, um, um, —*darts*,—um, um, um,—*beauty*,—um,—*charms*,—um, um, um,—*angel*,—um,—*goddess*,—um,—[*Kissing the letter.*] um, um, um,—*truest lover*,—um, um,—*eternal constancy*,—um, um, um,—*cruel*,—um, um, um,—*racks*,—um, um,—*tortures*, —um, um,—*fifty daggers*,—um, um,—*bleeding heart*,—um, um,—*dead man.*—Very well, a mighty civil letter I promise you ; not one smutty word in it : I'll go lock it up in my comb-box.   267

Flip. Well—but what does he say to you ?

Cor. Not a word of news, Flippanta ; 'tis all about business.

Flip. Does he not tell you he's in love with you ?

Cor. Ay, but he told me that before.

Flip. How so ? he never spoke to you.

Cor. He sent me word by his eyes.

Flip. Did he so ? mighty well ! I thought you had been to learn that language.   276

Cor. Oh, but you thought wrong, Flippanta. What, because I don't go a-visiting, and see the world, you think I know nothing ! But you should consider, Flippanta, that the more one's alone, the more one thinks ; and 'tis thinking that improves a girl. I'll have you to know, when I was younger than I am now, by more than I'll boast of, I thought of things would have made you stare again.

Flip. Well, since you are so well versed in your business, I suppose I need not inform you, that if you don't write your gallant an answer—he'll die.   286

Cor. Nay, now, Flippanta, I confess you tell me something I did not know before. Do you speak in serious sadness ? Are men given to die if their mistresses are sour to 'em ?

Flip. Um—I can't say they all die.—No, I can't say they all do; but truly, I believe it would go very hard with the colonel.

Cor. Lard, I would not have my hands in blood for thousands; and therefore, Flippanta—if you'll encourage me— 295

Flip. Oh, by all means an answer.

Cor. Well, since you say it then, I'll e'en in and do it, though I protest to you (lest you should think me too forward now) he's the only man that wears a beard, I'd ink my fingers for.—[*Aside.*] Maybe if I marry him, in a year or two's time I mayn't be so nice. [*Exit.*

Flip. Now Heaven give him joy; he's like to have a rare wife o' thee! But where there's money, a man has a plaster to his sore. They have a blessed time on't, who marry for love. See!—here comes an example—Araminta's dread lord. 306

Enter MONEYTRAP.

Mon. Ah, Flippanta! How do you do, good Flippanta? how do you do?

Flip. Thank you, sir, well, at your service.

Mon. And how does the good family, your master, and your fair mistress? Are they at home?

Flip. Neither of 'em; my master has been gone out these two hours, and my lady is just gone with your wife.

Mon. Well, I won't say I have lost my labour, however, as long as I have met with you, Flippanta. For I have wished a great while for an opportunity to talk with you a little. You won't take it amiss, if I should ask you a few questions? 318

Flip. Provided you leave me to my liberty in my answers.—[*Aside.*] What's this cotquean* going to pry into now?

Mon. Prithee, good Flippanta, how do your master and mistress live together?

Flip. Live! why—like man and wife; generally out of humour, quarrel often, seldom agree, complain of one another; and perhaps have both reason. In short, 'tis much as 'tis at your house.

Mon. Good lack! But whose side are you generally of?   329

Flip. O' the right side always, my lady's. And if you'll have me give you my opinion of these matters, sir, I do not think a husband can ever be in the right.

Mon. Ha!

Flip. Little, peaking, creeping, sneaking, stingy, covetous, cowardly, dirty, cuckoldly things.

Mon. Ha!

Flip. Fit for nothing but tailors and dry-nurses.

Mon. Ha!

Flip. A dog in a manger, snarling and biting, to starve gentlemen with good stomachs.   340

Mon. Ha!

Flip. A sentry upon pleasure, set to be a plague upon lovers, and damn poor women before their time.

Mon. A husband is indeed—

Flip. Sir, I say, he is nothing.—A beetle without wings, a windmill without sails, a ship in a calm.

---

* A man who busies himself with women's affairs.—*Johnson.*

Mon.   Ha !

Flip.   A bag without money—an empty bottle—dead small beer.

Mon.   Ha !   350

Flip.   A quack without drugs.

Mon.   Ha !

Flip.   A lawyer without knavery.

Mon.   Ha !

Flip.   A courtier without flattery.

Mon.   Ha !

Flip.   A king without an army, or a people with one. Have I drawn him, sir ?

Mon.   Why, truly, Flippanta, I can't deny but there are some general lines of resemblance. But you know there may be exceptions.   361

Flip.   Hark you, sir, shall I deal plainly with you ? Had I got a husband, I would put him in mind that he was married as well as I.   [*Sings.*

> *For were I the thing call'd a wife,*
>   *And my fool grew too fond of his power,*
> *He should look like an ass all his life,*
>   *For a prank that I'd play him in an hour.*
>   *Tol lol, la ra, tol tol, &c.*

Do you observe that, sir ?   370

Mon.   I do : and think you would be in the right on't. But, prithee, why dost not give this advice to thy mistress ?

Flip.   For fear it should go round to your wife, sir, for you know they are playfellows.

Mon.   Oh, there's no danger of my wife ; she knows I'm none of those husbands.

Flip.   Are you sure she knows that, sir ?

Mon. I'm sure she ought to know it, Flippanta, for really I have but four faults in the world.

Flip. And, pray, what may they be ?   380

Mon. Why, I'm a little slovenly, I shift but once a week.

Flip. Fough !

Mon. I am sometimes out of humour.

Flip. Provoking !

Mon. I don't give her so much money as she'd have.

Flip. Insolent !

Mon. And a—perhaps I mayn't be quite so young as I was.

Flip. The devil !   390

Mon. Oh, but then consider how 'tis on her side, Flippanta. She ruins me with washing, is always out of humour, ever wanting money, and will never be older.

Flip. That last article, I must confess, is a little hard upon you.

Mon. Ah, Flippanta ! didst thou but know the daily provocations I have, thou'dst be the first to excuse my faults. But now I think on't—thou art none of my friend, thou dost not love me at all ; no, not at all.

Flip. And whither is this little reproach going to lead us now ?   401

Mon. You have power over your fair mistress, Flippanta.

Flip. Sir !

Mon. But what then ? you hate me.

Flip. I understand you not.

Mon. There's not a moment's trouble her naughty husband gives her, but I feel it too.

Flip. I don't know what you mean.

Mon.   If she did but know what part I take in her
sufferings—   410

Flip.   Mighty obscure !

Mon.   Well, I'll say no more ; but—

Flip.   All Hebrew !

Mon.   If thou wouldst but tell her on't —

Flip.   Still darker and darker !

Mon.   I should not be ungrateful.

Flip.   Ah, now I begin to understand you.

Mon.   Flippanta—there's my purse.

Flip.   Say no more ; now you explain, indeed—you are
in love ?   420

Mon.   Bitterly—and I do swear by all the gods—

Flip.   Hold !—spare 'em for another time, you stand in
no need of 'em now.   A usurer that parts with his purse,
gives sufficient proof of his sincerity.

Mon.   I hate my wife, Flippanta.

Flip.   That we'll take upon your bare word.

Mon.   She's the devil, Flippanta.

Flip.   You like your neighbour's better ?

Mon.   Oh !—an angel !

Flip.   What pity it is the law don't allow trucking !

Mon.   If it did, Flippanta !   431

Flip.   But since it don't, sir,—keep the reins upon your
passion : don't let your flame rage too high, lest my lady
should be cruel, and it should dry you up to a mummy.

Mon.   'Tis impossible she can be so barbarous to let me
die.   Alas, Flippanta ! a very small matter would save my
life.

Flip.   Then y'are dead—for we women never grant
anything to a man who will be satisfied with a little.

Mon. Dear Flippanta, that was only my modesty ; but since you'll have it out—I am a very dragon : and so your lady'll find—if ever she thinks fit to be—Now I hope you'll stand my friend.   443

Flip. Well, sir, as far as my credit goes, it shall be employed in your service.

Mon. My best Flippanta !—Tell her—I'm all hers—tell her—my body's hers—tell her—my soul's hers—tell her— my estate's hers.   Lard have mercy upon me, how I'm in love !

Flip. Poor man ! what a sweat he's in ! But hark—I hear my master ; for Heaven's sake compose yourself a little, you are in such a fit, o' my conscience he'll smell you out.   453

Mon. Ah dear ! I'm in such an emotion, I dare not be seen ; put me in this closet for a moment.

Flip. Closet, man ! it's too little, your love would stifle you.   Go air yourself in the garden a little, you have need on't i'faith.—[*She puts him out.*]   A rare adventure, by my troth !   This will be curious news to the wives.   Fortune has now put their husbands into their hands, and I think they are too sharp to neglect its favours.

Enter GRIPE.

Gripe. Oh, here's the right hand ; the rest of the body can't be far off.—Where's my wife, huswife ?   463

Flip. An admirable question !—Why, she's gone abroad, sir.

Gripe. Abroad, abroad, abroad already !   Why, she uses to be stewing in her bed three hours after this time, as late as 'tis.   What makes her gadding so soon ?

Flip.　Business, I suppose.

Gripe.　Business! she has a pretty head for business truly.　O ho, let her change her way of living, or I'll make her change a light heart for a heavy one.　472

Flip.　And why would you have her change her way of living, sir?　You see it agrees with her.　She never looked better in her life.

Gripe.　Don't tell me of her looks, I have done with her looks long since.　But I'll make her change her life, or—

Flip.　Indeed, sir, you won't.

Gripe.　Why, what shall hinder me, Insolence?

Flip.　That which hinders most husbands—contradiction.　482

Gripe.　Suppose I resolve I won't be contradicted?

Flip.　Suppose she resolves you shall?

Gripe.　A wife's resolution is not good by law.

Flip.　Nor a husband's by custom.

Gripe.　I tell thee, I will not bear it.

Flip.　I tell you, sir, you will bear it.

Gripe.　Oons! I have borne it three years already.

Flip.　By that you see 'tis but giving your mind to it.

Gripe.　My mind to it! Death and the devil! My mind to it!　492

Flip.　Look ye, sir, you may swear and damn, and call the furies to assist you; but till you apply the remedy to the right place, you'll never cure the disease. You fancy you have got an extravagant wife, is't not so?

Gripe.　Prithee change me that word fancy, and it is so.

Flip.　Why there's it. Men are strangely troubled with the vapours of late. You'll wonder now, if I tell you, you have the most reasonable wife in town; and that all the disorders you think you see in her, are only here, here, here, in your own head. [*Thumping his forehead.*

Gripe. She is then, in thy opinion, a reasonable woman ? 504

Flip. By my faith I think so.

Gripe. I shall run mad !—Name me an extravagance in the world she is not guilty of.

Flip. Name me an extravagance in the world she is guilty of.

Gripe. Come then : does not she put the whole house in disorder ?

Flip. Not that I know of, for she never comes into it but to sleep.

Gripe. 'Tis very well : does she employ any one moment of her life in the government of her family ?

Flip. She is so submissive a wife, she leaves it entirely to you. 517

Gripe. Admirable ! Does she not spend more money in coach-hire, and chair-hire, than would maintain six children ?

Flip. She's too nice of your credit to be seen daggling in the streets.

Gripe. Good ! Do I set eye on her sometimes in a week together ?

Flip. That, sir, is because you are never stirring at the same time ; you keep odd hours ; you are always going to bed when she's rising, and rising just when she's coming to bed. 528

Gripe. Yes, truly, night into day, and day into night, bawdy-house play, that's her trade ! But these are trifles :

has she not lost her diamond necklace ?   Answer me to that, trapes.

Flip.   Yes; and has sent as many tears after it as if it had been her husband.

Gripe.   Ah !—the pox take her ! but enough.   'Tis resolved, and I will put a stop to the course of her life, or I will put a stop to the course of her blood, and so she shall know the first time I meet with her;—[*Aside.*] which, though we are man and wife, and lie under one roof, 'tis very possible may not be this fortnight.   [*Exit.* 540

Flip.   Nay, thou hast a blessed time on't, that must be confessed.   What a miserable devil is a husband !   Insupportable to himself, and a plague to everything about him. Their wives do by them as children do by dogs—tease and provoke 'em, till they make 'em so cursed, they snarl and bite at everything that comes in their reach.   This wretch here is grown perverse to that degree, he's for his wife's keeping home, and making hell of his house, so he may be the devil in it, to torment her.   How niggardly soever he is of all things he possesses, he is willing to purchase her misery, at the expense of his own peace.   But he had as good be still, for he'll miss of his aim.   If I know her (which I think I do) she'll set his blood in such a ferment, it shall bubble out at every pore of him ; whilst hers is so quiet in her veins, her pulse shall go like a pendulum.   [*Exit.*

ACT III.

SCENE I.—*A Room in* Mrs. AMLET'S *House.*

Enter DICK AMLET.

Dick. Where's this old woman?—A-hey! What the devil, nobody at home? Ha! her strong-box!—and the key in't! 'tis so. Now Fortune be my friend. What the deuce!—not a penny of money in cash!—nor a chequer note!—nor a bank bill!—[*Searching the strong box.*] Nor a crooked stick!* nor a—mum!—here's something.—A diamond necklace, by all the gods!—Oons, the old woman! —Zest!

> [*Claps the necklace in his pocket, then runs and asks her blessing.*]

Enter Mrs. AMLET.

Pray, mother, pray to, &c.

Mrs. Aml. Is it possible!—Dick upon his humble knee! Ah, my dear child!—May Heaven be good unto thee.   12

Dick. I'm come, my dear mother, to pay my duty to you, and to ask your consent to—

---

* *i.e.,* An Exchequer tally, which was "a crooked stick, about two feet long, cut into a peculiar shape, with certain notches cut in it, to denote the amount paid in pounds, shillings, and pence, the same being given as a receipt for money paid into the Exchequer."—*Notes and Queries,* Third Series, vol. x., p. 197.

Mrs. Aml. What a shape is there !

Dick. To ask your consent, I say, to marry a great fortune ; for what is riches in this world without a blessing ? and how can there be a blessing without respect and duty to parents ?

Mrs. Aml. What a nose he has!   20

Dick. And therefore, it being the duty of every good child not to dispose of himself in marriage, without the—

Mrs. Aml. Now the Lord love thee !—[*Kissing him.*] for thou art a goodly young man. Well, Dick,—and how goes it with the lady ? Are her eyes open to thy charms ? Does she see what's for her own good ? Is she sensible of the blessings thou hast in store for her ? Ha ! is all sure ? Hast thou broke a piece of money with her ? Speak, bird, do : don't be modest and hide thy love from thy mother, for I'm an indulgent parent.   30

Dick. Nothing under heaven can prevent my good fortune, but its being discovered I am your son—

Mrs. Aml. Then thou art still ashamed of thy natural mother—graceless ! Why, I'm no whore, sirrah.

Dick. I know you are not.—A whore ! bless us all !

Mrs. Aml. No ; my reputation's as good as the best of 'em ; and though I'm old, I'm chaste, you rascal you !

Dick. Lord, that is not the thing we talk of, mother ; but—

Mrs. Aml. I think, as the world goes, they may be proud of marrying their daughter into a vartuous family.

Dick. Oons ! Vartue is not the case—   42

Mrs. Aml. Where she may have a good example before her eyes.

Dick. O Lord ! O Lord ! O Lord !

Mrs. Aml. I'm a woman that don't so much as encourage an incontinent look towards me.

Dick. I tell you, 'sdeath, I tell you—

Mrs. Aml. If a man should make an uncivil motion to
me, I'd spit in his lascivious face : and all this you may tell
'em, sirrah.   51

Dick. Death and furies ! the woman's out of her—

Mrs. Aml. Don't you swear, you rascal you, don't you
swear ; we shall have thee damned at last, and then I shall
be disgraced.

Dick. Why, then in cool blood hear me speak to you.
I tell you it's a city fortune I'm about, she cares not a fig
for your vartue, she'll hear of nothing but quality. She has
quarrelled with one of her friends for having a better
complexion, and is resolved she'll marry, to take place of
her.   61

Mrs. Aml. What a cherry-lip is there !

Dick. Therefore, good dear mother now, have a care
and don't discover me ; for if you do, all's lost.

Mrs. Aml. Dear, dear, how thy fair bride will be
delighted ! Go, get thee gone, go ! Go fetch her home !
go fetch her home ! I'll give her a sack-posset, and a pillow
of down she shall lay her head upon. Go, fetch her home,
I say !

Dick. Take care then of the main chance, my dear
mother ; remember if you discover me—   71

Mrs. Aml. Go, fetch her home, I say !

Dick. You promise me then—

Mrs. Aml. March !

Dick. But swear to me—

Mrs. Aml. Begone, sirrah !

Dick. Well, I'll rely upon you.—But one kiss before I go. 　　　　　　　[*Kisses her heartily, and runs off.*

Mrs. Aml. Now the Lord love thee; for thou art a comfortable young man ! 　　　　　　　　　　　[*Exit.*

SCENE II.—*A Room in* GRIPE's *House.*

Enter CORINNA *and* FLIPPANTA.

Cor. But hark you, Flippanta, if you don't think he loves me dearly, don't give him my letter, after all.

Flip. Let me alone.

Cor. When he has read it, let him give it you again.

Flip. Don't trouble yourself.

Cor. And not a word of the pudding to my mother-in-law.

Flip. Enough.

Cor. When we come to love one another to the purpose, she shall know all. 　　　　　　　　　　　　　　10

Flip. Ay, then 'twill be time.

Cor. But remember 'tis you make me do all this now, so if any mischief comes on't, 'tis you must answer for't.

Flip. I'll be your security.

Cor. I'm young, and know nothing of the matter; but you have experience, so it's your business to conduct me safe.

Flip. Poor innocence !

Cor. But tell me in serious sadness, Flippanta, does he love me with the very soul of him ? 　　　　　　　20

Flip. I have told you so a hundred times, and yet you are not satisfied.

Cor. But, methinks, I'd fain have him tell me so himself.

Flip. Have patience, and it shall be done.

Cor. Why, patience is a virtue; that we must all confess.—But, I fancy, the sooner it's done the better, Flippanta.

Enter Jessamin.

Jes. Madam, yonder's your geography-master waiting for you.   [*Exit.*

Cor. Ah, how I am tired with these old fumbling fellows, Flippanta!   30

Flip. Well, don't let 'em break your heart, you shall be rid of 'em all ere long.

Cor. Nay, 'tis not the study I'm so weary of, Flippanta, 'tis the odious thing that teaches me. Were the colonel my master, I fancy I could take pleasure in learning everything he could show me.

Flip. And he can show you a great deal, I can tell you that. But get you gone in, here's somebody coming, we must not be seen together.

Cor. I will, I will, I will!—Oh, the dear colonel!

[*Exit, running.*

Enter Mrs. Amlet.

Flip. O ho, it's Mrs. Amlet.—What brings you so soon to us again, Mrs. Amlet?   42

Mrs. Aml. Ah, my dear Mrs. Flippanta, I'm in a furious fright!

Flip. Why, what's come to you?

Mrs. Aml. Ah, mercy on us all!—Madam's diamond necklace—

Flip. What of that?

Mrs. Aml. Are you sure you left it at my house?

Flip. Sure I left it! a very pretty question truly!

Mrs. Aml. Nay, don't be angry; say nothing to madam of it, I beseech you. It will be found again, if it be Heaven's good will. At least 'tis I must bear the loss on't. 'Tis my rogue of a son has laid his birdlime fingers on't.   54

Flip. Your son, Mrs. Amlet! Do you breed your children up to such tricks as these then?

Mrs. Aml. What shall I say to you, Mrs. Flippanta? Can I help it? He has been a rogue from his cradle, Dick has. But he has his deserts too. And now it comes in my head, mayhap he may have no ill design in this neither.

Flip. No ill design, woman! He's a pretty fellow if he can steal a diamond necklace with a good one.

Mrs. Aml. You don't know him, Mrs. Flippanta, so well as I that bore him. Dick's a rogue, 'tis true, but—mum!—

Flip. What does the woman mean?   66

Mrs. Aml. Hark you, Mrs. Flippanta, is not here a young gentlewoman in your house that wants a husband?

Flip. Why do you ask?

Mrs. Aml. By way of conversation only, it does not concern me; but when she marries, I may chance to dance at the wedding. Remember I tell you so; I who am but Mrs. Amlet.

Flip. You dance at her wedding! you!

Mrs. Aml. Yes I, I; but don't trouble madam about her necklace, perhaps it mayn't go out of the family. Adieu, Mrs. Flippanta.   [*Exit.*   77

Flip. What—what—what does the woman mean? Mad!

What a capilotade* of a story's here! The necklace lost;
and her son Dick; and a fortune to marry; and she shall
dance at the wedding; and—she does not intend, I hope, to
propose a match between her son Dick and Corinna? By
my conscience I believe she does. An old beldam!

Enter Brass.

Brass. Well, hussy, how stand our affairs? Has Miss
writ us an answer yet? my master's very impatient yonder.

Flip. And why the deuce does not he come himself?
What does he send such idle fellows as thee of his errands?
Here I had her alone just now.—He won't have such an
opportunity again this month, I can tell him that.   89

Brass. So much the worse for him; 'tis his business.—
But now, my dear, let thee and I talk a little of our own:
I grow most damnably in love with thee; dost hear
that?

Flip. Phu! thou art always timing things wrong; my
head is full at present of more important things than
love.

Brass. Then it's full of important things indeed. Dost
want a privy-counsellor?

Flip. I want an assistant.

Brass. To do what?   100

Flip. Mischief.

Brass. I'm thy man—touch.

Flip. But before I venture to let thee into my project,
prithee tell me whether thou findest a natural disposition to
ruin a husband to oblige his wife?

---

* See note *ante*, p. 52.

Brass.   Is she handsome?

Flip.   Yes.

Brass.   Why then, my disposition's at her service.

Flip.   She's beholding to thee.

Brass.   Not she alone neither, therefore don't let her grow vain upon't ; for I have three or four affairs of that kind going at this time.   112

Flip.   Well, go carry this epistle from Miss to thy master; and when thou comest back I'll tell thee thy business.

Brass.   I'll know it before I go, if you please.

Flip.   Thy master waits for an answer.

Brass.   I'd rather he should wait than I.

Flip.   Why then, in short, Araminta's husband is in love with my lady.

Brass.   Very well, child, we have a Rowland for her Oliver: thy lady's husband is in love with Araminta.

Flip.   Who told you that, sirrah?   122

Brass.   'Tis a negotiation I am charged with, pert.   Did not I tell thee I did business for half the town?   I have managed Master Gripe's little affairs for him these ten years, you slut you.

Flip.   Hark thee, Brass, the game's in our hands, if we can but play the cards.

Brass.   Pique and repique, you jade you, if the wives will fall into a good intelligence.

Flip.   Let them alone; I'll answer for 'em they don't slip the occasion.—See, here they come.   They little think what a piece of good news we have for 'em.   133

Enter CLARISSA *and* ARAMINTA.

Clar.   Jessamin!

Enter Jessamin.

Here, boy, carry up these things into my dressing-room, and break as many of 'em by the way as you can, be sure.— [*Exit* Jessamin.]   Oh, art thou there, Brass?   What news?

Brass.   Madam, I only called in as I was going by.— But some little propositions Mrs. Flippanta has been starting, have kept me here to offer your ladyship my humble service.

Clar.   What propositions?

Brass.   She'll acquaint you, madam.

Aram.   Is there anything new, Flippanta?

Flip.   Yes, and pretty too.   145

Clar.   That follows of course; but let's have it quick.

Flip.   Why, madam, you have made a conquest.

Clar.   Hussy!—But of who? quick!

Flip.   Of Mr. Moneytrap, that's all.

Aram.   My husband!

Flip.   Yes, your husband, madam.   You thought fit to corrupt ours, so now we are even with you.

Aram.   Sure thou art in jest, Flippanta!

Flip.   Serious as my devotions.

Brass.   And the cross intrigue, ladies, is what our brains have been at work about.   156

Aram.   [*To* Clarissa.]   My dear!

Clar.   My life!

Aram.   My angel!

Clar.   My soul!   [*Hugging one another.*

Aram.   The stars have done this.

Clar.   The pretty little twinklers.

Flip.   And what will you do for them now?

Clar. What grateful creatures ought; show 'em we don't despise their favours.   165

Aram. But is not this a wager between these two block-heads?

Clar. I would not give a shilling to go the winner's halves.

Aram. Then 'tis the most fortunate thing that ever could have happened.

Clar. All your last night's ideas, Araminta, were trifles to it.

Aram. Brass (my dear) will be useful to us.

Brass. At your service, madam.   175

Clar. Flippanta will be necessary, my life.

Flip. She waits your commands, madam.

Aram. For my part then, I recommend my husband to thee, Flippanta, and make it my earnest request thou won't leave him one half-crown.

Flip. I'll do all I can to obey you, madam.

Brass. [*To* CLARISSA.] If your ladyship would give me the same kind orders for yours.

Clar. Oh—if thou sparest him, Brass, I'm thy enemy till I die.   185

Brass. 'Tis enough, madam, I'll be sure to give you a reasonable account of him: But how do you intend we shall proceed, ladies? Must we storm the purse at once, or break ground in form, and carry it by little and little?

Clar. Storm, dear Brass, storm! Ever whilst you live, storm!

Aram. Oh, by all means!—Must it not be so, Flippanta?

Flip. In four-and-twenty hours, two hundred pounds a-piece, that's my sentence.

Brass. Very well.—But, ladies, you'll give me leave to put you in mind of some little expense in favours, 'twill be necessary you are at, to these honest gentlemen.   197

Aram. Favours, Brass?

Brass. Um—a—some small matters, madam, I doubt must be.

Clar. Now that's a vile article, Araminta; for that thing your husband is so like mine—

Flip. Phu, there's a scruple, indeed! Pray, madam, don't be so squeamish; though the meat be a little flat, we'll find you savoury sauce to it.

Clar. This wench is so mad.

Flip. Why, what in the name of Lucifer is it you have to do that's so terrible?

Brass. A civil look only.

Aram. There's no great harm in that.   210

Flip. An obliging word.

Clar. That one may afford 'em.

Brass. A little smile *à propos.*

Aram. That's but giving one's self an air.

Flip. Receive a little letter, perhaps.

Clar. Women of quality do that from fifty odious fellows.

Brass. Suffer (maybe) a squeeze by the hand.

Aram. One's so used to that one does not feel it.

Flip. Or if a kiss would do't?

Clar. I'd die first!   220

Brass. Indeed, ladies, I doubt 'twill be necessary to—

Clar. Get their wretched money, without paying so dear for it.

Flip. Well, just as you please for that, my ladies. But I suppose you'll play upon the square with your favours, and not pique yourselves upon being one more grateful than another?

Brass. And state a fair account of receipts and disbursements?

Aram. That I think should be indeed. 230

Clar. With all my heart, and Brass shall be our bookkeeper. So get thee to work, man, as fast as thou canst; but not a word of all this to thy master.

Brass. I'll observe my orders, madam. [*Exit.*

Clar. I'll have the pleasure of telling him myself; he'll be violently delighted with it. 'Tis the best man in the world, Araminta; he'll bring us rare company to-morrow, all sorts of gamesters; and thou shalt see my husband will be such a beast to be out of humour at it. 239

Aram. The monster!—But hush, here's my dear approaching: prithee let's leave him to Flippanta.

Flip. Ay, pray do, I'll bring you a good account of him, I'll warrant you.

Clar. Dispatch then, for the basset-table's in haste.

[*Exit with* ARAMINTA.

Flip. So, now have at him; here he comes. We'll try if we can pillage the usurer, as he does other folks.

Enter MONEYTRAP.

Mon. Well, my pretty Flippanta, is thy mistress come home?

Flip. Yes, sir.

Mon. And where is she, prithee? 250

Flip. Gone abroad, sir.

Mon. How dost mean?

Flip. I mean right, sir; my lady'll come home and go

abroad ten times in an hour, when she's either in very good humour or very bad.

Mon. Good lack! But I'll warrant, in general, 'tis her naughty husband that makes her house uneasy to her. But hast thou said a little something to her, chicken, for an expiring lover? ha?

Flip. Said!—yes, I have said! much good may it do me!   261

Mon. Well, and how?

Flip. And how!—And how do you think? You would have me do't. And you have such a way with you, one can refuse you nothing. But I have brought myself into a fine business by it.

Mon. Good lack!—But I hope, Flippanta—

Flip. Yes, your hopes will do much, when I am turned out of doors.

Mon. Was she then terrible angry?   270

Flip. Oh! had you seen how she flew, when she saw where I was pointing; for you must know I went round the bush and round the bush, before I came to the matter.

Mon. Nay, 'tis a ticklish point, that must be owned.

Flip. On my word is it—I mean where a lady's truly virtuous; for that's our case, you must know.

Mon. A very dangerous case indeed.

Flip. But I can tell you one thing—she has an inclination to you.

Mon. Is it possible?   280

Flip. Yes, and I told her so at last.

Mon. Well, and what did she answer thee?

Flip. Slap—and bid me bring it you for a token.

[*Giving him a slap on the face.*

Mon. [*Aside.*]   And you have lost none on't by the way, with a pox t'ye !

Flip.   Now this, I think, looks the best in the world.

Mon.   Yes, but really it feels a little oddly.

Flip.   Why, you must know, ladies have different ways of expressing their kindness, according to the humour they are in.   If she had been in a good one, it had been a kiss ; but as long as she sent you something, your affairs go well.

Mon.   Why, truly, I am a little ignorant in the mysterious paths of love, so I must be guided by thee. But, prithee, take her in a good humour, next token she sends me.   295

Flip.   Ah—good humour !

Mon.   What's the matter ?

Flip.   Poor lady !

Mon.   Ha !

Flip.   If I durst tell you all—

Mon.   What then ?

Flip.   You would not expect to see her in one a good while.

Mon.   Why, I pray ?

Flip.   I must own I did take an unseasonable time to talk of love-matters to her.   306

Mon.   Why, what's the matter ?

Flip.   Nothing.

Mon.   Nay, prithee tell me.

Flip.   I dare not.

Mon.   You must indeed.

Flip.   Why, when women are in difficulties, how can they think of pleasure ?

Mon.   Why, what difficulties can she be in ?

Flip.   Nay, I do but guess after all; for she has that grandeur of soul, she'd die before she'd tell.   316

Mon.   But what dost thou suspect?

Flip.   Why, what should one suspect, where a husband loves nothing but getting of money, and a wife nothing but spending on't?

Mon.   So she wants that same then?

Flip.   I say no such thing, I know nothing of the matter; pray make no wrong interpretation of what I say, my lady wants nothing that I know of.   'Tis true—she has had ill luck at cards of late; I believe she has not won once this month; but what of that?   326

Mon.   Ha!

Flip.   'Tis true, I know her spirit's that, she'd see her husband hanged before she'd ask him for a farthing.

Mon.   Ha!

Flip.   And then I know him again, he'd see her drowned before he'd give her a farthing; but that's a help to your affair, you know.

Mon.   'Tis so, indeed.

Flip.   Ah—well, I'll say nothing; but if she had none of these things to fret her—   336

Mon.   Why really, Flippanta—

Flip.   I know what you are going to say now; you are going to offer your service, but 'twon't do; you have a mind to play the gallant now, but it must not be; you want to be showing your liberality, but 'twon't be allowed; you'll be pressing me to offer it, and she'll be in a rage.   We shall have the devil to do.

Mon.   You mistake me, Flippanta; I was only going to say—   345

Flip. Ay, I know what you were going to say well enough ; but I tell you it will never do so. If one could find out some way now—ay—let me see—

Mon. Indeed I hope—

Flip. Pray be quiet—no—but I'm thinking—hum—she'll smoke that though—let us consider.—If one could find a way to—'Tis the nicest point in the world to bring about, she'll never touch it, if she knows from whence it comes.

Mon. Shall I try if I can reason her husband out of twenty pounds, to make her easy the rest of her life.   356

Flip. Twenty pound, man !—why, you shall see her set that upon a card. Oh, she has a great soul !—Besides, if her husband should oblige her, it might, in time, take off her aversion to him, and, by consequence, her inclination to you. No, no, it must never come that way.

Mon. What shall we do then ?

Flip. Hold still—I have it. I'll tell you what you shall do.

Mon. Ay.

Flip. You shall make her—a restitution—of two hundred pounds.   366

Mon Ha !—a restitution ?

Flip. Yes, yes, 'tis the luckiest thought in the world ; madam often plays, you know, and folks who do so meet now and then with sharpers. Now you shall be a sharper.

Mon. A sharper ?

Flip. Ay, ay, a sharper ; and having cheated her of two hundred pounds, shall be troubled in mind, and send it her back again. You comprehend me ?

Mon. Yes, I—I comprehend, but a—won't she suspect if it be so much ?   376

Flip. No, no, the more the better.

Mon. Two hundred pound?

Flip. Yes, two hundred pound.—Oh, let me see—so even a sum may look a little suspicious,—ay—let it be two hundred and thirty; that odd thirty will make it look so natural, the devil won't find it out.

Mon. Ha!

Flip. Pounds, too, look I don't know how; guineas I fancy were better:—ay, guineas, it shall be guineas. You are of that mind, are you not?   386

Mon. Um—a guinea, you know, Flippanta, is—

Flip. A thousand times genteeler; you are certainly in the right on't; it shall be as you say, two hundred and thirty guineas.

Mon. Ho—well, if it must be guineas, let's see, two hundred guineas.

Flip. And thirty; two hundred and thirty: if you mistake the sum, you spoil all. So go put 'em in a purse, while it's fresh in your head, and send 'em to me with a penitential letter, desiring I'll do you the favour to restore 'em to her.   397

Mon. Two hundred and thirty pounds in a bag?

Flip. Guineas, I say, guineas!

Mon. Ay, guineas, that's true. But, Flippanta, if she don't know they come from me, then I give my money for nothing, you know.

Flip. Phu! leave that to me; I'll manage the stock for you; I'll make it produce something, I'll warrant you.

Mon. Well, Flippanta, 'tis a great sum indeed; but I'll go try what I can do for her. You say, two hundred guineas in a purse?   407

Flip.   And thirty, if the man's in his senses !

Mon.   And thirty, 'tis true, I always forget that thirty.

[*Exit.*

Flip.   So, get thee gone ; thou art a rare fellow, i'faith.—
Brass !—it's thee, is't not ?

Re-enter BRASS.

Brass.   It is, huswife.   How go matters ?   I stayed till
thy gentleman was gone.   Hast done anything towards our
common purse ?

Flip.   I think I have ; he's going to make us a restitution
of two or three hundred pounds.

Brass.   A restitution !—good !   417

Flip.   A new way, sirrah, to make a lady take a present
without putting her to the blush.

Brass.   'Tis very well, mighty well, indeed.   Prithee,
where's thy master ? let me try if I can persuade him to be
troubled in mind too.

Flip.   Not so hasty ; he's gone into his closet to prepare
himself for a quarrel I have advised him to—with his wife.

Brass.   What to do ?

Flip.   Why, to make her stay at home, now she has
resolved to do it beforehand.   You must know, sirrah, we
intend to make a merit of our basset-table, and get a good
pretence for the merry companions we intend to fill his
house with.   430

Brass.   Very nicely spun, truly ; thy husband will be a
happy man.

Flip.   Hold your tongue, you fool you ! See, here comes
your master.

Brass.   He's welcome.

Enter Dick Amlet.

Dick.   My dear Flippanta, how many thanks have I to pay thee !

Flip.   Do you like her style?

Dick.   The kindest little rogue ! there's nothing but she gives me leave to hope.   I am the happiest man the world has in its care.   441

Flip.   Not so happy as you think for neither, perhaps ; you have a rival, sir, I can tell you that.

Dick.   A rival !

Flip.   Yes, and a dangerous one too.

Dick.   Who, in the name of terror ?

Flip.   A devilish fellow ; one Mr. Amlet.

Dick.   Amlet ! I know no such man.

Flip.   You know the man's mother though ; you met her here, and are in her favour, I can tell you.   If he worst you in your mistress, you shall e'en marry her, and disinherit him.   452

Dick.   If I have no other rival but Mr. Amlet, I believe I shan't be much disturbed in my amour.   But can't I see Corinna ?

Flip.   I don't know, she has always some of her masters with her: but I'll go see if she can spare you a moment, and bring you word.   [*Exit.*

Dick.   I wish my old hobbling mother han't been blabbing something here she should not do.   460

Brass.   Fear nothing, all's safe on that side yet.   But how speaks young mistress's epistle? soft and tender?

Dick.   As pen can write.

Brass.   So you think all goes well there ?

Dick.   As my heart can wish.

Brass.   You are sure on't?

Dick.   Sure on't.

Brass.   Why then, ceremony aside,—[*Putting on his hat.*] you and I must have a little talk, Mr. Amlet.   469

Dick.   Ah, Brass, what art thou going to do? Wou't ruin me?

Brass.   Look you, Dick, few words; you are in a smooth way of making your fortune; I hope all will roll on. But how do you intend matters shall pass 'twixt you and me in this business?

Dick.   Death and furies! what a time dost take to talk on't!

Brass.   Good words, or I betray you; they have already heard of one Mr. Amlet in the house.   479

Dick.   Here's a son of a whore!   [*Aside.*

Brass.   In short, look smooth, and be a good prince. I am your valet, 'tis true; your footman sometimes, which I'm enraged at; but you have always had the ascendant, I confess. When we were schoolfellows, you made me carry your books, make your exercise, own your rogueries, and sometimes take a whipping for you. When we were fellow-prentices, though I was your senior, you made me open the shop, clean my master's shoes, cut last at dinner, and eat all the crust. In our sins too, I must own you still kept me under; you soared up to adultery with our mistress, while I was at humble fornication with the maid. Nay, in our punishments you still made good your post; for when once upon a time I was sentenced but to be whipped, I cannot deny but you were condemned to be hanged. So that in all times, I must confess, your inclinations have been greater and nobler than mine. However, I cannot consent that you should at once fix fortune for life, and I dwell in my humilities for the rest of my days. 498

Dick. Hark thee, Brass, if I do not most nobly by thee, I'm a dog.

Brass. And when?

Dick. As soon as ever I am married.

Brass. Ah, the pox take thee!

Dick. Then you mistrust me?

Brass. I do, by my faith! Look you, sir, some folks we mistrust, because we don't know 'em; others we mistrust, because we do know 'em: and for one of these reasons I desire there may be a bargain beforehand. If not— [*Raising his voice*] look ye, Dick Amlet— 509

Dick. Soft, my dear friend and companion.—[*Aside.*] The dog will ruin me!—[*Aloud.*] Say, what is't will content thee?

Brass. O ho!

Dick. But how canst thou be such a barbarian?

Brass. I learned it at Algiers.

Dick. Come, make thy Turkish demand then.

Brass. You know you gave me a bank-bill this morning to receive for you.

Dick. I did so, of fifty pounds; 'tis thine. So, now thou art satisfied; all's fixed. 520

Brass. It is not, indeed. There's a diamond necklace you robbed your mother of e'en now.

Dick. Ah, you Jew!

Brass. No words.

Dick. My dear Brass!

Brass. I insist.

Dick.   My old friend !

Brass.   Dick Amlet—[*Raising his voice.*] I insist.

Dick.   Ah, the cormorant !—Well, 'tis thine : but thou'lt never thrive with't.   530

Brass.   When I find it begins to do me mischief, I'll give it you again.   But I must have a wedding-suit.

Dick.   Well.

Brass.   Some good lace.

Dick.   Thou shalt.

Brass.   A stock of linen.

Dick.   Enough.

Brass.   Not yet ; a silver sword.

Dick.   Well, thou shalt have that too.   Now thou hast everything.   540

Brass.   Gad forgive me !   I forgot a ring of remembrance. I would not forget all these favours for the world : a sparkling diamond will be always playing in my eye, and put me in mind of 'em.

Dick.   [*Aside.*] This unconscionable rogue !—[*Aloud.*] Well, I'll bespeak one for thee.

Brass.   Brilliant ?

Dick.   It shall.   But if the thing don't succeed after all ?—   549

Brass.   I'm a man of honour, and restore.   And so the treaty being finished, I strike my flag of defiance, and fall into my respects again.   [*Taking off his hat.*

Re-enter FLIPPANTA.

Flip.   I have made you wait a little, but I could not help it : her master is but just gone.   He has been showing her Prince Eugene's March into Italy.

Dick. Prithee, let me come to her, I'll show her a part of the world he has never shown her yet.

Flip. So I told her, you must know; and she said, she could like to travel in good company: so, if you'll slip up those back-stairs, you shall try if you can agree upon the journey. 561

Dick. My dear Flippanta !

Flip. None of your dear acknowledgments, I beseech you, but up stairs as hard as you can drive.

Dick. I'm gone. [*Exit.*

Flip. And do you follow him, Jack-a-dandy, and see he is not surprised.

Brass. I thought that was your post, Mrs. Useful. But if you'll come and keep me in humour, I don't care if I share the duty with you. 570

Flip. No words, sirrah, but follow him ; I have somewhat else to do.

Brass. The jade's so absolute, there's no contesting with her. One kiss though, to keep the sentinel warm.—[*Gives her a long kiss.*] So. [*Exit.*

Flip. [*Wiping her mouth.*] A nasty rogue. But let me see, what have I to do now? This restitution will be here quickly, I suppose; in the meantime I'll go know if my lady's ready for the quarrel yet. Master, yonder, is so full on't, he's ready to burst ; but we'll give him vent by and by, with a witness. [*Exit.*

ACT IV.

SCENE I.—*A Room in* GRIPE'S *House.*

Enter CORINNA, DICK AMLET, *and* BRASS.

Brass.   Don't fear, I'll give timely notice.

[*Goes to the door.*

Dick.   Come, you must consent, you shall consent.   How can you leave me thus upon the rack?   A man who loves you to that excess that I do.

Cor.   Nay, that you love me, sir, that I'm satisfied in, for you have sworn you do: and I'm so pleased with it, I'd fain have you do so as long as you live, so we must never marry.

Dick.   Not marry, my dear! why, what's our love good for if we don't marry?   10

Cor.   Ah!—I'm afraid 'twill be good for little if we do.

Dick.   Why do you think so?

Cor.   Because I hear my father and mother, and my uncle and aunt, and Araminta and her husband, and twenty other married folks, say so from morning to night.

Dick.   Oh, that's because they are bad husbands and bad wives; but, in our case, there will be a good husband and a good wife, and so we shall love for ever.

Cor.   Why, there may be something in that truly; and I'm always willing to hear reason, as a reasonable young woman ought to do. But are you sure, sir, though we are very good now, we shall be so when we come to be better acquainted?   23

Dick. I can answer for myself, at least.

Cor. I wish you could answer for me too. You see I'm a plain-dealer, sir, I hope you don't like me the worse for it.

Dick. Oh, by no means! 'Tis a sign of admirable morals; and I hope, since you practise it yourself, you'll approve of it in your lover. In one word, therefore, (for 'tis in vain to mince the matter) my resolution's fixed, and the world can't stagger me, I marry—or I die.

Cor. Indeed, sir, I have much ado to believe you; the disease of love is seldom so violent.   33

Dick. Madam, I have two diseases to end my miseries; if the first don't do't, the latter shall;—[*Drawing his sword.*] one's in my heart, the t'other's in my scabbard.

Cor. Not for a diadem!—[*Catching hold of him.*] Ah, put it up! put it up!

Dick. How absolute is your command !—[*Dropping his sword.*] A word, you see, disarms me.

Cor. [*Aside.*] What a power I have over him! The wondrous deeds of love!—[*Aloud.*] Pray, sir, let me have no more of these rash doings though; perhaps I mayn't be always in the saving humour.—[*Aside.*] I'm sure if I had let him stick himself, I should have been envied by all the great ladies in the town.   46

Dick. Well, madam, have I then your promise? You'll make me the happiest of mankind?

Cor. I don't know what to say to you; but I believe I had as good promise, for I find I shall certainly do't.

Dick. Then let us seal the contract thus.   [*Kisses her.*

Cor. [*Aside.*] Um—he has almost taken away my breath : he kisses purely !

Dick. Hark !—somebody comes.

Brass. [*Peeping in.*] Gare there ! the enemy !—No, hold ! y'are safe, 'tis Flippanta.   56

Enter FLIPPANTA.

Flip. Come, have you agreed the matter? If not, you must end it another time, for your father's in motion, so pray kiss and part.

Cor. That's sweet and sour.—[*They kiss.*] Adieu t'ye, sir !   [*Exeunt* DICK AMLET *and* CORINNA.

Enter CLARISSA.

Clar. Have you told him I'm at home, Flippanta ?

Flip. Yes, madam.

Clar. And that I'll see him ?

Flip. Yes, that too. But here's news for you ; I have just now received the restitution.   66

Clar. That's killing pleasure ; and how much has he restored me ?

Flip. Two hundred and thirty.

Clar. Wretched rogue ! But retreat ; your master's coming to quarrel.

Flip. I'll be within call, if things run high.   [*Exit.*

Enter GRIPE.

Gripe. O ho !—are you there, i'faith? Madam, your humble servant, I'm very glad to see you at home, I thought I should never have had that honour again.   75

Clar. Good-morrow, my dear, how d'ye do? Flippanta says you are out of humour, and that you have a mind to quarrel with me. Is it true, ha?—I have a terrible pain in my head, I give you notice on't beforehand.

Gripe. And how the pox should it be otherwise? It's a wonder you are not dead—[*A·ide*] as a' would you were!—[*Aloud*] with the life you lead. Are you not ashamed? and do you not blush to—

Clar. My dear child, you crack my brain; soften the harshness of your voice. Say what thou wou't, but let it be in an agreeable tone.   86

Gripe. Tone, madam! don't tell me of a tone—

Clar. Oh,—if you will quarrel, do it with temperance; let it be all in cool blood, even and smooth, as if you were not moved with what you said; and then I'll hear you as if I were not moved with it neither.

Gripe. Had ever man such need of patience! Madam, madam, I must tell you, madam—

Clar. Another key, or I walk off.

Gripe. Don't provoke me.   95

Clar. Shall you be long, my dear, in your remonstrances?

Gripe. Yes, madam, and very long.

Clar. If you would quarrel *en abrégé*, I should have a world of obligation to you.

Gripe. What I have to say, forsooth, is not to be expressed *en abrégé*, my complaints are too numerous.

Clar. Complaints! of what, my dear?—Have I ever given you subject of complaint, my life?

Gripe. O pox! my dear and my life! I desire none of your tendres.   106

Clar. How! find fault with my kindness, and my expressions of affection and respect? The world will guess by this what the rest of your complaints may be. I must tell you I'm scandalized at your procedure.

Gripe. I must tell you I am running mad with yours.

Clar. Ah! how insupportable are the humours of some husbands, so full of fancies, and so ungovernable! What have you in the world to disturb you?

Gripe. What have I to disturb me? I have you, death and the devil! 116

Clar. Ay, merciful Heaven! how he swears! You should never accustom yourself to such words as these; indeed, my dear, you should not; your mouth's always full of 'em.

Gripe. Blood and thunder! madam—

Clar. Ah, he'll fetch the house down! Do you know you make me tremble for you?—Flippanta! who's there? Flippanta!

Gripe. Here's a provoking devil for you! 125

Re-enter FLIPPANTA.

Flip. What in the name of Jove's the matter? you'll raise the neighbourhood.

Clar. Why, here's your master in a most violent fuss, and no mortal soul can tell for what.

Gripe. Not tell for what!

Clar. No, my life.—I have begged him to tell me his griefs, Flippanta; and then he swears, good Lord, how he does swear!

Gripe. Ah, you wicked jade! ah, you wicked jade!.

Clar. Do you hear him, Flippanta? do you hear him?

Flip. Pray, sir, let's know a little what puts you in all this fury? 137

Clar. Prithee stand near me, Flippanta, there's an odd froth about his mouth, looks as if his poor head were going wrong; I'm afraid he'll bite.

Gripe. The wicked woman, Flippanta, the wicked woman!

Clar. Can anybody wonder I shun my own house, when he treats me at this rate in it?

Gripe. At this rate! Why in the devil's name—

Clar. Do you hear him again?

Flip. Come, a little moderation, sir, and try what that will produce.   148

Gripe. Hang her, 'tis all a pretence to justify her going abroad.

Clar. A pretence! a pretence! Do you hear how black a charge he loads me with? Charges me with a pretence! Is this the return for all my downright open actions? You know, my dear, I scorn pretences: whene'er I go abroad, it is without pretence.

Gripe. Give me patience!

Flip. You have a great deal, sir.

Clar. And yet he's never content, Flippanta.

Gripe. What shall I do?   159

Clar. What a reasonable man would do; own yourself in the wrong, and be quiet. Here's Flippanta has under-standing, and I have moderation; I'm willing to make her judge of our differences.

Flip. You do me a great deal of honour, madam: but I tell you beforehand, I shall be a little on master's side.

Gripe. Right, Flippanta has sense. Come, let her decide.—Have I not reason to be in a passion? tell me that.

Clar. You must tell her for what, my life.

Gripe. Why, for the trade you drive, my soul.   169

Flip. Look you, sir, pray take things right. I know madam does fret you a little now and then, that's true; but in the fund she is the softest, sweetest, gentlest lady breathing. Let her but live entirely to her own fancy, and she'll never say a word to you from morning to night.

Gripe. Oons! let her but stay at home, and she shall do what she will: in reason, that is.

Flip. D'ye hear that, madam? Nay, now I must be on master's side; you see how he loves you, he desires only your company. Pray give him that satisfaction, or I must pronounce against you.   180

Clar. Well, I agree. Thou knowest I don't love to grieve him: let him be always in good humour, and I'll be always at home.

Flip. Look you there, sir, what would you have more?

Gripe. Well, let her keep her word, and I'll have done quarrelling.

Clar. I must not, however, so far lose the merit of my consent, as to let you think I'm weary of going abroad, my dear. What I do, is purely to oblige you; which, that I may be able to perform without a relapse, I'll invent what ways I can to make my prison supportable to me.

Flip. Her prison! pretty bird! her prison! don't that word melt you, sir?   193

Gripe. I must confess I did not expect to find her so reasonable.

Flip. Oh, sir, soon or late wives come into good humour. Husbands must only have a little patience to wait for it.

Clar. The innocent little diversions, dear, that I shall content myself with, will be chiefly play and company.

Gripe. Oh, I'll find you employment, your time shan't lie upon your hands; though if you have a mind now for such a companion as a—let me see—Araminta, for example, why I shan't be against her being with you from morning till night. 204

Clar. You can't oblige me more, 'tis the best woman in the world.

Gripe. Is not she?

Flip. Ah, the old satyr! [*Aside.*

Gripe. Then we'll have, besides her, maybe sometimes— her husband; and we shall see my niece that writes verses, and my sister Fidget; with her husband's brother that's always merry; and his little cousin, that's to marry the fat curate; and my uncle the apothecary, with his wife and all his children. Oh, we shall divert ourselves rarely! 214

Flip. Good! [*Aside.*

Clar. Oh, for that, my dear child, I must be plain with you, I'll see none of 'em but Araminta, who has the manners of the court; for I'll converse with none but women of quality.

Gripe. Ay, ay, they shall all have one quality or other.

Clar. Then, my dear, to make our home pleasant, we'll have concerts of music sometimes.

Gripe. Music in my house!

Clar. Yes, my child, we must have music, or the house will be so dull I shall get the spleen, and be going abroad again. 226

Flip. Nay, she has so much complaisance for you, sir, you can't dispute such things with her.

Gripe. Ay, but if I have music—

Clar. Ay, but, sir, I must have music—

Flip. Not every day, madam don't mean.

Clar. No, bless me, no; but three concerts a week: three days more we'll play after dinner, at ombre, picquet, basset, and so forth, and close the evening with a handsome supper and a ball. 235

Gripe. A ball!

Clar. Then, my love, you know there is but one day more upon our hands, and that shall be the day of conversation; we'll read verses, talk of books, invent modes, tell lies, scandalize our friends, be pert upon religion; and in short, employ every moment of it in some pretty witty exercise or other.

Flip. What order you see 'tis she proposes to live in! a most wonderful regularity!

Gripe. Regularity with a pox! [*Aside.*

Clar. And as this kind of life, so soft, so smooth, so agreeable, must needs invite a vast deal of company to partake of it, 'twill be necessary to have the decency of a porter at our door, you know. 249

Gripe. A porter!—a scrivener have a porter, madam!

Clar. Positively, a porter.

Gripe. Why, no scrivener since Adam ever had a porter, woman!

Clar. You will therefore be renowned in story, for having the first, my life.

Gripe. Flippanta!

Flip. [*Aside to* GRIPE.] Hang it, sir, never dispute a trifle; if you vex her, perhaps she'll insist upon a Swiss.

Gripe. But, madam— 259

Clar. But, sir, a porter, positively a porter; without that the treaty's null, and I go abroad this moment.

Flip. Come, sir, never lose so advantageous a peace for a pitiful porter.

Gripe. Why, I shall be hooted at, the boys will throw stones at my porter. Besides, where shall I have money for all this expense ?

Clar. My dear, who asks you for any ? Don't be in a fright, chicken.

Gripe. Don't be in a fright, madam ! But where, I say—   270

Flip. Madam plays, sir, think on that ; women that play have inexhaustible mines, and wives who receive least money from their husbands, are many times those who spend the most.

Clar. So, my dear, let what Flippanta says content you. Go, my life, trouble yourself with nothing, but let me do just as I please, and all will be well. I'm going into my closet, to consider of some more things to enable me to give you the pleasure of my company at home, without making it too great a misery to a yielding wife.   [*Exit.*

Flip. Mirror of goodness ! Pattern to all wives ! Well sure, sir, you are the happiest of all husbands !   282

Gripe. Yes — and a miserable dog for all that too, perhaps.

Flip. Why, what can you ask more than this matchless complaisance ?

Gripe. I don't know what I can ask, and yet I'm not satisfied with what I have neither, the devil mixes in it all, I think ; complaisant or perverse, it feels just as't did.

Flip. Why, then, your uneasiness is only a disease, sir ; perhaps a little bleeding and purging would relieve you.

Clar. [*Calling within.*] Flippanta !   292

Flip. Madam calls.—I come, madam.—Come, be merry, be merry, sir, you have cause, take my word for't.—[*Aside.*] Poor devil!　　　　　　　　　　　　　　　　[*Exit.*

Gripe. I don't know that, I don't know that: but this I do know, that an honest man, who has married a jade, whether she's pleased to spend her time at home or abroad, had better have lived a bachelor.

Enter BRASS.

Brass. Oh, sir, I'm mighty glad I've found you.　　300

Gripe. Why, what's the matter, prithee?

Brass. Can nobody hear us?

Gripe. No, no, speak quickly.

Brass. You han't seen Araminta since the last letter I carried her from you?

Gripe. Not I, I go prudently; I don't press things like your young firebrand lovers.

Brass. But seriously, sir, are you very much in love with her?

Gripe. As mortal man has been.　　　　　　　310

Brass. I'm sorry for't.

Gripe. Why so, dear Brass?

Brass. If you were never to see her more now? Suppose such a thing, d'you think 'twould break your heart?

Gripe. Oh!

Brass. Nay, now I see you love her; would you did not!

Gripe. My dear friend!

Brass. I'm in your interest deep; you see it.

Gripe. I do: but speak, what miserable story hast thou for me?　　　　　　　　　　　　　　320

Brass. I had rather the devil had, phu!—flown away

with you quick, than to see you so much in love, as I perceive you are, since—

Gripe. Since what?—ho !

Brass. Araminta, sir—

Gripe. Dead ?

Brass. No.

Gripe. How then ?

Brass. Worse.

Gripe. Out with't.   330

Brass. Broke.

Gripe. Broke !

Brass. She is, poor lady, in the most unfortunate situation of affairs.   But I have said too much.

Gripe. No, no, 'tis very sad, but let's hear it.

Brass. Sir, she charged me, on my life, never to mention
it to you, of all men living.

Gripe. Why, who shouldst thou tell it to, but to the best
of her friends ?   339

Brass. Ay, why there's it now, it's going just as I fancied.
Now will I be hanged if you are not enough in love to be
engaging in this matter.   But I must tell you, sir, that as
much concern as I have for that most excellent, beautiful, agreeable, distressed, unfortunate lady, I'm too much
your friend and servant, ever to let it be said, 'twas the
means of your being ruined for a woman—by letting you
know she esteemed you more than any other man upon
earth.

Gripe. Ruined ! what dost thou mean ?

Brass. Mean ! why, I mean that women always ruin those
that love 'em, that's the rule.   351

Gripe. The rule !

Brass. Yes, the rule ; why, would you have 'em ruin those that don't ?   How shall they bring that about ?

Gripe. But is there a necessity then, they should ruin somebody ?

Brass. Yes, marry is there ; how would you have 'em support their expense else ?   Why, sir, you can't conceive now —you can't conceive what Araminta's privy-purse requires : only her privy-purse, sir !   Why, what do you imagine now she gave me for the last letter I carried her from you ?   'Tis true, 'twas from a man she liked, else, perhaps, I had had my bones broke.   But what do you think she gave me ?

Gripe. Why, mayhap—a shilling.   364

Brass. A guinea, sir, a guinea !   You see by that how fond she was on't, by the by.   But then, sir, her coach-hire, her chair-hire, her pin-money, her play-money, her china, and her charity—would consume peers.   A great soul, a very great soul ! but what's the end of all this ?

Gripe. Ha !

Brass. Why, I'll tell you what the end is—a nunnery.

Gripe. A nunnery !

Brass. A nunnery.—In short, she is at last reduced to that extremity, and attacked with such a battalion of duns, that rather than tell her husband, (who you know is such a dog, he'd let her go if she did) she has e'en determined to turn papist, and bid the world adieu for life.   377

Gripe. O terrible ! a papist !

Brass. Yes, when a handsome woman has brought herself into difficulties, the devil can't help her out of—to a nunnery, that's another rule, sir.

Gripe. But, but, but, prithee Brass, but—

Brass. But all the buts in the world, sir, won't stop her ;

she's a woman of a noble resolution. So, sir, your humble
servant; I pity her, I pity you, turtle and mate; but the
fates will have it so, all's packed up, and I am now going to
call her a coach, for she resolves to slip off without saying a
word; and the next visit she receives from her friends will
be through a melancholy grate, with a veil instead of a top-
knot.   [*Going.*

Gripe. It must not be, by the powers it must not! she
was made for the world, and the world was made for
her.   393

Brass. And yet you see, sir, how small a share she has
on't.

Gripe. Poor woman! is there no way to save her?

Brass. Save her! no; how can she be saved? Why, she
owes above five hundred pound.

Gripe. Oh!

Brass. Five hundred pound, sir; she's like to be saved
indeed!—Not but that I know them in this town would give
me one of the five if I would persuade her to accept of
t'other four: but she has forbid me mentioning it to any
soul living; and I have disobeyed her only to you; and so
—I'll go and call a coach.   405

Gripe. Hold!—Dost think, my poor Brass, one might
not order it so as to compound those debts for—for—
twelve pence in the pound?

Brass. Sir, d'ye hear? I have already tried 'em with ten
shillings, and not a rogue will prick up his ear at it.
Though after all, for three hundred pounds all in glittering
gold I could set their chaps a-watering. But where's that to
be had with honour? there's the thing, sir.—I'll go and call
a coach.   414

Gripe. Hold, once more : I have a note in my closet of two hundred, ay—and fifty, I'll go and give it her myself.

Brass. You will; very genteel truly ! Go, slap dash, and offer a woman of her scruples money bolt in her face ! Why, you might as well offer her a scorpion, and she'd as soon touch it.

Gripe. Shall I carry it to her creditors then, and treat with them ?

Brass. Ay, that's a rare thought.

Gripe. Is not it, Brass ?

Brass. Only one little inconvenience by the way.

Gripe. As how?   426

Brass. That they are your wife's creditors as well as hers ; and perhaps it might not be altogether so well to see you clearing the debts of your neighbour's wife, and leaving those of your own unpaid.

Gripe. Why, that's true now.

Brass. I'm wise, you see, sir.

Gripe. Thou art; and I'm but a young lover. But what shall we do then ?

Brass. Why, I'm thinking, that if you give me the note, do you see, and that I promise to give you an account of it—

Gripe. Ay, but look you, Brass—   437

Brass. But look you !—Why, what, d'ye think I'm a pickpocket ? D'ye think I intend to run away with your note ? your paltry note !

Gripe. I don't say so—I say only that in case—

Brass. Case, sir ! there's no case but the case I have put you ; and since you heap cases upon cases, where there is but three hundred rascally pounds in the case—I'll go and call a coach.   445

Gripe. Prithee don't be so testy; come, no more words, follow me to my closet, and I'll give thee the money.

Brass. A terrible effort you make indeed ; you are so much in love, your wits are all upon the wing, just a-going ; and for three hundred pounds you put a stop to their flight. Sir, your wits are worth that, or your wits are worth nothing. Come away.

Gripe. Well, say no more, thou shalt be satisfied.

[*Exeunt.*

Enter Dick Amlet.

Dick. S't !—Brass ! S't !—

Re-enter Brass.

Brass. Well, sir ?   455

Dick. 'Tis not well, sir, 'tis very ill, sir ; we shall be all blown up.

Brass. What, with pride and plenty ?

Dick. No, sir, with an officious slut that will spoil all. In short, Flippanta has been telling her mistress and Araminta of my passion for the young gentlewoman ; and truly to oblige me (supposed no ill match by the by) they are resolved to propose it immediately to her father.

Brass. That's the devil ! We shall come to papers and parchments, jointures and settlements, relations meet on both sides ; that's the devil !   466

Dick. I intended this very day to propose to Flippanta the carrying her off: and I'm sure the young housewife would have tucked up her coats, and have marched.

Brass. Ay, with the body and the soul of her.

Dick. Why, then, what damned luck is this !

Brass. 'Tis your damned luck, not mine. I have

P 2

always seen it in your ugly phiz, in spite of your powdered
periwig.—Pox take ye !—he'll be hanged at last.—Why don't
you try to get her off yet ?   475

Dick.   I have no money, you dog ; you know you have
stripped me of every penny.

Brass.   Come, damn it, I'll venture one cargo more upon
your rotten bottom : but if ever I see one glance of your
hempen fortune again, I'm off of your partnership for ever.
—I shall never thrive with him.

Dick.   An impudent rogue ! but he's in possession of my
estate, so I must bear with him.   [*Aside.*

Brass.   Well, come, I'll raise a hundred pounds for your
use, upon my wife's jewels here.—[*Pulling out the necklace.*]
Her necklace shall pawn for't.   486

Dick.   Remember, though, that if things fail, I'm to have
the necklace again ; you know you agreed to that.

Brass.   Yes, and if I make it good, you'll be the better
for't ; if not, I shall : so you see where the cause will
pinch.

Dick.   Why, you barbarous dog, you won't offer to—

Brass.   No words now ; about your business, march !
Go stay for me at the next tavern : I'll go to Flippanta, and
try what I can do for you.   495

Dick.   Well, I'll go, but don't think to—O pox, sir !—
                                                    [*Exit.*

Brass.   Will you be gone?   A pretty title you'd have to
sue me upon truly, if I should have a mind to stand upon
the defensive, as perhaps I may.   I have done the rascal
service enough to lull my conscience upon't, I'm sure : but
'tis time enough for that.   Let me see—first I'll go to Flippanta, and put a stop to this family way of match-making,

then sell our necklace for what ready money 'twill produce ;
and by this time to-morrow, I hope we shall be in possession
of—t'other jewel here ; a precious jewel, as she's set in gold :
I believe for the stone itself we may part with't again to a
friend—for a tester.   [*Exit.*

ACT V.

SCENE I.—*A Room in* GRIPE'S *House.*

Enter BRASS *and* FLIPPANTA.

Brass. Well, you agree I'm in the right, don't you ?

Flip. I don't know ; if your master has the estate he talks of, why not do't all above-board ? Well, though I am not much of his mind, I'm much in his interest, and will therefore endeavour to serve him in his own way.

Brass. That's kindly said, my child, and I believe I shall reward thee one of these days, with as pretty a fellow to thy husband for't, as—

Flip. Hold your prating, Jack-a-dandy, and leave me to my business.   10

Brass. I obey—adieu !   [*Kisses her, and exit.*

Flip. Rascal !

Enter CORINNA.

Cor. Ah, Flippanta, I'm ready to sink down ! my legs tremble under me, my dear Flippy !

Flip. And what's the affair ?

Cor. My father's there within, with my mother and Araminta ; I never saw him in so good humour in my life.

Flip. And is that it that frightens you so ?

Cor. Ah, Flippanta, they are just going to speak to him about my marrying the colonel.   20

Flip. Are they so? so much the worse; they're too hasty.

Cor. Oh no, not a bit; I slipped out on purpose, you must know, to give 'em an opportunity; would 'twere done already!

Flip. I tell you no; get you in again immediately, and prevent it.

Cor. My dear, dear, I am not able: I never was in such a way before.

Flip. Never in a way to be married before, ha? is not that it?   31

Cor. Ah, Lord, if I'm thus before I come to't, Flippanta, what shall I be upon the very spot? Do but feel with what a thumpaty thump it goes. [*Putting her hand to her heart.*

Flip. Nay, it does make a filthy bustle, that's the truth on't, child. But I believe I shall make it leap another way, when I tell you, I'm cruelly afraid your father won't consent after all.

Cor. Why, he won't be the death o' me, will he?

Flip. I don't know, old folks are cruel; but we'll have a trick for him. Brass and I have been consulting upon the matter, and agreed upon a surer way of doing it in spite of his teeth.   43

Cor. Ay, marry, sir, that were something.

Flip. But then he must not know a word of anything towards it.

Cor. No, no.

Flip. So, get you in immediately.

Cor. One, two, three, and away!   [*Running off.*

Flip. And prevent your mother's speaking on't.

Cor. But is t'other way sure, Flippanta?   51

Flip.   Fear nothing, 'twill only depend upon you.

Cor.   Nay then—O ho! ho! ho! how pure that is!

                                                                [*Exit.*

Flip.   Poor child! we may do what we will with her, as
far as marrying her goes: when that's over, 'tis possible she
mayn't prove altogether so tractable.   But who's here? my
sharper, I think: yes.

Enter MONEYTRAP.

Mon.   Well, my best friend, how go matters?   Has the
restitution been received, ha?   Was she pleased with it?

Flip.   Yes, truly; that is, she was pleased to see there
was so honest a man in this immoral age.   61

Mon. . Well, but a—does she know that 'twas I that—

Flip.   Why, you must know I begun to give her a little
sort of a hint, and—and so—why, and so she begun to put
on a sort of a severe, haughty, reserved, angry, forgiving air.
But soft; here she comes.   You'll see how you stand with
her presently: but don't be afraid.   Courage!

Mon.   He, hem!

Enter CLARISSA.

'Tis no small piece of good fortune, madam, to find you at
home: I have often endeavoured it in vain.   70

Clar.   'Twas then unknown to me, for if I could often
receive the visits of so good a friend at home, I should be
more reasonably blamed for being so much abroad.

Mon.   Madam, you make me—

Clar.   You are the man of the world whose company I
think is most to be desired.   I don't compliment you when
I tell you so, I assure you.

Mon.   Alas, madam; your poor humble servant—

Clar. My poor humble servant however (with all the esteem I have for him) stands suspected with me for a vile trick I doubt he has played me, which if I could prove upon him, I'm afraid I should punish him very severely.   82

Mon. I hope, madam, you'll believe I am not capable of—

Clar. Look you, look you, you are capable of whatever you please, you have a great deal of wit, and know how to give a nice and gallant turn to everything; but if you will have me continue your friend, you must leave me in some uncertainty in this matter.

Mon. Madam, I do then protest to you—

Clar. Come, protest nothing about it, I am but too penetrating, as you may perceive; but we sometimes shut our eyes rather than break with our friends; for a thorough knowledge of the truth of this business would make me very seriously angry.   94

Mon. 'Tis very certain, madam, that—

Clar. Come, say no more on't, I beseech you, for I'm in a good deal of heat while I but think on't; if you'll walk in, I'll follow you presently.

Mon. Your goodness, madam, is—

Flip. [*Aside to* Moneytrap.] War horse! No fine speeches, you'll spoil all.

Mon. Thou art a most incomparable person.

Flip. Nay, it goes rarely; but get you in, and I'll say a little something to my lady for you, while she's warm.

Mon. But s't, Flippanta, how long dost think she may hold out?   106

Flip. Phu! not a twelvemonth.

Mon. Boo!

Flip. Away, I say!   [*Pushing him out.*

Clar. Is he gone? What a wretch it is! he never was quite such a beast before.

Flip. Poor mortal, his money's finely laid out truly!

Clar. I suppose there may have been much such another scene within between Araminta and my dear. But I left him so insupportably brisk, 'tis impossible he can have parted with any money. I'm afraid Brass has not succeeded as thou hast done, Flippanta.   117

Flip. By my faith but he has, and better too; he presents his humble duty to Araminta, and has sent her— this.   [*Showing the note.*

Clar. A bill from my love for two hundred and fifty pounds! The monster! he would not part with ten to save his lawful wife from everlasting torment.

Flip. Never complain of his avarice, madam, as long as you have his money.

Clar. But is not he a beast, Flippanta? methinks the restitution looked better by half.

Flip. Madam, the man's beast enough, that's certain; but which way will you go to receive his beastly money, for I must not appear with his note?   130

Clar. That's true; why, send for Mrs. Amlet; that's a mighty useful woman, that Mrs. Amlet.

Flip. Marry is she; we should have been basely puzzled how to dispose of the necklace without her, 'twould have been dangerous offering it to sale.

Clar. It would so, for I know your master has been laying out for't amongst the goldsmiths. But I stay here too long, I must in and coquette it a little more to my lover, Araminta will get ground on me else.   [*Exit* CLARISSA.

Flip. And I'll go send for Mrs. Amlet. [*Exit* FLIPPANTA.

SCENE II.—*Another Room in the same.*

ARAMINTA, CORINNA, GRIPE, *and* MONEYTRAP, *are discovered at a tea-table, very gay and laughing.*

All.   Ha! ha! ha! ha!

Mon.   Mighty well, O mighty well indeed!

Enter CLARISSA.

Clar.   Save you, save you, good folks! you are all in rare
humour methinks.

Gripe.   Why, what should we be otherwise for, madam?

Clar.   Nay, I don't know, not I, my dear; but I han't
had the happiness of seeing you so since our honeymoon
was over, I think.

Gripe.   Why, to tell you the truth, my dear, 'tis the joy of
seeing you at home.—[*Kisses her.*]   You see what charms
you have when you are pleased to make use of 'em.

Aram.   Very gallant truly.   12

Clar.   Nay, and what's more, you must know, he's never
to be otherwise henceforwards; we have come to an agreement about it.

Mon.   Why, here's my love and I have been upon just
such another treaty too.

Aram.   Well, sure there's some very peaceful star rules
at present.   Pray Heaven continue its reign.

Mon.   Pray do you continue its reign, you ladies; for 'tis
all in your power.   [*Leering at* CLARISSA.

Gripe.   My neighbour Moneytrap says true; at least I'll
confess frankly [*Ogling* ARAMINTA] 'tis in one lady's power
to make me the best-humoured man on earth.   24

Mon.　And I'll answer for another that has the same over me.　　　　　　　　　　　　　　　　[*Ogling* CLARISSA.

Clar.　'Tis mighty fine, gentlemen! mighty civil husbands, indeed!

Gripe.　Nay, what I say's true, and so true, that all quarrels being now at an end, I am willing, if you please, to dispense with all that fine company we talked of to-day, be content with the friendly conversation of our two good neighbours here, and spend all my toying hours alone with my sweet wife.　　　　　　　　　　　　　　　　34

Mon.　Why, truly, I think now, if these good women pleased, we might make up the prettiest little neighbourly company between our two families, and set a defiance to all the impertinent people in the world.

Clar.　The rascals!　　　　　　　　　　　　[*Aside.*

Aram.　Indeed I doubt you'd soon grow weary, if we grew fond.

Gripe.　Never, never, for our wives have wit, neighbour, and that never palls.

Clar.　And our husbands have generosity, Araminta, and that seldom palls.　　　　　　　　　　　　45

Gripe.　So, that's a wipe for me now, because I did not give her a new-year's-gift last time; but be good, and I'll think of some tea-cups for you, next year.

Mon.　And perhaps I mayn't forget a fan, or as good a thing—hum, hussy.

Clar.　Well, upon these encouragements, Araminta, we'll try how good we can be.

Gripe. [*Aside.*] Well, this goes most rarely! Poor Moneytrap, he little thinks what makes his wife so easy in his company.　　　　　　　　　　　　　　　55

Mon. [*Aside.*] I can but pity poor neighbour Gripe. Lard, Lard, what a fool does his wife and I make of him!

Clar. [*Aside to* Araminta.] Are not these two wretched rogues, Araminta?

Aram. [*Aside to* Clarissa.] They are indeed.

Enter JESSAMIN.

Jes. Sir, here's Mr. Clip, the goldsmith, desires to speak with you.

Gripe. Cods so, perhaps some news of your necklace, my dear. 65

Clar. That would be news indeed.

Gripe. Let him come in. [*Exit* JESSAMIN.

Enter Mr. CLIP.

Gripe. Mr. Clip, your servant; I'm glad to see you: how do you do?

Clip. At your service, sir, very well.—Your servant, madam Gripe.

Clar. Horrid fellow! [*Aside.*

Gripe. Well, Mr. Clip, no news yet of my wife's necklace?

Clip. If you please to let me speak with you in the next room, I have something to say to you. 75

Gripe. Ay, with all my heart. Shut the door after us.— [*They come forward, and the scene shuts behind them.*] Well, any news?

Clip. Look you, sir, here's a necklace brought me to sell, at least very like that you described to me.

Gripe. Let's see't.—*Victoria!* the very same. Ah, my dear Mr. Clip! [*Kisses him.*] But who brought it you? you should have seized him.

Clip. 'Twas a young fellow that I know: I can't tell whether he may be guilty, though it's like enough. But he has only left it me now, to show a brother of our trade, and will call upon me again presently.   87

Gripe. Wheedle him hither, dear Mr. Clip. Here's my neighbour Moneytrap in the house; he's a justice, and will commit him presently.

Clip. 'Tis enough.

Enter BRASS.

Gripe. Oh, my friend Brass!

Brass. Hold, sir, I think that's a gentleman I'm looking for.—Mr. Clip, oh, your servant! What, are you acquainted here? I have just been at your shop.   95

Clip. I only stepped here to show Mr. Gripe the neck-lace you left.

Brass. [*To* GRIPE.] Why, sir, do you understand jewels? I thought you had dealt only in gold. But I smoke the matter, hark you—a word in your ear—you are going to play the gallant again, and make a purchase on't for Araminta; ha, ha?

Gripe. Where had you the necklace?

Brass. Look you, don't trouble yourself about that; it's in commission with me, and I can help you to a penny-worth on't.   106

Gripe. A pennyworth on't, villain?   [*Strikes at him.*

Brass. Villain! ahey, ahey! Is't you or me, Mr. Clip, he's pleased to compliment?

Clip. What do you think on't, sir?

Brass. Think on't! now the devil fetch me if I know what to think on't.

Gripe. You'll sell a pennyworth, rogue! of a thing you have stolen from me.

Brass. Stolen! pray, sir—what wine have you drank to-day? It has a very merry effect upon you.   116

Gripe. You villain! either give me an account how you stole it, or—

Brass. O ho, sir, if you please, don't carry your jest too far; I don't understand hard words, I give you warning on't. If you han't a mind to buy the necklace, you may let it alone; I know how to dispose on't. What a pox!—

Gripe. Oh, you shan't have that trouble, sir.—Dear Mr. Clip, you may leave the necklace here. I'll call at your shop, and thank you for your care.   125

Clip. Sir, your humble servant.   [*Going.*

Brass. O ho, Mr. Clip, if you please, sir, this won't do!—[*Stopping him.*] I don't understand raillery in such matters.

Clip. I leave it with Mr. Gripe; do you and he dispute it.   [*Exit.*

Brass. Ay, but 'tis from you, by your leave, sir, that I expect it.   [*Going after him.*

Gripe. You expect, you rogue, to make your escape, do you? But I have other accounts besides this, to make up with you. To be sure the dog has cheated me of two hundred and fifty pound. Come, villain, give me an account of—   138

Brass. Account of!—sir, give me an account of my necklace, or I'll make such a noise in your house I'll raise the devil in't.

Gripe. Well said, Courage!

Brass. Blood and thunder, give it me, or—

Gripe.   Come, hush, be wise, and I'll make no noise of this affair.

Brass.   You'll make no noise ! but I'll make a noise, and a damned noise too.   Oh, don't think to—

Gripe.   I tell thee I will not hang thee.

Brass.   But I tell you I will hang you, if you don't give me my necklace.   I will, rot me !   150

Gripe.   Speak softly, be wise ; how came it thine ? who gave it thee ?

Brass.   A gentleman, a friend of mine.

Gripe.   What's his name ?

Brass.   His name !—I'm in such a passion I have forgot it.

Gripe.   Ah, brazen rogue—thou hast stole it from my wife ! 'tis the same she lost six weeks ago.

Brass.   This has not been in England a month.

Gripe.   You are a son of a whore.   160

Brass.   Give me my necklace.

Gripe.   Give me my two hundred and fifty pound note.

Brass.   Yet I offer peace : one word without passion. The case stands thus, either I am out of my wits, or you are out of yours : now 'tis plain I am not out of my wits, ergo—

Gripe.   My bill, hang-dog, or I'll strangle thee !

                                        [*They struggle.*

Brass.   Murder ! murder !

Enter CLARISSA, ARAMINTA, CORINNA, FLIPPANTA,
         MONEYTRAP, *and* JESSAMIN.

Flip.   What's the matter ? what's the matter here ?

Gripe.   I'll matter him !   170

Clar.   Who makes thee cry out thus, poor Brass?

Brass.   Why, your husband, madam, he's in his altitudes here.

Gripe.   Robber!

Brass.   Here, he has cheated me of a diamond necklace.

Cor.   Who, papa? ah, dear me!

Clar.   Prithee what's the meaning of this great emotion, my dear?

Gripe.   The meaning is that—I'm quite out of breath— this son of a whore has got your necklace, that's all.   181

Clar.   My necklace!

Gripe.   That birdlime there—stole it.

Clar.   Impossible!

Brass.   Madam, you see master's a little—touched, that's all.   Twenty ounces of blood let loose would set all right again.

Gripe.   Here, call   a   constable   presently.—[*Exit* Jessamin.]   Neighbour Moneytrap, you'll commit him?

Brass.   D'ye hear? d'ye hear?   See how wild he looks: how his eyes roll in his head: tie him down, or he'll do some mischief or other.   192

Gripe.   Let me come at him.

Clar.   Hold!—prithee, my dear, reduce things to a little temperance, and let us coolly into the secret of this disagreeable rupture.

Gripe.   Well then, without passion.   Why, you must know (but I'll have him hanged), you must know that he came to Mr. Clip, to Mr. Clip the dog did!—with a necklace to sell; so Mr. Clip having notice before that (can you deny this, sirrah?) that you had lost yours, brings it to

me. Look at it here, do you know it again?—Ah, you
traitor !   [*To* BRASS.

Brass. He makes me mad! Here's an appearance of
something now to the company, and yet nothing in't in the
bottom.   206

Enter Constable.

Clar. Flippanta !—
                    [*Aside to* FLIPPANTA, *showing the necklace.*
Flip. 'Tis it, faith ; here's some mystery in this, we must
look about us.

Clar. The safest way is point blank to disown the
necklace.

Flip. Right, stick to that.

Gripe. Well, madam, do you know your old acquaintance, ha?

Clar. Why, truly, my dear, though (as you may all
imagine) I should be very glad to recover so valuable a
thing as my necklace, yet I must be just to all the world,
this necklace is not mine.   218

Brass. Huzza!—Here, constable, do your duty.—Mr.
Justice, I demand my necklace, and satisfaction of him.

Gripe. I'll die before I part with it, I'll keep it, and have
him hanged.

Clar. But be a little calm, my dear, do, my bird, and
then thou'lt be able to judge rightly of things.

Gripe. O good lack ! O good lack !

Clar. No, but don't give way to fury and interest both,
either of 'em are passions strong enough to lead a wise man
out of the way. The necklace not being really mine, give
it the man again, and come drink a dish of tea.   229

Brass. Ay, madam says right.

Gripe. Oons, if you, with your addle head, don't know your own jewels, I with my solid one do : and if I part with it, may famine be my portion !

Clar. But don't swear and curse thyself at this fearful rate : don't, my dove. Be temperate in your words, and just in all your actions, 'twill bring a blessing upon you and your family.

Gripe. Bring thunder and lightning upon me and my family, if I part with my necklace !   239

Clar. Why, you'll have the lightning burn your house about your ears, my dear, if you go on in these practices.

Mon. A most excellent woman this !   [*Aside.*

Enter Mrs. AMLET.

Gripe. I'll keep my necklace.

Brass. Will you so ? then here comes one has a title to it, if I han't.—[*Aside.*] Let Dick bring himself off with her as he can. —[*Aloud.*] Mrs. Amlet, you are come in a very good time ; you lost a necklace t'other day, and who do you think has got it ?

Mrs. Aml. Marry, that know I not, I wish I did.

Brass. Why, then, here's Mr. Gripe has it, and swears 'tis his wife's.   251

Gripe. And so I do, sirrah !—Look here, mistress, do you pretend this is yours ?

Mrs. Aml. Not for the round world I would not say it ; I only kept it, to do madam a small courtesy, that's all.

Clar. Ah, Flippanta, all will out now !

[*Aside to* FLIPPANTA.

Gripe. Courtesy ! what courtesy ?

Q 2

Mrs. Aml. A little money only that madam had present need of; please to pay me that, and I demand no more.   260

Brass. So here's fresh game; I have started a new hare, I find.   •   [*Aside.*

Gripe. How, forsooth, is this true?   [*To* CLARISSA.

Clar. You are in a humour at present, love, to believe anything, so I won't take the pains to contradict it.

Brass. This damned necklace will spoil all our affairs, this is Dick's luck again.   [*Aside.*

Gripe. Are you not ashamed of these ways? Do you see how you are exposed before your best friends here? don't you blush at it?   270

Clar. I do blush, my dear, but 'tis for you, that here it should appear to the world, you keep me so bare of money, I am forced to pawn my jewels.

Gripe. Impudent housewife !   .

[*Raising his hand to strike her.*

Clar. Softly, chicken; you might have prevented all this by giving me the two hundred and fifty pound you sent to Araminta e'en now.

Brass. You see, sir, I delivered your note. How I have been abused to-day !   279

Gripe. I'm betrayed !—Jades on both sides, I see that !

[*Aside.*

Mon. But, madam, madam, is this true I hear? Have you taken a present of two hundred and fifty pound? Pray what were you to return for these pounds, madam, ha ?

Aram. Nothing, my dear; I only took 'em to reimburse you of about the same sum you sent to Clarissa.

Mon. Hum, hum, hum !

Gripe. How, gentlewoman, did you receive money from him ?

Clar. Oh, my dear, 'twas only in jest; I knew you'd give it again to his wife. 290

Mrs. Aml. But amongst all this tintamar,* I don't hear a word of my hundred pounds. Is it madam will pay me, or master ?

Gripe. I pay! the devil shall pay!

Clar. Look you, my dear, malice apart, pay Mrs. Amlet her money, and I'll forgive you the wrong you intended my bed with Araminta. Am not I a good wife now ?

Gripe. I burst with rage, and will get rid of this noose, though I tuck myself up in another.

Mon. Nay, pray, e'en tuck me up with you. 300

[*Exeunt* Moneytrap *and* Gripe.

Clar. and Aram. Bye, dearies !

Enter Dick Amlet.

Cor. Look, look, Flippanta, here's the colonel come at last !

Dick. Ladies, I ask your pardon, I have stayed so long, but—

Mrs. Aml. Ah, rogue's face, have I got thee, old Good-for-nought ? Sirrah, sirrah, do you think to amuse me with your marriages, and your great fortunes ? Thou hast played me a rare prank, by my conscience ! Why, you ungracious rascal, what do you think will be the end of all this ? Now

---

* Noise; hubbub. From the French *tintamarre ; bruit éclatant, accompagné de confusion et de désordre.*—Littré.

Heaven forgive me, but I have a great mind to hang thee
for't.   312

Cor.   She talks to him very familiarly, Flippanta !

Flip.   So methinks, by my faith !

Brass.   Now the rogue's star is making an end of him.
                                                    [*Aside.*

Dick.   What shall I do with her ?   [*Aside.*

Mrs. Aml.   Do but look at him, my dames : he has the
countenance of a cherubim, but he's a rogue in his heart.

Clar.   What is the meaning of all this, Mrs. Amlet ?

Mrs. Aml.   The meaning, good lack !   Why, this all-to-
be-powdered rascal here is my son, an't please you.—Ha,
Graceless !   Now I'll make you own your mother, vermin !

Clar.   What, the colonel your son ?   323

Mrs. Aml.   'Tis Dick, madam, that rogue Dick I have
so often told you of, with tears trickling down my old
cheeks.

Aram.   The woman's mad, it can never be.

Mrs. Aml.   Speak, rogue, am I not thy mother, ha ?
Did I not bring thee forth ? say then.

Dick.   What will you have me say ? you had a mind to
ruin me, and you have done't ; would you do any more ?

Clar.   Then, sir, you are son to good Mrs. Amlet ?

Aram.   And have had the assurance to put upon us all
this while ?   334

Flip.   And the confidence to think of marrying Corinna ?

Brass.   And the impudence to hire me for your servant,
who am as well born as yourself ?

Clar.   Indeed I think he should be corrected.

Aram.   Indeed I think he deserves to be cudgelled.

Flip.   Indeed I think he might be pumped.

Brass. Indeed I think he will be hanged.

Mrs. Aml. Good lack a-day! Good lack a-day! there's no need to be so smart upon him neither: if he is not a gentleman, he's a gentleman's fellow.—Come hither, Dick, they shan't run thee down neither; cock up thy hat, Dick, and tell 'em, though Mrs. Amlet is thy mother, she can make thee amends with ten thousand good pounds to buy thee some lands, and build thee a house in the midst on't.

All. How!

Clar. Ten thousand pounds, Mrs. Amlet! 350

Mrs. Aml. Yes, forsooth, though I should lose the hundred you pawned your necklace for.—Tell 'em of that, Dick.

Cor. Look you, Flippanta, I can hold no longer, and I hate to see the young man abused.—And so, sir, if you please, I'm your friend and servant, and what's mine is yours; and when our estates are put together, I don't doubt but we shall do as well as the best of 'em.

Dick. Sayest thou so, my little queen? Why, then, if dear mother will give us her blessing, the parson shall give us a tack. We'll get her a score of grandchildren, and a merry house we'll make her. [*They kneel to* Mrs. AMLET.

Mrs. Aml. Ah—ha! ha! ha! ha! the pretty pair, the pretty pair! Rise, my chickens, rise, rise and face the proudest of 'em. And if madam does not deign to give her consent, a fig for her, Dick!—Why, how now? 366

Clar. Pray, Mrs. Amlet, don't be in a passion, the girl is my husband's girl, and if you can have his consent, upon my word you shall have mine, for anything belongs to him.

Flip. Then all's peace again, but we have been more lucky than wise.

Aram.   And I suppose for us, Clarissa, we are to go on with our dears, as we used to do.

Clar.   Just in the same tract, for this late treaty of agreement with 'em was so unnatural you see it could not hold. But 'tis just as well with us as if it had.   Well, 'tis a strange fate, good folks !   But while you live, everything gets well out of a broil but a husband.   [*Exeunt omnes.*

EPILOGUE.

SPOKEN BY MRS. BARRY.

I'VE heard wise men in politics lay down
What feats by little England might be done,
Were all agreed, and all would act as one.
Ye wives a useful hint from this might take,
The heavy, old, despotic kingdom shake,
And make your matrimonial monsieurs quake.
Our heads are feeble, and we're cramp'd by laws;
Our hands are weak, and not too strong our cause:
Yet would those heads and hands, such as they are,
In firm confed'racy resolve on war,   10
You'd find your tyrants—what I've found my dear.
What only two united can produce
You've seen to-night, a sample for your use:
Single, we found we nothing could obtain;
We join our force—and we subdued our men.
Believe me (my dear sex) they are not brave;
Try each your man; you'll quickly find your slave.
I know they'll make campaigns, risk blood and life;
But this is a more terrifying strife;
They'll stand a shot, who'll tremble at a wife.   20
Beat then your drums, and your shrill trumpets sound,
Let all your visits of your feats resound,
And deeds of war in cups of tea go round:

The stars are with you, fate is in your hand,
In twelve months' time you've vanquish'd half the land ;
Be wise, and keep 'em under good command.
This year will to your glory long be known,
And deathless ballads hand your triumphs down ;
Your late achievements ever will remain,
For though you cannot boast of many slain,   30
Your pris'ners show you've made a brave campaign.

THE MISTAKE.

INTRODUCTION TO "THE MISTAKE."

This comedy was represented for the first time on the 27th of December, 1705, at the theatre in the Haymarket. Genest states that it ran for nine nights; but it appears, from the advertisements in the *Daily Courant*, that it was actually played only six times consecutively, the last performance taking place on Wednesday, the 2nd of January, 1706. It was published, in 4to, and without the author's name, on the 11th of January, 1706. * The title-page of the original edition is as follows: " *The Mistake. A Comedy. As it is Acted at the Queen's Theatre in the Hay-Market. By Her Majesty's Sworn Servants. By the Author of The Provok'd Wife, &c. London, Printed for Jacob Tonson, within Grays-Inn Gate next Grays-Inn Lane.* 1706."

The Mistake is a translation of *Le Dépit Amoureux*, one of the earliest of Molière's comedies, first produced at Béziers in 1656, at Paris in 1658, and published in 1663. The translation, though not literal, is in general tolerably close, and follows the original scene by scene. What

---

* The following announcement of its publication appeared in the *Daily Courant* of January 11, 1706. "'The Mistake, a Comedy, as it was acted at the Queen's Theatre in the Hay-Market, by her Majesty's sworn Servants. By the Author of the Provoked Wife. Printed for Jacob Tonson within Grays-Inn Gate next Grays-Inn Lane."

Molière has said in rhyme, Vanbrugh has rendered in plain prose; with less dignity, it is true, but with undeniable briskness and movement. He has added occasional touches of a homelier humour than that of Molière, and also, unfortunately, occasional outbursts of fustian entirely unwarranted by the original. The rant which is put into the mouth of Don Carlos, in his scene with Leonora in the fourth act, has no other effect than seriously to disfigure a scene which, in the French, is the most charming in the whole play.

DRAMATIS PERSONÆ.

MEN.

Don *Alvarez*, Father to *Leonora*	Mr. *Betterton*.
Don *Felix*, Father to *Lorenzo*	Mr. *Bright*.
Don *Carlos*, in Love with *Leonora*	Mr. *Booth*.
Don *Lorenzo*, in Love with *Leonora*	Mr. *Husbands*.
Metaphrastus, Tutor to *Camillo*	Mr. *Freeman*.
Sancho, Servant to *Carlos*	Mr. *Dogget*.
Lopez, Servant to *Lorenzo*	... Mr. *Pack*.
A Bravo.	

WOMEN.

Leonora, Daughter to *Alvarez*	Mrs. *Bowman*.
Camillo, supposed Son to *Alvarez*	Mrs. *Harcourt*.
Isabella, her Friend	Mrs. *Porter*.
Jacinta, Servant to *Leonora*	Mrs. *Baker*.

[SCENE.—A Town in SPAIN.]

PROLOGUE.

Written by Mr. STEELE.

SPOKEN BY MR. BOOTH.

OUR author's wit and raillery to-night
Perhaps might please, but that your stage-delight
No more is in your minds, but ears and sight.
With audiences compos'd of belles and beaux,
The first dramatic rule is, have good clothes.
To charm the gay spectator's gentle breast,
In lace and feather tragedy's express'd,
And heroes die unpitied, if ill dress'd.
    The other style you full as well advance ;
If 'tis a comedy, you ask—Who dance ?   10
For oh ! what dire convulsions have of late   –
Torn and distracted each dramatic state,
On this great question, which house first should sell
The new French steps, imported by Ruel ?
Desbarques can't rise so high, we must agree,
They've half a foot in height more wit than we.*

---

* Messieurs du Ruel and Desbarques (or de Barques) were French
dancers, who were performing in London at this time, the former at the
Theatre Royal, the latter at the Queen's Theatre in the Haymarket.
It was just then the fashion to introduce entertainments of dancing into
comedies of all kinds, and the names of Ruel and Desbarques are
continually to be met with in the theatrical announcements of the

But though the genius of our learned age
Thinks fit to dance and sing quite off the stage
True action, comic mirth, and tragic rage ;
Yet, as your taste now stands, our author draws 20
Some hopes of your indulgence and applause.
For that great end this edifice* he made,
Where humble swain at lady's feet is laid ;
Where the pleased nymph her conquer'd lover spies,
Then to glass pillars turns her conscious eyes,
And points anew each charm, for which he dies.

The Muse, before nor terrible nor great,
Enjoys by him this awful gilded seat :
By him theatric angels mount more high,
And mimic thunders shake a broader sky. 30

Thus all must own, our author has done more
For your delight than ever bard before.
His thoughts are still to raise your pleasures fill'd ;
To write, translate, to blazon, or to build.
Then take him in the lump, nor nicely pry
Into small faults, that 'scape a busy eye ;
But kindly, sirs, consider, he to-day
Finds you the house, the actors, and the play :
So, though we stage-mechanic rules omit,
You must allow it in a wholesale wit. 40

Daily Courant. Thus we find announced for performance at the Hay-
market on the 7th of January, 1706, "The Committee : or, The
Faithful Irishman. With several Entertainments of Dancing by
Monsieur de Barques, Mrs. Elford and others." On the 16th and 23rd
of the same month, *The Mistake* was acted, on both occasions with
entertainments of dancing by de Barques.

* The theatre built by Vanbrugh in the Haymarket.

THE MISTAKE.

A COMEDY.

ACT I.

SCENE.—*The Street.*

Enter CARLOS *and* SANCHO.

Car. I tell thee, I am not satisfied ; I'm in love enough to be suspicious of everybody.

San. And yet methinks, sir, you should leave me out.

Car. It may be so ; I can't tell ; but I'm not at ease. If they don't make a knave, at least they'll make a fool of thee.

San. I don't believe a word on't. But good faith, master, your love makes somewhat of you ; I don't know what 'tis, but methinks when you suspect me, you don't seem a man of half those parts I used to take you for. Look in my face, 'tis round and comely, not one hollow line of a villain in it. Men of my fabric don't use to be suspected for knaves ; and when you take us for fools, we never take you for wise men. For my part, in this present case, I take myself to be mighty deep. A stander-by, sir, sees more than a gamester. You are pleased to be jealous of your poor mistress without a cause. She uses you but too well, in my humble opinion. She sees you, and talks with you, till I am quite tired on't sometimes; and your rival, that you are so scared about, forces a visit upon her about once in a fortnight.   21

Car. Alas! thou art ignorant in these affairs: he that's the civilly'st received is often the least cared for. Women appear warm to one, to hide a flame for another. Lorenzo, in short, appears too composed of late to be a rejected lover; and the indifference he shows upon the favours I seem to receive from her, poisons the pleasure I else should taste in 'em, and keeps me on a perpetual rack. No! I would fain see some of his jealous transports; have him fire at the sight o' me, contradict me whenever I speak, affront me wherever he meets me, challenge me, fight me—   31

San. Run you through the guts.

Car. But he's too calm, his heart's too much at ease, to leave me mine at rest.

San. But, sir, you forget that there are two ways for our hearts to get at ease: when our mistresses come to be very fond of us, or we—not to care a fig for them. Now suppose, upon the rebukes you know he has had, it should chance to be the latter.

Car. Again thy ignorance appears. Alas! a lover who has broke his chain will shun the tyrant that enslaved him. Indifference never is his lot; he loves or hates for ever; and if his mistress prove another's prize, he cannot calmly see her in his arms.   44

San. For my part, master, I'm not so great a philosopher as you be, nor (thank my stars) so bitter a lover, but what I see—that I generally believe; and when Jacinta tells me she loves me dearly, I have good thoughts enough of my person never to doubt the truth on't. See, here the baggage comes.

Enter JACINTA *with a letter.*

Hist, Jacinta, my dear!

Jac. Who's that? Blunderbuss! Where's your master?

San. Hard by. . [*Shewing him.*

Jac. O, sir! I'm glad I have found you at last; I believe I have travelled five miles after you, and could neither find you at home, nor in the walks, nor at church, nor at the opera, nor— 57

San. Nor anywhere else, where he was not to be found. If you had looked for him where he was, 'twas ten to one but you had met with him.

Jac. I had, Jack-a-dandy?

Car. But, prithee, what's the matter? who sent you after me?

Jac. One who's never well but when she sees you, I think; 'twas my lady. 65

Car. Dear Jacinta, I fain would flatter myself, but am not able; the blessing's too great to be my lot. Yet 'tis not well to trifle with me: how short soe'er I am in other merit, the tenderness I have for Leonora claims something from her generosity. I should not be deluded.

Jac. And why do you think you are? methinks she's pretty well above-board with you. What must be done more to satisfy you?

San. Why, Lorenzo must hang himself, and then we are content. 75

Jac. How? Lorenzo?

San. If less will do, he'll tell you.

Jac. Why, you are not mad, sir, are you? Jealous of him! Pray which way may this have got into your head? I took you for a man of sense before.—[*To* Sancho.] Is this your doings, Log?

San. No, forsooth, Pert! I'm not much given to suspicion, as you can tell, Mrs. Forward : if I were, I might find more cause, I guess, than your mistress has given our master here. But I have so many pretty thoughts of my own person, housewife, more than I have of yours, that I stand in dread of no man. 87

Jac. That's the way to prosper, however; so far I'll confess the truth to thee ; at least, if that don't do, nothing else will. Men are mighty simple in love-matters, sir. When you suspect a woman's falling off, you fall a-plaguing her to bring her on again, attack her with reason, and a sour face. Udslife, sir! attack her with a fiddle, double your good-humour; give her a ball—powder your periwig at her—let her cheat you at cards a little—and I'll warrant all's right again. But to come upon a poor woman with the gloomy face of jealousy, before she gives the least occasion for't, is to set a complaisant rival in too favourable a light. Sir, sir! I must tell you, I have seen those have owed their success to nothing else. 100

Car. Say no more, I have been to blame; but there shall be no more on't.

Jac. I should punish you but justly, however, for what's past, if I carried back what I have brought you ; but I'm good-natured, so here 'tis ; open it, and see how wrong you timed your jealousy !

Car. [*Reads.*] *If you love me with that tenderness you*

have made me long believe you do, this letter will be welcome;
'tis to tell you, you have leave to plead a daughter's weakness
to a father's indulgence; and if you prevail with him to lay
his commands upon me, you shall be as happy as my obedience
to 'em can make you.　　　　　　　LEONORA.　112

Then I shall be what man was never yet.—[*Kissing the*
letter.] Ten thousand blessings on thee for thy news!—I
could adore thee as a deity!　　[*Embracing* JACINTA.

　San.　True flesh and blood, every inch of her, for all that.

　Car. [*Reads again.*] *And if you prevail with him to lay*
his commands upon me, you shall be as happy as my obedience
to 'em can make you.—O happy, happy Carlos!—But what
shall I say to thee for this welcome message? Alas! I
want words.—But let this speak for me, and this, and this,
and—　　　　　　[*Giving her his ring, watch, and purse.*

　San.　Hold, sir; pray leave a little something for our
board-wages.—[*To* JACINTA.] You can't carry 'em all, I
believe: shall I ease thee of this?　　　　　125
　　　　　　　　[*Offering to take the purse.*

　Jac.　No; but you may carry—that, sirrah.
　　　　　　　　[*Giving him a box o' the ear.*

　San.　The jade's grown purse-proud already.

　Car.　Well, dear Jacinta, say something to your charming
mistress, that I am not able to say myself; but, above all,
excuse my late unpardonable folly, and offer her my life to
expiate my crime.

　Jac.　The best plea for pardon will be never to repeat
the fault.

　Car.　If that will do, 'tis sealed for ever.

　Jac.　Enough. But I must begone; success attend you
with the old gentleman. Good-bye t'ye, sir.　　136

Car.　Eternal blessings follow thee !　　*[Exit* JACINTA.

San.　I think she has taken 'em all with her; the jade has got her apron full.

Car.　Is not that Lorenzo coming this way?

San.　Yes, 'tis he ; for my part now I pity the poor gentleman.

Enter LORENZO.

Car.　I'll let him see at last I can be cheerful too.—Your servant, Don Lorenzo ; how do you do this morning?

Lor.　I thank you, Don Carlos, perfectly well, both in body and in mind.　　　　　　　　　　　　　146

Car.　What ! cured of your love then?

Lor.　No, nor I hope I never shall.　May I ask you how 'tis with yours?

Car.　Increasing every hour ; we are very constant both.

Lor.　I find so much delight in being so, I hope I never shall be otherwise.

Car.　Those joys I am well acquainted with, but should lose 'em soon were I to meet a cool reception.

Lor.　That's every generous lover's case, no doubt; an angel could not fire my heart, but with an equal flame.

Car.　And yet you said you still loved Leonora?　　157

Lor.　And yet I said I loved her.

Car.　Does she then return you—

Lor.　Everything my passion can require.

Car.　Its wants are small, I find.

Lor.　Extended as the heavens.

Car.　I pity you.

Lor.　He must be a deity that does so.

Car.　Yet I'm a mortal, and once more can pity you.

Alas! Lorenzo, 'tis a poor cordial to an aching heart, to have the tongue alone announce it happy; besides, 'tis mean; you should be more a man. 168

Lor. I find I have made you an unhappy one, so can forgive the boilings of your spleen.

Car. This seeming calmness might have the effect your vanity proposes by it, had I not a testimony of her love would (should I show it) sink you to the centre.

Lor. Yet still I'm calm as ever.

Car. Nay, then have at your peace. Read that, and end the farce. [*Gives him* LEONORA'S *letter.*

Lor. [*After reading.*] I have read it.

Car. And know the hand?

Lor. 'Tis Leonora's; I have often seen it.

Car. I hope you then at last are satisfied. 180

Lor. [*Smiling.*] I am. Good morrow, Carlos! [*Exit.*

San. Sure he's mad, master.

Car. Mad, say'st thou?

San. And yet, by'r Lady, that was a sort of a dry sober smile at going off.

Car. A very sober one! Had he shown me such a letter, I had put on another countenance.

San. Ay, o' my conscience had you.

Car. Here's mystery in this—I like it not.

San. I see his man and confidant there, Lopez. Shall I draw him on a Scotch pair of boots,* master, and make him tell all? 192

---

* An allusion to the torture of the boot, employed in Scotland during the persecution of the Covenanters.

Car. Some questions I must ask him ; call him hither.

San. Hem, Lopez, hem !

Enter LOPEZ.

Lop. Who calls ?

San. I and my master.

Lop. I can't stay.

San. You can indeed, sir.   [*Laying hold on him.*

Car. Whither in such haste, honest Lopez ? What ! upon some love-errand ?   200

Lop. Sir, your servant ; I ask your pardon, but I was going—

Car. I guess where ; but you need not be shy of me any more, thy master and I are no longer rivals ; I have yielded up the cause ; the lady will have it so, so I submit.

Lop. Is it possible, sir ? Shall I then live to see my master and you friends again ?

San. Yes ; and what's better, thou and I shall be friends too. There will be no more fear of Christian bloodshed, I give thee up Jacinta ; she's a slippery housewife, so master and I are going to match ourselves elsewhere.   210

Lop. But is it possible, sir, your honour should be in earnest ? I'm afraid you are pleased to be merry with your poor humble servant.

Car. I'm not at present much disposed to mirth, my indifference in this matter is not so thoroughly formed ; but my reason has so far mastered my passion, to show me 'tis in vain to pursue a woman whose heart already is another's. 'Tis what I have so plainly seen of late, I have roused my resolution to my aid, and broke my chains for ever.   219

Lop. Well, sir, to be plain with you, this is the joyfullest news I have heard this long time ; for I always knew you to be a mighty honest gentleman, and good faith it often went to the heart o' me to see you so abused. Dear, dear, have I often said to myself (when they have had a private meeting just after you have been gone)—

Car. Ha !

San. Hold, master, don't kill him yet. [*To* CARLOS *aside.*

Lop. I say I have said to myself, what wicked things are women, and what pity it is they should be suffered in a Christian country ! what a shame they should be allowed to play will-in-the-wisp with men of honour, and lead 'em through thorns and briars, and rocks, and rugged ways, till their hearts are torn in pieces, like an old coat in a fox chase ! I say, I have said to myself—   234

Car. Thou hast said enough to thyself, but say a little more to me. Where were these secret meetings thou talkest of ?

Lop. In sundry places, and by divers ways ; sometimes in the cellar, sometimes in the garret, sometimes in the court, sometimes in the gutter ; but the place where the kiss of kisses was given was—

Car. In hell !

Lop. Sir ?

Car. Speak, fury, what dost thou mean by the kiss of kisses ?   · 245

Lop. The kiss of peace, sir ; the kiss of union ; the kiss of consummation.

Car. Thou liest, villain !

Lop. I don't know but I may, sir.—[*Aside.*] What the devil's the matter now ?

Car. There's not one word of truth in all thy cursed tongue has uttered.

Lop. No, sir, I—I—believe there is not.

Car. Why then didst thou say it, wretch?

Lop. O—only in jest, sir.   255

Car. I am not in a jesting condition.

Lop. Nor I—at present, sir.

Car. Speak then the truth, as thou wouldst do it at the hour of death.

Lop. Yes, at the gallows, and be turned off as soon as I've done.   [*Aside.*

Car. What's that you murmur?

Lop. Nothing but a short prayer.

Car. [*Aside.*] I am distracted, and fright the wretch from telling me what I am upon the rack to know.—[*Aloud.*] Forgive me, Lopez, I am to blame to speak thus harshly to thee. Let this obtain thy pardon.—[*Gives him money.*] Thou seest I am disturbed.   268

Lop. Yes, sir, I see I have been led into a snare; I have said too much.

Car. And yet thou must say more; nothing can lessen my torment but a farther knowledge of what causes my misery. Speak then! have I anything to hope?

Lop. Nothing; but that you may be a happier bachelor, than my master may probably be a married man.

Car. Married, say'st thou?

Lop. I did, sir; and I believe he'll say so too in a twelvemonth.

Car. Oh torment!—But give me more on't: when, how, to who, where?   280

Lop. Yesterday, to Leonora, by the parson, in the pantry.

Car. Look to't, if this be false, thy life shall pay the torment thou hast given me. Begone!

Lop. With the body and the soul o' me. [*Exit.*

San. Base news, master.

Car. Now my insulting rival's smile speaks out: O cursed, cursed woman !

Enter JACINTA.

Jac. I'm come in haste to tell you, sir, that as soon as the moon's up, my lady'll give you a meeting in the close-walk by the back door of the garden ; she thinks she has something to propose to you, will certainly get her father's consent to marry you. 292

Car. Past sufferance ! This aggravation is not to be borne. Go, thank her—with my curses. Fly !—and let 'em blast her, while their venom's strong. [*Exit.*

Jac. Won't thou explain ? What's this storm for ?

San. And dar'st thou ask me questions, smooth-faced iniquity, crocodile of Nile, siren of the rocks ?* Go, carry back the too gentle answer thou hast received ; only let me add with the poet :— 300

> We are no fools, trollop, my master, nor me ;
> And thy mistress may go—to the devil, with thee.
> [*Exit.*

Jac. Am I awake ?—I fancy not ; a very idle dream this. Well : I'll go talk in my sleep to my lady about it ; and when I awake, we'll try what interpretation we can make on't. [*Exit.*

---

* Gros-René, in Molière, goes a flight beyond Sancho in classical allusion :—

> " Crocodile trompeur, de qui le cœur félon
> Est pire qu'un satrape, ou bien qu'un Lestrigon ! "

ACT II.

SCENE.—*An open Court near the House of* DON ALVAREZ.

Enter CAMILLO *and* ISABELLA.

Isab. How can you doubt my secrecy? have you not proofs of it?

Cam. Nay, I am determined to trust you; but are we safe here? can nobody overhear us?

Isab. Safer much than in a room. Nobody can come within hearing before we see 'em.

Cam. And yet how hard 'tis for me to break silence!

Isab. Your secret sure must be of great importance.

Cam. You may be sure it is, when I confess 'tis with regret I own it even to you; and, were it possible, you should not know it.　　　　　　　　　　11

Isab. 'Tis frankly owned indeed; but 'tis not kind, perhaps not prudent, after what you know I already am acquainted with. Have I not been bred up with you? and am I ignorant of a secret which, were it known—

Cam. Would be my ruin; I confess it would. I own you know why both my birth and sex are thus disguised; you know how I was taken from my cradle to secure the estate which had else been lost by young Camillo's death; but which is now safe in my supposed father's hands, by my passing for his son; and 'tis because you know all this, I have resolved to open farther wonders to you. But, before

I say any more, you must resolve one doubt, which often gives me great disturbance ; whether Don Alvarez ever was himself privy to the mystery which has disguised my sex, and made me pass for his son ?   26

Isab. What you ask me is a thing has often perplexed my thoughts as well as yours, nor could my mother ever resolve the doubt. You know, when that young child Camillo died, in whom was wrapped up so much expectation, from the great estate his uncle's will (even before he came into the world) had left him ; his mother made a secret of his death to her husband Alvarez, and readily fell in with a proposal made her to take you (who then were just Camillo's age) and bring you up in his room. You have heard how you were then at nurse with my mother, and how your own was privy and consenting to the plot ; but Don Alvarez was never let into it by 'em.

Cam. Don't you then think it probable his wife might after tell him ?   40

Isab. 'Twas ever thought nothing but a death-bed repentance could draw it from her to any one ; and that was prevented by the suddenness of her exit to t'other world, which did not give her even time to call Heaven's mercy on her. And yet, now I have said all this, I own the correspondence and friendship I observe he holds with your real mother gives me some suspicion, and the presents he often makes her (which people seldom do for nothing) confirm it. But, since this is all I can say to you on that point, pray let us come to the secret, which you have made me impatient to hear.   51

Cam. Know, then, that though Cupid is blind, he is not to be deceived : I can hide my sex from the world, but not from him ; his dart has found the way through the manly garb I wear, to pierce a virgin's tender heart.—I love—

Isab.   How !

Cam.   Nay, ben't surprised at that, I have other wonders for you.

Isab.   Quick, let me hear 'em.

Cam.   I love Lorenzo.   60

Isab.   Lorenzo ! Most nicely hit ! The very man from whom your imposture keeps this vast estate ; and who, on the first knowledge of your being a woman, would enter into possession of it.   This is indeed a wonder.

Cam.   Then, wonder farther still, I am his wife.

Isab.   Ha ! his wife !

Cam.   His wife, Isabella ; and yet thou hast not all my wonders, I am his wife without his knowledge : he does not even know I am a woman.

Isab.   Madam, your humble servant ; if you please to go on, I won't interrupt you, indeed I won't.   71

Cam.   Then hear how these strange things have passed : Lorenzo, bound unregarded in my sister's chains, seemed in my eyes a conquest worth her care.   Nor could I see him treated with contempt without growing warm in his interest : I blamed Leonora for not being touched with his merit ; I blamed her so long, till I grew touched with it myself : and the reasons I urged to vanquish her heart insensibly made a conquest of my own.   'Twas thus, my friend, I fell.   What was next to be done my passion pointed out ; my heart I felt was warmed to a noble enterprise, I gave it way, and boldly on it led me.   Leonora's name and voice, in the dark shades of night, I borrowed, to engage the object of my wishes.   I met him, Isabella, and so deceived him ; he cannot blame me sure, for much I blessed him. But to finish this strange story : in short, I owned I long had loved ; but, finding my father most averse to my desires, I at last had forced myself to this secret correspondence; I urged the mischiefs would attend the knowledge on't, I urged 'em so, he thought 'em full of weight, so yielded to observe what rules I gave him. They were, to pass the day with cold indifference, to avoid even sign or looks of intimacy, but gather for the still, the secret night, a flood of love to recompense the losses of the day. I will not trouble you with lovers' cares, nor what contrivances we formed to bring this toying to a solid bliss. Know only, when three nights we thus had passed, the fourth it was agreed should make us one for ever ; each kept their promise, and last night has joined us. 99

Isab. Indeed your talents pass my poor extent; you serious ladies are well formed for business. What wretched work a poor coquette had made on't ! But still there's that remains will try your skill; you have your man, but—

Cam. Lovers think no farther. The object of that passion possesses all desire. However, I have opened to you my wondrous situation, if you can advise me in my difficulties to come, you will. But see—my husband !

Enter LORENZO.

Lor. You look as if you were busy ; pray tell me if I interrupt you ; I'll retire. 110

Cam. No, no, you have a right to interrupt us, since you were the subject of our discourse.

Lor. Was I ?

Cam. You were; nay, I'll tell you how you entertained us too.

Lor. Perhaps I had as good avoid hearing that.

Cam. You need not fear, it was not to your disadvantage; I was commending you, and saying, if I had been a woman, I had been in danger; nay, I think I said I should infallibly have been in love with you.   120

Lor. While such an if is in the way, you run no great risk in declaring; but you'd be finely catched now, should some wonderful transformation give me a claim to your heart.

Cam. Not sorry for't at all, for I ne'er expect to find a mistress please me half so well as you would do, if I were yours.

Lor. Since you are so well inclined to me in your wishes, sir, I suppose (as the fates have ordained it) you would have some pleasure in helping me to a mistress, since you can't be mine yourself.   131

Cam. Indeed I should not.

Lor. Then my obligation is but small to you.

Cam. Why, would you have a woman, that is in love with you herself, employ her interest to help you to another?

Lor. No, but you being no woman might.

Cam. Sir, 'tis as a woman I say what I do, and I suppose myself a woman when I design all these favours to you. Therefore, out of that supposition, I have no other good intentions to you than you may expect from any one that says he's—sir, your humble servant.   141

Lor. So, unless Heaven is pleased to work a miracle, and from a sturdy young fellow make you a kind-hearted young lady, I'm to get little by your good opinion of me.

Cam. Yes, there is one means yet left (on this side a miracle) that would perhaps engage me ; if with an honest oath you could declare, were I woman, I might dispute your heart, even with the first of my pretending sex.

Lor. Then solemnly and honestly I swear, that had you been a woman, and I the master of the world, I think I should have laid it at your feet.   151

Cam. Then honestly and solemnly I swear, henceforwards all your interest shall be mine.

Lor. I have a secret to impart to you will quickly try your friendship.

Cam. I have a secret to unfold to you will put you even to a fiery trial.

Lor. What do you mean, Camillo?

Cam. I mean that I love where I never durst yet own it, yet where 'tis in your power to make me the happiest of—   161

Lor. Explain, Camillo; and be assured, if your happiness is in my power, 'tis in your own.

Cam. Alas ! you promise me you know not what.

Lor. I promise nothing but what I will perform ; name the person.

Cam. 'Tis one who's very near to you.

Lor. If 'tis my sister, why all this pain in bringing forth the secret?

Cam. Alas ! it is your—   170

Lor. Speak !

Cam. I cannot yet ; farewell !

Lor. Hold ! pray speak it now.

Cam. I must not : but when you tell me your secret, you shall know mine.

Lor. Mine is not in my power, without the consent of another.

Cam. Get that consent, and then we'll try who best will keep their oaths.

Lor. I am content.　　　　180

Cam. And I. Adieu!

Lor. Farewell.　　　　[*Exit.*

　　　　Enter LEONORA *and* JACINTA.

Leo. 'Tis enough: I will revenge myself this way: if it does but torment him, I shall be content to find no other pleasure in it.—Brother, you'll wonder at my change; after all my ill usage of Lorenzo, I am determined to be his wife.

Cam. How, sister! so sudden a turn? This inequality of temper indeed is not commendable.

Leo. Your change, brother, is much more justly surprising; you hitherto have pleaded for him strongly; accused me of blindness, cruelty, and pride; and now I yield to your reasons, and resolve in his favour, you blame my compliance, and appear against his interest.　　　　193

Cam. I quit his service for what's dearer to me, yours. I have learned from sure intelligence, the attack he made on you was but a feint, and that his heart is in another's chain: I would not therefore see you so exposed, to offer up yourself to one who must refuse you.

Leo. If that be all, leave me my honour to take care of; I am no stranger to his wishes; he won't refuse me, brother, nor I hope will you, to tell him of my resolution: if you do, this moment with my own tongue (through all a virgin's blushes) I'll own to him I am determined in his favour.— You pause as if you'd let the task lie on me.　　　　204

Cam. Neither on you, nor me; I have a reason you are
yet a stranger to.   Know then, there is a virgin, young and
tender, whose peace and happiness so much are mine, I
cannot see her miserable; she loves him with that torrent
of desire, that were the world resigned her in his stead, she'd
still be wretched.   I will not pique you to a female strife,
by saying you have not charms to tear him from her; but I
would move you to a female softness, by telling you her
death would wait your conquest.   What I have more to
plead is as a brother, I hope that gives me some small
interest in you; whate'er it is, you see how I'd employ it.

Leo. You ne'er could put it to a harder service.   I beg
a little time to think: pray leave me to myself a while. 217

Cam.   I shall; I only ask that you would think, and then
you won't refuse me.   [*Exeunt* CAMILLO *and* ISABELLA.

Jac. Indeed, madam, I'm of your brother's mind, though
for another cause; but sure 'tis worth thinking twice on for
your own sake.   You are too violent.

Leo. A slighted woman knows no bounds.   Vengeance
is all the cordial she can have, so snatches at the nearest.
Ungrateful wretch ! to use me with such insolence.

Jac. You see me as much enraged at it as you are yourself, yet my brain is roving after the cause, for something
there must be; never letter was received by man with
more passion and transport; I was almost as charming a
goddess as yourself, only for bringing it.   Yet when in a
moment after I come with a message worth a dozen on't,
never was witch so handled; something must have passed
between one and t'other, that's sure.   233

Leo. Nothing could pass worth my inquiring after, since
nothing could happen that can excuse his usage of me;

he had a letter under my hand which owned him master of
my heart; and till I contradicted it with my mouth he
ought not to doubt the truth on't.

Jac. Nay, I confess, madam, I han't a word to say for
him, I'm afraid he's but a rogue at bottom, as well as my
Shameless that attends him; we are bit, by my troth, and
haply well enough served, for listening to the glib tongues
of the rascals. But be comforted, madam; they'll fall into
the hands of some foul sluts or other, before they die, that
will set our account even with 'em.   245

Leo. Well, let him laugh; let him glory in what he has
done: he shall see I have a spirit can use him as I ought.

Jac. And let one thing be your comfort by the way,
madam, that in spite of all your dear affections to him, you
have had the grace to keep him at arm's end. You han't
thank'd me for't; but good faith, 'twas well I did not stir
out of the chamber that fond night. For there are times
the stoutest of us are in danger, the rascals wheedle so.

Leo. In short, my very soul is fired with this treatment:
and if ever that perfidious monster should relent, though he
should crawl like a poor worm beneath my feet, nay, plunge
a dagger in his heart, to bleed for pardon; I charge thee
strictly, charge thee on thy life, thou do not urge a look to
melt me toward him, but strongly buoy me up in brave
resentment; and if thou seest (which Heavens avert!) a
glance of weakness in me, rouse to my memory the vile
wrongs I've borne, and blazon 'em with skill in all their
glaring colours.   263

Jac. Madam, never doubt me; I'm charged to the
mouth with fury, and if ever I meet that fat traitor of mine,
such a volley will I pour about his ears!—Now Heaven

prevent all hasty vows ; but in the humour I am, methinks I'd carry my maidenhead to my cold grave with me, before I'd let it simper at the rascal. But soft ! here comes your father.   270

Enter ALVAREZ.

Alv. Leonora, I'd have you retire a little, and send your brother's tutor to me, Metaphrastus.—[*Exeunt* LEONORA *and* JACINTA.] I'll try if I can discover, by his tutor, what 'tis that seems so much to work his brain of late ; for something more than common there plainly does appear, yet nothing sure that can disturb his soul, like what I have to torture mine on his account. Sure nothing in this world is worth a troubled mind ! What racks has avarice stretched me on ! I wanted nothing : kind Heaven had given me a plenteous lot, and seated me in great abundance. Why then approve I of this imposture ? What have I gained by it ? Wealth and misery. I have bartered peaceful days for restless nights ; a wretched bargain ! and he that merchandises thus must be undone at last.   284

Enter METAPHRASTUS.

Metaph. *Mandatum tuum curo diligenter.*

Alv. Master, I had a mind to ask you—

Metaph. The title, master, comes from *magis* and *ter,* which is as much as to say, *thrice worthy.*

Alv. I never heard so much before, but it may be true for aught I know. But, master—

Metaph. Go on.

Alv. Why so I will if you'll let me, but don't interrupt me then.

Metaph. Enough, proceed.   294

Alv. Why then, master, for the third time, my son Camillo gives me much uneasiness of late ; you know I love him, and have many careful thoughts about him.

Metaph. 'Tis true. *Filio non potest præferri, nisi filius.*

Alv. Master, when one has business to talk on, these scholastic expressions are not of use; I believe you a great Latinist; possibly you may understand Greek; those who recommended you to me, said so, and I am willing it should be true: but the thing I want to discourse you about at present, does not properly give you an occasion to display your learning. Besides, to tell you truth, 'twill at all times be lost upon me; my father was a wise man, but he taught me nothing beyond common sense ;* I know but one tongue in the world, which luckily being understood by you as well as me, I fancy whatever thoughts we have to communicate to one another, may reasonably be conveyed in that, without having recourse to the language of Julius Cæsar. 313

Metaph. You are wrong, but may proceed.

Alv. I thank you. What is the matter I do not know ; but though it is of the utmost consequence to me to marry my son, what match soever I propose to him, he still finds some pretence or other to decline it.

Metaph. He is, perhaps, of the humour of a brother of Marcus Tullius, who—

Alv. Dear master, leave the Greeks, and the Latins, and

---

* The French is somewhat different :—" Ne m'a jamais rien fait apprendre que mes Heures."

the Scotch, and the Welsh, and let me go on in my business ;
what have those people to do with my son's marriage ?

Metaph. Again you are wrong; but go on.　324

Alv. I say then, that I have strong apprehensions, from
his refusing all my proposals, that he may have some secret
inclination of his own ; and to confirm me in this fear, I
yesterday observed him (without his knowing it) in a
corner of the grove where nobody comes—

Metaph. A place out of the way, you would say; a
place of retreat.

Alv. Why, the corner of the grove, where nobody comes,
is a place of retreat, is it not ?

Metaph. In Latin, *secessus.*

Alv. Ha ?

Metaph. As Virgil has it, *Est in secessu locus.*　336

Alv. How could Virgil have it, when I tell you no soul
was there but he and I ?

Metaph. Virgil is a famous author ; I quote his saying as
a phrase more proper to the occasion than that you use, and
not as one who was in the wood with you.

Alv. And I tell you, I hope to be as famous as any
Virgil of 'em all, when I have been dead as long, and have no
need of a better phrase than my own to tell you my meaning.

Metaph. You ought however to make choice of the
words most used by the best authors. *Tu vivendo bonos,* as
they say, *scribendo sequare peritos.*　347

Alv. Again !

Metaph. 'Tis Quintilian's own precept.

Alv. Oons !

Metaph. And he has something very learned upon it,
that may be of service to you to hear.

Alv. You son of a whore, will you hear me speak?

Metaph. What may be the occasion of this unmanly passion? What is it you would have with me?

Alv. What you might have known an hour ago, if you had pleased.

Metaph. You would then have me hold my peace—I shall.

Alv. You will do very well.   360

Metaph. You see I do; well, go on.

Alv. Why then, to begin once again, I say my son Camillo—

Metaph. Proceed; I shan't interrupt you.

Alv. I say, my son Camillo—

Metaph. What is it you say of your son Camillo?

Alv. That he has got a dog of a tutor, whose brains I'll beat out if he won't hear me speak.

Metaph. That dog is a philosopher, contemns passion, and yet will hear you.   370

Alv. I don't believe a word on't, but I'll try once again. I have a mind to know from you, whether you have observed anything in my son—

Metaph. Nothing that is like his father. Go on.

Alv. Have a care!

Metaph. I do not interrupt you; but you are long in coming to a conclusion.

Alv. Why, thou hast not let me begin yet!

Metaph. And yet it is high time to have made an end.

Alv. Dost thou know thy danger? I have not—thus much patience left.   [*Showing the end of his finger.*

Metaph. Mine is already consumed. I do not use to be thus treated; my profession is to teach, and not to hear, yet

I have hearkened like a schoolboy, and am not heard,
although a master.   385

Alv.   Get out of the room!

Metaph.   I will not.   If the mouth of a wise man be
shut, he is, as it were, a fool; for who shall know his
understanding?   Therefore a certain philosopher said well,
Speak, that thou may'st be known; great talkers, without
knowledge, are as the winds that whistle; but they who have
learning should speak aloud.   If this be not permitted, we
may expect to see the whole order of nature o'erthrown;
hens devour foxes, and lambs destroy wolves, nurses suck
children, and children give suck; generals mend stockings,
and chambermaids take towns; we may expect, I say—

Alv.   That, and that, and that, and—

[*Strikes him and kicks him; then follows him off
with a bell at his ear.*

Metaph.   *O tempora!   O mores!*   [*Exeunt.*

ACT III.

SCENE.—*The Street before the House of* DON ALVAREZ.

Enter LOPEZ.

Lop. Sometimes Fortune seconds a bold design, and when folly has brought us into a trap, impudence brings us out on't. I have been caught by this hot-headed lover here, and have told like a puppy what I shall be beaten for like a dog. Come! courage, my dear Lopez; fire will fetch out fire. Thou hast told one body thy master's secret, e'en tell it to half-a-dozen more, and try how that will thrive; go tell it to the two old Dons, the lovers' fathers. The thing's done, and can't be retrieved; perhaps they'll lay their two ancient heads together, club a pennyworth of wisdom a-piece, and with great penetration at last find out, that 'tis best to submit, where 'tis not in their power to do otherwise. This being resolved, there's no time to be lost.

[*Knocks at* ALVAREZ'S *door.*

Alv. [*Within.*] Who knocks?   14

Lop. Lopez.

Alv. [*Looking out.*] What dost want?

Lop. To bid you good-morrow, sir.

Alv. Well, good-morrow to thee again.   [*Retires.*

Lop. What a—I think he does not care for my company.

[*Knocks again.*

Alv. [*Within.*] Who knocks?

Lop. Lopez.

Alv. [*Looking out.*] What wouldst have?

Lop. My old master, sir, gives his service to you, and desires to know how you do. 24

Alv. How I do? why, well; how should I do? Service to him again. [*Retires.*

Lop. Sir!

Alv. [*Returning.*] What the deuce wouldst thou have with me, with thy good-morrows and thy services?

Lop. [*Aside.*] This man does not understand good breeding, I find.—[*Aloud.*] Why, sir, my master has some very earnest business with you.

Alv. Business! about what? What business can he have with me?

Lop. I don't know, truly; but 'tis some very important matter. He has just now (as I hear) discovered some great secret, which he must needs talk with you about. 37

Alv. Ha! a secret, say'st thou?

Lop. Yes; and bid me bring him word if you were at home, he'd be with you presently. Sir, your humble servant. [*Exit.*

Enter DON ALVAREZ, *from the house.*

Alv. A secret! and must speak with me about it! Heavens, how I tremble! What can this message mean? I have very little acquaintance with him, what business can he have with me? An important secret 'twas, he said, and that he had just discovered it. Alas! I have in the world but one: if it be that—I'm lost; an eternal blot must fix upon me. How unfortunate am I, that I have not followed the honest counsels of my heart, which have often

urged me to set my conscience at ease, by rendering to him
the estate that is his due, and which by a foul imposture I
keep from him! But 'tis now too late; my villainy is out,
and I shall not only be forced with shame to restore him
what is his, but shall be perhaps condemned to make him
reparation with my own. O terrible view!   55

Enter DON FELIX.

Don Fel. [*Aside.*] My son to go and marry her without
her father's knowledge! This can never end well. I don't
know what to do; he'll conclude I was privy to it, and his
power and interest are so great at court, he may with ease
contrive my ruin: I tremble at his sending to speak with
me.—Mercy on me, there he is!

Alv. [*Aside.*] Ah! shield me, kind Heaven! there's
Don Felix come. How I am struck with the sight of him!
Oh, the torment of a guilty mind!   64

Don Fel. What shall I say to soften him?   [*Aside.*

Alv. How shall I look him in the face?   [*Aside.*

Don Fel. 'Tis impossible he can forgive it.   [*Aside.*

Alv. To be sure he'll expose me to the whole world.

          [*Aside.*

Don Fel. I see his countenance change.   [*Aside.*

Alv. With what contempt he looks upon me!   [*Aside.*

Don Fel. I see, Don Alvarez, by the disorder of your
face, you are but too well informed of what brings me
here.

Alv. 'Tis true.   74

Don Fel. The news may well surprise you, 'tis what I
have been far from apprehending.

Alv. Wrong, very wrong, indeed.

Don Fel. The action is certainly to the last point to be condemned, and I think nobody should pretend to excuse the guilty.

Alv. They are not to be excused, though Heaven may have mercy.

Don Fel. That's what I hope you will consider.

Alv. We should act as Christians.

Don Fel. Most certainly.   85

Alv. Let mercy then prevail.

Don Fel. It is indeed of heavenly birth.

Alv. Generous Don Felix

Don Fel. Too indulgent Alvarez !

Alv. I thank you on my knee.

Don Fel. 'Tis I ought to have been there first.

[*They kneel.*

Alv. Is it then possible we are friends ?

Don Fel. Embrace me to confirm it.   [*They embrace.*

Alv. Thou best of men !

Don Fel. Unlooked-for bounty !   95

Alv. [*Rising.*] Did you know the torment this unhappy action has given me—

Don Fel. 'Tis impossible it could do otherwise ; nor has my trouble been less.

Alv. But let my misfortune be kept secret.

Don Fel. Most willingly ; my advantage is sufficient by it, without the vanity of making it public to the world.

Alv. [*Aside.*] Incomparable goodness ! That I should thus have wronged a man so worthy !—[*Aloud.*] My honour then is safe ?   105

Don Fel. For ever, even for ever let it be a secret, I am content.

Alv. [*Aside.*]   Noble   gentleman !—[*Aloud.*]   As to
what advantages ought to accrue to you by it, it shall be
all to your entire satisfaction.

Don Fel. [*Aside.*]   Wonderful bounty !—[*Aloud.*]   As
to that, Don Alvarez, I leave it entirely to you, and shall be
content with whatever you think reasonable.

Alv. I thank you, from my soul I must, you know I
must.—[*Aside.*] This must be an angel, not a man.   115

Don Fel. The thanks lie on my side, Alvarez, for this
unexpected generosity ; but may all faults be forgot, and
Heaven ever prosper you !

Alv. The same prayer I, with a double fervour, offer up
for you.

Don Fel. Let us then once more embrace, and be
forgiveness sealed for ever.

Alv. Agreed ; thou best of men, agreed. [*They embrace.*

Don Fel. This thing then being thus happily terminated,
let me own to you, Don Alvarez, I was in extreme
apprehensions of your utmost resentment on this occasion ;
for I could not doubt but you had formed more happy
views in the disposal of so fair a daughter as Leonora, than
my poor son's inferior fortune e'er can answer ; but since
they are joined, and that—   130

Alv. Ha !

Don Fel. Nay, 'tis very likely to discourse of it may not
be very pleasing to you, though your Christianity and
natural goodness have prevailed on you so generously to
forgive it. But to do justice to Leonora, and screen her
from your too harsh opinion in this unlucky action, 'twas
that cunning wicked creature that attends her, who by
unusual arts wrought her to this breach of duty, for her own

inclinations were disposed to all the modesty and resignation a father could ask from a daughter; my son I can't excuse, but since your bounty does so, I hope you'll quite forget the fault of the less guilty Leonora.   142

Alv. [*Aside.*] What a mistake have I lain under here! and from a groundless apprehension of one misfortune, find myself in the certainty of another.

Don Fel. He looks disturbed! what can this mean?

[*Aside.*

Alv. [*Aside.*] My daughter married to his son!— Confusion!—But I find myself in such unruly agitation, something wrong may happen if I continue with him; I'll therefore leave him.

Don Fel. You seem thoughtful, sir; I hope there's no—   152

Alv. A sudden disorder I am seized with; you'll pardon me, I must retire.   [*Exit.*

Don Fel. I don't like this:—he went oddly off.—I doubt he finds this bounty difficult to go through with. His natural resentment is making an attack upon his acquired generosity: pray Heaven it ben't too strong for't. The misfortune is a great one, and can't but touch him nearly. It was not natural to be so calm; I wish it don't yet drive him to my ruin. But here comes this young hot-brained coxcomb, who with his midnight amours has been the cause of all this mischief to me.   163

Enter LORENZO.

So, sir, are you come to receive my thanks for your noble exploit? You think you have done bravely now, ungracious offspring, to bring perpetual troubles on me. Must there never pass a day, but I must drink some bitter potion or other of your preparation for me?

Lor. I am amazed, sir; pray what have I done to deserve your anger? 170

Don Fel. Nothing; no manner of thing in the world; nor never do. I am an old testy fellow, and am always scolding, and finding fault for nothing; complaining that I have got a coxcomb of a son that makes me weary of my life, fancying he perverts the order of nature, turning day into night, and night into day; getting whims in my brain, that he consumes his life in idleness, unless he rouses now and then to do some noble stroke of mischief; and having an impertinent dream at this time, that he has been making the fortune of the family, by an underhand marriage with the daughter of a man who will crush us all to powder for it. Ah—ungracious wretch, to bring an old man into all this trouble! The pain thou gav'st thy mother to bring thee into the world, and the plague thou hast given me to keep thee here, make the getting thee (though 'twas in our honeymoon) a bitter remembrance to us both. [*Exit.* 186

Lor. So, all's out!—Here's a noble storm arising, and I'm at sea in a cock-boat! But which way could this business reach him? By this traitor Lopez; it must be so; it could be no other way; for only he, and the priest that married us, know of it. The villain will never confess though: I must try a little address with him, and conceal my anger.—Oh! here he comes.

Enter Lopez.

Lopez

Lop. Do you call, sir?

Lor. I find all's discovered to my father; the secret's out; he knows my marriage.   197

Lop. He knows your marriage! How the pest should that happen? Sir, 'tis impossible!—that's all.

Lor. I tell thee 'tis true; he knows every particular of it.

Lop. He does?—Why then, sir, all I can say is, that Satan and he are better acquainted than the devil and a good Christian ought to be.

Lor. Which way he has discovered it I can't tell, nor am I much concerned to know, since, beyond all my expectations, I find him perfectly easy at it, and ready to excuse my fault with better reasons than I can find to do it myself.   209

Lop. Say you so?—I'm very glad to hear that; then all's safe.   [*Aside.*

Lor. 'Tis unexpected good fortune; but it could never proceed purely from his own temper; there must have been pains taken with him to bring him to this calm. I'm sure I owe much to the bounty of some friend or other; I wish I knew where my obligation lay, that I might acknowledge it as I ought.

Lop. [*Aside.*] Are you thereabouts, i'faith? Then sharp's the word; egad, I'll own the thing, and receive his bounty for't.—[*Aloud.*] Why, sir—not that I pretend to make a merit o' the matter, for, alas! I am but your poor hireling, and therefore bound in duty to render you all the service I can;—but—'tis I have done't.   223

Lor. What hast thou done?

Lop. What no man else could have done—the job, sir; told him the secret, and then talked him into a liking on't.

Lor. 'Tis impossible; thou dost not tell me true.

Lop. Sir, I scorn to reap anything from another man's labours; but if this poor piece of service carries any merit with it, you now know where to reward it.

Lor. Thou art not serious?

Lop. I am, or may hunger be my messmate!

Lor. And may famine be mine, if I don't reward thee for't as thou deserv'st!—Dead!　　　[*Making a pass at him.*

Lop. Have a care there!—[*Leaping on one side.*] What do you mean, sir? I bar all surprise.

Lor. Traitor! is this the fruit of the trust I placed in thee—villain?　　　[*Making another thrust at him.*

Lop. Take heed, sir! you'll do one a mischief before y'are aware.　　　240

Lor. What recompense canst thou make me, wretch, for this piece of treachery? Thy sordid blood can't expiate the thousandth—but I'll have it, however.　[*Thrusts again.*

Lop. Look you there again! Pray, sir, be quiet; is the devil in you? 'Tis bad jesting with edged tools. Egad, that last push was within an inch o' me! I don't know what you make all this bustle about; but I'm sure I've done all for the best, and I believe 'twill prove for the best too at last, if you'll have but a little patience. But if gentlemen will be in their airs in a moment——Why, what the deuce— I'm sure I have been as eloquent as Cicero in your behalf; and I don't doubt, to good purpose too, if you'll give things time to work. But nothing but foul language, and naked swords about the house!—Sa, sa! run you through, you dog! Why, nobody can do business at this rate.　　　255

Lor. And suppose your project fail, and I'm ruined by't, sir?

T 2

Lop. Why, 'twill be time enough to kill me then, sir; won't it? What should you do it for now? Besides, I an't ready, I'm not prepared; I might be undone by't.

Lor. But what will Leonora say to her marriage being known, wretch?

Lop. Why, maybe she'll draw—her sword too.—[*Showing his tongue.*] But all shall be well with you both, if you will but let me alone.   265

Lor. Peace! here's her father.

Lop. That's well: we shall see how things go presently.

Enter DON ALVAREZ.

Alv. [*Aside.*] The more I recover from the disorder this discourse has put me in, the more strange the whole adventure appears to me. Leonora maintains there is not a word of truth in what I have heard; that she knows nothing of marriage: and, indeed, she tells me this with such a naked air of sincerity, that, for my part, I believe her. What then must be their project? Some villainous intention, to be sure; though which way, I yet am ignorant.—But here's the bride-groom; I'll accost him.—[*Aloud.*] I am told, sir, you take upon you to scandalize my daughter, and tell idle tales of what can never happen.   278

Lop. Now methinks, sir, if you treated your son-in-law with a little more civility, things might go just as well in the main.

Alv. What means this insolent fellow by my son-in-law? I suppose 'tis you, villain, are the author of this impudent story.

Lop. You seem angry, sir;—perhaps without cause.

Alv. Cause, traitor! Is a cause wanting, where a daughter's defamed, and a noble family scandalized?

Lop.   There he is ; let him answer you.

Alv.   I should be glad he'd answer me, why, if he had any desires to my daughter, he did not make his approaches like a man of honour.   290

Lop.   Yes ; and so have had the doors bolted against him, like a house-breaker.   [*Aside.*

Lor.   Sir, to justify my proceeding, I have little to say ; but to excuse it, I have much, if any allowance may be made to a passion which, in your youth, you have yourself been swayed by.   I love your daughter to that excess—

Alv.   You would undo her for a night's lodging.

Lor.   Undo her, sir !

Alv.   Yes, that's the word.   You knew it was against her interest to marry you, therefore you endeavoured to win her to't in private ; you knew her friends would make a better bargain for her, therefore you kept your designs from their knowledge ; and yet you love her to that excess—

Lor.   I'd readily lay down my life to serve her.   304

Alv.   Could you readily lay down fifty thousand pistoles to serve her, your excessive love would come with better credentials : an offer of life is very proper for the attack of a counterscarp, but a thousand ducats will sooner carry a lady's heart.   You are a young man, but will learn this when you are older.

Lop.   But since things have succeeded better this once, sir, and that my master will prove a most incomparable good husband (for that he'll do, I'll answer for him), and that 'tis too late to recall what's already done, sir—

Alv.   What's done, villain ?   315

Lop.   Sir, I mean—that since my master and my lady are married, and—

Alv. Thou liest! they are not married.

Lop. Sir!—I say, that since they are married, and that they love each other so passing dearly, indeed I fancy that—

Alv. Why, this impudence is beyond all bearing! Sir, do you put your rascal upon this?

Lor. Sir, I am in a wood! I don't know what it is you mean.   325

Alv. And I am in a plain, sir, and think I may be understood. Do you pretend you are married to my daughter?

Lor. Sir, 'tis my happiness on one side, as it is my misfortune on another.

Alv. And you do think this idle project can succeed? You do believe your affirming you are married to her will induce both her and me to consent it shall be so?

Lop. Sir, I see you make my master almost out of his wits to hear you talk so; but I, who am but a stander-by now, as I was at the wedding, have mine about me, and desire to know, whether you think this project can succeed? Do you believe your affirming they are not married, will induce both him and I to give up the lady? One short question to bring this matter to an issue—why do you think they are not married?   341

Alv. Because she utterly renounces it.

Lop. And so she will her religion, if you attack it with that dreadful face. D'ye hear, sir? the poor lady is in love heartily, and I wish all poor ladies that are so, would dispose of themselves so well as she has done; but you scare her out of her senses. Bring her here into the room, speak gently to her, tell her you know the thing is done, that you have it from a man of honour—me : that maybe you wish it had been otherwise, but are a Christian, and profess mercy, and therefore have resolved to pardon her. Say this, and I shall appear a man of reputation, and have satisfaction made me.   353

Alv. Or an impudent rogue, and have all your bones broke.

Lop. Content !

Alv. Agreed !—Leonora !—Who's there ? call Leonora.

Lop. All will go rarely, sir ; we shall have shot the gulf in a moment.   [*Aside to* LORENZO.

Enter LEONORA.

Alv. Come hither, Leonora.

Lop. So, now we shall see.   361

Alv. I called you to answer for yourself ; here's a strong claim upon you ; if there be anything in the pretended title, conceal it no farther, it must be known at last, it may as well be so now.   Nothing is so uneasy as uncertainty, I would therefore be gladly freed from it.   If you have done what I am told you have, 'tis a great fault indeed ; but as I fear 'twill carry much of its punishment along with it, I shall rather reduce my resentment into mourning your misfortune, than suffer it to add to your affliction ; therefore speak the truth.

Lop. Well, this is fair play ; now I speak, sir.—You see, fair lady, the goodness of a tender father ; nothing need therefore hinder you from owning a most loving husband. We had like to have been all together by the ears about this business, and pails of blood were ready to run about the house ; but, thank Heaven, the sun shines out again, and one word from your sweet mouth makes fair weather for ever.   My master has been forced to own your marriage, he begs you'll do so too.   379

Leo.   What does this impudent rascal mean?

Lop.   Ha!—madam!

Leo.   [*To* LORENZO.]   Sir, I should be very glad to know what can have been the occasion of this wild report; sure you cannot be yourself a party in it?

Lop.   He, he—

Lor.   Forgive me, dear Leonora, I know you had strong reasons for the secret being longer kept; but 'tis not my fault, our marriage is disclosed.

Leo.   Our marriage, sir!—   389

Lor.   'Tis known, my dear, though much against my will; but since it is so, 'twould be in vain for us to deny it longer.

Leo.   Then, sir, I am your wife?   I fell in love with you, and married you without my father's knowledge?

Lor.   I dare not be so vain to think 'twas love; I humbly am content to owe the blessing to your generosity; you saw the pains I suffered for your sake, and in compassion eased'em.

Leo.   I did, sir? Sure this exceeds all human impudence!

Lop.   Truly, I think it does.   She'd make an incomparable actress.   [*Aside.* 399

Lor.   I begin to be surprised, madam, at your carrying this thing so far; you see there's no occasion for it, and for the discovery, I have already told you 'twas not my fault.

Lop.   My master's! no, 'twas I did it.   Why, what a bustle's here!   I knew things would go well, and so they do, if folks would let 'em.   But if ladies will be in their merriments, when gentlemen are upon serious business, why, what a deuce can one say to 'em?

Leo.   I see this fellow is to be an evidence in your plot.

Where you hope to drive, it is hard to guess; for if anything can exceed its impudence, it is its folly. A noble
stratagem indeed to win a lady by! I could be diverted
with it, but that I see a face of villainy requires a rougher
treatment: I could almost, methinks, forget my sex, and be
my own avenger.   414

Lor. Madam, I am surprised beyond all—

Lop. Pray, sir, let me come to her; you are so surprised,
you'll make nothing on't: she wants a little snubbing.—
Look you, madam, I have seen many a pleasant humour
amongst ladies, but you outcut 'em all. Here's contradiction with a vengeance! You han't been married eight-and-
forty hours, and you are slap—at your husband's beard
already. Why, do you consider who he is?—who this
gentleman is?—and what he can do—by law? Why, he
can lock you up—knock you down—tie you neck and heels—

Lor. Forbear, you insolent villain, you!   425

> [*Offering to strike him.*

Leo. That—for what's past however.

> [*Giving him a box o' the ear.*

Lop. I think—she gave me a box o' th' ear; ha!—[*Exit*
Leonora.] Sir, will you suffer your old servants to be used
thus by new comers? It's a shame, a mere shame. Sir,
will you take a poor dog's advice for once? She denies
she's married to you: take her at her word; you have seen
some of her humours,—let her go.

Alv. Well, gentlemen, thus far you see I have heard all
with patience; have you content? or how much farther do
you design to go with this business?   435

Lop. Why truly, sir, I think we are near at a stand.

Alv. 'Tis time, you villain you!

Lop. Why, and I am a villain now, if every word I've spoke be not as true as—as the Gazette: and your daughter's no better than a—a—a whimsical young woman, for making disputes among gentlemen. And if everybody had their deserts, she'd have a good—I won't speak it out to inflame reckonings ; but let her go, master.

Alv. Sir, I don't think it well to spend any more words with your impudent and villainous servant here.   445

Lop. Thank you, sir : but I'd let her go.

Alv. Nor have I more to say to you than this: that you must not think so daring an affront to my family can go long unresented. Farewell!   [*Exit.*

Lor. Well, sir, what have you to say for yourself now ?

Lop. Why, sir, I have only to say, that I am a very unfortunate—middle-aged man ; and that I believe all the stars upon heaven and earth have been concerned in my destiny. Children now unborn will hereafter sing my downfall, in mournful lines, and notes of doleful tune: I am at resent troubled in mind ; despair around me, signified in appearing gibbets, with a great bundle of dog-whips by way of preparation.   458

I therefore will go seek some mountain high,
If high enough some mountain may be found,
With distant valley, dreadfully profound,
And from the horrid cliff—look calmly all around.*

Farewell !   [*Aside.*

---

* "Aussi, pour être en paix dans ce désordre extrême,
Je me vais d'un rocher précipiter moi-même,
Si, dans le désespoir dont mon cœur est outré,
Je puis en rencontrer d'assez haut à mon gré."—*Molière.*

Lor. No, sirrah; I'll see your wretched end myself. Die here, villain ! [*Drawing his sword.*

Lop. I can't, sir, if anybody looks upon me.

Lor. Away, you trifling wretch ! but think not to escape, for thou shalt have thy recompense. [*Exit.*

Lop. Why, what a mischievous jade is this, to make such an uproar in a family the first day of her marriage ! Why, my master won't so much as get a honeymoon out of her ! Egad, I'd let her go. If she be thus in her soft and tender youth, she'll be rare company at threescore. Well ; he may do as he pleases, but were she my dear, I'd let her go—such a foot at her tail, I'd make the truth bounce out at her mouth like a pellet out of a pop-gun. [*Exit.*

ACT IV.

SCENE.—*A Street.*

Enter CAMILLO *and* ISABELLA.

Isab. 'Tis an unlucky accident indeed !

Cam. Ah, Isabella, fate has now determined my undoing ! This thing can ne'er end here ; Leonora and Lorenzo must soon come to some explanation ; the dispute is too monstrous to pass over without further inquiry, which must discover all ; and what will be the consequence I tremble at. For whether Don Alvarez knows of the imposture, or whether he is deceived with the rest of the world, when once it breaks out, and that the consequence is the loss of that great wealth he now enjoys by it, what must become of me ? All paternal affections then must cease, and regarding me as an unhappy instrument in the trouble which will then o'erload him, he will return me to my humble birth, and then I'm lost for ever. For what, alas ! will the deceived Lorenzo say? A wife, with neither fortune, birth, nor beauty, instead of one most plenteously endowed with all. O Heavens ! what a sea of misery I have before me !   18

Isab. Indeed you reason right, but these reflections are ill-timed ; why did you not employ 'em sooner ?

Cam. Because I loved.

Isab. And don't you do so now?

Cam. I do, and therefore 'tis I make these cruel just reflections.

Isab. So that love, I find, can do anything.

Cam. Indeed it can. Its powers are wondrous great; its pains no tongue can tell, its bliss no heart conceive, crowns cannot recompense its torments, Heaven scarce supplies its joys. My stake is of this value. Oh, counsel me how I shall save it!   30

Isab. Alas! that counsel's much beyond my wisdom's force, I see no way to help you.

Cam. And yet 'tis sure there's one.

Isab. What?

Cam. Death.

Isab. There possibly may be another; I have a thought this moment—perhaps there's nothing in't; yet a small passage comes to my remembrance, that I regarded little when it happened—I'll go and search for one may be of service. But hold; I see Don Carlos. He'll but disturb us now, let us avoid him.   [*Exeunt.* 41

Enter CARLOS *and* SANCHO.

Car. Repulsed again! this is not to be borne. What though this villain's story be a falsehood, was I to blame to hearken to it? This usage cannot be supported: how was it she treated thee?

San. Never was ambassador worse received. Madam, my master asks ten thousand pardons, and humbly begs one moment's interview:—Begone, you rascal you!—Madam, what answer shall I give my master?—Tell him he's a villain.—Indeed, fair lady, I think this is hasty treatment.—Here, my footmen! toss me this fellow out at the window;—and away she went to her devotions.　　　52

Car. Did you see Jacinta?

San. Yes; she saluted me with half a score rogues and rascals too. I think our destinies are much alike, sir : and, o' my conscience, a couple of scurvy jades we are hampered with.

Car. Ungrateful woman! to receive with such contempt so quick a return of a heart so justly alarmed.

San. Ha! ha! ha!

Car. What, no allowance to be made to the first transports of a lover's fury, when roused by so dreadful an appearance! As just as my suspicions were, have I long suffered 'em to arraign her?　　　64

San. No.

Car. Have I waited for oaths or imprecations to clear her?

San. No.

Car. Nay, even now; is not the whole world still in suspense about her? whilst I alone conclude her innocent.

San. 'Tis very true.

Car. She might, methinks, through this profound respect, observe a flame another would have cherished; she might support me against groundless fears, and save me from a rival's tyranny; she might release me from these cruel racks, and would, no doubt, if she could love as I do.　　　77

San. Ha! ha! ha!

Car. But since she don't, what do I whining here? Curse on the base humilities of love!

San. Right.

Car. Let children kiss the rod that flays 'em, let dogs lie down, and lick the shoe that spurns 'em.

San. Ay.

Car. I am a man, by nature meant for power; the sceptre's given us to wield, and we betray our trust whene'er we meanly lay it at a woman's feet.　　　87

San. True, we are men; boo—Come, master, let us both be in a passion; here's my sceptre.—[*Showing a cudgel.*] Subject Jacinta, look about you. Sir, was you ever in Muscovy? the women there love the men dearly: why? because—[*shaking his stick*] there's your love-powder for you. Ah, sir, were we but wise and stout, what work should we make with 'em! But this humble love-making spoils 'em all. A rare way indeed to bring matters about with 'em! We are persuading 'em all day they are angels and goddesses, in order to use 'em at night like human creatures; we are like to succeed truly!

Car. For my part, I never yet could bear a slight from anything, nor will I now. There's but one way, however, to resent it from a woman; and that's to drive her bravely from your heart, and place a worthier in her vacant throne.　　　103

San. Now, with submission to my betters, I have another way, sir; I'll drive my tyrant from my heart, and place myself in her throne. Yes; I will be lord of my own tenement, and keep my household in order. Would you would do so too, master! For, look you, I have been servitor in a college at Salamanca, and read philosophy with the doctors; where I found that a woman, in all times, has been observed to be an animal hard to understand, and much inclined to mischief. Now, as an animal is always an animal, and a captain always a captain, so a woman is always a woman : whence it is that a certain Greek says, her head is like a bank of sand ; or, as another, a solid rock ; or, according to a third, a dark lantern. Pray, sir, observe, for this is close reasoning ; and so, as the head is the head of the body ; and that the body without a head, is like a head without a tail ; and that where there is neither head nor tail, 'tis a very strange body : so I say a woman is by comparison, do you see (for nothing explains things like comparisons), I say by comparison, as Aristotle has often said before me, one may compare her to the raging sea. For as the sea, when the wind rises, knits its brows like an angry bull, and that waves mount upon rocks, and rocks mount upon waves ; that porpoises leap like trouts, and whales skip about like gudgeons ; that ships roll like beer-barrels, and mariners pray like saints ; just so, I say, a woman——A woman, I say, just so, when her reason is shipwrecked upon her passion, and the hulk of her understanding lies thumping against the rock of her fury ; then it is, I say, that by certain immotions, which—um—cause, as one may suppose, a sort of convulsive—yes—hurricanious—um—like—in short, a woman is like the devil, sir.   135

Car.   Admirably reasoned indeed, Sancho !

San.   Pretty well, I thank Heaven.—But here come the crocodiles, to weep us into mercy.

Enter LEONORA *and* JACINTA.

Master, let us show ourselves men, and leave their briny tears to wash their dirty faces.

Car.   It is not in the power of charms to move me.

San. Nor me, I hope ; and yet I fear those eyes
Will look out sharp to snap up such a prize.

[*Pointing to* JACINTA.

Jac. He's coming to us, madam, to beg pardon; but
sure you'll never grant it him ? 145

Leo. If I do, may Heaven never grant me mine.

Jac. That's brave.

Car. You look, madam, upon me as if you thought I
came to trouble you with my usual importunities; I'll ease
you of that pain, by telling you, my business now is calmly
to assure you, but I assure it you with heaven and hell for
seconds; for may the joys of one fly from me, whilst the
pains of t'other overtake me, if all your charms displayed
e'er shake my resolution ; I'll never see you more.

San. Bon ! 155

Leo. You are a man of that nice honour, sir, I know
you'll keep your word : I expected this assurance from you,
and came this way only to thank you for't.

Jac. Very well !

Car. You did, imperious dame, you did ! How base is
woman's pride ! How wretched are the ingredients it is
formed of ! If you saw cause for just disdain, why did you
not at first repulse me ? Why lead a slave in chains, that
could not grace your triumphs? If I am thus to be contemned,
think on the favours you have done the wretch, and hide
your face for ever. 166

San. Well argued.

Leo. I own you have hit the only fault the world can
charge me with : the favours I have done to you I am
indeed ashamed of; but, since women have their frailties,
you'll allow me mine.

Car. 'Tis well, extremely well, madam. I'm happy, however, you at last speak frankly. I thank you for it; from my soul I thank you : but don't expect me grovelling at your feet again ; don't ! for if I do—   175

Leo. You will be treated as you deserve ; trod upon.

Car. Give me patience !—But I don't want it; I am calm. Madam, farewell; be happy if you can ; by Heavens I wish you so, but never spread your net for me again; for if you do—

Leo. You'll be running into it.

Car. Rather run headlong into fire and flames ; rather be torn with pincers bit from bit ; rather be broiled like martyrs upon gridirons !—But I am wrong ; this sounds like passion, and Heaven can tell I am not angry. Madam, I think we have no farther business together ; your most humble servant.   186

Leo. Farewell t'ye, sir.

Car. [*To* SANCHO.] Come along.—[*Goes to the scene and returns.*] Yet once more before I go (lest you should doubt my resolution), may I starve, perish, rot, be blasted, dead, damned, or any other thing that men or gods can think on, if on any occasion whatever, civil or military, pleasure or business, love or hate, or any other accident of life, I, from this moment, change one word or look with you.   [*Going off,* SANCHO *claps him on the back.*

Leo. Content !—Come away, Jacinta.   196

CARLOS *returns.*

Car. Yet one word, madam, if you please. I have a little thing here belongs to you, a foolish bauble I once was fond of.—[*Twitching her picture from his breast.*] Will you accept a trifle from your servant ?

Leo. Willingly, sir. I have a bauble too I think you have some claim to; you'll wear it for my sake.

> [*Breaks a bracelet from her arm, and gives it him.*

Car. Most thankfully. This too I should restore you, it once was yours.—[*Giving her a table-book.*] By your favour, madam—there is a line or two in it I think you did me once the honour to write with your own fair hand. Here it is.   [*Reads.*

> You love me, Carlos, and would know
>   The secret movements of my heart :
> Whether I give you mine or no,   210
>   With yours, methinks, I'd never, never part.

Thus you have encouraged me, and thus you have deceived me.

San. Very true.

Leo. [*Pulling out a table-book.*] I have some faithful lines too; I think I can produce 'em.   [*Reads.*

> How long soe'er, to sigh in vain,
>   My destiny may prove,
> My fate (*in spite of your disdain*)
> Will let me glory in your chain,   220
>   And give me leave eternally to love.

There, sir, take your poetry again.—[*Throwing it at his feet.*] 'Tis not much the worse for my wearing; 'twill serve again upon a fresh occasion.

Jac. Well done!

Car. I believe I can return the present, madam, with —a pocketful of your prose.—There !

> [*Throwing a handful of letters at her feet.*

U 2

Leo. Jacinta, give me his letters.—There, sir, not to be behindhand with you.

> [*Takes a handful of his letters out of a box and throws 'em in his face.*

Jac. And there! and there! and there, sir!   230

> [JACINTA *throws the rest at him.*

San. 'Cods my life, we want ammunition! but for a shift—there! and there! you saucy slut you!

> [SANCHO *pulls a pack of dirty cards out of his pocket, and throws 'em at her ; then they close ; he pulls off her head-clothes, and she his wig, and then part, running, she to her mistress, he to his master.*

Jac. I think, madam, we have clearly the better on't.

Leo. For a proof, I resolve to keep the field.

Jac. Have a care he don't rally and beat you yet though : pray walk off.

Leo. Fear nothing.

San. How the armies stand and gaze at one another after the battle ! What think you, sir, of showing yourself a great general, by making an honourable retreat ?   240

Car. I scorn it !—O Leonora ! Leonora ! a heart like mine should not be treated thus !

Leo. Carlos! Carlos! I have not deserved this usage !

Car. Barbarous Leonora ! but 'tis useless to reproach you ; she that is capable of what you have done, is formed too cruel ever to repent of it. Go on then, tyrant ; make your bliss complete ; torment me still ; for still, alas ! I love enough to be tormented.

Leo. Ah, Carlos ! little do you know the tender movements of that thing you name ; the heart where love presides, admits no thought against the honour of its ruler.   252

Car.   'Tis not to call that honour into doubt, if, conscious of our own unworthiness, we interpret every frown to our destruction.

Leo.   When jealousy proceeds from such humble apprehensions, it shows itself with more respect than yours has done.

Car.   And where a heart is guiltless, it easily forgives a greater crime.

Leo.   Forgiveness is not now in our debate ; if both have been in fault, 'tis fit that both should suffer for it; our separation will do justice on us.   263

Car.   But since we are ourselves the judges of our crimes, what if we should inflict a gentler punishment ?

Leo.   'Twould but encourage us to sin again.

Car.   And if it should—

Leo.   'Twould give a fresh occasion for the pleasing exercise of mercy.

Car.   Right ; and so we act the part of earth and heaven together, of men and gods, and taste of both their pleasures.

Leo.   The banquet's too inviting to refuse it.

Car.   Then thus let us fall on, and feed upon't for ever.

   [*Carries her off, embracing her, and kissing her*
         hand.

Jac.   Ah, woman ! foolish, foolish woman ! *   274

---

* This line is given to Leonora in former editions, but it evidently belongs to Jacinta. So in the French, as Lucile and Eraste go out, Marinette, Lucile's maid, exclaims, "Oh ! la lâche personne !"

San.   Very foolish indeed.

Jac.   But don't expect I'll follow her example.

San.   You would, Mopsy, if I'd let you.

Jac.   I'd sooner tear my eyes out; ah—that she had had a little of my spirit in her !

San.   I believe I shall find thou hast a great deal of her flesh, my charmer; but 'twon't do; I am all rock, hard rock, very marble.

Jac.   A very pumice stone, you rascal you, if one would try thee ! But to prevent thy humilities, and show thee all submission would be vain; to convince thee thou hast nothing but misery and despair before thee, here—take back thy paltry thimble, and be in my debt, for the shirts I have made thee with it.   288

San.   Nay, if y'are at that sport, mistress, I believe I shall lose nothing by the balance of the presents. There, take thy tobacco-stopper, and stop thy—

Jac.   Here—take thy satin pincushion, with thy curious half hundred of pins in't, thou madest such a vapouring about yesterday. Tell 'em carefully, there is not one wanting.

San.   There's thy ivory-hafted knife again, whet it well; 'tis so blunt 'twill cut nothing but love.

Jac.   And there's thy pretty pocket scissars thou hast honoured me with, they'll cut off a leg or an arm, Heaven bless 'em !   300

San.   Here's the enchanted handkerchief you were pleased to endear with your precious blood, when the violence of your love at dinner t'other day made you cut your fingers.—There.   [*Blows his nose in't and gives it her.*

Jac.   The rascal so provokes me, I won't even keep his

paltry garters from him.　D'you see these?　You pitiful beggarly scoundrel you!—There, take 'em, there.

[*She takes her garters off, and flaps 'em about his face.*

San.　I have but one thing more of thine.—[*Showing his cudgel.*] I own 'tis the top of all thy presents, and might be useful to me; but that thou may'st have nothing to upbraid me with, e'en take it again with the rest of 'em.　　　311

[*Lifting it up to strike her, she leaps about his neck.*

Jac.　Ah, cruel Sancho!—Now beat me, Sancho, do.

San.　Rather, like Indian beggars, beat my precious self.

[*Throws away his stick, and embraces her.*

Rather let infants' blood about the streets,
Rather let all the wine about the cellar,
Rather let—Oh Jacinta—thou hast o'ercome.
How foolish are the great resolves of man!
Resolves, which we neither would keep, nor can.
When those bright eyes in kindness please to shine,
Their goodness I must needs return with mine:
Bless my Jacinta in her Sancho's arms—

Jac.　And I my Sancho with Jacinta's charms.　　[*Exeunt.*

ACT V.

SCENE.—*The Street.*

Enter LOPEZ.

Lop.   As soon as it is night, says my master to me, though
it cost me my life, I'll enter Leonora's lodgings ; therefore
make haste, Lopez, prepare everything necessary, three pair
of pocket-pistols, two wide-mouthed blunderbusses, some
six ells of sword-blade, and a couple of dark lanterns. When
my master said this to me ; Sir, said I to my master, (that
is, I would have said it if I had not been in such a fright I
could say nothing ; however, I'll say it to him now, and shall
probably have a quiet hearing,) look you, sir, by dint of
reason I intend to confound you.   You are resolved, you
say, to get into Leonora's lodgings, though the devil stand
in the doorway?—Yes, Lopez, that's my resolution.—Very
well ; and what do you intend to do when you are there ?
—Why, what an injured man should do; make her sensible of
—Make her sensible of a pudding! don't you see she's a
jade ?   She'll raise the house about your ears, arm the whole
family, set the great dog at you.—Were there legions of
devils to repulse me, in such a cause I could disperse 'em
all.—Why then you have no occasion for help, sir, you may
leave me at home to lay the cloth.—No ; thou art my
ancient friend, my fellow traveller, and to reward thy faith-

ful services, this night thou shalt partake my danger and my glory.—Sir, I have got glory enough under you already, to content any reasonable servant for his life.—Thy modesty makes me willing to double my bounty; this night may bring eternal honour to thee and thy family.—Eternal honour, sir, is too much in conscience for a serving-man; besides, ambition has been many a great soul's undoing.— I doubt thou art afraid, my Lopez; thou shalt be armed with back, with breast, and head-piece. — They will encumber me in my retreat.—Retreat, my hero ! thou never shalt retreat.—Then by my troth, I'll never go, sir.—But here he comes.   33

Enter LORENZO.

Lor. Will it never be night? sure 'tis the longest day the sun e'er travelled.

Lop. Would 'twere as long as those in Greenland, sir, that you might spin out your life t'other half year. I don't like these nightly projects; a man can't see what he does. We shall have some scurvy mistake or other happen; a brace of bullets blunder through your head in the dark perhaps, and spoil all your intrigue.

Lor. Away, you trembling wretch, away !

Lop. Nay, sir, what I say is purely for your safety; for as to myself—uds-death, I no more value the losing a quart of blood, than I do drinking a quart of wine. Besides, my veins are too full; my physician advised me but yesterday to let go twenty ounces for my health. So you see, sir, there's nothing of that in the case.   48

Lor. Then let me hear no other objections; for till I see Leonora I must lie upon the rack. I cannot bear her

resentment, and will pacify her this night, or not live to see
to-morrow.

Lop. Well, sir, since you are so determined, I shan't be
impertinent with any farther advice ; but I think you have
laid your design to—[*He coughs*] (I have got such a cold to-
day !) to get in privately, have you not?

Lor. Yes ; and have taken care to be introduced as far
as her chamber-door, with all secrecy.   58

Lop. (*Coughing.*)   This unlucky cough ! I had rather
have had a fever at another time.   Sir, I should be sorry to
do you more harm than good upon this occasion : if this
cough should come upon me in the midst of the action,
[*Coughs*] and give the alarm to the family, I should not forgive myself as long as I lived.

Lor. I have greater ventures than that to take my chance
for, and can't dispense with your attendance, sir.

Lop. This 'tis to be a good servant, and make one's self
necessary !   68

Enter TOLEDO.

Tol. Sir—I am glad I have found you.   I am a man of
honour, you know, and do always profess losing my life upon
a handsome occasion.   Sir, I come to offer you my service.
I am informed from unquestionable hands, that Don Carlos
is enraged against you to a dangerous degree ; and that old
Alvarez has given positive directions to break the legs and
arms of your servant Lopez.

Lop. Look you there now ; I thought what 'twould come
to ! What do they meddle with me for ? what have I to do
in my master's amours?   The old Don's got out of his
senses, I think ; have I married his daughter ?   79

Lor. Fear nothing, we'll take care o' thee.— Sir, I thank you for the favour of your intelligence, 'tis nothing however but what I expected, and am provided for.

Tol. Sir, I would advise you to provide yourself with good friends ; I desire the honour to keep your back hand myself.

Lop. 'Tis very kind indeed. Pray, sir, have you ne'er a servant with you could hold a racket for me too ?

Tol. I have two friends fit to head two armies ; and yet —a word in your ear, they shan't cost you above a ducat a piece.   90

Lop. Take 'em by all means, sir, you were never offered a better pennyworth in your life.

Tol. Ah, sir !—little Diego—you have heard of him; he'd have been worth a legion upon this occasion. You know, I suppose, how they have served him ?—They have hanged him, but he made a noble execution; they clapped the rack and the priest to him at once, but could neither get a word of confession nor a groan of repentance; he died mighty well truly.

Lor. Such a man is indeed much to be regretted : as for the rest of your escort, captain, I thank you for 'em, but shall not use 'em.   102

Tol. I'm sorry for't, sir, because I think you go in very great danger; I'm much afraid your rival won't give you fair play.

Lop. If he does I'll be hanged ! he's a damned passionate fellow, and cares not what mischief he does.

Lor. I shall give him a very good opportunity ; for I'll have no other guards about me but you, sir. So come along.   110

Lop. Why, sir, this is the sin of presumption; setting Heaven at defiance, making jack-pudding of a blunderbuss.

Lor. No more, but follow.—Hold! turn this way; I see Camillo there. I would avoid him, till I see what part he takes in this odd affair of his sister's. For I would not have the quarrel fixed with him, if it be possible to avoid it.

[*Exit.*

Lop. Sir!—Captain Toledo! one word if you please, sir. I'm mighty sorry to see my master won't accept of your friendly offer. Look ye, I'm not very rich; but as far as the expense of a dollar went, if you'd be so kind to take a little care of me, it should be at your service.   121

Tol. Let me see;—a dollar you say? but suppose I'm wounded?

Lop. Why, you shall be put to no extraordinary charge upon that: I have been prentice to a barber, and will be your surgeon myself.

Tol. 'Tis too cheap in conscience; but my land-estate is so ill paid this war time—

Lop. That a little industry may be commendable; so say no more, that matter's fixed.   [*Exeunt.*   130

Enter CAMILLO.

Cam. How miserable a perplexity have I brought myself into! Yet why do I complain? since, with all the dreadful torture I endure, I can't repent of one wild step I've made. O love! what tempests canst thou raise, what storms canst thou assuage! To all thy cruelties I am resigned. Long years, through seas of torment, I'm content to roll, so thou wilt guide me to the happy port of my Lorenzo's arms, and bless me there with one calm day at last.

Enter ISABELLA.

What news, dear Isabella? Methinks there's something
cheerful in your looks may give a trembling lover hopes.
If you have comfort for me, speak, for I indeed have need
of it.   142

Isab. Were your wants yet still greater than they are, I
bring a plentiful supply.

Cam. O Heavens! is't possible?

Isab. New mysteries are out, and if you can find charms
to wean Lorenzo from your sister, no other obstacle is in
your way to all you wish.

Cam. Kind messenger from Heaven, speak on.

Isab. Know then, that you are daughter to Alvarez.

Cam. How! daughter to Alvarez?   151

Isab. You are: the truth this moment's come to light;
and till this moment he, although your father, was a stranger
to it; nay, did not even know you were a woman. In
short, the great estate, which has occasioned these
uncommon accidents, was left but on condition of a son;
great hopes of one there was, when you destroyed 'em, and
to your parents came a most unwelcome guest. To repair
the disappointment, you were exchanged for that young
Camillo, who few months after died. Your father then was
absent, but your mother, quick in contrivance, bold in
execution, during that infant's sickness, had resolved his death
should not deprive her family of those advantages his life
had given it; so ordered things with such dexterity that
once again there passed a change between you. Of this
(for reasons yet unknown to me) she made a secret to her
husband, and took such wise precautions, that till this hour

'twas so to all the world, except the person from whom I
now have heard it.   169

Cam. This news indeed affords a view of no unhappy
termination.   Yet there are difficulties still may be of fatal
hindrance.

Isab. None, except that one I just now named to you ;
for to remove the rest, know I have already unfolded all
both to Alvarez and Don Felix.

Cam. And how have they received it ?

Isab. To your wishes both.   As for Lorenzo, he is yet a
stranger to all has passed, and the two old fathers desire he
may some moments longer continue so.   They have agreed
to be a little merry with the heats he is in, and engage you
in a family quarrel with him.   181

Cam. I doubt, Isabella, I shall act that part but faintly.

Isab. No matter, you'll make amends for it in the
scene of reconciliation.

Cam. Pray Heaven it be my lot to act it with him.

Isab. Here comes Don Felix to wish you joy.

Enter DON FELIX.

Don Fel. Come near, my daughter, and with extended
arms of great affection let me receive thee.—[*Kisses her.*]
Thou art a dainty wench, good faith thou art, and 'tis a
mettled action thou hast done ; if Lorenzo don't like thee
the better for't, cods my life, he's a pitiful fellow, and I
shan't believe the bonny old man had the getting of
him.

Cam. I'm so encouraged by your forgiveness, sir,
methinks I have some flattering hopes of his.   195

Don Fel. Of his ! egad, and he had best ; I believe he'll

meet with his match if he don't. What dost think of trying his courage a little, by way of a joke or so?

Isab. I was just telling her your design, sir.

Don Fel. Why, I'm in a mighty witty way upon this whimsical occasion. But I see him coming. You must not appear yet; go your way in to the rest of the people there, and I'll inform him what a squabble he has worked himself into here. [*Exeunt* CAMILLO *and* ISABELLA.

Enter LORENZO *and* LOPEZ.

Lop. Pray, sir, don't be so obstinate now, don't affront Heaven at this rate. I had a vision last night about this business on purpose to forewarn you; I dreamt of goose-eggs, a blunt knife, and the snuff of a candle; I'm sure there's mischief towards. 209

Lor. You cowardly rascal, hold your tongue.

Don Fel. Lorenzo, come hither, my boy, I was just going to send for thee. The honour of our ancient family lies in thy hands; there is a combat preparing, thou must fight, my son.

Lop. Look you there now, did not I tell you? Oh, dreams are wondrous things! I never knew that snuff of a candle fail yet.

Lor. Sir, I do not doubt but Carlos seeks my life, I hope he'll do it fairly. 219

Lop. Fairly, do you hear, fairly! give me leave to tell you, sir, folks are not fit to be trusted with lives that don't know how to look better after 'em.—Sir, you gave it him; I hope you'll make him take a little more care on't.

Don Fel. My care shall be to make him do as a man of honour ought to do.

Lop.   What, will you let him fight then? let your own
flesh and blood fight?

Don Fel.   In a good cause, as this is.

Lop.   *O monstrum horrendum!* Now I have that
humanity about me, that if a man but talks to me of fighting,
I shiver at the name on't.   231

Lor.   What you do on this occasion, sir, is worthy of
you : and had I been wanting to you in my due regards
before, this noble action would have stamped that impression, which a grateful son ought to have for so generous a
father.

Lop.   [*Aside.*]   Very generous truly! gives him leave to
be run through the guts, for his posterity to brag on a
hundred years hence.

Lor.   I think, sir, as things now stand, it won't be right
for me to wait for Carlos's call; I'll, if you please, prevent him.

Lop.   Ay, pray sir, do prevent him by all means; 'tis
better made up, as you say, a thousand times.   243

Don Fel.   Hold your tongue, you impertinent jack-a-
napes! I will have him fight, and fight like a fury too; if
he don't he'll be worsted, I can tell him that.—For know,
son, your antagonist is not the person you name, it is an
enemy of twice his force.

Lop.   O dear! O dear! O dear! and will nobody keep
'em asunder?

Lor.   Nobody shall keep us asunder, if once I know
the man I have to deal with.

Don Fel.   Thy man then is—Camillo.

Lor.   Camillo!   254

Don Fel.   'Tis he; he'll suffer nobody to decide this
quarrel but himself.

Lop.   Then there are no seconds, sir?

Don Fel.   None.

Lop.   He's a brave man.

Don Fel.   No, he says nobody's blood shall be spilled on this occasion, but theirs who have a title to it.

Lop.   I believe he'll scarce have a lawsuit upon the claim.

Don Fel.   In short, he accuses thee of a shameful false-hood, in pretending his sister Leonora was thy wife; and has upon it prevailed with his father, as thou hast done with thine, to let the debate be ended by the sword 'twixt him and thee.

Lop.   And pray, sir, with submission, one short question if you please; what may the gentle Leonora say of this business?   269

Don Fel.   She approves of the combat, and marries Carlos.

Lop.   Why, God a-mercy!

Lor.   Is it possible? sure she's a devil, not a woman.

Lop.   Ecod, sir, a devil and a woman both, I think.

Don Fel.   Well, thou sha't have satisfaction of some of 'em.—Here they all come.

Enter Alvarez, Leonora, Carlos, Sancho, *and* Jacinta.

Alv.   Well, Don Felix, have you prepared your son? for mine, he's ready to engage.

Lor.   And so is his.   My wrongs prepare me for a thousand combats.   My hand has hitherto been held, by the regard I've had to everything of kin to Leonora; but since the monstrous part she acts has driven her from my heart, I call for reparation from her family.   282

Alv.   You'll have it, sir; Camillo will attend you instantly.

Lop.   O lack! O lack! will nobody do a little some-thing to prevent bloodshed?—[*To* Leonora.]   Why, madam, have you no pity, no bowels? Stand and see one of your husbands stotered before your face? 'Tis an arrant shame.

Leo. If widowhood be my fate, I must bear it as I can.

Lop. Why, did you ever hear the like?   290

Lor. Talk to her no more. Her monstrous impudence is no otherwise to be replied to than by a dagger in her brother's heart.

Leo. Yonder he's coming to receive it. But have a care, brave sir, he does not place it in another's.

Lor. It is not in his power. He has a rotten cause upon his sword, I'm sorry he's engaged in't; but since he is, he must take his fate.—[*To* CARLOS.] For you, my bravo, expect me in your turn.

Car. You'll find Camillo, sir, will set your hand out.

Lor. A beardless boy! You might have matched me better, sir; but prudence is a virtue.   302

Don Fel. Nay, son, I would not have thee despise thy adversary neither; thou'lt find Camillo will put thee hardly to't.

Lor. I wish we were come to the trial. Why does he not appear?

Jac. Now do I hate to hear people brag thus. Sir, with my lady's leave, I'll hold a ducat he disarms you. [*They laugh.*

Lor. Why, what!—I think I'm sported with. Take heed, I warn you all; I am not to be trifled with.   311

Enter CAMILLO *and* ISABELLA.

Leo. You shan't, sir; here's one will be in earnest with you.

Lor. He's welcome: though I had rather have drawn my sword against another.—I'm sorry, Camillo, we should meet on such bad terms as these ; yet more sorry your sister should be the wicked cause on't : but since nothing will serve her but the blood either of a husband or brother, she shall be glutted with't.   Draw !

Lop.   Ah Lard ! ah Lard ! ah Lard !

Lor.   And yet, before I take this instrument of death into my fatal hand, hear me, Camillo ; hear, Alvarez; all !   I imprecate the utmost powers of Heaven, to shower upon my head the deadliest of its wrath ; I ask that all hell's torments may unite, to round my soul with one eternal anguish, if wicked Leonora ben't my wife.   325

All.   O Lord ! O Lord ! O Lord !

Leo.   Why then, may all those curses pass him by, and wrap me in their everlasting pains, if ever once I had a fleeting thought of making him my husband.

Lop.   O Lord ! O Lord ! O Lord !

Leo.   Nay more : to strike him dumb at once, and show what men with honest looks can practise, know, he's married to another.

Alv. and Fel.   How !

Leo.   The truth of this is known to some are here.

Jac.   Nay, 'tis certainly so.   336

Isab.   'Tis to a friend of mine.

Car.   I know the person.

Lor.   'Tis false ! and thou art a villain for thy testimony.

Cam.   Then let me speak ; what they aver is true, and I myself was, in disguise, a witness of its doing.

Lor.   Death and confusion ! he a villain too !—Have at thy heart.   [*He draws.*

Lop.   Ah !—I can't bear the sight on't.

Cam.   Put up that furious thing, there's no business for't.

X 2

Lor.   There's business for a dagger, stripling; 'tis that
should be thy recompense.   347

Cam.   Why then, to show thee naked to the world, and
close thy mouth for ever—I am myself thy wife—

Lor.   What does the dog mean?

Cam.   To fall upon the earth and sue for mercy.

> [*Kneels and lets her periwig fall off.*

Lor.   A woman!—

Lop.   Ecod, and a pretty one too; you wags you!

Lor.   I'm all amazement!—Rise, Camillo, (if I am still
to call you by that name) and let me hear the wonders you
have for me.   356

Isab.   That part her modesty will ask from me. I'm to
inform you then, that this disguise hides other mysteries
besides a woman; a large and fair estate was covered by't,
which with the lady now will be resigned you.   'Tis true, in
justice it was yours before; but 'tis the god of love has done
you right.   To him you owe this strange discovery;
through him you are to know, the true Camillo's dead, and
that this fair adventurer is daughter to Alvarez.

Lor.   Incredible!   But go on; let me hear more.

Don Fel.   She'll tell thee the rest herself, the next dark
night she meets thee in the garden.   367

Lor.   Ha!—Was it Camillo then, that I—

Isab.   It was Camillo who there made you happy; and
who has virtue, beauty, wit, and love—enough to make you
so while life shall last you.

Lor.   The proof she gives me of her love deserves a large
acknowledgment indeed.   Forgive me, therefore, Leonora,
if what I owe this goodness and these charms, I with my
utmost care, my life, my soul, endeavour to repay.

Cam. Is it then possible you can forgive me ?   376

Lor. Indeed I can ; few crimes have such a claim to
mercy.   But join with me then, dear Camillo, (for still I
know you by no other name) join with me to obtain your
father's pardon.   Yours, Leonora, too, I must implore ; and
yours, my friend, for now we may be such.—[*To* Carlos.]
Of all I ask forgiveness.   And since there is so fair a cause
of all my wild mistakes, I hope I by her interest shall obtain
it.

Alv. You have a claim to mine, Lorenzo, I wish I had
so strong a one to yours ; but if by future services, (though
I lay down my life amongst 'em) I may blot out of your
remembrance a fault (I cannot name), I then shall leave the
world in peace.   389

Lor. In peace then, sir, enjoy it ; for from this very hour,
whate'er is past with me is gone for ever.   Your daughter is
too fair a mediatrix to be refused his pardon, to whom she
owes the charms she pleads with for it.

From this good day, then, let all discord cease ;
Let those to come be harmony and peace ;
Henceforth let all our diff'rent int'rests join,
Let fathers, lovers, friends, let all combine,
To make each other's days as bless'd as she will mine.

[*Exeunt omnes.*

EPILOGUE.

WRITTEN BY MR. MOTTEUX.*

I'M thinking, now good husbands are so few,
To get one like my friend, what I must do.†
Camillo ventur'd hard ; yet at the worst,
She stole love's honeymoon, and tried her lover first.
Many poor damsels, if they dar'd to tell,
Have done as much, but have not 'scap'd so well.
'Tis well the scene's in Spain ; thus in the dark,
I should be loath to trust a London spark.
Some accident might, for a private reason,
Silence a female, all this acting season.   10
Hard fate of woman ! Any one would vex,
To think what odds you men have of our sex.
Restraint and customs share our inclination,
You men can try, and run o'er half the nation.

---

* Peter Antony Motteux was a Frenchman who settled in England
after the revocation of the Edict of Nantes, and divided his time
between the tea trade and literature. His translation of *Don Quixote*
is well known. He continued Urquhart's translation of *Rabelais*, and
produced various dramatic pieces, songs, epilogues, &c. He died in
1718, aged fifty-eight.

† This epilogue was spoken by Mrs. Porter, in the character o
Isabella.

We dare not, even to avoid reproach,
When y'are at White's, peep out of hackney coach ;
Nor with a friend at night, our fame regarding,
With glass drawn up, drive about Covent-garden.
If poor town-ladies steal in here, you rail,
Though like chaste nuns, their modest looks they veil ;   20
With this decorum they can hardly gain
To be thought virtuous, even in Drury-lane.
Though this you'll not allow, yet sure you may
A plot to snap you, in an honest way.
In love-affairs, one scarce would spare a brother :
All cheat ; and married folks may keep a pother,
But look as if they cheated one another.
You may pretend, our sex dissembles most,
But of your truth none have much cause to boast :
You promise bravely ; but for all your storming,   30
We find y'are not so valiant at performing.
    Then sure Camillo's conduct you'll approve :
Would you not do as much for one you love ?
Wedlock's but a blind bargain at the best,
You venture more, sometimes, to be not half so blest.
All, soon or late, that dang'rous venture make,
And some of you may make a worse mistake.

A JOURNEY TO LONDON.

This comedy, being left unfinished by the author at his
death, was revised and completed by Colley Cibber, who
brought it upon the stage under the title of *The Provok'd
Husband; or, A Journey to London*. The play, as finished
by Cibber, was published, in 8vo, on the 31st of January,
1728,* and from a note, at the foot of the *Dramatis
Personæ*, we learn that the fragment written by Vanbrugh
was published separately on the same day. In the preface
to *The Provok'd Husband*, Cibber writes : " I have, for the
Satisfaction of the Curious, printed the whole of what he
wrote, separately, under the Single Title he gave it, of
A Journey to London, without presuming to alter a Line."

The original edition of Vanbrugh's unfinished play is in
8vo, and has the following title-page: "*A Journey to
London. Being Part of a Comedy Written by the Late Sir
John Vanbrugh, Knt. And Printed after His own Copy :
Which (since his Decease) has been made an Intire Play, By
Mr. Cibber, And call'd The Provok'd Husband, &c. London :
Printed for John Watts, at the Printing Office in Wild-Court,
near Lincoln's-Inn-Fields*, 1728."

On the 10th of January, 1728, *The Provok'd Husband*
was produced at Drury Lane. The part of Sir Francis
Wronghead, as Cibber had re-christened Sir Francis

---

* The *Daily Post*.

Headpiece, was played by Cibber himself; that of Lord Townly (Vanbrugh's Lord Loverule), by Wilks; while Mrs. Oldfield "out-did her usual excellence" in the character of Lady Townly (Vanbrugh's Lady Arabella). The piece ran for twenty-eight nights, and continued a favourite stock-play throughout the whole of the eighteenth century. It is, indeed, an excellent *eighteenth-century* comedy, and as unlike as possible to what it would have been, had Vanbrugh himself completed it. The reformation of the stage was going on briskly, and Cibber's production was eminently adapted to the new taste of the times. He has watered down the scenes which he has taken from Vanbrugh, and added a plentiful supply of the sententious and sentimental morality which reformed audiences were beginning to delight in.

It is greatly to be regretted that Vanbrugh did not finish the play. The scenes, as they stand, show him at his best: in wit and humour, invention, observation, and satire, they are scarcely surpassed by anything that he has written. Completed by him, *A Journey to London* would undoubtedly have proved a masterpiece, equal, perhaps, to the very best of his earlier plays. Of his purpose in the catastrophe, we know only what Cibber tells us—that Lady Arabella, after running her course of folly and dissipation to the last extremity, was to be turned fairly out of doors by her husband. Cibber, more tender-hearted, preserves the lady's chastity, and allows her to reform.

In Hunter's *Chorus Vatum Anglicanorum,** I find an idle story in reference to this play, as follows. " His

---

* British Museum. Add. MSS. 24488. Vol. vi. p. 194.

[Vanbrugh's] wife was a daughter of a Yorkshire knight, Sir Thomas Yarborough of Snaith, and I remember being told by my old friend Mr. John Milnes, that having quarrelled with the Yarboroughs, he ridiculed them in Sir Francis Wronghead and his family, in those scenes of *The Provok'd Husband* which answer to the title, *The Journey to London.* Sir Thomas indeed was twice returned member for the borough of Pontefract, viz: in 1685 and 1688, and the Servant in the play is made to speak of the Humber as near the residence of the Wronghead family."

The story, on the face of it, is not entitled to credit. To begin with, Sir Thomas Yarburgh, the member of Parliament, was not Henrietta Vanbrugh's father, but her grandfather. He was, without doubt, a gentleman of consideration in his county, and his wife, who, previously to her marriage, had been maid of honour to the Duchess of York, was daughter to a distinguished Royalist, Colonel Thomas Blagge (or Blague), and sister to Lady Godolphin. Their son, James Yarburgh, the father of Lady Vanbrugh, had been at court in his youth, and served in the army as lieutenant-colonel and aide-de-camp to the Duke of Marlborough. In fact, all that we know of the Yarburghs renders utterly inadmissible the assumption that Vanbrugh designed to ridicule them as a parcel of country boors. The allusion to the Humber, moreover, and an allusion to York, which would have been even more to the purpose, are to be found only in Cibber.

I have not thought it necessary to reprint here *The Provok'd Husband.* All that is in it of lasting value is contained in the following fragment, which is wholly the work of Vanbrugh.

DRAMATIS PERSONÆ.

MEN.

Sir *Francis Headpiece*, a Country Gentleman.
Lord *Loverule*.
Sir *Charles*.
Uncle *Richard*, Uncle to Sir *Francis*.
Squire *Humphry*, Son to Sir *Francis*.
Colonel *Courtly*.
Captain *Toupee*.
John Moody, ⎫
George, ⎬ Servants to Sir *Francis*.
Tom,   ⎭
James, Servant to Uncle *Richard*.
Moneybag, Steward to Lord *Loverule*.
Shortyard, a Mercer.

WOMEN.

Lady *Headpiece*, Wife to Sir *Francis*.
Miss *Betty*, her Daughter.
Lady *Arabella*, Wife to Lord *Loverule*.
Clarinda, a young unmarried Lady.
Mrs. *Motherly*, one that lets Lodgings.
Martilla, her Niece.
Mrs. *Handy*, Maid to Lady *Headpiece*.
Doll Tripe, the Cook.
Deborah, Maid to Mrs. *Motherly*.
Trusty, Lady *Arabella's* Woman.

[SCENE.—London.]

A
JOURNEY TO LONDON.

A COMEDY.

[UNFINISHED.]

ACT I.

SCENE I.—*A Room in* UNCLE RICHARD'S *House*.

Enter UNCLE RICHARD.

Unc. Rich. What prudent cares does this deep foreseeing nation take for the support of its worshipful families ! In order to which, and that they may not fail to be always significant and useful in their country, it is a settled foundation-point that every child that is born shall be a beggar, except one ; and that he—shall be a fool. My grandfather was bred a fool, as the country report ; my father was a fool, as my mother used to say ; my brother was a fool, to my own knowledge, though a great justice of the peace ; and he has left a son that will make his son a fool, or I am mistaken. The lad is now fourteen years old, and but just out of his Psalter. As to his honoured father, my much-esteemed nephew—here I have him.—[*Shewing a letter.*] In this profound epistle (which I have just now received) there is the top and bottom of him. Forty years and two is the age of him ; in which it is computed by his butler, his own person has drank two-and-thirty tun of ale. The rest of his time has been employed in persecuting all the poor four-legged creatures round, that would but run away fast enough from him, to give him the high-mettled pleasure of running after them.   In this noble employ he has broke his right arm, his left leg, and both his collar-bones.   Once he broke his neck, but that did him no harm ; a nimble hedge-leaper, a brother of the stirrup, that was by, whipped off of his horse and mended it.   His estate being left him with two jointures and three weighty mortgages upon it, he, to make all easy, and pay his brother's and sister's portions, married a profuse young housewife for love, with never a penny of money.   Having done all this, like his brave ancestors, for the support of the family, he now finds children and interest-money make such a bawling about his ears, that he has taken the friendly advice of his neighbour, the good lord Courtlove, to run his estate two thousand pounds more in debt, that he may retrieve his affairs by being a parliament-man, and bringing his wife to London to play off a hundred pounds at dice with ladies of quality before breakfast.   But let me read this wiseacre's letter once over again.—[*Reads.*]   *Most honoured uncle, I do not doubt but you have much rejoiced at my success in my election.   It has cost me some money, I own ; but what of all that ! I am a parliament-man, and that will set all to rights.   I have lived in the country all my days, 'tis true ; but what then ! I have made speeches at the sessions,- and in the vestry too, and can elsewhere, perhaps, as well as some others that do ; and I have a noble friend hard by, who has let me into some small knowledge of what's what at Westminster.   And so, that I*

may be always at hand to serve my country, I have consulted
with my wife about taking a house at London, and bringing
her and my family up to town ; which, her opinion is, will be
the rightest thing in the world.—My wife's opinion about
bringing her to London !—I'll read no more of thee—beast !
　　　　　[*Strikes the letter down with his stick.*

　　　　　Enter James *hastily.*

James.　Sir, sir! do you hear the news ?　They are all
a-coming.　　　　　　　　　　　　　　　　　　　53
　Unc. Rich.　Ay, sirrah, I hear it, with a pox to it !
　James.　Sir, here's John Moody arrived already ; he's
stumping about the streets in his dirty boots, and asking
every man he meets, if they can tell where he may have a
good lodging for a parliament-man, till he can hire such a
house as becomes him.　He tells them his lady and all
the family are coming too ;　and that they are so nobly
attended, they care not a fig for anybody.　Sir, they have
added two cart-horses to the four old geldings, because
my lady will have it said she came to town in her coach-and-
six ; and—ha ! ha !—heavy George the ploughman rides
postillion !　　　　　　　　　　　　　　　　　　65
　Unc. Rich.　Very well ; the journey begins as it should
do.—James !
　James.　Sir !
　Unc. Rich.　Dost know whether they bring all the children
with them ?
　James.　Only squire Humphry and Miss Betty, sir ; the
other six are put to board at half-a-crown a week a head,
with Joan Growse at Smoke-dung-hill farm.
　Unc. Rich.　The Lord have mercy upon all good folks !

what work will these people make ! Dost know when they'll
be here?   76

James. John says, sir, they'd have been here last night,
but that the old wheezy-belly horse tired, and the two fore-
wheels came crash down at once in Waggonrut-lane. Sir,
they were cruelly loaden, as I understand ; my lady herself,
he says, laid on four mail-trunks, besides the great deal-box,
which fat Tom sat upon behind.

Unc. Rich. So!

James. Then within the coach there was sir Francis, my
lady, the great fat lapdog, squire Humphry, Miss Betty, my
lady's maid, Mrs. Handy, and Doll Tripe the cook; but she
puked with sitting backward, so they mounted her into the
coach-box.   88

Unc. Rich. Very well.

James. Then, sir, for fear of a famine before they should
get to the baiting-place, there was such baskets of plumcake, Dutch-gingerbread, Cheshire-cheese, Naples biscuits,
maccaroons, neat's-tongues, and cold boiled beef;—and in
case of sickness, such bottles of usquebaugh, black-cherry
brandy, cinnamon-water, sack, tent, and strong beer, as made
the old coach crack again.

Unc. Rich. Well said !

James. And for defence of this good cheer and my lady's
little pearl necklace, there was the family basket-hilt sword,
the great Turkish cimeter, the old blunderbuss, a good
bag of bullets, and a great horn of gunpowder.   101

Unc. Rich. Admirable !

James. Then for bandboxes, they were so bepiled up to
sir Francis's nose, that he could only peep out at a chance
hole with one eye, as if he were viewing the country through

a perspective-glass.—But, sir, if you please, I'll go look after
John Moody a little, for fear of accidents ; for he never was
in London before, you know, but one week, and then he was
kidnapped into a house of ill repute, where he exchanged all
his money and clothes for a——um ! So I'll go look after
him, sir.   [*Exit.* 111

Unc. Rich. Nay, I don't doubt but this wise expedition
will be attended with more adventures than one. This
noble head and supporter of his family will, as an honest
country gentleman, get credit enough amongst the tradesmen,
to run so far in debt in one session, as will make him just
fit for a jail when he's dropped at the next election. He
will make speeches in the house, to show the government of
what importance he can be to them, by which they will see
he can be of no importance at all ; and he will find, in time,
that he stands valued at (if he votes right) being sometimes
—invited to dinner. Then his wife (who has ten times
more of a jade about her than she yet knows of) will so
improve in this rich soil, she will, in one month, learn every
vice the finest lady in the town can teach her. She will be
extremely courteous to the fops who make love to her in
jest, and she will be extremely grateful to those who do it in
earnest. She will visit all ladies that will let her into their
houses, and she will run in debt to all the shop-keepers that
will let her into their books. In short, before her husband
has got five pound by a speech at Westminster, she will have
lost five hundred at cards and dice in the parish of St.
James's.—Wife and family to London with a pox ! [*Exit.*

SCENE II.—*A Room in* Mrs. Motherly's *House.*

Enter James, *and* John Moody.

James. Dear John Moody, I am so glad to see you in London once more.

John. And I you, dear Mr. James. Give me a kiss.— Why, that's friendly.

James. I wish they had been so, John, that you met with when you were here before.

John. Ah—murrain upon all rogues and whores! I say; but I am grown so cunning now, the de'il himself can't handle me. I have made a notable bargain for these lodgings here; we are to pay but five pounds a-week, and have all the house to ourselves.   11

James. Where are the people that belong to it to be then?

John. Oh! there's only the gentlewoman, her two maids, and a cousin, a very pretty, civil young woman truly, and the maids are the merriest grigs—

James. Have a care, John.

John. Oh, fear nothing; we did so play together last night.

James. Hush! here comes my master.   20

Enter Uncle Richard.

Unc. Rich. What! John has taken these lodgings, has he?

James. Yes, sir, he has taken 'em.   [*Exit.*

Unc. Rich.   O John! how dost do, honest John?   I am glad to see thee with all my heart.

John.   I humbly thank your worship.   I'm staut still, and a faithful awd servant to th' family.   Heaven prosper aw that belong to't.

Unc. Rich.   What, they are all upon the road?

John.   As mony as the awd coach would hauld, sir: the Lord send 'em well to tawn.   31

Unc. Rich.   And well out on't again, John, ha?

John.   Ah, sir! you are a wise man, so am I: home's home, I say   I wish we get any good here.   I'se sure we ha' got little upo' the road.   Some mischief or other aw the day long.   Slap! goes one thing, crack! goes another; my lady cries out for driving fast; the awd cattle are for going slow; Roger whips, they stand still and kick; nothing but a sort of a contradiction aw the journey long.   My lady would gladly have been here last night, sir, though there were no lodgings got; but her ladyship said, she did naw care for that, she'd lie in the inn where the horses stood, as long as it was in London.   43

Unc. Rich.   These ladies, these ladies, John!—

John.   Ah, sir, I have seen a little of 'em, though not so much as my betters.   Your worship is naw married yet?

Unc. Rich.   No, John, no; I am an old bachelor still.

John.   Heavens bless you, and preserve you, sir.

Unc. Rich.   I think you have lost your good woman, John?

John.   No, sir, that have I not; Bridget sticks to me still.   Sir, she was for coming to London too, but, no, says I, there may be mischief enough done without you.

Unc. Rich.   Why, that was bravely spoken, John, and like a man.   54

John. Sir, were my measter but hafe the mon that I am, gadswookers !—though he'll speak stautly too sometimes, but then he canno' hawd it ; no, he canno' hawd it.

Enter DEBORAH.

Deb. Mr. Moody, Mr. Moody, here's the coach come.
John. Already ! no sure.
Deb. Yes, yes, it's at the door, they are getting out ; my mistress is run to receive 'em.
John. And so will I, as in duty bound.

[*Exit with* DEBORAH.

Unc. Rich. And I will stay here, not being in duty bound to do the honours of this house.   64

Enter Sir FRANCIS HEADPIECE, Lady HEADPIECE, Squire HUMPHRY, Miss BETTY, Mrs. HANDY, JOHN MOODY, *and* Mrs. MOTHERLY.

Lady Head. Do you hear, Moody, let all the things be first laid down here, and then carried where they'll be used.
John. They shall, an't please your ladyship.
Lady Head. What, my Uncle Richard here to receive us ! This is kind indeed : sir, I am extremely glad to see you.
Unc. Rich. [*Salutes her.*] Niece, your servant.—[*Aside.*] I am extremely sorry to see you, in the worst place I know in the world for a good woman to grow better in.—[*Aloud.*] Nephew, I am your servant too ; but I don't know how to bid you welcome.   75

Sir Fran. I am sorry for that, sir.
Unc. Rich. Nay, 'tis for your own sake : I'm not concerned.

Sir Fran. I hope, uncle, I shall give you such weighty reasons for what I have done, as shall convince you I am a prudent man.

Unc. Rich. That wilt thou never convince me of, whilst thou shalt live. [*Aside.*

Sir Fran. Here, Humphry, come up to your uncle.— Sir, this is your godson. 85

Squire Hum. Honoured uncle and godfather, I crave leave to ask your blessing. [*Kneels.*

Unc. Rich. [*Aside.*] Thou art a numskull I see already.— [*Puts his hand on his head.*] There, thou hast it. And if it will do thee any good, may it be, to make thee, at least, as wise a man as thy father.

Lady Head. Miss Betty, don't you see your uncle?

Unc. Rich. And for thee, my dear, mayst thou be, at least, as good a woman as thy mother.

Miss Bet. I wish I may ever be so handsome, sir. 95

Unc. Rich. Ha! Miss Pert! now that's a thought that seems to have been hatched in the girl on this side Highgate. [*Aside.*

Sir Fran. Her tongue is a little nimble, sir.

Lady Head. That's only from her country education, sir Francis, she has been kept there too long; I therefore brought her to London, sir, to learn more reserve and modesty.

Unc. Rich. Oh, the best place in the world for it! Every woman she meets will teach her something of it. There's the good gentlewoman of the house looks like a knowing person, even she perhaps will be so good to read her a lesson, now and then, upon that subject.—[*Aside.*] An arrant bawd, or I have no skill in physiognomy! 107

Mrs. Moth. Alas, sir, miss won't stand long in need of

my poor instructions; if she does, they'll be always at her service.

Lady Head.   Very obliging indeed, Mrs. Motherly.

Sir Fran.   Very kind and civil truly; I believe we are got into a mighty good house here.

Unc. Rich.   [*Aside.*] For good business very probable.— [*Aloud.*] Well, niece, your servant for to-night; you have a great deal of affairs upon your hands here, so I won't hinder you.

Lady Head.   I believe, sir, I shan't have much less every day, while I stay in this town, of one sort or other.   119

Unc. Rich.   Why, 'tis a town of much action indeed.

Miss Bet.   And my mother did not come to it to be idle, sir.

Unc. Rich.   Nor you neither, I dare say, young mistress.

Miss Bet.   I hope not, sir.

Unc. Rich.   Um! miss Mettle.—[*Going,* Sir FRANCIS *following him.*] Where are you going, nephew?

Sir Fran.   Only to attend you to the door, sir.

Unc. Rich.   Phu! no ceremony with me; you'll find I shall use none with you or your family.   128

Sir Fran.   I must do as you command me, sir.

[*Exit* UNCLE RICHARD.

Miss Bet.   This uncle Richard, papa, seems but a crusty sort of an old fellow.

Sir Fran.   He is a little odd, child; but you must be very civil to him, for he has a great deal of money, and nobody knows who he may give it to.

Lady Head.   Phu, a fig for his money! you have so many projects of late about money, since you are a parliament-man, we must make ourselves slaves to his testy humours, seven years perhaps, in hopes to be his heirs; and then he'll be

just old enough to marry his maid.—But pray let us take care
of our things here : are they all brought in yet? 140

Mrs. Hand. Almost, my lady ; there are only some of
the bandboxes behind, and a few odd things.

Lady Head. Let 'em be fetched in presently.

Mrs. Hand. They are here.—Come, bring the things in.

Enter Servant.

Is there all yet ?

Serv. All but the great basket of apples, and the goose-
pie.

Enter DOLL TRIPE.

Doll. Ah, my lady ! we're aw undone ; the goose-pie's
gwon.

All. Gone? 150

Sir Fran. The goose-pie gone ? how ?

Doll. Why, sir, I had got it fast under my arm to bring
it in, but being almost dark, up comes two of these thin
starved London rogues, one gives me a great kick o' the
—here ; [*Laying her hand upon her backside.*] while t'other
hungry varlet twitched the dear pie out of my hands, and
away they run dawn street like two greyhounds. I cried
out fire ! but heavy George and fat Tom are after 'em with
a vengeance ; they'll sauce their jackets for 'em, I'll warrant
'em. 160

Enter GEORGE *with a bloody face, and* TOM.

So, have you catched 'em ?

George. Catched 'em ! the gallows catch 'em for me ! I
had naw run hafe the length of our bearn, before somewhat
fetched me such a wherry across the shins, that dawn came

I flop o' my feace all along in the channel, and thought I should ne'er ha' gotten up again ; but Tom has skawer'd after them, and cried murder as he'd been stuck.

Tom. Yes, and straight upo' that, swap comes somewhat across my forehead, with such a force, that dawn came I like an ox.   170

Squire Hum. So the poor pie's quite gone then !

Tom. Gone, young measter ? yeaten I believe by this time. These I suppose are what they call sharpers in this country.

Squire Hum. It was a rare good pie.

Doll. As e'er these hands put pepper to.

Lady Head. Pray, Mrs. Motherly, do they make a practice of these things often here ?

Mrs. Moth. Madam, they'll twitch a rump of beef out of a boiling copper ; and for a silver tankard, they make no more conscience of that, than if it were a Tunbridge sugar-box.   182

Sir Fran. I wish the coach and horses, George, were safe got to the inn. Do you and Roger take special care that nobody runs away with them, as you go thither.

George. I believe, sir, aur cattle woant yeasily be run away with to-night ; but weest take best care we con of them, poor sauls !   [*Exit.*

Sir Fran. Do so, pray now.

Squire Hum. Feather, I had rather they had run away with heavy George than the goose-pie, a slice of it before supper to-night would have bcen pure.   192

Lady Head. This boy is always thinking of his belly.

Sir Fran. But, my dear, you may allow him to be a little hungry after a journey.

Lady Head. Pray, good sir Francis, he has been constantly eating in the coach, and out of the coach, above seven hours this day. I wish my poor girl could eat a quarter as much.

Miss Bet. Mamma, I could eat a good deal more than I do, but then I should grow fat mayhap, like him, and spoil my shape.

Lady Head. Mrs. Motherly, will you be so kind to tell them where they shall carry the things?

Mrs. Moth. Madam, I'll do the best I can: I doubt our closets will scarce hold 'em all, but we have garrets and cellars, which, with the help of hiring a store-room, I hope may do.—[*To* TOM.] Sir, will you be so good to help my maids a little in carrying away the things?

Tom. With all my heart, forsooth, if I con but see my way; but these whoresons have awmost knocked my eyen aut. [*They carry off the things.*

Mrs. Moth. Will your ladyship please to refresh yourself with a dish of tea, after your fatigue? I think I have pretty good. 215

Lady Head. If you please, Mrs. Motherly.

[*Exit* Mrs. MOTHERLY.

Squire Hum. Would not a good tankard of strong beer, nutmeg, and sugar, do better, feather, with a toast and some cheese?

Sir Fran. I think it would, son.—Here, John Moody, get us a tankard of good hearty stuff presently.

John. Sir, here's Norfolk-nog * to be had at next door.

---

* A strong ale.

Squire Hum. That's best of all, feather; but make haste
with it, John.   [*Exit* JOHN MOODY.

Lady Head. Well, I wonder, sir Francis, you will
encourage that lad to swill his guts thus with such beastly,
lubberly liquor: if it were burgundy, or champagne, something might be said for't; they'd perhaps give him some wit
and spirit; but such heavy, muddy stuff as this will make
him quite stupid.   230

Sir Fran. Why, you know, my dear, I have drank good
ale and strong beer these thirty years, and, by your permission,
I don't know that I want wit.

Miss Bet. But you might have had more, papa, if you'd
have been governed by my mother.

Re-enter JOHN MOODY, *with a tankard, &c.*

Sir Fran. Daughter, he that is governed by his wife, has
no wit at all.

Miss Bet. Then I hope I shall marry a fool, father, for
I shall love to govern dearly.

Sir Fran. Here, Humphry, here's to thee.—[*Drinks.*]
You are too pert, child, it don't do well in a young woman.

Lady Head. Pray, Sir Francis, don't snub her, she has
a fine growing spirit, and if you check her so, you'll make
her as dull as her brother there.   244

Squire Hum. Indeed, mother, I think my sister is too
forward.   [*After drinking a long draught.*

Miss Bet. You? you think I'm too forward? what have
you to do to think, brother Heavy? you are too fat to
think of anything but your belly.

Lady Head. Well said, miss; he's none of your master,
though he's your elder brother.

Re-enter George.

George. Sir, I have no good opinion of this tawn, it's made up of mischief, I think.

Sir Fran. Why, what's the matter now?   254

George. I'se tell your worship; before we were gotten to the street end, a great luggerheaded cart, with wheels as thick as a good brick wall, laid hawld of the coach, and has pood it aw to bits. An this be London, wa'd we were all weel i' th' country again.

Miss Bet. What have you to do, sir, to wish us all in the country again, lubber? I hope we shan't go in the country again these seven years, mama, let twenty coaches be pulled to pieces.

Sir Fran. Hold your tongue, Betty.—[*To* George.] Was Roger in no fault in this?   265

George. No, sir, nor I neither. Are not you ashamed, says Roger to the carter, to do such an unkind thing to strangers? No, says he, you bumpkin.—Sir, he did the thing on very purpose, and so the folks said that stood by; but they said your worship need na be concerned, for you might have a lawsuit with him when you pleased, that would not cost you above a hundred pounds, and mayhap you might get the better of him.

Sir Fran. I'll try what I can do with him, egad, I'll make such—   275

Squire Hum. Feather, have him before the parliament.

Sir Fran. And so I will: I'll make him know who I am. Where does he live?

George. I believe in London, sir.

Sir Fran. What's the villain's name?

George. I think I heard somebody call him Dick.

Sir Fran. Where did he go ?

George. Sir, he went home.

Sir Fran. Where's that ?

George. By my troth I do naw knaw. I heard him say he had nothing more to do with us to-night, and so he'd go home and smoke a pipe.   287

Lady Head. Come, sir Francis, don't put yourself in a heat, accidents will happen to people in travelling abroad to see the world. Eat your supper heartily, go to bed, sleep quietly, and to-morrow see if you can buy a handsome second-hand coach for present use, bespeak a new one, and then all's easy.   [*Exeunt.*

SCENE III.—*Another Room in the same.*

Enter Colonel COURTLY.

Col. Who's that, Deborah ?

Enter DEBORAH.

Deb. At your service, sir.

Col. What, do you keep open house here ? I found the street door as wide as it could gape.

Deb. Sir, we are all in a bustle, we have lodgers come in to-night, the house full.

Col. Where's your mistress ?   7

Deb. Prodigious busy with her company ; but I'll tell Mrs. Martilla you are here, I believe she'll come to you.

Col. That will do as well.—[*Exit* Deborah.]   Poor
Martilla ! she's a very good girl, and I have loved her a great
while, I think ; six months it is, since, like a merciless
highwayman, I made her deliver all she had about her ; she
begged hard, poor thing, I'd leave her one small bauble.
Had I let her keep it, I believe she had still kept me.
Could women but refuse their ravenous lovers that one dear
destructive moment, how long might they reign over them !
—But for a bane to both their joys and ours, when they have
indulged us with such favours as make us adore them, they
are not able to refuse us that one which puts an end to our
devotion.   21

Enter Martilla.

Martilla, how dost thou do, my child ?
    Mar. As well as a losing gamester can.
    Col. Why, what have you lost ?
    Mar. I have lost you.
    Col. How came you to lose me ?
    Mar. By losing myself.
    Col. We can be friends still.
    Mar. Dull ones.
    Col. Useful ones perhaps.   Shall I help thee to a good
husband ?   31
    Mar. Not if I were rich enough to live without one.
    Col. I'm sorry I am not rich enough to make thee so ;
but we won't talk of melancholy things.   Who are these
folks your aunt has got in her house ?
    Mar. One sir Francis Headpiece and his lady, with a
son and daughter.
    Col. Headpiece ! cotso, I know 'em a little.   I met

with 'em at a race in the country two years since; a sort of
blockhead, is not he?   40

Mar. So they say.

Col. His wife seemed a mettled gentlewoman, if she had
had but a fair field to range in.

Mar. That she won't want now, for they stay in town
the whole winter.

Col. Oh, that will do to show all her parts in.

Enter Mrs. Motherly.

How do you do, my old acquaintance?

Mrs. Moth. At your service you know always, colonel.

Col. I hear you have got good company in the house.

Mrs. Moth. I hope it will prove so; he's a parliament-
man only, colonel, you know there's some danger in that.

Col. Oh, never fear, he'll pay his landlady, though he
don't pay his butcher.   53

Mrs. Moth. His wife's a clever woman.

Col. So she is.

Mrs. Moth. How do you know?

Col. I have seen her in the country, and I begin to
think I'll visit her in town.

Mrs. Moth. You begin to look like a rogue.

Col. What, your wicked fancies are stirring already?

Mrs. Moth. Yours are, or I'm mistaken. But—I'll have
none of your pranks played upon her.

Col. Why, she's no girl, she can defend herself.   63

Mrs. Moth. But what if she won't?

Col. Why, then, she can blame neither you nor me.

Mrs. Moth. You'll never be quiet till you get my windows
broke; but I must go and attend my lodgers, so good night.

Col. Do so, and give my service to my lady, and tell her, if she'll give me leave, I'll do myself the honour to-morrow to come and tender my services to her, as long as she stays in town.—[*Aside.*] If it ben't too long.

Mrs. Moth. I'll tell her what a devil you are, and advise her to have a care of you.   73

Col. Do, that will make her every time she sees me think of what I'd be at.—[*Exit* Mrs. Motherly.] Dear Martilla, good night ; I know you won't be my hindrance ; I'll do you as good a turn some time or other. Well, I am so glad, you don't love me too much.

Mar. When that's our fate, as too, too oft we prove,
How bitterly we pay the past delights of love !
                                                    [*Exeunt.*

ACT II.

SCENE I.—*A Room in* Lord LOVERULE's *House.*

Enter Lord LOVERULE *and* Lady ARABELLA.

Lady Ara. Well, look you, my lord, I can bear it no longer; nothing still but about my faults, my faults! an agreeable subject truly!

Lord Love. But, madam, if you won't hear of your faults, how is it likely you should ever mend 'em?

Lady Ara. Why, I don't intend to mend 'em. I can't mend 'em, I have told you so a hundred times; you know I have tried to do it, over and over, and it hurts me so I can't bear it. Why, don't you know, my lord, that whenever (just to please you only) I have gone about to wean myself from a fault (one of my faults, I mean, that I love dearly), han't it put me so out of humour, you could scarce endure the house with me?   13

Lord Love. Look you, my dear, it is very true, that in weaning one's self from—

Lady Ara. Weaning! why, ay, don't you see, that even in weaning poor children from the nurse, it's almost the death of 'em? and don't you see your true religious people, when they go about to wean themselves, and have solemn days of fasting and praying, on purpose to help them, does it not so disorder them, there's no coming near 'em? are they not as cross as the devil? and then they don't do the business neither; for next day their faults are just where they were the day before. 24

Lord Love. But, madam, can you think it a reasonable thing to be abroad till two o'clock in the morning, when you know I go to bed at eleven?

Lady Ara. And can you think it a wise thing (to talk your own way now) to go to bed at eleven, when you know I am likely to disturb you by coming there at three?

Lord Love. Well, the manner of women's living of late is insupportable, and some way or other— 32

Lady Ara. It's to be mended, I suppose.—Pray, my lord, one word of fair argument. You complain of my late hours; I of your early ones; so far we are even, you'll allow. But which gives us the best figure in the eye of the polite world? My two o'clock speaks life, activity, spirit, and vigour; your eleven has a dull, drowsy, stupid, good-for-nothing sound with it. It savours much of a mechanic, who must get to bed betimes that he may rise early to open his shop! Faugh!

Lord Love. I thought to go to bed early and rise so, was ever esteemed a right practice for all people. 43

Lady Ara. Beasts do it.

Lord Love. Fie, fie, madam, fie! But 'tis not your ill hours alone disturb me; but the ill company who occasion those ill hours.

Lady Ara. And pray what ill company may those be?

Lord Love. Why, women that lose their money, and men that win it: especially when 'tis to be paid out of their husband's estate; or if that fail, and the creditor be a little pressing, the lady will perhaps be obliged to try if the gentleman, instead of gold, will accept of a trinket. 53

Lady Ara. My lord, you grow scurrilous, and you'll make me hate you. I'll have you to know I keep company with the politest people in the town, and the assemblies I frequent are full of such.

Lord Love. So are the churches now and then.

Lady Ara. My friends frequent them often, as well as the assemblies.

Lord Love. They would do it oftener, if a groom of the chamber there were allowed to furnish cards and dice to the company. 63

Lady Ara. You'd make a woman mad !

Lord Love. You'd make a man a fool !

Lady Ara. If Heaven has made you otherwise, that won't be in my power.

Lord Love. I'll try if I can prevent your making me a beggar at least.

Lady Ara. A beggar ! Crœsus ! I'm out of patience !— I won't come home till four to-morrow morning.

Lord Love. I'll order the doors to be locked at twelve.

Lady Ara. Then I won't come home till to-morrow night.

Lord Love. Then you shall never come home again, madam. [*Exit.* 75

Lady Ara. There he has knocked me down. My father upon our marriage said, wives were come to that pass, he did not think it fit they should be trusted with pin-money, and so would not let this man settle one penny upon his poor wife, to serve her at a dead lift for separate maintenance.

Enter CLARINDA.

Clar. Good-morrow, madam ; how do you do to-day? you seem to be in a little fluster.

Lady Ara. My lord has been in one, and as I am the most complaisant poor creature in the world, I put myself into one too, purely to be suitable company to him.   85

Clar. You are prodigious good; but surely it must be mighty agreeable when a man and his wife can give themselves the same turn of conversation.

Lady Ara. Oh, the prettiest thing in the world !

Clar. But yet, though I believe there's no life so happy as a married one, in the main ; yet I fancy, where two people are so very much together, they must often be in want of something to talk upon.   93

Lady Ara. Clarinda, you are the most mistaken in the world ; married people have things to talk of, child, that never enter into the imagination of others. Why now, here's my lord and I, we han't been married above two short years, you know, and we have already eight or ten things constantly in bank, that whenever we want company, we can talk of any one of them for two hours together, and the subject never the flatter. It will be as fresh next day, if we have occasion for it, as it was the first day it entertained us.

Clar. Why, that must be wonderful pretty.   103

Lady Ara. Oh, there's no life like it ! This very day now, for example, my lord and I, after a pretty cheerful *tête-à-tête* dinner, sat down by the fireside, in an idle, indolent, picktooth way for a while, as if we had not thought of one another's being in the room. At last (stretching himself, and yawning twice), my dear, says he, you came home very late last night. 'Twas but two in the morning, says I. I was in bed (yawning) by eleven, says he. So you are every night, says I. Well, says he, I am amazed how you can sit up so late. How can you be amazed, says I, at a thing that happens so often? Upon which we entered into conversation. And though this is a point has entertained us above fifty times already, we always find so many pretty new things to say upon't, that I believe in my soul it will last as long as we live.

Clar. But in such sort of family dialogues (though extremely well for passing of time) don't there now and then enter some little witty sort of bitterness? 　　120

Lady Ara. O yes; which don't do amiss at all; a little something that's sharp, moderates the extreme sweetness of matrimonial society, which would else perhaps be cloying. Though to tell you the truth, Clarinda, I think we squeezed a little too much lemon into it this bout; for it grew so sour at last, that I think I almost told him he was a fool; and he talked something oddly of turning me out of doors.

Clar. Oh, but have a care of that! 　　128

Lady Ara. Why, to be serious, Clarinda, what would you have a woman do in my case? There is no one thing he can do in this world to please me—except giving me money; and that he is growing weary of; and I at the same time (partly by nature, and partly perhaps by keeping the best company) do with my soul love almost everything that he hates. I dote upon assemblies, adore masquerades, my heart bounds at a ball; I love play to distraction, cards enchant me, and dice—put me out of my little wits.—Dear, dear hazard, what music there is in the rattle of the dice, compared to a sleepy opera! Do you ever play at hazard, Clarinda? 　　140

Clar. Never; I don't think it sits well upon women; it's very masculine, and has too much of a rake; you see how it makes the men swear and curse. Sure it must incline the women to do the same too, if they durst give way to it.

Lady Ara. So it does; but hitherto, for a little decency, we keep it in; and when, in spite of our teeth, an oath gets into our mouths, we swallow it.

Clar. That's enough to burst you; but in time perhaps you'll let 'em fly as they do.   149

Lady Ara. Why, 'tis probable we may, for the pleasure of all polite women's lives now, you know, is founded upon entire liberty to do what they will. But shall I tell you what happened t'other night? Having lost all my money but ten melancholy guineas, and throwing out for them, what do you think slipped from me?

Clar. An oath?

Lady Ara. Gud soons!

Clar. O Lord! O Lord! did not it frighten you out of your wits?   159

Lady Ara. Clarinda, I thought a gun had gone off.— But I forget, you are a prude, and design to live soberly.

Clar. Why, 'tis true; both my nature and my education do in a good degree incline me that way.

Lady Ara. Well, surely to be sober is to be terribly dull. You will marry, won't you?

Clar. I can't tell but I may.

Lady Ara. And you'll live in town?

Clar. Half the year I should like it very well.

Lady Ara. And you would live in London half a year, to be sober in it?   170

Clar. Yes.

Lady Ara. Why can't you as well go and be sober in the country?

Clar. So I would the t'other half year.

Lady Ara. And pray what pretty scheme of life would

you form now, for your summer and winter sober entertainments?

Clar. A scheme that, I think, might very well content us.

Lady Ara. Let's hear it. 179

Clar. I could in summer pass my time very agreeably,
in riding soberly, in walking soberly, in sitting under a tree
soberly, in gardening soberly, in reading soberly, in hearing
a little music soberly, in conversing with some agreeable
friends soberly, in working soberly, in managing my family
and children (if I had any) soberly; and possibly by these
means I might induce my husband to be as sober as
myself.

Lady Ara. Well, Clarinda, thou art a most contemptible creature. But let's have the sober town scheme too,
for I am charmed with the country one. 190

Clar. You shall, and I'll try to stick to my sobriety there
too.

Lady Ara. If you do, you'll make me sick of you. But
let's hear it, however.

Clar. I would entertain myself in observing the new
fashions soberly, I would please myself in new clothes
soberly, I would divert myself with agreeable friends at home
and abroad soberly, I would play at quadrille soberly, I
would go to court soberly, I would go to some plays soberly,
I would go to operas soberly, and I think I could go
once, or, if I liked my company, twice to a masquerade
soberly. 202

Lady Ara. If it had not been for that last piece of
sobriety, I was going to call for some surfeit-water.

Clar. Why, don't you think, that with the further aid of
breakfasting, dining, supping, and sleeping (not to say a

word of devotion), the four and twenty hours might roll over in a tolerable manner ?

Lady Ara.   How I detest that word, tolerable !   And so will a country relation of ours, that's newly come to town, or I'm mistaken.

Clar.   Who is that?

Lady Ara.   Even my dear lady Headpiece.   213

Clar.   Is she come?

Lady Ara.   Yes, her sort of a tolerable husband has gotten to be chosen parliament-man at some simple town or other, upon which she has persuaded him to bring her and her folks up to London.

Clar.   That's good; I think she was never here before.

Lady Ara.   Not since she was nine years old ; but she has had an outrageous mind to it ever since she was married.

Clar.   Then she'll make the most of it, I suppose, now she is come.   223

Lady Ara.   Depend upon that.

Clar.·   We must go and visit her.

Lady Ara.   By all means ; and may be you'll have a mind to offer her your tolerable scheme for her London diversion this winter ; if you do, mistress, I'll show her mine too, and you shall see, she'll so despise you and adore me, that if I do but chirrup to her, she'll hop after me like a tame sparrow, the town round.   But there's your admirer I see coming in, I'll oblige him, and leave you to receive part of his visit, while I step up to write a letter.   Besides, to tell you the truth, I don't like him half so well as I used to do : he falls off of late from being the company he was, in our way.   In short, I think he's growing to be a little like my lord.   [*Exit.* 237

Enter Sir CHARLES.

Sir Char. Madam, your servant; they told me lady Arabella was here.

Clar. She's only stepped up to write a letter; she'll come down presently.

Sir Char. Why, does she write letters? I thought she had never time for't: pray how may she have disposed of the rest of the day?

Clar. A good deal as usual; she has visits to make till six; she's then engaged to the play; from that till court-time she's to be at cards at Mrs. Idle's; after the drawing-room she takes a short supper with lady Hazard, and from thence they go together to the assembly.   249

Sir Char. And are you to do all this with her?

Clar. The visits and the play, no more.

Sir Char. And how can you forbear all the rest?

Clar. 'Tis easy to forbear what we are not very fond of.

Sir Char. I han't found it so. I have passed much of my life in this hurry of the ladies, yet was never so pleased as when I was at quiet without 'em.

Clar. What then induced you to be with 'em?

Sir Char. Idleness and the fashion.

Clar. No mistresses in the case?   259

Sir Char. To speak honestly, yes. When one is in a toyshop, there was no forbearing the baubles; so I was per-petually engaging with some coquette or other, whom I could love perhaps just enough to put it into her power to plague me.

Clar. Which power I suppose she sometimes made use of.

Sir Char. The amours of a coquette, madam, generally mean nothing farther; I look upon them and prudes to be nuisances much alike, though they seem very different : the first are always disturbing the men, and the latter always abusing the women.   271

Clar. And all I think is to establish the character of being virtuous.

Sir Char. That is, being chaste they mean, for they know no other virtue ; therefore indulge themselves in every-thing else that's vicious ; they (against nature) keep their chastity, only because they find more pleasure in doing mischief with it, than they should have in parting with it. But, madam, if both these characters are so odious, how highly to be valued is that woman who can attain all they aim at, without the aid of the folly or vice of either !   281

Re-enter Lady Arabella.

Lady Ara. Your servant, sir. I won't ask your pardon for leaving you alone a little with a lady that I know shares so much of your good opinion.

Sir Char. I wish, madam, she could think my good opinion of value enough to afford me a small part in hers.

Lady Ara. I believe, sir, every woman, who knows she has a place in a fine gentleman's good opinion, will be glad to give him one in hers, if she can. But however you two may stand in one another's, you must take another time if you desire to talk farther about it, or we shan't have enough to make our visits in ; and so your servant, sir.—Come, Clarinda.   293

Sir Char. I'll stay and make my lord a visit, if you will give me leave.

Lady Ara. You have my leave, sir, though you were a lady.   [*Exit with* CLARINDA.

Enter Lord LOVERULE.

Lord Love. Sir Charles, your servant; what, have the ladies left you?

Sir Char. Yes; and the ladies in general I hope will leave me too.

Lord Love. Why so?   302

Sir Char. That I mayn't be put to the ill-manners of leaving them first.

Lord Love. Do you then already find your gallantry inclining to an ebb?

Sir Char. 'Tis not that I am yet old enough to justify myself in an idle retreat, but I have got, I think, a sort of surfeit on me, that lessens much the force of female charms.

Lord Love. Have you then been so glutted with their favours?   312

Sir Char. Not with their favours, but with their service; it is unmerciful. I once thought myself a tolerable time-killer; I drank, I played, I intrigued, and yet I had hours enow for reasonable uses; but he that will list himself a lady's man of mettle now, she'll work him so at cards and dice, she won't afford him time enough to play with her at anything else, though she herself should have a tolerable good mind to it.

Lord Love. And so the disorderly lives they lead make you incline to a reform of your own.   322

Sir Char. 'Tis true; for bad examples (if they are but bad enough) give us as useful reflections as good ones do.

Lord Love. 'Tis pity anything that's bad should come from women.

Sir Char. 'Tis so indeed; and there was a happy time when both you and I thought there never could.

Lord Love. Our early first conceptions of them, I well remember, were, that they never could be vicious, nor never could be old.   331

Sir Char. We thought so then; the beauteous form we saw them cast in, seemed designed a habitation for no vice, nor no decay; all I had conceived of angels I conceived of them; true, tender, gentle, modest, generous, constant, I thought was writ in every feature; and in my devotions, Heaven, how did I adore thee, that blessings like them should be the portion of such poor inferior creatures as I took myself and all men else (compared with them) to be! —But where's that adoration now?   340

Lord Love. 'Tis with such fond young fools as you and I were then.

Sir Char. And with such it ever will be.

Lord Love. Ever. The pleasure is so great in believing women to be what we wish them, that nothing but a long and sharp experience can ever make us think them otherwise. That experience, friend, both you and I have had; but yours has been at other men's expense; mine—at my own.

Sir Char. Perhaps you'd wonder, should you find me disposed to run the risk of that experience too.   351

Lord Love. I should indeed.

Sir Char. And yet 'tis possible I may; know, at least I still have so much of my early folly left, to think there's yet one woman fit to make a wife of. How far such a one can answer the charms of a mistress, married men are silent in, so pass—for that, I'd take my chance; but could she make a home easy to her partner, by letting him find there a cheerful companion, an agreeable intimate, a useful assistant, a faithful friend, and (in its time perhaps) a tender mother, such change of life, from what I lead, seems not unwise to think of.   362

Lord Love. Not unwise to purchase, if to be had for millions; but—

Sir Char. But what?

Lord Love. If the reverse of this should chance to be the bitter disappointment, what would the life be then?

Sir Char. A damned one.

Lord Love. And what relief?

Sir Char. A short one; leave it, and return to that you left, if you can't find a better.   371

Lord Love. [*Aside.*] He says right.—That's the remedy, and a just one—for if I sell my liberty for gold, and I am foully paid in brass, shall I be held to keep the bargain?

Sir Char. What are you thinking of?

Lord Love. Of what you have said.

Sir Char. And was it well said?

Lord Love. I begin to think it might.

Sir Char. Think on, 'twill give you ease.—The man who has courage enough to part with a wife, need not much dread the having one; and he that has not, ought to tremble at being a husband.—But perhaps I have said too much; you'll pardon, however, the freedom of an old friend, because you know I am so; so your servant.   384

Lord Love. Charles, farewell! I can take nothing as ill meant that comes from you.—[*Exit* Sir CHARLES.] Nor ought my wife to think I mean amiss to her, if I convince her I'll endure no longer that she should thus expose herself and me. No doubt 'twill grieve her sorely. Physic's a loathsome thing till we find it gives us health, and then we are thankful to those who made us take it. Perhaps she may do so by me; if she does 'tis well; if not, and she resolves to make the house ring with reprisals, I believe (though the misfortune's great) he'll make a better figure in the world, who keeps an ill wife out of doors, than he that keeps her within. [*Exit.*

ACT III.

SCENE I.—*A Room in* Mrs. MOTHERLY'S *House.*

Enter Lady HEADPIECE *and* Mrs. MOTHERLY.

Lady Head. So, you are acquainted with Lady Arabella, I find.

Mrs. Moth. Oh, madam, I have had the honour to know her ladyship almost from a child, and a charming woman she has made.

Lady Head. I like her prodigiously; I had some acquaintance with her in the country two years ago; but she's quite another woman here.

Mrs. Moth. Ah, madam, two years keeping company with the polite people of the town will do wonders in the improvement of a lady, so she has it but about her.   11

Lady Head. Now 'tis my misfortune, Mrs. Motherly, to come late to school.

Mrs. Moth. Oh! don't be discouraged at that, madam, the quickness of your ladyship's parts will easily recover your loss of a little time.

Lady Head. Oh, you flatter me! But I'll endeavour, by industry and application, to make it up; such parts as I have shall not lie idle. My lady Arabella has been so good to offer me already her introduction to those assemblies where a woman may soonest learn to make herself valuable to everybody.   22

Mrs. Moth. [*Aside.*] But her husband.—[*Aloud.*] Her ladyship, madam, can indeed, better than anybody, introduce you where everything that accomplishes a fine lady is practised to the last perfection.   Madam, she herself is at the very tip top of it—'tis pity, poor lady, she should meet with any discouragements.

Lady Head. Discouragements! from whence, pray?

Mrs. Moth. From home sometimes—my lord a—

Lady Head. What does he do? 31

Mrs. Moth. But one should not talk of people of quality's family concerns.

Lady Head. Oh, no matter, Mrs. Motherly, as long as it goes no farther.   My lord, you were saying—

Mrs. Moth. Why, my lord, madam, is a little humoursome, they say.

Lady Head. Humoursome?

Mrs. Moth. Yes, they say he's humoursome.

Lady Head. As how, pray? 40

Mrs. Moth. Why, if my poor lady perhaps does but stay out at night maybe four or five hours after he's in bed, he'll be cross.

Lady Head. What, for such a thing as that?

Mrs. Moth. Yes, he'll be cross; and then, if she happens, it may be, to be unfortunate at play, and lose a great deal of money, more than she has to pay, then, madam, —he'll snub.

Lady Head. Out upon him, snub such a woman as she is? I can tell you, Mrs. Motherly, I that am but a country lady, should sir Francis take upon him to snub me, in London, he'd raise a spirit would make his hair stand an end. 53

Mrs. Moth.   Really, madam, that's the only way to deal with 'em.

Enter Miss BETTY.

And here comes pretty Miss Betty, that I believe will never be made a fool of when she's married.

Miss Bet.   No, by my troth won't I.   What, are you talking of my being married, mother?

Lady Head.   No, miss ; Mrs. Motherly was only saying what a good wife you would make when you were so.

Miss Bet.   The sooner it's tried, mother, the sooner it will be known.—Lord, here's the colonel, madam.   63

Enter Colonel COURTLY.

Lady Head.   Colonel, your servant.

Miss Bet.   Your servant, colonel.

Col.   Ladies, your most obedient.—I hope, madam, the town air continues to agree with you?

Lady Head.   Mighty well, sir.

Miss Bet.   Oh, prodigious well, sir.   We have bought a new coach, and an ocean of new clothes, and we are to go to the play to-night, and to-morrow we go to the opera, and next night we go to the assembly, and then the next night after, we—

Lady Head.   Softly, miss.—Do you go to the play to-night, colonel?   75

Col.   I did not design it, madam ; but now I find there is to be such good company, I'll do myself the honour (if you'll give me leave, ladies) to come and lead you to your coach.

Lady Head.   It's extremely obliging.

Miss Bet.   It is, indeed, mighty well-bred.—Lord, colonel,

what a difference there is between your way and our country
companions! One of them would have said, What, you are
aw gooing to the playhouse, then? Yes, says we, won't you
come and lead us out? No, by good feggings, says he, ye
ma' e'en ta' care o' yoursels, y'are awd enough; and so he'd
ha' gone to get drunk at the tavern against we came home
to supper.   88

Mrs. Moth. Ha! ha! ha! well, sure, madam, your ladyship is the happiest mother in the world to have such a
charming companion to your daughter.

Col. The prettiest creature upon earth!

Miss Bet. D'ye hear that, mother? Well, he's a fine
gentleman really, and I think a man of admirable sense.

Lady Head. Softly, miss, he'll hear you.

Miss Bet. If he does, madam, he'll think I say true, and
he'll like me never the worse for that, I hope.—Where's
your niece Martilla, Mrs. Motherly?—Mamma, won't you
carry Martilla to the play with us?

Lady Head. With all my heart, child.   100

Col. She's a very pretty civil sort of woman, madam,
and miss will be very happy in having such a companion in
the house with her.

Miss Bet. So I shall indeed, sir, and I love her dearly
already, we are growing very great together.

Lady Head. But what's become of your brother, child?
I han't seen him these two hours, where is he?

Miss Bet. Indeed, mother, I don't know where he is; I
saw him asleep about half an hour ago by the kitchen fire.

Col. Must not he go to the play too?   110

Lady Head. Yes, I think he should go, though he'll be
weary on't before it's half done.

Miss Bet. Weary! yes, and then he'll sit, and yawn, and stretch like a greyhound by the fireside, till he does some nasty thing or other, that they'll turn him out of the house, so it's better to leave him at home.

Mrs. Moth. Oh, that were pity, miss. Plays will enliven him.—See, here he comes, and my niece with him.

Enter Squire HUMPHRY *and* MARTILLA.

Col. Your servant, sir; you come in good time, the ladies are all going to the play, and wanted you to help gallant them.   121

Squire Hum. And so 'twill be nine o'clock before one shall get ony supper!

Miss Bet. Supper! why, your dinner is not out of your mouth yet, at least 'tis all about the brims of it.—See how greasy his chaps is, mother.

Lady Head. Nay, if he han't a mind to go, he need not. —You may stay here till your father comes home from the parliament house, and then you may eat a broiled bone together.   130

Miss Bet. Yes, and drink a tankard of strong beer together, and then he may tell you all he has been doing in the parliament house, and you may tell him all you have been thinking of when you were asleep in the kitchen; and then if you'll put it all down in writing, when we come from the play, I'll read it to the company.

Squire Hum. Sister, I don't like your joking, and you are not a well-behaved young woman; and although my mother encourages you, my thoughts are, you are not too big to be whipped.   140

Miss Bet. How, sirrah?

Squire Hum. There's a civil young gentlewoman stands there, is worth a hundred of you.   And I believe she'll be married before you.

Miss Bet. Cots my life, I have a good mind to pull your eyes out!

Lady Head. Hold, miss, hold, don't be in such a passion neither.

Miss Bet. Mamma, it is not that I am angry at anything he says to commend Martilla, for I wish she were to be married to-morrow, that I might have a dance at her wedding; but what need he abuse me for?—[*Aside.*] I wish the lout had mettle enough to be in love with her, she'd make pure sport with him.—[*To him.*] Does your heaviness find any inclinations moving towards the lady you admire? —Speak! are you in love with her?   156

Squire Hum. I am in love with nobody; and if anybody be in love with me, mayhap they had as good be quiet.

Miss Bet. Hold your tongue, I'm quite sick of you.— Come, Martilla, you are to go to the play with us.

Mart. Am I, miss? I am ready to wait upon you.

Lady Head. I believe it's time we should be going, colonel, is not it?

Col. Yes, madam, I believe it is.

Lady Head. Come then; who is there?   165

Enter TOM.

Is the coach at the door?

Tom. It has been there this hafe haur, so please your ladyship.

Miss Bet. And are all the people in the street gazing at it, Tom?

Tom. That are they, madam; and Roger has drank so much of his own beverage, that he's e'en as it were gotten a little drunk.

Lady Head. Not so drunk, I hope, but that he can drive us?   175

Tom. Yes, yes, madam, he drives best when he's a little upish. When Roger's head turns, raund go the wheels, i' faith.

Miss Bet. Never fear, mamma, as long as it's to the playhouse, there's no danger.

Lady Head. Well, daughter, since you are so courageous, it shan't be said I make any difficulty; and if the colonel is so gallant to have a mind to share our danger, we have room for him, if he pleases.

Col. Madam, you do me a great deal of honour, and I'm sure you give me a great deal of pleasure.   186

Miss Bet. Come, dear mamma, away we go.

[*Exeunt all but* Squire, MARTILLA, *and* Mrs. MOTHERLY.]

Squire Hum. [*To* MARTILLA.] I did not think you would have gone.

Mart. Oh, I love a play dearly.   [*Exit.*

Mrs. Moth. I wonder, squire, that you would not go to the play with 'em.

Squire Hum. What needed Martilla have gone? they were enow without her.

Mrs. Moth. Oh, she was glad to go to divert herself; and, besides, my lady desired her to go with them.   196

Squire Hum. And so I am left alone!

Mrs. Moth. Why, should you have cared for her company?

Squire Hum. Rather than none.

Mrs. Moth. [*Aside.*]   On my conscience, he's ready to cry; this is matter to think of; but here comes sir Francis.

Enter Sir FRANCIS.

How do you do, sir? I'm afraid these late parliament hours won't agree with you.

Sir Fran.   Indeed, I like them not, Mrs. Motherly; if they would dine at twelve o'clock, as we do in the country, a man might be able to drink a reasonable bottle between that and supper-time.

Mrs. Moth. That would be much better indeed, sir Francis.   210

Sir Fran. But then when we consider that what we undergo is in being busy for the good of our country—Oh, the good of our country is above all things! What a noble and glorious thing it is, Mrs. Motherly, that England can boast of five hundred zealous gentlemen, all in one room, all of one mind, upon a fair occasion, to go all together by the ears for the good of their country!—Humphry, perhaps you'll be a senator in time, as your father is now; when you are, remember your country; spare nothing for the good of your country; and when you come home at the end of the sessions, you will find yourself so adored, that your country will come and dine with you every day in the week.—Oh, here's my uncle Richard.   223

Enter UNCLE RICHARD.

Mrs. Moth.   I think, sir, I had best get you a mouthful of something to stay your stomach till supper.

Sir Fran. With all my heart, for I'm almost famished.

[*Exit* Mrs. MOTHERLY.

Squire Hum. And so shall I before my mother comes from the playhouse, so I'll go get a buttered toast. [*Exit.*

Sir Fran. Uncle, I hope you are well.

Unc. Rich. Nephew, if I had been sick, I would not have come abroad ; I suppose you are well, for I sent this morning and was informed you went out early ; was it to make your court to some of the great men ?   233

Sir Fran. Yes, uncle, I was advised to lose no time, so I went to one great man, whom I had never seen before.

Unc. Rich. And who had you got to introduce you ?

Sir Fran. Nobody. I remembered I had heard a wise man say, My son, be bold ; so I introduced myself.

Unc. Rich. As how, I pray ?

Sir Fran. Why thus, uncle ; Please your lordship, says I, I am sir Francis Headpiece, of Headpiece-hall, and member of parliament for the ancient borough of Gobble-guinea. Sir, your humble servant, says my lord, though I have not the honour to know your person, I have heard you are a very honest gentleman, and I am very glad your borough has made choice of so worthy a representative ; have you any service to command me ? Those last words, uncle, gave me great encouragement ; and though I know you have not any very great opinion of my parts, I believe you won't say I missed it now.   250

Unc. Rich. I hope I shall have no cause.

Sir Fran. My lord, says I, I did not design to say anything to your lordship to-day about business ; but since your lordship is so kind and free, as to bid me speak if I have any service to command you, I will.

Unc. Rich. So I

Sir Fran. I have, says I, my lord, a good estate, but it's

a little aut at elbows, and as I desire to serve my king as well
as my country, I shall be very willing to accept of a place at
court.   260

Unc. Rich. This was bold indeed.

Sir Fran. Ecod, I shot him flying, uncle ; another man
would have been a month before he durst have opened his
mauth about a place.   But you shall hear.   Sir Francis,
says my lord, what sort of a place may you have turned
your thoughts upon ? My lord, says I, beggars must not be
choosers ; but some place about a thousand a-year, I believe,
might do pretty weel to begin with.   Sir Francis, says he, I
shall be glad to serve you in anything I can ; and in saying
these words he gave me a squeeze by the hand, as much as
to say, I'll do your business.   And so he turned to a lord
that was there, who looked as if he came for a place too.

Unc. Rich. And so your fortune's made.   273

Sir Fran. Don't you think so, uncle?

Unc. Rich. Yes, for just so mine was made—twenty
years ago.

Sir Fran. Why, I never knew you had a place, uncle !

Unc. Rich. Nor I neither, upon my faith, nephew.   But
you have been down at the house since you made your
court, have not you ?

Sir Fran. O yes ; I would not neglect the house for
ever so much.

Unc. Rich. And what may they have done there to-day,
I pray ?   284

Sir Fran. Why truly, uncle, I cannot well tell what they
did, but I'll tell you what I did.   I happened to make a
little sort of a mistake.

Unc. Rich. How was that ?

Sir Fran. Why, you must know, uncle, they were all got into a sort of a hodge-podge argument for the good of the nation, which I did not well understand.   However, I was convinced, and so resolved to vote aright, according to my conscience; but they made such a puzzling business on't, when they put the question, as they call it, that, I believe, I cried Ay when I should have cried No; for a sort of a Jacobite that sat next me, took me by the hand, and said,—Sir, you are a man of honour, and a true Englishman, and I should be glad to be better acquainted with you; and so he pulled me along with the crowd into the lobby with him, when, I believe, I should have stayed where I was.   300

Unc. Rich. And so, if you had not quite made your fortune before, you have clenched it now.—[*Aside.*] Ah, thou head of the Headpieces!—[*Aloud.*] How now, what's the matter here?

Re-enter Lady HEADPIECE, Miss BETTY, Colonel COURTLY,
   Squire HUMPHRY, *and* MARTILLA, *in disorder,*
   some dirty, some lame, some bloody.

Sir Fran. Mercy on us! they are all killed.

Miss Bet. Not for a thousand pounds; but we have been all down in the dirt together.

Lady Head. We have had a sad piece of work on't, sir Francis; overturned in the channel as we were going to the playhouse.   310

Miss Bet. Over and over, papa; had it been coming from the playhouse, I should not have cared a farthing.

Sir Fran. But, child, you are hurt, your face is all bloody.

Miss Bet. O sir, my new gown is all dirty.

Lady Head.   The new coach is all spoiled.

Miss Bet.   The glasses are all to bits.

Lady Head.   Roger has put out his arm.

Miss Bet.   Would he had put out his neck, for making us lose the play !   320

Squire Hum. ˙ Poor Martilla has scratched her little finger.

Lady Head.   And here's the poor colonel ; nobody asks what he has done.—I hope, sir, you have got no harm ?

Col.   Only a little wounded with some pins I met with about your ladyship.

Lady Head.   I am sorry anything about me should do you harm.

Col.   If it does, madam, you have that about you, if you please, will be my cure.   I hope your ladyship feels nothing amiss ?   331

Lady Head.   Nothing at all, though we did roll about together strangely.

Col.   We did indeed.   I'm sure we rolled so, that my poor hands were got once—I don't know where they were got.—But her ladyship I see will pass by slips.   [*Aside.*

Sir Fran.   It would have been pity the colonel should have received any damage in his services to the ladies ; he is the most complaisant man to 'em, uncle ; always ready when they have occasion for him.   340

Unc. Rich.   Then I believe, nephew, they'll never let him want business.

Sir Fran.   Oh, but they should not ride the free horse to death neither.—Come, colonel, you'll stay and drink a bottle, and eat a little supper with us, after your misfortune ?

Col.   Sir, since I have been prevented from attending

the ladies to the play, I shall be very proud to obey their commands here at home.

Sir Fran. A prodigious civil gentleman, uncle ; and yet as bold as Alexander upon occasion.   350

Unc. Rich. Upon a lady's occasion.

Sir Fran. Ha, ha, you are a wag, uncle; but I believe he'd storm anything.

Unc. Rich. Then I believe your citadel may be in danger.
                                                              [*Aside.*

Sir Fran. Uncle, won't you break your rule for once, and sup from home?

Unc. Rich. The company will excuse me, nephew; they'll be freer without me ; so good night to them and you.

Lady Head. Good night to you, sir, since you won't stay.—Come, colonel.   360

Unc. Rich. [*Aside.*] Methinks this facetious colonel is got upon a pretty familiar, easy foot already with the family of the Headpieces—hum.   [*Exit.*

Sir Fran. Come, my lady, let's all in, and pass the evening cheerfully. And d'ye hear, wife—a word in your ear—I have got a promise of a place at court, of a thousand a-year, he, hem !   [*Exeunt.*

ACT IV.

SCENE I.— Lady Arabella's *Dressing-room.*

Enter Lady Arabella, *as just up, walking pensively to her toilet, followed by* Trusty.

Lady Ara. Well, sure never woman had such luck!— these devilish dice!—Sit up all night; lose all one's money, and then—how like a hag I look!—[*Sits at her toilet, turning her purse inside out.*] Not a guinea—worth less by a hundred pounds than I was at one o'clock this morning—and then—I was worth nothing—what is to be done, Trusty?

Trus. I wish I were wise enough to tell you, madam : but if there comes in any good company to breakfast with your ladyship, perhaps you may have a run of better fortune.

Lady Ara. But I han't a guinea to try my fortune.—Let me see—who was that impertinent man, that was so saucy last week about money, that I was forced to promise, once more, he should have what I owed him this morning?

Trus. Oh, I remember, madam; it was your old mercer Shortyard, that you turned off a year ago, because he would trust you no longer. 16

Lady Ara. That's true; and I think I bid the steward keep thirty guineas out of some money he was paying me, to stop his odious mouth.

Trus. Your ladyship did so.

Lady Ara. Prithee, Trusty, run and see whether the

wretch has got the money yet; if not, tell the steward I have occasion for it myself; run quickly.

[TRUSTY *runs to the door.*

Trus. Ah, madam, he's just a-paying it away now, in the hall.

Lady Ara. Stop him! quick, quick, dear Trusty.

Trus. Hem, hem, Mr. Moneybag, a word with you quickly. 28

Mon. [*Within.*] I'll come presently.

Trus. Presently won't do, you must come this moment.

Mon. I'm but just paying a little money.

Trus. Cods my life, paying money! is the man distracted? Come here, I tell you, to my lady this moment, quick.

MONEYBAG *comes to the door, with a purse in's hand.*

My lady says, you must not pay the money to-day, there's a mistake in the account, which she must examine; and she's afraid too there was a false guinea or two left in the purse, which might disgrace her.—[*Twitches the purse from him.*] But she's too busy to look for 'em just now, so you must bid Mr. What-d'ye-call-'em come another time.—[*Exit* MONEY-BAG.] There they are, madam.—[*Gives her the money.*] The poor things were so near gone, they made me tremble. I fancy your ladyship will give me one of those false guineas for good luck.—[*Takes a guinea.*] Thank you, madam.

Lady Ara. Why, I did not bid you take it. 44

Trust. No, but your ladyship looked as if you were just going to bid me, so I took it to save your ladyship the trouble of speaking.

Lady Ara. Well, for once—but hark—I think I hear the man making a noise yonder.

Trus.   Nay, I don't expect he'll go out of the house quietly.   I'll listen.   [*Goes to the door.*

Lady Ara.   Do.

Trus.   He's in a bitter passion with poor Moneybag; I believe he'll beat him.—Lord, how he swears!   54

Lady Ara.   And a sober citizen too! that's a shame.

Trus.   He says he will speak with you, madam, though the devil held your door.—Lord! he's coming hither full drive, but I'll lock him out.

Lady Ara.   No matter, let him come: I'll reason with him.

Trus.   But he's a saucy fellow for all that.

Enter SHORTYARD.

What would you have, sir?

Short.   I would have my due, mistress.

Trus.   That would be—to be well cudgelled, master, for coming so familiarly where you should not come.   64

Lady Ara.   Do you think you do well, sir, to intrude into my dressing-room?

Short.   Madam, I sold my goods to you in your dressing-room, I don't know why I mayn't ask for my money there.

Lady Ara.   You are very short, sir.

Short.   Your ladyship won't complain of my patience being so?

Lady Ara.   I complain of nothing that ought not to be complained of; but I hate ill-manners.

Short.   So do I, madam—but this is the seventeenth time I have been ordered to come, with good manners, for my money, to no purpose.   76

Lady Ara.   Your money, man! is that the matter? Why, it has lain in the steward's hands this week for you.

Short. Madam, you yourself appointed me to come this very morning for it.

Lady Ara. But why did you come so late then?

Short. So late! I came soon enough, I thought.

Lady Ara. That thinking wrong makes us liable to a world of disappointments; if you had thought of coming one minute sooner, you had had your money.   85

Short. Gad bless me, madam: I had the money as I thought; I'm sure it was telling out, and I was writing a receipt for't.

Trus. Why, there you thought wrong again, master.

Lady Ara. Yes, for you should never think of writing a receipt till the money is in your pocket.

Short. Why, I did think 'twas in my pocket.

Trus. Look you, thinking again! Indeed, Mr. Short-yard, you make so many blunders, 'tis impossible but you must suffer by it, in your way of trade. I'm sorry for you, and you'll be undone.   96

Short. And well I may, when I sell my goods to people that won't pay me for 'em, till the interest of my money eats out all my profit: I sold them so cheap, because I thought I should be paid the next day.

Trus. Why, there again! there's another of your thoughts. Paid the next day! and you han't been paid this twelve-month, you see.

Short. Oons, I han't been paid at all, mistress.

Lady Ara. Well, tradesmen are strange, unreasonable creatures, refuse to sell people any more things, and then quarrel with 'em because they don't pay for those they have had already. Now, what can you say to that, Mr. Short-yard?   109

Short. Say! why—'sdeath, madam, I don't know what you talk of, I don't understand your argument.

Lady Ara. Why, what do you understand, man?

Short. Why, I understand that I have had above a hundred pounds due to me, a year ago; that I came by appointment just now to receive it; that it proved at last to be but thirty instead of a hundred and ten; and that, while the steward was telling even that out, and I was writing the receipt, comes Mrs. Pop here, and the money was gone. But I'll be bantered no longer if there's law in England. Say no more, Shortyard.   [*Exit.*

Trus. What a passion the poor devil's in!   121

Lady Ara. Why, truly, one can't deny but he has some present cause for a little ill humour; but when one has things of so much greater consequence on foot, one can't trouble oneself about making such creatures easy; so call for breakfast, Trusty, and set the hazard-table ready; if there comes no company, I'll play a little by myself.

Enter Lord Loverule.

Lord Love. Pray what offence, madam, have you given to a man I met with just now as I came in?

Lady Ara. People who are apt to take offence, do it for small matters, you know.   131

Lord Love. I shall be glad to find this so; but he says you have owed him above a hundred pounds this twelve-month; that he has been here forty times by appointment for it, to no purpose; and that coming here this morning upon positive assurance from yourself, he was tricked out of the money while he was writing a receipt for it, and sent away without a farthing.

Lady Ara. Lord, how these shopkeepers will lie!

Lord Love. What then is the business? For some ground the man must have to be in such a passion.   141

Lady Ara. I believe you'll rather wonder to see me so calm, when I tell you, he had the insolence to intrude into my very dressing-room here, with a story without head or tail.—You know, Trusty, we could not understand one word he said, but when he swore—good Lord! how the wretch did swear!

Trus. I never heard the like, for my part.

Lord Love. And all this for nothing?

Lady Ara. So it proved, my lord, for he got nothing by it.   151

Lord Love. His swearing I suppose was for his money, madam. Who can blame him?

Lady Ara. If he swore for money, he should be put in the pillory.

Lord Love. Madam, I won't be bantered, nor sued by this man for your extravagances. Do you owe him the money or not?

Lady Ara. He says I do, but such fellows will say anything.   160

Lord Love. [*Aside.*] Provoking!—[*Aloud.*] Did not I desire an account from you, of all your debts, but six months since, and give you money to clear them?

Lady Ara. My lord, you can't imagine how accounts make my head ache.

Lord Love. That won't do. The steward gave you two hundred pounds besides, but last week; where's that?

Lady Ara. Gone.

Lord Love. Gone! where?   169

Lady Ara.   Half the town over, I believe, by this time.

Lord Love.   Madam, madam, this can be endured no longer! and before a month passes expect to find me—

Lady Ara.   Hist, my lord, here's company.

Enter Captain Toupee.

Captain Toupee, your servant; what, nobody with you? do you come quite alone?

Capt.   'Slife, I thought to find company enough here.— My lord, your servant.—What a deuce, you look as if you had been up all night. I'm sure I was in bed but three hours; I would you'd give me some coffee.   179

Lady Ara.   Some coffee there; tea too, and chocolate.
                                        [*Exit* Trusty.

Capt.   [*Singing a minuet and dancing.*]   Well, what a strange fellow am I to be thus brisk, after losing all my money last night!—but upon my soul you look sadly.

Lady Ara.   No matter for that, if you'll let me win a little of your money this morning.

Capt.   What, with that face? Go, go wash it, go wash it, and put on some handsome things; you looked a good likely woman last night; I would not much have cared if you had run five hundred pounds in my debt; but if I play with you this morning, egad, I'd advise you to win, for I won't take your personal security at present for a guinea.

Lord Love.   [*Aside.*]   To what a nauseous freedom do women of quality of late admit these trifling fops! and there's a morning exercise will give 'em claim to greater freedoms still.—[*Points to the hazard-table.*]   Some course must be taken.   [*Exit.*   196

Capt.   What, is my lord gone? He looked, methought,

as if he did not delight much in my company. Well, peace
and plenty attend him for your ladyship's sake, and those —
who have now and then the honour to win a hundred
pounds of you.　　　　　*[Goes to the table singing and throws.*

Lady Ara. [*Twitching the box from him.*] What, do
you intend to win all the money upon the table?—Seven's
the main—set me a million, Toupee.

　　Capt. I set you two, my queen—six to seven !　　205
　　Lady Ara. Six.—The world's my own.
　　Both. Ha! ha! ha!
　　Lady Ara. Oh, that my lord had but spirit enough about
him to let me play for a thousand pounds a night—but here
comes country company.

Enter Lady HEADPIECE, Miss BETTY, Mrs. MOTHERLY, *and*
Colonel COURTLY.

Your servant, madam, good morrow to you.

Lady Head. And to you, madam. We are come to
breakfast with you. Lord, are you got to those pretty things
already?　　　　　　　　　　　　　*[Points to the dice.*

Lady Ara. You see we are not such idle folks in town as
you country ladies take us to be; we are no sooner out of
our beds, but we are at our work.　　　　　　　　217

Miss Bet. Will dear Lady Arabella give us leave, mother,
to do a stitch or two with her?　　*[Takes the box and throws.*

　　Capt. The pretty lively thing !

Lady Ara. With all her heart; what says your mamma?

Lady Head. She says, she don't love to sit with her hands
before her, when other people's are employed.

　　Capt. And this is the prettiest little sociable work, men
and women can all do together at it.

Lady Head. Colonel, you are one with us, are you not? 227

Lady Ara. O, I'll answer for him, he'll be out at nothing.

Capt. In a facetious way; he is the politest person; he will lose his money to the ladies so civilly, and will win theirs with so much good breeding; and he will be so modest to 'em before company, and so impudent to 'em in a dark corner.—Ha! colonel!

Lady Head. So I found him, I'm sure, last night.— Mercy on me, an ounce of virtue less than I had, and sir Francis had been undone. 237

Capt. Colonel, I smoke you.

Col. And a fine character you give the ladies of me, to help me.

Capt. I give 'em just the character of you they like, modest and brave.—Come, ladies, to business; look to your money, every woman her hand upon her purse.

Miss Bet. Here's mine, captain.

Capt. Oh, the little soft velvet one!—and it's as full.— Come, lady Blowze, rattle your dice and away with 'em.

Lady Ara. Six—at all—five to six—five—eight—at all again—nine to eight—nine. 248

Enter Sir Francis, *and stands gazing at 'em.*

Seven's the main—at all for ever! [*Throws out.*

Miss Bet. Now, mamma, let's see what you can do.
[Lady Headpiece *takes the box.*

Lady Head. Well, I'll warrant you, daughter.

Miss Bet. If you do, I'll follow a good example.

Lady Head. Eight's the main—don't spare me, gentle

men, I fear you not—have at you all—seven to eight—
seven.

Capt.   Eight, lady, eight.—Five pounds, if you please.

Lady Ara.   Three, kinswoman.

Col.   Two, madam.   258

Miss Bet.   And one for miss, mamma.—And now let's see
what I can do.—[*Aside.*]   If I should win enough this
morning to buy me another new gown—O bless me! there
they go!—Seven!—Come, captain, set me boldly, I want to
be at a handful.

Capt.   There's two for you, miss.

Miss Bet.   I'll at 'em, though I die for't.

Sir Fran.   Ah, my poor child, take care!

                                      [*Runs to stop the throw.*

Miss Bet.   There.

Capt.   Out—twenty pounds, young lady.

Sir Fran.   False dice, sir.   269

Capt.   False dice, sir! I scorn your words.—Twenty
pounds, madam.

Miss Bet.   Undone! undone!

Sir Fran.   She shan't pay you a farthing, sir; I won't
have miss cheated.

Capt.   Cheated, sir!

Lady Head.   What do you mean, sir Francis, to disturb
the company, and abuse the gentleman thus?

Sir Fran.   I mean to be in a passion.

Lady Head.   And why will you be in a passion, sir
Francis?   280

Sir Fran.   Because I came here to breakfast with my
lady there, before I went down to the house, expecting to
find my family set round a civil table with her, upon some

plumcake, hot rolls, and a cup of strong beer; instead of which, I find these good women staying their stomachs with a box and dice, and that man there, with the strange periwig, making a good hearty meal upon my wife and daughter—

CÆTERA DESUNT.

" INTRODUCTION TO " A SHORT VINDICATION."

THE Collier controversy, and Vanbrugh's part therein, have been discussed at some length in the Introduction to these volumes, nor does it seem necessary to add to what has already been said upon the subject. Vanbrugh's *Short Vindication* was published on the 9th of June, 1698, in the form of a small 8vo volume of seventy-nine pages. The publication is thus announced in the *Flying Post* of June 7-9, 1698 : " A Short Vindication of the Relapse, and the provok'd Wife, from Immorality and Prophaneness. By the (same) Author. Sold by *H. Walwyn,* at the *Three Leggs* in the *Poultry,* over-against *Stocks Market.*"

The title-page of the original edition reads as follows : " *A Short Vindication of the Relapse and the Provok'd Wife, from Immorality and Prophaneness. By the Author. London: Printed for H. Walwyn, at the Three Legs in the Poultrey, against the Stocks-Market. MDCXCVIII.*"

A Short Vindication of the Relapse and the Provok'd Wife, from Immorality and Profaneness.

WHEN first I saw Mr. *Collier's* performance upon the irregularities of the stage (in which amongst the rest of the gentlemen, he's pleased to afford me some particular favours), I was far from designing to trouble either myself or the town with a vindication ; I thought his charges against me for immorality and profaneness were grounded upon so much mistake, that every one (who had had the curiosity to see the plays, or on this occasion should take the trouble to read 'em) would easily discover the root of the invective, and that 'twas the quarrel of his gown, and not of his God, that made him take arms against me.

I found the opinion of my friends and acquaintance the same (at least they told me so), and the righteous as well as the unrighteous persuaded me, the attack was so weak, the town would defend itself ; that the general's head was too hot for his conduct to be wise ; his shot too much at random ever to make a breach ; and that the siege would be raised, without my taking the field.

I easily believed, what my laziness made me wish ; but I have since found, that by the industry of some people, whose temporal interest engages 'em in the squabble ; and the natural propensity of others, to be fond of anything that's abusive ; this lampoon has got credit enough in some places to brand the persons it mentions with almost as bad a character, as the author of it has fixed upon himself, by his life and conversation in the world.*

I think 'tis therefore now a thing no farther to be laughed at. Should I wholly sit still, those people who are so much mistaken to think I have been busy to encourage immorality, may double their mistake, and fancy I profess it : I will therefore endeavour, in a very few pages, to convince the world I have brought nothing upon the stage, that proves me more an atheist than a bigot.

I may be blind in what relates to myself; 'tis more than possible, for most people are so : but if I judge right, what I have done is in general a discouragement to vice and folly ; I am sure I intended it, and I hope I have performed it. Perhaps I have not gone the common road, nor observed the strictest prescriptions : but I believe those who know this town, will agree, that the rules of a college of divines will, in an infinity of cases, fall as short of the disorders of the mind, as those of the physicians do in the diseases of the body ; and I think a man may vary from 'em both, without being a quack in either.

The real query is, Whether the way I have varied be likely to have a good effect, or a bad one? That's the true state of the case ; which if I am cast in, I don't question however to gain at least thus much of my cause, that it shall be allowed I aimed at the mark, whether I hit it or not. This, if it won't vindicate my sense, will justify my morals ; and shew the world, that this honest gentleman, in stretching his malice, and curtailing his

---

* Collier was a violent nonjuror, who had been more than once arrested for writing against the government. In 1696, Sir John Friend and Sir William Perkins were executed for conspiring to assassinate King William, and Collier, with two other clergymen, gave them public absolution on the scaffold. His two associates were committed to Newgate, but Collier saved himself by absconding, and remained in concealment for about a year. He was outlawed, however, and although the prosecution was allowed to drop, the outlawry was never removed.

charity, has played a part which would have much better become a licentious poet, than a reverend divine.

Though I resolve to use very few words, I would willingly observe some method, were it possible ; that the world, who is the judge, might sum up the evidence the easier, and bring the right and wrong into the shorter (and by consequence the clearer) view. But his play is so wild, I must be content to take the ball as it comes, and return it if I can ; which whether I always do or not, however, I believe will prove no great matter, since I hope 'twill appear, where he gives me the rest, he makes but a wide chase : his most threatening strokes end in nothing at all ; when he cuts, he's under line ; when he forces, he's up in the nets. But to leave tennis, and come to the matter.

The first chapter in his book is upon the Immodesty of the Stage ; where he tells you how valuable a qualification modesty is in a woman. For my part I am wholly of his mind ; I think 'tis almost as valuable in a woman as in a clergyman ; and had I the ruling of the roast, the one should neither have a husband, nor the t'other a benefice without it. If this declaration won't serve to shew I'm a friend to't, let us see what proof this gentle-man can give of the contrary.

I don't find him over-stocked with quotations in this chapter : he's forced, rather than say nothing, to fall upon poor Miss *Hoyden.* He does not come to particulars, but only mentions her with others, for an immodest character. What kind of immodesty he means, I can't tell : but I suppose he means lewdness, because he generally means wrong. For my part, I know of no bawdy she talks : if the strength of his imagination gives any of her discourse that turn, I suppose it may be owing to the number of bawdy plays he has read, which have debauched his taste, and made every thing seem salt, that comes in his way.

He has but one quotation more in this long chapter, that I am concerned in : and there he points at the *Provok'd Wife*, as if there were something in the 41st page of that play, to discountenance modesty in women. But since he did not think fit to acquaint the reader what it was, I will.

Lady *Brute* and *Belinda* speaking of the smuttiness of some plays, *Belinda* says,

> *Why don't some reformer or other beat the poet for it ?*

Lady BRUTE. *Because he is not so sure of our private approbation, as of our public thanks: Well, sure there is not upon earth so impertinent a thing as women's modesty.*

BELINDA. *Yes, men's fantasque, that obliges us to it: If we quit our modesty, they say we lose our charms; and yet they know that very modesty is affectation, and rail at our hypocrisy.**

Now which way this gentleman will extract anything from hence, to the discouragement of modesty, is beyond my chymistry : 'tis plainly and directly the contrary. Here are two women (not over virtuous, as their whole character shews), who being alone, and upon the rallying pin, let fall a word between jest and earnest, as if now and then they found themselves cramped by their modesty. But lest this should possibly be mistaken by some part of the audience, less apprehensive of right and wrong than the rest, they are put in mind at the same instant, that (with the men) if they quit their modesty, they lose their charms. Now I thought 'twas impossible to put the ladies in mind of anything more likely to make 'em preserve it. I have nothing more laid to my charge in the first chapter.

---

* See *ante*, vol. i. pp. 332-3.

The second is entitled, *The Profaneness of the Stage*; which he ranges under two heads : their Cursing and Swearing ; and their Abuse of Religion and the Holy Scriptures.

As to swearing, I agree with him in what he says of it in general : that 'tis contrary both to religion and good manners, especially before women. But I say, what he calls swearing in the play-house (at least where I have to answer for it), is a breach upon neither.

And here I must desire the reader to observe, his accusations against me run almost always in general terms, he scarce ever comes to particulars : I hope 'twill be allowed a good sign on my side, that it always falls to my turn to quote the thing at length in my defence, which he huddles together in my charge. What follows will be an instance of it.

He says in the 57th page (where the business of swearing is upon the *tapis*), with a great deal of honesty and charity, that in this respect the *Relapse* and the *Provok'd Wife* are particularly rampant and scandalous.

Would not anybody imagine from hence, that the oaths that were used there, were no less than those of a losing bully at backgammon, or a bilked hackney-coachman ? Yet after all, the stretch of the profaneness lies in Lord *Foppington's Gad*, and Miss *Hoyden's Icod*. This is all this gentleman's zeal is in such a ferment about.

Now whether such words are entirely justifiable or not, there's this at least to be said for 'em : that people of the nicest rank both in their religion and their manners throughout Christendom use 'em.

In France you meet with *par die, par bleu, ma foi*, &c., in the constant conversation of the ladies and the clergy, I mean those who are religious even up to bigotry itself ; and accordingly we see they are always allowed in their plays.   And in England, we meet with an infinity of people, clergy as well as laity, and of the best lives and conversations, who .use the words *I-gad, I-faith*,

Codsfish, *Cot's my life*, and many more, which all lie liable to the same objection.

Now whether they are right or wrong in doing it, I think at least their example is authority enough for the stage ; and should have been enough to have kept so good a Christian as Mr. *Collier* from loading his neighbour with so foul a charge as blasphemy and profaneness, unless he had been better provided to make it good.

The next thing he takes to task in this chapter, is the abuse of religion and Holy Scripture. Now here I think he should first clearly have proved, that no story, phrase, or expression whatsoever in the Scripture, whether in the divine, moral, or historical part of it, should be either repeated, or so much as alluded to, upon the stage, to how useful an end soever it might be applied. This I say he should have first put past a dispute, before he fell upon me for an abuser of the Holy Scripture ; for unless that be to abuse it, I am innocent.

The Scripture is made up of history, prophecy, and precept ; which are things in their nature capable of no other burlesque than what calls in question either their reality or their sense.* Now if any allusion I have made be found even to glance at either of them, I shall be ready to ask pardon both of God and the church. But to the trial.

The first accusation lies upon the *Provok'd Wife*, where *Rasor* is highly blamed by Mr. *Collier* for, in the 77th page, pleading the same excuse to an untoward prank he had newly played, which *Adam* did heretofore upon a more unfortunate occasion : that woman having tempted him, the devil overcame him.†
How the Scripture is affronted by this, I can't tell ; here's ›

---

* " The *Vindicator* is out in his notion of burlesque. To *burlesque* a book, is to turn it into *ridicule*. Now this may be done without questioning the history, or mistaking the text."—Collier's *Defence of the Short View*, p. 103.

† See *ante*, vol. i. p. 382.

nothing that reflects upon the truth of the story : it may indeed put the audience in mind of their forefather's crime, and his folly, which, in my opinion, like Gunpowder-Treason, ought never to be forgot.

The line in *Rasor*'s confession, which Mr. *Collier*'s modesty ties him from repeating, makes the close of this sentence : *And if my prayers were to be heard, her punishment for so doing should be like the Serpent's of old, she should lie upon her face all the days of her life.*

All I shall say to this is, that an obscene thought must be buried deep indeed, if he don't smell it out ; and that I find he has a much greater veneration for the Serpent than I have, who shall always make a very great distinction between my respects to God and the devil.

He runs amuck at all. The next he lances at is my Lord *Foppington.* And here he's as angry at me for being *for* religion, as before for being *against* it (which shews you the man's resolved to quarrel with me) :* for I think his Lordship's words which he quotes about St. *James*'s Church, are beyond all dispute on the minister's side, though not on his congregation's.† The indecencies of the place, the levity of the women, and the unseasonable gallantry of the men, are exposed in the very lines this gentleman is pleased to quote for their profaneness. For though my Lord *Foppington* is not supposed to speak what he does to a religious end, yet 'tis so ordered, that his manner of speaking it, together with the character he represents, plainly and obviously instructs the audience (even to the meanest capacity) that what he says of his church-behaviour is designed for their contempt, and not for their imitation. This is so

---

* Collier, rather disingenuously, interprets this remark of Vanbrugh's as "a frank confession, that he was against religion before."—*Defence of the Short View*, p. 106.

† See *ante*, vol. i. p. 46.

notorious, that no school-boy could mistake it : I therefore hope those who observe this man of reformation is capable of giving so good an intention so pernicious a turn, will conclude, when he sat down to write upon the profaneness of the poets, he had nothing less in his head, than to refine the morals of the age.

From the elder brother he falls upon the younger ; I suppose, because he takes me to be his friend, for I find no other reason for his quarrel. He accuses him for assuring his man *Lory*, that he has kicked his conscience downstairs ;* and he observes, he says, by the way, that this loose young gentleman is the author's favourite. Now the author observes by the way, that he's always observing wrong ; for he has no other proof of his being his favourite, than that he has helped him to a wife, who's likely to make his heart ache : † but I suppose Mr. *Collier* is of opinion, that gold can never be bought too dear.

The next flirt is at *Worthy* and *Berinthia;* and here he tells you two characters of figure determine the point in defence of pimping. I can pardon his mistake in the business of pimping, because I charitably believe the University may have been the only place he has had any experience of it in, and there 'tis not managed indeed by people of any extraordinary figure : but he may be informed if he pleases, that in this righteous town the profession soars somewhat higher, and that (out of my Lord Mayor's Liberties) there are such things as *Worthy* and *Berinthia* to be found. I brought 'em upon the stage to shew

---

* *Ante*, vol. i. p. 65.

† "Indeed so says the *Vindicator*. But *Young Fashion* tells another story. He is in no fright about the matter. Upon observing some signs of extravagance in *Hoyden*, he says to himself (and then you may be sure *he delivers his real thoughts to the audience*), '*Tis no matter. She brings me an estate will afford me a separate maintenance.* We see here's no danger of mortification. This soliloquy is extremely moral ! It teaches the art of marrying the estate without the woman, and makes a noble settlement upon lewdness."—*Defence of the Short View*, p. 109.

the world how much the trade was improved ; but this gentle-man I find won't take my word for't.

Nurse is to have the next kick o' the breech, and 'tis for being too profane. But that's left for me to quote again : for his part, all he repeats from her is, *That his Worship* (*young* Fashion) *overflows with his mercy and his bounty : he is not only pleased to forgive us our sins, but which is more than all, has prevailed with me to become the wife of thy bosom.**

This he says is dull. Why, so 'tis ; and so is he, for thinking it worth his finding fault with, unless it had been spoke by some-body else than a nurse, and to somebody else than Mr. *Bull.* But the profane stuff he says precedes it, I'll acquaint the reader with. She says (speaking to the chaplain) : Roger, *are not you a wicked man*, Roger, *to set your strength against a weak woman, and persuade her it was no sin to conceal Miss's nuptials ? My conscience flies in my face for it, thou priest of* Baal ; *and I find by weful experience, thy absolution is not worth an old cassock.*

The reader may here be pleased to take notice what this gentleman would conster profaneness, if he were once in the saddle with a good pair of spurs upon his heels. I have all manner of respect for the clergy, but I should be very sorry to see the day that a nurse's cracking a jest upon a chaplain (where it has no allusion to religion) should be brought within the verge of profaneness : but the next chapter, about the Abuse of the Clergy, will give occasion for some more remarks of this kind.

Amanda comes next ; I thought she might have 'scaped, but it seems, with all her virtue, she charges the Bible with un-truths, and says :

Good Gods, what slippery stuff are men compos'd of ! Sure

----

* *Ante,* vol. i. p. 129.

*the account of their creation's false, and 'twas the woman's rib that they were form'd of.**

I'm sorry the gentleman who writ this speech of *Amanda's*, is not here to defend himself; but he being gone away with the Czar, who has made him Poet Laureate of *Muscovy*, I can do no less for the favour he intended me, than to say this in his justification : that to my knowledge he has too much veneration for the Bible, to intend this a charge upon the truth of it ; and that it appears very plain to me, *Amanda* intended no more to call it in question by those words, than Mr. *Collier's* wife might be supposed to do, if from some observations upon his book, she should say : *Sure 'tis a mistake in the New Testament, that the fruits of the Spirit are modesty, temperance, justice, meekness, charity, &c.; for my* Jeremy *is a spiritual person, yet has not one of these marks about him.*

Worthy follows ; and I am threatened with no less than eternal damnation, for making him say to his procuress (when she had promised to do what he'd have her), *Thou Angel of Light, let me fall down and adore thee.*† But I am not commended for the answer she makes him, to put the audience in mind, she was not supposed to deserve that compliment : *Thou Minister of Darkness, get up again, for I hate to see the devil at his devotions.*‡ If Mr. *Collier* had quoted this too, he had given a better character of me, and I think of himself.

A page or two farther, he has a snap, as he goes by, at the *Provok'd Wife.* And here he's at foul play again. He accuses

---

* *Ante*, vol. i. p. 131.

† Vol. i. p. 120.

‡ "*Berinthia's* answer looks rather like a design of carrying on the profaneness, and continuing the religious banter."—*Defence of the Short View*, p. 112. A fair rejoinder, from Collier's point of view ; but a fuss about nothing, all the same.

Lady *Brute* for setting down as a precept, that the part of a wife is to cuckold her husband ; whereas her words are these : *In short*, Belinda, *he has used me so barbarously of late, I could almost resolve to play the downright wife, and cuckold him.**

This indeed is saying, wives do cuckold their husbands : I ask the ladies' pardons for lying. But 'tis not saying they should do so : I hope Mr. *Collier* will ask mine.

Lady *Brute* in her next reply to *Belinda*, says, what I own at first view seems much more liable to exception. Yet lest the audience should mistake her raillery for her serious opinion, there is care taken immediately to inform 'em otherwise, by making her reprimand herself in these words to *Belinda : But I shall play the fool and jest on, till I make you begin to think I'm in earnest.*†

Here, methinks, he should have commended me for my caution. But he was surly, and would not.

Young Fashion is next accused for saying to *Lory* (when he had a prospect of getting Miss *Hoyden*), *Providence, thou seest at last, takes care of men of merit.*‡

This surely is a very poor charge, and a critic must be reduced to short commons to chop at it. Everybody knows the word Providence in common discourse goes for Fortune. If it be answered, let it go for what it will, it is in strictness God Almighty ; I answer again, that if you go to strictness, Fortune is God Almighty as much as Providence, and yet no one ever thought it blasphemy to say, Fortune's blind, or Fortune favours fools : and the reason why it is not thought so, is because 'tis known it is not meant so.

Berinthia comes again, and is blamed for telling *Amanda* that *Worthy* had taken her to pieces like a text, and preached upon every part of her :§ this is called a lewd and profane allegory. I

---

* Vol. i. p. 279.   † Vol. i. p. 280.   ‡ Vol. i. p. 34.   § Vol. i. p. 91.

confess it has at a glance, the appearance of somewhat which it is not, and that, methinks, Mr. *Collier* might have been content to have charged it with ; but he always takes care to stretch that way that becomes him least, and so is sure to be in the wrong himself, whether I am so or not.

Neither the woman in general, nor any particular part about her, is likened to the text ; the simile lies between the manner of a minister's using his text, and *Worthy's* flourishing upon his mistress ; so that the profanation's got in the wrong place here again. But supposing the minister to be as Mr. *Collier* would have him, as sacred a thing as his text, there's nothing here that burlesques him. 'Tis a simile indeed, but a very inoffensive one, for it abuses nobody ; and as to the lewdness on't, I refer myself to the reader here again, whether this gentleman does not give us another instance of his having a very quick nose, when some certain things are in the wind. I believe, had the obscenity he has routed up here, been buried as deep in his church-yard, the yarest boar in his parish would hardly have tossed up his snout at it.

Berinthia's close of her speech, *Now consider of what has been said, and Heaven give you grace to put it in practice,* brings up the rear of the attack in this chapter. These I own are words often used at the close of a sermon, and therefore perhaps might as well have been let alone here. A known pulpit-expression sounds loose upon the stage, though nothing is really affronted by it ; for that I think in this case is very plain, to any body that considers who it is that speaks these words, and her manner of doing it. There's nothing serious in't, as if she would persuade either *Amanda* or the audience that Heaven approved what she was doing : 'tis only a loose expression, suitable to the character she represents, which, throughout the play, sufficiently shows, she's brought upon the stage to ridicule something that's off on't.

These three or four last quotations Mr. *Collier* says are

downright blasphemy, and within the law.   I hope the reader
will perceive he says wrong.

The next chapter is upon the Abuse of the Clergy : and here
we are come to the spring of the quarrel.   I believe whoever
reads Mr. *Collier*, need take very little pains to find out, that in
all probability, had the poets never discovered a rent in the
gown, he had done by religion, as I do by my brethren, left
it to shift for itself.

In starting this point, he opens a large field for an adversary
to rove in ; he unbars the gate of the town, forgetting the weakness of the garrison : were I the governor on't, I'd commend him
for his courage, much more than for his prudence.

I once thought to have said a great deal upon this occasion ;
but I have changed my mind, and will trouble the reader with
no more than I think is necessary to clear myself from the
charge of ridiculing the function of a clergyman.

I am as fully convinced as the most pious divine, or the most
refined politician, can wish me, how necessary the practice of
all moral virtues is to our happiness in this world, as well as to
that of another.   And this opinion has its natural consequence
with me, which is, to give me a regard to every instrument of
their promotion.

The institution of the clergy, I own to be both in the intention
and capacity the most effectual of all ; I have therefore for the
function all imaginable deference, and would do all things to
support it in such a kind of credit, as will render it most formidable in the execution of its design.   But in this Mr. *Collier* and
I, I doubt, are not like to agree.

He is of opinion, that riches and plenty, title, state and
dominion, give a majesty to precept, and cry *Place* for it wherever it comes ; that Christ and his Apostles took the thing by
the wrong handle ; and that the Pope and his Cardinals have
much refined upon 'em in the policy of instruction.   That

should a vicar, like St. *John*, feed on locusts and wild honey, his parish would think he had too ill a taste for himself, to cater for them ; and that a bishop, who, like St. *Paul*, should decline temporal dominion, would show himself such an **ass**, his advice would go for nothing.

This I find is Mr. *Collier*'s opinion ; and if ever I take orders, I won't swear it shan't be mine : but [till]* then I fear I shall continue in my heresy ; three articles of which are these :

    1. That the shepherd, who has least business at home in his house, is likely to take the most care of his flock.

    2. That he who finds fault with the sauce he greedily sops his bread in, gives very good cause to suspect he'd fain keep it all to himself.†

    3. That he who is strict in the performance of his duty, needs no other help, to be respected in his office.

These pills, I own, are as bitter to the flesh, as they are agreeable to the spirit ; but the physic's sound, and the prescription is so necessary, that when nothing else will persuade some people to swallow 'em, I think 'tis not amiss, they should be forced down by the stage. If any poet has gone farther, let him answer for't ; I'll endeavour to show I have not. And first I'm to answer for Sir *John Brute*'s putting on a gown to abuse the clergy.

If a Sir *John Brute* off the stage should put on a gown in his cups, and pass his lewdness upon the world, for the extrava-

---

* The word "till" is evidently required here, although it does not appear in the original edition.

† "The Vindicator in his 2d Article discourses of *Sauce* and *Sops*, &c. But he has cooked the allegory so oddly, that I know not well what to make on't. If he reasons from the kitchen upon these subjects, he must talk by himself."—*Defence of the Short View*, p. 120.

gances of a churchman ; this, I own, would be an abuse and a
prejudice to the clergy.   But to expose this very man upon the
stage, for putting this affront upon the gown ; to put the
audience in mind, that there were laymen so wicked, they
cared not what they did to bring religion in contempt, and were
therefore always ready to throw dirt upon the pilots of it : this, I
believe, nobody but a man of Mr. *Collier's* heat could have
mistaken so much, to quote it under the head of the Clergy
abused by the Stage.   But men that ride post, with the reins
loose upon the neck, must expect to get falls.   When he writes
again, he'll take up perhaps, and mix a little lead with his quick-
silver.

The Justice does indeed drop a word which alludes to the
jolly doings of some boon companions in the Fens * ; and
if I had let him drop a word or two more, I think I had made
him a better Justice than I have.

In the *Relapse*, Mr. *Collier* complains that his Brother *Bull*
wishes the married couple joy in language so horribly smutty
and profane, to transcribe it would blot the paper too much.
I'm therefore put upon the old necessity to transcribe it for him,
that the world may see what this honest gentleman would pass
upon them as well as me for profane, had he as long a sword
in his hand as the Pope has in his.

Bull's words are these.   *I most humbly thank your honours;
and I hope, since it has been my lot to join you in the holy bands
of wedlock, you will so well cultivate the soil, which I have craved
a blessing on, that your children may swarm about you, like bees
about a honey-comb.*†   These are the words he calls horribly
smutty and profane.

The next quarrel's about I don't know what ; nor can light of
anybody that can tell me.   He says, *Young Fashion's* desiring

---

Mr. *Bull* to make haste to Sir *Tunbelly ;* he answers him very decently, *I fly, my good Lord.** What this gentleman means by this quotation, I can't imagine ; but I can answer for t'other gentleman, he only meant he'd make haste.

He quotes two or three sentences more of *Bull's*, which are just as profane as the rest. He concludes, that the chaplain has a great deal of heavy stuff upon his hands ; and his chief quarrel to me here is, that I have not made him a wit.

I ask pardon, that I could suppose a Deputy-Lieutenant's chaplain could be a blockhead ; but I thought, if there was such a thing, he was as likely to be met with in Sir *Tunbelly's* house, as anywhere. If ever I write the character of a gentleman where a chaplain like Mr. *Collier* is to have the direction of the family, I'll endeavour to give him more sense, that I may qualify him for more mischief.

He has now left lashing me in particular, and I only have my share in his general stroke upon all such sinful wretches, who *attack religion under every form, and pursue the priesthood through all the sub-divisions of opinion.* He says, *Neither* Jews *nor Heathens,* Turks *nor Christians,* Rome *nor* Geneva, *church nor conventicle, can escape us.* And we say, They'll all escape us, if he can defend 'em. Priest or Presbyter, Pope or *Calvin,* Mufti or Brammen, ambassador from God or envoy from the devil, if they have but their credentials from t'other world, they are (with him) all brothers of the sacred string ; there's no more discord than is necessary to make up the harmony ; and if a poet does but touch the worst instrument they play upon, the holy consort of religion and morality, he'll tell you, is quite out of tune.

Thus violently does his zeal to the priesthood run away with him. Some clergyman, methinks, should help to stop him

---

* Vol. i. p. 99.

and I almost persuade myself there will. There is still in the
gown of the Church of England a very great number of men,.
both learned, wise, and good, who thoroughly understand
religion, and truly love it : from amongst these I flatter myself
some hero will start up, and with the naked virtue of an old
generous *Roman*, appear a patriot for religion indeed ; with a
trumpet before him proclaim the secrets of the cloister, and by
discovering the disease, guide the world to the cure on't.

He may shew (if he pleases), that the contempt of the clergy
proceeds from another kind of want, than that of power and
revenue : that piety and learning, charity and humility, with so
visible a neglect of the things of this life, that no one can doubt
their expectations from another ; is the way to be believed in
their doctrine, followed in their precepts, and (by a most
infallible consequence) respected in their function. Religion is
not a cheat, and therefore has no need of trappings : its beauty
is in its nature, and wants no dress. An ambassador who comes
with advantageous proposals, stands in no need of equipage to
procure him respect. He who teaches piety and morality to the
world, is so great a benefactor to mankind, he need never doubt
their thanks, if he does not ask too much of their money. But
here's the sand, where religion runs aground ; avarice and
ambition in its teachers, are the rocks on which 'tis dashed to
pieces. It, with many weak people, brings the whole matter
into doubt. Men naturally suspect the foundation of a project,
where the projector is eager for a larger contribution than they
see is necessary to carry on the work. But this case is so
plain, there needs nothing to illustrate it. 'Tis the clergy's
invasion into the temporal dominion, that has raised the alarm
against 'em : it has made their doctrine suspected, and by consequence, their persons despised. I own I have sometimes
doubted whether *Pharaoh*, with all the hardness of his heart,
would have pursued the Children of *Israel* to the *Red Sea*, as
he did, if they had not meddled with the riches of his subjects

at their parting ; but that action renewed the doubts of a faith so weak as his, and made him, in spite of all the miracles he had seen, question whether *Moses* had his commission from God. He paid indeed for his infidelity, as others may happen to do upon a parallel mistake ; I wish none have done't already : but I'm afraid those very instances Mr. *Collier* gives us of the grandeur of the clergy, are the things that have destroyed both them and their flocks.

They owe their fall to their ambition ; their soaring so high has melted their wings ; in a word, had they never been so great, they had never been so little. But lest I should be mistaken, and make myself enemies of men I am no enemy to, I must declare, my thoughts are got to *Rome*, while I am talking thus of the clergy ; for the charge is in no measure so heavy at home. The Reformation has reduced things to a tolerable medium ; and I believe what quarrel we have to our clergy here, points more at the conduct of some, than the establishment of the whole. I wish it may never go farther, and I believe it won't, if those who I don't question are still by much the majority, will to so good an end (as the curbing their ambitious brethren, and reforming their lewd ones) for once make a league with the wicked, and agree, that whilst *they* play their great artillery at 'em from the pulpit, the poets shall pelt 'em with their small shot from the stage. But since Mr. *Collier* is violently bent against this, I'll tell him why I am for it. And 'tis,—

Because he has put me in mind, in the first words of his book, that the business of plays *is to recommend virtue and discountenance vice: to shew the uncertainty of human greatness; the sudden turns of fate, and the unhappy conclusions of violence and injustice: that 'tis to expose the singularities of pride and fancy; to make folly and falsehood contemptible, and to bring everything that is ill, under infamy and neglect.*

The next chapter is upon the Encouragement of Immorality by the Stage : and here *Constant* is fallen upon, for pretending to be a fine gentleman, without living up to the exact rules of religion.   If Mr. *Collier* excludes every one from that character, that does not, I doubt he'll have a more general quarrel to make up with the gentlemen of *England,* than I have with the lords, though he tells 'em I have highly affronted 'em.

But I would fain know after all, upon what foundation he lays so positive a position, that *Constant* is my model for a fine gentleman ; and that he is brought upon the stage for imitation.

He might as well say, if I brought *his* character upon the stage, I designed it a model to the clergy: and yet I believe most people would take it t'other way.   O, but these kind of fine gentlemen, he says, are always prosperous in their undertakings, and their vice under no kind of detection ; for in the fifth act of the play, they are usually rewarded with a wife or a mistress. And suppose I should reward him with a bishopric in the fifth act, would that mend his character?   I have too great a veneration for the clergy, to believe that would make 'em follow his steps. And yet (with all due respect to the ladies) take one amour with another, the bishopric may prove as weighty a reward as a wife or a mistress either.   He says Mr. *Bull* was abused upon the stage, yet he got a wife and a benefice too.   Poor *Constant* has neither ; nay, he has not got even his mistress yet ; he had not, at least, when the play was last acted.   But this honest Doctor, I find, does not yet understand the nature of Comedy, though he has made it his study so long.   For the business of Comedy is to shew people what they should do, by representing them upon the stage, doing what they should not.   Nor is there any necessity a philosopher should stand by, like an interpreter at a puppet-show, to explain the moral to the audience.   The mystery is seldom so deep, but the pit and boxes can dive into it ; and 'tis their example out of the play-house, that chiefly influences the galleries. \ The stage is a glass for the world to view itself in ; people ought therefore to see themselves as they are ; if it makes their faces too fair, they won't know they are dirty, and by consequence will neglect to wash 'em. If therefore I have shew'd *Constant* upon the stage, what generally the thing called a fine gentleman is off on't, I think I have done what I should do. I have laid open his vices as well as his virtues : 'tis the business of the audience to observe where his flaws lessen his value ; and by considering the deformity of his blemishes, become sensible how much a finer thing he would be without 'em. But after all, *Constant* says nothing to justify the life he leads, except where he's pleading with Lady *Brute* to debauch her ; and sure nobody will suppose him there to be speaking much of his mind. Besides, his mistress in all her answers makes the audience observe the fallacy of his arguments. And I think young ladies may without much penetration make this use of the dialogue, that they are not to take all for Gospel, men tell 'em upon such occasions.

The *Provok'd Wife* is charged with nothing more, except *Belinda* for declaring she'd be glad of a gallant, and Lady *Brute* for saying, *Virtue's an ass, and a gallant's worth forty on't.**

I need make no other defence for the ladies, than I have already done for the gentlemen, the case being much the same. However, to show how unfair an adversary I have to deal with, I must acquaint the reader, that *Belinda* only says, *If her pride should make her marry a man she hated, her virtue would be in danger from the man she loved.†* Now her reflection upon this, I take to be a useful caution both to mothers and daughters (who

---

* Vol. i. p. 279.

† See vol. 1, p. 364. " His play will soon decide the controversy, and shew on which side the unfairness lies. *Belinda*'s words are these : *O' my conscience, were't not for your affair in the balance, I should go near to pick up some odious man of quality yet, and only take poor* Heartfree *for a gallant.*"—*Defence of the Short View*, p. 127.

think chastity a virtue) to consider something in their matches, besides a page and a coronet.

Lady *Brute's* words are fairly recited, but wrongly applied. Mr. *Collier's* mistaken ; 'tis not virtue she exposes, but herself, when she says 'em ; nor is it me he exposes, but himself, when he quotes 'em.

He gives me no farther occasion to mention the *Provok'd Wife ;* I'll therefore take this to make an observation or two upon the moral of it, it being upon that account he has called it in question, and endeavoured to make it pass for a play that has none.

This play was writ many years ago, and when I was very young ; if therefore there had been some small flaws in the moral, I might have been excused for the writing, though liable to some blame for the publishing it. But I hope it is not so loose, but I may be pardoned for both, whether Mr. *Collier* sets his seal to't or not.

As for Sir *John Brute,* I think there are an infinity of husbands who have a very great share of his vices : and I think his business throughout the play is a visible burlesque upon his character. 'Tis this gentleman that gives the spring to the rest of the adventures : and though I own there is no mighty plot in the whole matter, yet what there is, tends to the reformation of manners. For besides the hateful idea his figure needs must give of his character, the ill consequence of his brutality appears in the miscarriage of his wife : for though his ill usage of her does not justify her intrigue, her intriguing upon his ill usage may be a caution for some. I don't find our women in *England* have much of the *Muscovite* temper in 'em : if you'll make 'em think you are their friend, you must give 'em softer strokes of your kindness ; if you don't, the gallant has a dangerous plea, and such a one as, I doubt, has carried many a cause. Religion, I own (when a woman has it), is a very great bulwark for her husband's security : and so is modesty, and so is fear, and so is pride; and yet all are little enough, if the gallant has a friend in the garrison. I therefore think that play has a very good end, which puts the governor in mind, let his soldiers be ever so good, 'tis possible he may provoke 'em to a mutiny.

The rest of the characters, as they have no very great good, so they have very little mischief in 'em. Lady *Fanciful* is ridiculed for her vanity and her affectation. *Mademoiselle* brings to mind what may often be expected from a *suivante* of her country. *Heartfree* is catch'd for his extravagant railing at womankind : and *Constant* gives himself a great deal of trouble, for a thing that is not worth his pains. In short, they are most of 'em busy about what they should not be ; and those who observe they are so, may take warning to employ their time better.

I have nothing more to answer for in this chapter, but making the women speak against their own sex : and having the presumption to bring a fop upon the stage with the title of a lord.

This is a bungling piece of policy, to make the women and the nobility take up arms in his quarrel. I'm ashamed a churchman should spin his mischief no finer : the solicitors to the Holy War had almost as good a plea. But he had one consideration farther in this : he remembered he had positively declared, let a clergyman be guilty of what crimes he would, he was God's ambassador, and therefore a privileged person, whom the poets ought never to take into custody. This, upon second thoughts, he found would hardly go down, if he monopolized the privilege to them alone ; and so lest the company should bring their charter to a dispute, he has opened the books for new subscriptions. The lords and the ladies are invited to come in ; the gentlemen, I suppose, may do so too, if they please ; and, in short, rather than the committee of religion shall be exposed for their faults, all mankind shall be admitted to trade in sin as they please.

But I dare answer for the laity, of what quality soever they may be, they are willing their vices should be scourged upon the stage ; at least, I never yet heard one of 'em declare the contrary. If the clergy insist upon being exempted by themselves, I believe they may obtain it : but I'm apt to fancy, if they protect their loose livers from being exposed in the play-house, they'll find 'em grow the bolder to expose themselves in the streets. A clergyman is not in any country exempted from the gallows : and Mr. *Collier* has seen one of his brethren peep through a worse place than a garret-window : nay, (in a reign he reckons a just one) amble through the town at the tail of a cart, with his sins in red letters upon his shoulders.*   A hangman then may jerk him ; why not a poet ?   Perhaps 'tis feared he might give him more sensible strokes.

I am now come to thank the gentleman for the last of his favours ; in which he is so generous to bestow a chapter entire upon me.

I'm extremely obliged to him for it, since 'tis more than ever he promised me ; for in the title of his book, he designs to correct the stage only for the immorality and profaneness of it. And indeed I think that was all his business with't.   But he has since considered better of the matter, and rather than *quit his hold*, falls a criticizing upon plots, characters, words, dialogue, &c., even to telling us when our fine gentlemen make love in the prevailing strain, and when not.   This gives us a farther view of his studies ; but, I think, if he kept to his text, he had given us a better view of a clergyman.

It may, perhaps, be expected I should say more in answer to

---

* He alludes, no doubt, to the whipping of the Reverend Titus Oates, from Aldgate to Newgate, and from Newgate to Tyburn, in the reign of King James II.

this chapter, than to all that has gone before it ; the sense of the play being attacked here, much more than the moral, which those who will take Mr. *Collier*'s word for my principles, must believe I am least concerned for. But I shall satisfy 'em of the contrary, by leaving the sense to answer for itself if it can. I'll only say this for't in general : that it looks as if a play were not overloaded with blunders, when so pains-taking a corrector is reduced to the wretched necessity of spending his satire upon *Fire* and *Flames* being in the same line ; and *Arms* twice in the same speech, though at six lines distance one from t'other. This looks as if the critic were rather duller than the poet. But when men fight in a passion, 'tis usual to make insignificant thrusts : most of his are so wide, they need no parrying ; and those that hit, are so weak, they make no wound.

I don't pretend, however, to have observed the nicety of rule in this play.* I writ it in as much haste (though not in so much fury) as he has done his remarks upon't ; 'tis therefore possible I may have made as many foolish mistakes.

I could, however, say a great deal against the too exact observance of what's called the rules of the stage, and the crowding a comedy with a great deal of intricate plot. I believe I could shew, that the chief entertainment, as well as the moral, lies much more in the characters and the dialogue, than in the business and the event. And I can assure Mr. *Collier*, if I would have weakened the diversion, I could have avoided all his objections, and have been at the expense of much less pains than I have. And this is all the answer I shall make to 'em, except what tumbles in my way, as I'm observing the foul play he shews me, in setting the *Relapse* in so wrong a light as he does, at his opening of the fable on't.

In the first page of his remarks upon this play, he says I

---

* *I.e., The Relapse.*

have given it a wrong title ; the *Relapse,* or *Virtue in Danger,* relating only to *Loveless* and *Amanda,* who are characters of an inferior consideration ; and that the *Younger Brother,* or the *Fortunate Cheat,* had been much more proper ; because *Young Fashion* is, without competition, the principal person in the comedy.

In reading this gentleman's book, I have been often at loss to know when he's playing the knave, and when he's playing the fool ; nor can I decide which he's at now. But this I'm sure, *Young Fashion* is no more the principal person of the play, than *he's* the best character in the church ; nor has he any reason to suppose him so, but because he brings up the rear of the most insignificant part of the play, and happens to be the bridegroom in the close on't.

I won't say anything here irreverently of matrimony, because *à la Françoise* bigotry runs high, and by all I see, we are in a fair way to make a sacrament on't again. But this I may say, that I had full as much respect for *Young Fashion,* while he was a bachelor ; and yet I think while he was so, *Loveless* had a part that, from people who desire to be the better for plays, might draw a little more attention. In short ; my Lord *Foppington,* and the *Bridegroom,* and the *Bride,* and the *Justice,* and the *Match-maker,* and the *Nurse,* and the *Parson* at the rear of 'em, are the inferior persons of the play (I mean as to their business), and what they do, is more to divert the audience, by something particular and whimsical in their humours, than to instruct 'em in anything that may be drawn from their morals ; though several useful things may in passing be picked up from 'em too.

This is as distinct from the main intention of the play, as the business of *Gomez* is in the *Spanish Friar.** I shan't here

---

* *The Spanish Friar, or The Double Discovery;* one of Dryden's best comedies, brought out in 1681.

enter into the contest, whether it be right to have two distinct designs in one play ; I'll only say, I think when there are so, if they are both entertaining, then 'tis right ; if they are not, 'tis wrong.   But the dispute here is, where lies the principal business in the *Relapse ?*   Mr. *Collier* decides it roundly for the wedding-house, because there's best cheer; his patron, Sir *Tun-belly*, has got a good venison-pasty for him, and such a tankard of ale, as has made him quite forget the moral reflections he should have made upon the disorders that are slipped into *Loveless*'s house, by his being too positive in his own strength, and forgetting, that *Lead us not into Temptation*, is a petition in our prayers, which was thought fit to be tacked to that for our daily bread.

And here my design was such, I little thought it would ever have been ridiculed by a clergyman.   'Twas in few words this.

I observed in a play, called *Love's Last Shift, or the Fool in Fashion*, a debauchee pay so dear for his lewdness and his folly, as from a plentiful fortune, and a creditable establishment in the world, to be reduced by his extravagance to want even the common supports of life.

In this distress, Providence (I ask Mr. *Collier*'s pardon for using the word) by an unexpected turn in his favour, restores him to peace and plenty : and there is that in the manner of doing it, and the instrument that brings it to pass, as must necessarily give him the most sensible view, both of his misery past, from the looseness of his life ; and his happiness to come, in the reform of it.   In the close of the play, he's left thoroughly convinced it must therefore be done, and as fully determined to do it.

For my part, I thought him so undisputably in the right ; and he appeared to me to be got into so agreeable a tract of life, that I often took a pleasure to indulge a musing fancy, and suppose myself in his place.   The happiness I saw him possessed of, I

D D 2

looked upon as a jewel of a very great worth, which naturally
led me to the fear of losing it ; I therefore considered by what
enemies 'twas most likely to be attacked, and that directed me
in the plan of the works that were most probable to defend it.
I saw but one danger in solitude and retirement, and I saw
a thousand in the bustle of the world ; I therefore in a moment
determined for the country, and supposed *Loveless* and *Amanda*
gone out of town.

I found these reflections of some service to myself, and so
(being drawn into the folly of writing a play) I resolved the
town should share 'em with me. But it seems they are so little
to Mr. *Collier*'s taste, he'll neither eat the meat himself, nor say
grace to't for anybody else. I'll try, however, if the following
account will recommend it to him.

Loveless and his wife appear in the start of the play, happy in
their retirement, and in all human prospect, likely to continue
so, if they continue where they are. As for *Amanda*, she's so
pleased with her solitude, she desires never to leave it ; and the
adventures that happen upon her being forced to it, may caution
a husband (if he pleases) against being so very importunate to
bring his wife (how virtuous soever) into the way of mischief,
when she herself is content to keep out of it.

Loveless, he's so thoroughly weaned from the taste of his
debauches, he has not a thought toward the stage where they
used to be acted. 'Tis business, not pleasure, brings him thither
again, and his wife can't persuade him there's the least danger
of a relapse : he's proud to think on what a rock his reformation
is built, and resolves she herself shall be a witness, that though
the winds blow, and the billows roar, yet nothing can prevail
against it.

To town in short they come, and temptation's set at defiance.
Lead us not into it, is a request he has no farther occasion for.
The first place he tries his strength, is where he used to be the
most sensible of his weakness.

He could resist no woman heretofore ; he'll now shew he can stand a battalion of 'em ; so to the playhouse he goes, and with a smile of contempt looks coolly into the boxes. But *Berinthia* is there to chastise his presumption : he discovers her beauty, but despises her charms ; and is fond of himself, that so unmoved he can consider 'em. He finds a pleasure indeed, in viewing the curiosity, but 'tis only to contemplate the skill of the Contriver. As for desire, he's satisfied he has none ; let the symptoms be what they will, he's free from the disease ; he may gaze upon the lady till he grows a statue in the place, but he's sure he's in love with none but his wife. Home he comes, and gives her an account of what he had seen ; she's alarmed at the story, and looks back to her retirement : he blames her suspicion, and all's silent again. When Fate (here's blasphemy again) so disposes things, that the temptation's brought home to his door, and his wife has the misfortune to invite it into her house. In short, *Berinthia* becomes one of the family : she's beautiful in her person, gay in her temper, coquet in her behaviour, and warm in her desires. In a word, the battery is so near, there's no standing the shot ; constancy's beaten down ; the breach is made, resolution gives ground, and the town's taken.

This I designed for a natural instance of the frailty of mankind, even in his most fixed determinations ; and for a mark upon the defect of the most steady resolve, without that necessary guard, of keeping out of temptation. But I had still a farther end in *Loveless*'s relapse, and indeed much the same with that in the *Provok'd Wife*, though in different kind of characters ; these latter * being a little more refined, which places the moral in a more reasonable, and I think a more agreeable view. There ; the provocation is from a *Brute*, and by consequence cannot be supposed to sting a woman so much,

---

* *I.e.*, Loveless and Amanda.

as if it had come from a more reasonable creature : the lady therefore that gives herself a loose upon it, could not naturally be represented the best of her sex. Virtuous (upon some ground or other) there was a necessity of making her ; but it appears by a strain of levity that runs through her discourse, she owed it more to form, or apprehension, or at best to some few notions of gratitude to her husband, for taking her with an inferior fortune, than to any principle of religion, or an extraordinary modesty. 'Twas therefore not extremely to be wondered at, that when her husband made her house uneasy to her at home, she should be prevailed with to accept of some diversions abroad. However, since she was regular while he was kind, the fable may be a useful admonition to men who have wives, and would keep 'em to themselves, not to build their security so entirely upon their lady's principles, as to venture to pull from under her all the political props of her virtue.

But in the adventures of *Loveless* and *Amanda*, the caution is carried farther. Here's a woman whose virtue is raised upon the utmost strength of foundation : religion, modesty, and love, defend it. It looks so sacred, one would think no mortal durst approach it ; and seems so fixed, one would believe no engine could shake it : yet loosen one stone, the weather works in, and the structure moulders apace to decay. She discovers her husband's return to his inconstancy. The unsteadiness of his love gives her a contempt of his person ; and what lessens her opinion, declines her inclination. As her passion for him is abated, that against him's inflamed ; and as her anger increases, her reason's confused. Her judgment in disorder, her religion's unhinged ; and that fence being broken, she lies widely exposed : *Worthy's* too sensible of the advantage, to let slip the occasion : he has intelligence of the vacancy, and puts in for the place.

Poor *Amanda's* persuaded he's only to be her friend, and that all he asks, is to be admitted as a comforter in her afflictions. But when people are sick, they are so fond of a cordial, that when they get it to their nose, they are apt to take too much on't.

She finds in his company such a relief to her pain, she desires the physician may be always in her sight. She grows pleased with his person as well as his advice, yet she's sure he can never put her Virtue in Danger. But she might have remembered her husband was once of the same opinion ; and have taken warning from him, as the audience, I intended, should do from 'em both.

This was the design of the play ; which I think is something of so much greater importance than *Young Fashion*'s marrying Miss *Hoyden*, that if I had called it the *Younger Brother*, or the *Fortunate Cheat*, instead of the *Relapse, or Virtue in Danger*, I had been just as much in the wrong, as Mr. *Collier* is now.

His reason, I remember, why *Loveless* can't be reckoned a principal part, is, because he sinks in the fourth act. But I can tell him, if the play had sunk in the fourth act too, it had been better than 'tis, by just twenty *per cent.** However, though *Loveless*'s affair is brought about in the fourth act, *Amanda*'s last adventure is towards the end of the fifth. But this is only a cavil from the formality of the critics ; which is always well broken into, if the diversion's increased by't, and nature not turned top-side-turvy. If therefore nothing but the critics (I mean such as Mr. *Collier*) find themselves shocked by the disorders of this play, I think I need trouble myself as little to justify what's past, as I own I should to mend it, in anything to

---

* Vanbrugh would have done better to "sink" this very foolish sentence, which elicits from Collier the obvious retort, that if the play had sunk in the *third* act, it had been more valuable still. "For some entertainments," says the divine, "like dirty ways, are always the better for being short."— *Defence*, p. 130.

come ; had I thoughts of meddling any more with the stage. But to draw to an end.

I have reserved for the close of this paper one observation (a home one I think) upon the unfair dealing of this reverend gentleman ; which shews at once the rancour of his venom, the stretch of his injustice, and by a moral consequence, I think, the extremity of his folly : for sure there cannot be a greater, than for a man of his coat, at the very instant he's declaiming against the crimes of the age, to lay himself so open, to be hit in the most immoral blot of life, which that of slander undisputably is.

To explain. I beg the reader will bestow one moment's reflection upon the pains he has taken to make *Young Fashion* and his affair pass for the principal concern of the comedy ; which he only has done, in hopes to sink the useful moral of the play, which he knew lay in t'other part of it, and would unavoidably have appeared in judgment against his reflections upon the whole, if he had not taken this way to stifle the evidence. He therefore carries on the imposture to that degree, as at last to slubber over the conclusive scene between *Worthy* and *Amanda*, as if there were no meaning of importance in it. Nay, his rage is so great (to find the stamp of immorality he would fain have fixed upon this play, so cleanly washed off by the close of this scene) that he cares not what folly he commits : and therefore in his heats, rather than commend it for the alarm it gives to lewdness, by *Worthy's* reflections upon *Amanda's* refusal, he turns him into ridicule for an insipid *Platonic :* by which we may guess, had he been in the fine gentleman's place, the lady would not have 'scaped as she did. I'll repeat *Worthy's* words, with the Doctor's use of 'em, and so have done.

Sure there's divinity about her, and sh'as dispens'd some portion on't to me : For what but now was the wild flame of love, or (to dissect that specious term) the vile, the gross desires of flesh and blood, is in a moment turn'd to adoration: the coarser appetite of nature's gone, and 'tis methinks the food of angels I require. How long this influence may last, Heaven knows: but in this moment of my purity, I could on her own terms accept her heart. Yes, lovely woman, I can accept it, for now 'tis doubly worth my care: your charms are much increas'd since thus adorn'd: when truth's extorted from us, then we own the robe of virtue is a graceful habit.

> *Could women but our secret councils scan;*
> *Could they but reach the deep reserves of man;*
> *They'd wear it on, that that of love might last:*
> *For when they throw off one, we soon the other cast.*
> *Their sympathy is such ——*
> *The fate of one, the other scarce can fly,*
> *They live together, and together die.*

This reflection *Worthy* makes to himself, upon *Amanda's* having virtue enough to resist him, when he plainly saw she lay under a pressing temptation.

Now when 'tis considered, that upon the stage the person who speaks in a soliloquy is always supposed to deliver his real thoughts to the audience: I think it must be granted, there never was a homer check given to the lewdness of women in any play whatsoever. For what in nature can touch 'em nearer, than to see a man, after all the pains he has taken, and the eager arguments he has used, lay open his heart, and frankly confess, had he gained his mistress, she had lost her gallant.

This I thought was a turn so little suited to comedy, that I confess I was afraid the rigour of the moral would have damned the play. But it seems everybody could relish it but a clergyman. Mr. *Collier's* words are these:

Amanda continues obstinate, and is not in the usual humour of the stage: upon this, like a well-bred lover, he seizes her by force, and threatens to kill her: (By the way, this purblind divine might have seen 'twas himself, not his mistress, he, threatened.) *In this rencounter the lady proves too nimble, and slips through his fingers.   Upon this disappointment he cries,* There's divinity about her, and she has dispensed some portion on't to me.   *His passion is metamorphosed in the turn of a hand : he's refined into a* platonic *admirer, and goes off as like a town-spark as you would wish.   And so much for the poet's fine gentleman.*

The world may see by this, what a contempt the Doctor has for a spark that can make no better use of his mistress, than to admire her for her virtue.   This methinks is something so very extraordinary in a clergyman, that I almost fancy when he and I are fast asleep in our graves, those who shall read what we both have produced, will be apt to conclude there's a mistake in the tradition about the authors ; and that 'twas the reforming divine writ the play, and the scandalous poet the remarks upon't.*

THE END.

---

* In justice to Collier, I append the following extract from his reply to this concluding thrust. "In this reflection upon *Worthy*, I was not examining the *moral*, but the *dramatic* virtues of the play. . . . My business here was to shew the inconsistency of *Worthy's* character, and the unlikelihood of his reformation. . . . What can be more improbable than that so profane and finished a debauchee, so weak in principle, and so violent in passion, should run from one extreme to another? Should break through custom, and metamorphose desire at so short a warning? To solicit to rudeness, and talk sentences and morality, to be pious and profane in the same breath, must be very extraordinary. To be all pleasure and mortification so just together, a madman one minute and a hermit the next, is, one would think, somewhat forced, and unnatural : it looks at best but like the grimace of a disappointment, the fox's virtue when the grapes were above his reach. . . . The soil and the plant, the man and the morals won't agree."—*Defence of the Short View*, pp. 130-32.

www.ingramcontent.com/pod-product-compliance
Lightning Source LLC
Chambersburg PA
CBHW030819110726
47900CB00006B/1673